This book should be returned to any branch of the
Lancashire County Library on or before the date shown

CAINE BAMB 17/4/17. SR NSL MORAL 10/17 Hulme 3/18 Cassey P/19 1 - 12. 20 Yatchsman 12/20		

Lancashire County Library
Bowran Street
Preston PR1 2UX
www.lancashire.gov.uk/libraries

Lancashire
County
Council

LL1(A)

THE SWAN MAID

Lottie Lane is a chambermaid at one of London's busiest inns. Condemned to a life of drudgery and at the mercy of a vicious landlady, Lottie is too worn out to even dream of a better life. Until one night an injured soldier is brought to The Swan. Lottie nurses him back from the dead and suddenly everything changes. She finds herself following the drum of the soldiers, from the docks of Chatham to the despair of a far flung battlefield. When tragedy strikes, the threat of destitution nips at her heels and Lottie is in dire need of a miracle...

THE SWAN MAID

THE SWAN MAID

by

Dilly Court

Magna Large Print Books
Long Preston, North Yorkshire,
BD23 4ND, England.

British Library Cataloguing in Publication Data.

Court, Dilly
    The swan maid.

        A catalogue record of this book is
        available from the British Library

        ISBN   978-0-7505-4330-9

First published in Great Britain by HarperCollins*Publishers* 2016

Published in Large Print 2016 by arrangement with
HarperCollins Publishers Ltd.

Magna Large Print is an imprint of Library Magna Books Ltd.

Printed and bound in Great Britain by
T.J. (International) Ltd., Cornwall, PL28 8RW

19145922

For Teresa Chris, my excellent agent
and trusted friend.

Acknowledgements

Although *The Swan Maid* is a work of fiction, I have done my utmost to ensure that the historical facts are correct, and I found the following works both fascinating and useful:

Wonderful Adventures of Mrs Seacole in Many Lands, by Mary Seacole (Penguin Classics)

Mary Seacole, by Jane Robinson (Constable & Robinson Ltd)

Crimean Journal, by Fanny Duberly (Classic Travel Book)

Narrative of Personal Experiences & Impressions During a Residence on the Bosphorus Throughout the Crimean War, by Lady Alicia Blackwood (National Army Museum)

Lonely Planet India (Travel Guide), by Lonely Planet

Chapter One

Cheapside, London, 1854

'Lottie, you wretched girl, where are you?' Mrs Filby's strident voice echoed around the galleries of The Swan with Two Necks, and the galleried coaching inn seemed to shake on its foundations.

Lottie was in the stable yard and had been emptying chamber pots onto the dung heap, which lay festering in the heat of the late summer sun. She had been up since five o'clock that morning and had not yet had breakfast, but the rooms had to be serviced, and the guests must be looked after. Their needs came before those of the inn servants, and the mail coach from Exeter would be arriving at any moment.

'Lottie, answer me at once.' Prudence Filby leaned over the balustrade on the first floor, shielding her eyes from the sunlight. 'Is that you down there in the horse muck?'

'Yes, ma'am.' Lottie had hoped that the short-sighted landlady might not see her, but it seemed that her luck was out. It was better to answer, and receive a tirade of abuse, than to hide, only to be accused later of every shortcoming and misdemeanour that came to Mrs Filby's mind.

'That's where you belong, you idle slut, but I have need of you in the dining parlour. Come in at once, and wash your filthy hands.'

'Coming, ma'am.' Lottie hurried indoors, leaving the chamber pots in the scullery to be scoured clean when she could find the time. She washed her hands in the stone sink and was about to dry them on her apron, when she realised that this would leave a wet mark, which would be enough to earn a swift clout round the head from her employer. Mrs Filby had a right hook that would be the envy of champion bare-knuckle fighters, and had been seen to wrestle a drunk to the ground on many an occasion. Her husband Shem, who was by no means a small man, treated her with due deference, and spent most of his time in the taproom, drinking ale with his customers.

Lottie hitched up her skirts and raced across the cobblestones to the kitchen on the far side of the stable yard. The heat from the range hit her with the force of a cannonball, and the smell of rancid bacon fat and the bullock's head being boiled for soup made her feel sick.

She acknowledged the cook with a nod, and hurried on until she reached the dining parlour, where she came to a halt, peering at her hazy reflection in a fly-spotted mirror on the wall. Strands of fair hair had escaped from the knot at the nape of her neck, and she tucked them under her frilled mobcap. She straightened her apron, braced her shoulders and entered the room.

Prudence Filby stood by the sideboard, arms akimbo. She glowered at Lottie. 'You took your time,' she hissed. 'Clear the plates and don't offer them more coffee. The Exeter mail coach is due any minute, and I want this lot out of here.'

'More bread, girl.' A portly man clicked his

14

fingers. 'And a slab of butter. I paid good money for my breakfast.'

Lottie hurried to his side. 'I'll do what I can, sir.'

'You'll do more than that. Bring me bread and butter, and a pot of jam wouldn't go amiss.'

'Is there jam?' A woman seated with her husband at the next table leaned over to tug at Lottie's skirt. 'Why didn't we get any jam? I don't like dry bread, and I'll swear the flour had chalk added to it. My mouth is full of grit.'

'No wonder this place is half empty.' Her husband turned his head to stare at Mrs Filby. 'This is your establishment, madam. Why have we been deprived of jam?'

Mrs Filby folded her arms across her ample bosom and advanced on him, eyes narrowed, lips pursed. 'You paid for bed and breakfast, sir. No one never mentioned jam. Jam costs extra.'

'Don't make a fuss, Nathaniel.' The man's wife reached out across the table to touch his hand. 'Suddenly I've lost my appetite.'

The City gentlemen at a table by the window had been listening attentively, and they too started demanding more coffee, and bread and butter: one went so far as to ask for marmalade.

Mrs Filby answered their requests by dragging Lottie from the parlour. She closed the door, and boxed Lottie's ears. 'That's what you get for nothing – see what you get for something. I've told you time and time again that bread, butter, coffee and the like should be given sparingly. We're here to make money, and you must wait until the last minute before the coach arrives to serve the coffee or soup. It has to be so hot that the customers leave it.' She caught Lottie by the ear. 'What happens then, girl? Do you remember anything you've been taught?'

'It goes back in the pot, ma'am.'

Mrs Filby released her, wiping her hands on her skirt. 'That's right. Then we can sell it twice over and we make more money. You do know, so why don't you carry out my orders?'

'I'm sorry, ma'am. It won't happen again.'

'Go and fetch hot coffee, and make sure the bread is straight from the oven. I heard the post horn. This miserable lot of complainers will be leaving in the time it takes to change horses and turn the coach around.'

'What about jam?'

'Jam?' Mrs Filby's voice rose to a screech.

Lottie fled to the kitchen.

The next mail coach arrived just as the disgruntled passengers from the dining parlour were boarding the one about to leave. The lady who had been refused jam climbed into the coach declaring that they would be travelling by train next time. Her husband followed her, saying nothing.

Lottie stood to attention, waiting to show the new arrivals to the dining room. London might be the end of the journey for some, but others would want to rest and refresh themselves before travelling on. It was a never-ending cycle of weary travellers arriving and departing, with only minutes to achieve a swift turnaround. The ostlers worked with impressive speed and dexterity, and Jem, the potboy, raced about doing the jobs that no one else wanted to do. He nudged Lottie as he went to offload the luggage.

'Save us a slice of bacon,' he said, grinning. 'I'm starving.'

She nodded. 'I will, if I can.'

He dashed forward to catch a carpet bag thrown from the coach roof by the guard, resplendent in his livery of scarlet and gold. Trotter was a regular on this route, and Lottie had observed that he liked to show off his strength in front of an appreciative audience. She looked up and, sure enough, the other chambermaids, May and Ruth, were leaning over the balustrade on the top floor, waving their cleaning cloths in an attempt to attract his attention.

Jem followed her gaze. 'You're a randy old goat, Trotter,' he said, chuckling. 'How do you do it, mate?'

Trotter's answer was to hurl a leather valise at Jem that almost brought him to his knees. 'Cheeky devil.' Trotter flexed his muscles. 'You could learn a thing or two from me, son.' He turned and waved at the maids before leaping to the ground, and swaggering off in the direction of the tap-room.

'You'd best get that lot indoors before Mrs Filby sees you,' Lottie said hastily. 'She's already given me a clout round the head that made me see stars.'

Jem tucked two smaller cases under his arms and then lifted the heavier bags, one in each hand. 'She'd have to stand on a box to reach my head, but she punched me in the bread-basket last time I made her mad. She's a nasty piece of work, and that's the truth, but we're better than her, Lottie.

Keep that in mind, my girl.' He strolled off, whistling.

Lottie looked up, but May and Ruth had vanished, and a quick glance over her shoulder revealed the cause. Mrs Filby was standing in the doorway, scowling at her. 'Don't loaf around doing nothing, you lazy little slut. Get on with your work.'

'How does she do it?' Lottie muttered as she hurried into the scullery to take up where she had left off. 'She's got eyes in the back of her head.'

'Talking to yourself, are you? That's the first sign of madness.' Ruth edged past her, carrying two dangerously full chamber pots. 'You'd think the horses had pissed in these. I was all for emptying them over the balustrade, but May stopped me just in time.'

'That would have taken Trotter down a peg or two,' Lottie said, laughing. 'He wouldn't have been so cocky then.'

Ruth backed out into the yard, taking care not to spill a drop. 'Maybe I'll be in time to have a few words with him before the coach leaves. It's me he fancies, not May.'

'I expect he's got a wife and half a dozen nippers at home. I'd watch out for him if I were you, Ruth.'

'I will, don't you fret, ducks.' Ruth stepped outside, leaving Lottie to finish her unenviable task.

That done, she returned to the bedrooms, and made them ready for the next occupants. When she was satisfied that Mrs Filby could find nothing to criticise in her work, she went downstairs to help Cook prepare the midday meal.

Jezebel Pretty did not live up to her name. She was tall, raw-boned and ungainly, with a lean, mean face and a fiery temperament. She had served a two-year sentence in Coldbath Fields prison, commonly known as The Steel, for inflicting grievous bodily harm on her former lover, and had been employed at the inn for almost a year. Lottie, Ruth and May had often spoken about her in the privacy of the attic room where they laid their heads at night, but it was not the fact that the Filbys had taken on an ex-convict that shocked them. What they found hard to believe was that anyone as patently ugly as Jezebel could have found a man who fancied her in the first place, or one who was foolish enough to take on a woman whose volatile temper simmered beneath the surface, erupting every now and then like a volcano.

Even so, Lottie had discovered a different side to Jezebel. Not long after the cook had started work at the inn, a small mongrel terrier had got in the way of one of the mail coach horses. The poor creature had been flung up in the air and had landed on the cobblestones in a pathetic heap. Jezebel had happened to be in the yard, smoking her clay pipe, when the accident occurred, and Lottie had seen her rush to the animal's aid. She had picked it up and, cradling it in her arms like a baby, carried it into the kitchen. Lottie had followed, offering to help and had watched Jezebel examining the tiny body for broken bones with the skill of an experienced surgeon, and the tender-

19

ness of a mother caring for her child.

Despite two broken ribs and several deep cuts, Lad – as Jezebel named him – survived, and they became inseparable, despite Mrs Filby's attempts to banish the dog from the kitchen, or any part of the building other than the stables. Lad, quite naturally, had developed a deep distrust of horses and he refused to be parted from his saviour. Jezebel, who was a good cook and worked for next to nothing, was the one person Mrs Filby treated with a certain amount of restraint and respect, and Lad was allowed to stay.

Lottie entered the kitchen and received an enthusiastic greeting from the small dog, who seemed to remember that she was one of the first people who had shown him any kindness. Having been flea-ridden and undernourished when he first arrived, he was now plump and lively, with a shiny white coat and comical brown patches over one eye and the tip of one ear.

'Where've you been?' Jezebel demanded. 'The bullock's head is done and the meat needs to be taken off the bone, and the vegetables need preparing to go in the stew. I've been run off me feet. I was better off in The Steel than I am here.'

'I would have come sooner, but I had to wait on in the dining parlour and I hadn't finished the bedchambers, but I'm here now.'

'And where are those two flibbertigibbets? I suppose they're making sheep's eyes at that fellow Trotter. My Bill was just like him until I spoiled his beauty with my chiv. Trotter had best look out, that's all I can say.'

Lottie lifted the heavy saucepan off the range.

She knew better than to argue the point with Jezebel. It was easier and safer to keep her mouth shut and get on with her work; that way the long days passed without unpleasantness and everyone was happy in his or her own way. She had learned long ago that it was pointless to bemoan the fate that had brought her to The Swan with Two Necks. Born into an army family, her early years had been spent in India, and when her mother died of a fever, which also took Lottie's younger brothers and sister, she had been sent to England with a family who were returning on leave, and left with her Uncle Sefton in Clerkenwell. A confirmed bachelor, he had little time for children and Lottie had been packed off to boarding school, although her uncle had made it plain that he considered educating females to be a total waste of money.

She had received a basic education until the age of twelve, when she returned home to find that her uncle had married a rich widow. Lottie's childhood had ended when her new aunt, supposedly acting with her niece's best interests at heart, had sent Lottie to work for the Filbys. It was just another form of slavery: she worked from the moment she rose in the morning until late at night, when she fell exhausted into her bed.

'Are you doing what I told you, or are you daydreaming again, Lottie Lane? D'you want to feel the back of my hand, girl?' Jezebel reared up in front of Lottie, bringing her back to the present with a start.

'Sorry, ma'am.'

'Get on with it, or you'll get another clout round the head, and I ain't as gentle as the missis.' Jezebel stomped out into the yard, snatching up her pipe and tobacco pouch on the way. Lad trotted at her heels, growling and baring his teeth at the horses.

Lottie set to work and dissected the head, taking care not to waste a scrap of meat. Mrs Filby would check the bones later, and woe betide her if there was any waste. Parsimonious to the last, Prudence Filby ruled her empire with a rod of iron.

Minutes later, Jezebel marched back into the room. 'Where's Jem? The butcher has delivered the mutton. I want the carcass boned and ready for the pot. Go and find him, girl.'

'But I haven't finished what I'm doing.'

Jezebel moved with the speed of a snake striking its prey. The sound of the slap echoed round the beamed kitchen, and Lottie clutched her hand to her cheek. 'The bullock's going nowhere, but you are. Find the boy and tell him to get started or I'll be after him.'

Lottie found Jem in the taproom, serving ale to the newly arrived male passengers, while Mrs Filby shepherded the ladies to the dining parlour, where they would be plied with coffee, tea and toast, all of which were added onto the bill. Each day was the same, and everyone knew their part in the carefully choreographed routine designed to make the travellers part with their money in as short a time as possible. Jem had taken too long offloading the last coach and was now behindhand with his tasks. Normally cheerful and easy-going, he was looking flushed and flustered.

'Cook wants you, Jem.' Lottie took the pint mug from his hand. 'I'll finish up in here. There's only minutes before the coach leaves.'

'I suppose she's in a foul mood, as usual.'

'You'll soon find out if you don't hurry up.' Lottie passed the mug of ale to a man seated at the nearest table. She had just finished serving when the call came for the passengers to board, and she heard the clatter of hoofs and the rumble of wheels as yet another mail coach pulled into the stable yard. She was relieved by Shem Filby, who escorted the new guests into the taproom, enabling her to hurry back to the kitchen to prepare the vegetables.

Early mornings were always hectic, and she was used to the rush, although by midday everyone was beginning to flag, but there was no time to rest. Private carriages made up most of their custom during the day. Filby was pleased to point out that some people preferred the convenience of being transported from door to door, a luxury not provided when travelling by train, and others feared that the speed reached by steam engines would have serious effects on their health. The railways, he said, would one day put them out of business, but that was a long way off, or so he hoped.

Lottie did not have time to worry about such matters. She alternated between the kitchen, the dining room and the bedchambers, as did Ruth and May. They met briefly at mealtimes, with rare moments of free time during the afternoon lull, and then there was dinner to be prepared and served. After everything was cleared away and the dishes were washed and dried, there were beds to be turned back and aired, using copper warming pans filled with live coals. The constant need to provide washing facilities necessitated regular trips from the kitchen to the bedrooms, carrying ewers of hot water, and there was always someone who wanted something extra. Lottie had been sent out to buy all manner of things, mainly for ladies on their travels who had forgotten to bring a hairbrush or a comb. Sometimes it was a bottle of laudanum for pain, or oil of cloves for toothache, and these were always needed as a matter of urgency. Lottie had once been sent out to purchase a gift for a man's wife as he had forgotten her birthday. Sometimes guests tipped generously, while others gave nothing in return, not even a thank you.

The only time the girls had to chat was during the brief period before they fell asleep on their straw-filled palliasses, and even then they might be awakened at any hour of the night and called upon to serve travellers who stopped at the inn.

Such a call came in the early hours of the next morning. Lottie was in a deep sleep when she was shaken awake by Ruth. 'Get up. We're wanted in the kitchen.'

'What's the matter?'

'Soldiers,' Ruth said excitedly. 'I leaned over the balustrade and saw their red jackets. I love a man in uniform. Come on, they'll be in need of sustenance.'

Half asleep, Lottie made her way downstairs, still struggling with the buttons on her blouse.

The stable yard was illuminated by gaslight and

filled with the sound of booted feet, the clatter of horses' hoofs and men's raised voices. Above them the night sky formed a dark canopy, creating a theatrical backdrop to the dramatic scene. An officer was issuing orders, and Shem Filby was standing in the midst of the chaos, bellowing instructions to the ostlers that seemed to countermand those given by the young lieutenant. It had become a competition to see whose voice was the loudest, and in the end it was Mrs Filby, wearing a dressing robe over her nightgown, whose strident tones were heard above all others.

'Silence.' She waded into their midst, seizing a young private by the collar and thrusting him out of her way. 'Gentlemen, have a thought for our other guests.' She faced the officer with a contemptuous curl of her lip. 'You will be more comfortable in the dining parlour, sir. Ruth will show you the way.'

'Thank you, ma'am.' As meekly as a schoolboy caught scrumping apples, he followed Ruth into the building.

'Take the men into the kitchen, May.' Mrs Filby marched up to two soldiers who were supporting a comrade who appeared to be unconscious. 'What's the matter with him? Is he sick? If so, you can take him to hospital.'

The elder of the two privates stood to attention. 'If you please, ma'am, he's suffered a knock on the head. A cracked skull ain't catching.'

'I don't need any of your cheek, soldier.' Mrs Filby peered at the injured man. 'Has he been drinking?'

'Only Adam's ale, ma'am. We've been working

25

on the telegraph lines in the Strand for two days, but now we're heading for Chatham, and then on to the Crimea. All he needs is a bed for the night and some tender care, such as would be given by a kind lady like yourself.'

'Well, then, I'm sure we can do something for one of our brave men who will soon depart for battle.' Mrs Filby spun round to face Lottie. 'Take them to my parlour. See that they have everything they need.'

'Yes'm.' Lottie made a move towards the door-way. 'This way, please, gents.'

'One moment.' The lieutenant had obviously had second thoughts and had returned. 'I'm grateful for your help, ma'am, but I am in charge of my men. Private Ellis needs medical attention.'

'What is your name, sir?' Mrs Filby bristled vis-ibly. 'You are on my property now, not the battle-field.'

He doffed his shako with a bow and a flourish. 'Lieutenant Farrell Gillingham, Corps of Royal Sappers and Miners, at your service.'

'Well, Lieutenant Gillingham, if you wish to take your man to hospital, feel free to do so, but we cannot incur the expense of the doctor's fees, unless, of course, you wish to stump up for them yourself.'

'Perhaps we will wait until daylight, ma'am. If Ellis is not well enough to be moved, I'll think again.' Gillingham spoke in a tone that did not invite argument. He bowed smartly and followed Ruth into the building.

'Go with the men, Lottie,' Mrs Filby said in a low voice. 'You're a sensible girl, for the most part, anyway. See to their needs as best you can.' She lowered her voice to a whisper. 'But don't make them too comfortable. Their sort don't pay well.' She glanced round the yard, which was empty except for the ostlers who were attending to the horses. 'Filby, where are you? Speak to me.'

Lottie beckoned to the soldiers. 'Let's get the poor fellow inside.'

The Filbys' parlour was dominated by a huge walnut chiffonier, upon which were set out Prudence Filby's treasured china tea set and small ornaments that had no intrinsic value, but must surely have a meaning for her. Lottie knew each piece intimately, having had to dust them every day since her arrival at The Swan with Two Necks. For some reason best known to herself, Mrs Filby had made the cleaning of her private parlour Lottie's responsibility, insisting that the hand-hooked rugs with vibrant floral designs had to be taken out into the yard and beaten daily, and the heavy crimson velvet curtains and portière had to be brushed free from dust and cobwebs at least once a week.

Lottie held the door open, and while the soldiers settled Private Ellis on the sofa she raked the glowing embers of the fire into life.

'What happened to him?' she asked.

The younger of the two men eyed her up and down. 'What makes a pretty girl like you want to work in a place like this?'

'I think we should send for the doctor.' Lottie chose to ignore the compliment. 'Your friend looks very poorly.'

'You've got eyes the colour of the cornflowers

27

in the fields at home,' he said earnestly, 'and hair the colour of ripe wheat. I never seen such a pretty face in all me born days.'

'That's enough of that, Frank. You're a sapper, not a poet.' The older man held his hand out to Lottie. 'Private Joe Benson, miss. Don't take no notice of my mate. He can't help hisself when he meets a young lady.'

Lottie smiled. 'I don't mind being called pretty, but I still think that your friend looks very unwell.'

Benson leaned over to examine the unconscious man. 'I'd say he's got concussion. I seen it afore, miss. We was undergoing training at the Electric Telegraph Company, working on the underground wiring in the Strand, and Ellis was on the ladder when it gave way.'

'He should have been taken straight to hospital,' Lottie said worriedly.

'He could die.' Frank moved closer to the fire. 'Is there any chance of a bite to eat and a drink, miss? We can't do much for young Gideon, but the living has to be taken care of too.'

Lottie turned on him. 'How can you be so heartless? If you're hungry go to the kitchen and Mrs Pretty will feed you.'

Frank's tanned features split into a wide grin. 'Does she take after her name? Is she good-looking like you?'

It was on the tip of Lottie's tongue to put him straight, but she changed her mind. 'The only way you'll find out is to do as I say.' She shot a sideways glance at Private Benson. 'You look as though you could do with some sustenance. I'll stay with your friend while you get some food, but don't be too long.'

Benson tipped his cap. 'Ta, miss. Much obliged. We ain't eaten since midday.' He pushed Frank towards the door. 'Hurry up, then. If we don't hurry we'll find the greedy gannets have ate everything in the kitchen.'

Lottie stared down at the inert figure on the couch. A livid bruise marked his otherwise smooth forehead, and his light brown hair was matted with blood from a cut on the temple. He looked young and defenceless, despite the army uniform, and if she had not known better she might have thought him to be sleeping peacefully. She left the room briefly to look for Jem who was rushing about, fetching food and ale for their new guests.

She beckoned to him. 'When you've done that, could you bring me a bowl of warm water and some clean rags? I daren't leave the poor fellow on his own.'

'What a to-do! But the officer is a toff,' Jem chuckled and patted his trouser pocket. 'He gave me a handsome tip, so I don't mind running after him and his mates. I'll bring the water as soon as I can.' He raced off towards the kitchen, balancing a jug of ale with the expertise of long practice.

When she had bathed the soldier's cuts, and placed a cold compress on his bruised forehead, Lottie could do no more, and she settled down by the fire. It was warm in the Filbys' parlour and the chair was comfortable. She was tired and very sleepy...

She awakened with a start at the sound of someone calling out in distress.

Chapter Two

Lottie almost fell off the chair in her haste to be at the young private's side. His eyes were open, but unfocused, and he was babbling incoherently. She clutched his hand. 'It's all right, Gideon. That's your name, I believe.'

'Mother?' He attempted to sit up, but she pressed him back against the cushions.

'Lie still, there's a good boy.'

'You're not my mother?' He gazed at her, puzzled and frowning. 'Is she here?'

Lottie swallowed hard. The lump in her throat threatened to choke her but she managed a smile as she held his hand to her cheek. 'Your ma isn't here, Gideon, but I'm sure you'll see her soon.'

'I need to send her money. I have to make sure she's taken care of while I'm away.'

'You mustn't worry. She'll be all right.'

His hazel eyes, framed by ridiculously long and thick brown lashes, focused with difficulty on her face. 'Where am I? I don't know you, do I?'

'My name is Charlotte Lane, although everyone here calls me Lottie.'

'Lottie.' He closed his eyes with a sigh.

'Gideon.' Alarmed, she shook him by the shoulders. 'Don't die. Please don't die.'

'It's all right, miss. We're back now.' Joe Benson had come into the room unnoticed. He leaned over Gideon. 'He ain't dead. It's the bump on the

30

head that's making him like this. We'll take over now. You get yourself back to bed.'

'I'll go with you if you want company.' Frank stood in the doorway with a tankard clutched in his hand. He was grinning stupidly, and it was obvious that he was in the early stages of being drunk.

'No, ta, very much. I'll say good night, then.' She hesitated, staring down at Gideon. 'Are you sure there's nothing we can do for him?'

Benson patted her on the shoulder. 'We'll take care of him tonight, and we'll see how he is in the morning.'

'But where will you sleep?' Lottie asked anxiously.

'We're sappers, miss.' Frank saluted drunkenly. 'We can doss down anywhere.'

'He's right. Don't worry about us.' Benson moved swiftly to the door and held it open. 'We'll probably be off before you're up and about. This was an unplanned stopover, thanks to Ellis falling down a hole in the road.'

'I hope he gets better soon.'

Lottie tried to convince herself that Private Ellis was in good hands as she made her way back to the attic, but she had the nagging feeling she could have done more for the injured man. Ruth and May were already in bed, snoring gently, and Lottie had to feel her way in almost complete darkness. She lay down on the prickly palliasse, and, despite her worries, sank into a deep sleep.

Her first thoughts when she awakened next morning were for Private Ellis, and she dressed quickly.

It was still dark, but she could hear movement in the stable yard below.

She nudged Ruth, who slept next to her. 'Wake up. I think the soldiers are leaving.'

Ruth snapped to a sitting position, although her eyes were still shut. 'What's the time?'

'It's early, I think, but I'm going down anyway.' Lottie did not wait for a reply. She hurried to the stable yard, where she found men assembled, and Lieutenant Gillingham and his sergeant about to mount their horses. Mrs Filby was conspicuous by her absence, and it was Filby himself who was in charge.

Lottie knew better than to put herself forward, but she could not see Private Ellis and she was alarmed. He might have been taken to hospital, or his cold corpse might be lying on the sofa awaiting the arrival of the undertaker. Her imagination was rapidly getting the better of her, and some of her anxiety seemed to have communicated itself to the lieutenant. He handed the reins to his sergeant.

'Miss...' he hesitated, smiling ruefully. 'I'm afraid I don't know your name.'

'Lottie, sir. Lottie Lane.'

'Well, Miss Lane, I want to thank you for turning out in the middle of the night to assist my men.'

'It was nothing, sir. How is Private Ellis?'

'Mr Filby has kindly agreed to allow Ellis to remain here for a day or two, until he's fit to travel on to Chatham. My men moved him to one of the guest rooms, first thing, but unfortunately I cannot spare anyone to stay with him. Mr Filby assures me that he will be well cared for.'

'He will indeed,' Lottie said firmly. 'I'll do everything I can for him.'

Gillingham's serious expression melted into a smile that crinkled the corners of his grey eyes. 'From what Benson has told me you would make a good nurse, Miss Lane.'

'Oh, no, sir. I did what anyone would have done.'

'Don't underestimate yourself, Miss Lane. Did you know that Miss Nightingale is recruiting nurses to take with her to the Crimea?'

'Don't put ideas in her head, I beg you, sir.' Filby had come up behind them, and, although he was smiling, Lottie knew him well enough to realise that he was growing impatient.

'I am just a chambermaid, sir,' she said hastily.

'Yes, indeed.' Filby jerked his head in the direction of the kitchen. 'I think Mrs Pretty is preparing some gruel for the patient, Lottie. You'll find him in room fifteen, but don't loiter longer than necessary. There's a mail coach due from Exeter in half an hour.'

'Thank you for your hospitality, landlord.' Gillingham mounted his horse, tossing a coin to the ostler as he rode through the archway that led into Gresham Street.

Frank Jenkins marched past Lottie without a glance, but Joe Benson saluted and winked. It was obvious from his tight-lipped expression that Frank was sober now and suffering the consequences of drinking too much ale. He must, Lottie thought, have received quite a shock when he discovered that Jezebel Pretty did not live up to her name. She could picture the scene, and was still chuckling as she entered the kitchen, but her smile faded when she came face to face with Jezebel, who did not look too pleased.

'Gruel,' she said bitterly. 'As if I hadn't got enough to do without cooking pap for a sick soldier. They should have taken him with them.'

'It's all right, Mrs Pretty. I'll see to it.' Lottie took the wooden spoon from her and stirred the mess of oatmeal and water in the soot-blackened saucepan. 'I'll take it to him.'

'You'd best watch out. Military men are all the same. My man was a soldier. He was a conceited turkeycock, always showing off and putting hisself about. He ain't so handsome now, and that's a fact.' Jezebel picked up a cleaver and severed the head off a chicken carcass before tossing it into a stew pot. She threw the head to Lad, who pounced on it and ran under the table with it in his mouth.

Lottie filled a bowl with gruel, and poured the tea, adding a generous dash of milk to both. 'I'll be back in a tick, Cook.'

'You'd better, or I'll come looking for you. I ain't handling breakfasts on me own, not with her ladyship yelling at me to hurry up with the bacon and make more toast. I dunno why I stick it here.'

Lottie escaped from the kitchen and crossed the yard, making for the stairs on the far side. The ostlers were preparing the horses that would take the mail coach on to its next stop, but they were unusually silent and barely raised a nod of acknowledgement when Lottie passed by. She met Ruth and May on the way to room fifteen, but they too seemed tired and listless. Lottie could see that it was going to be a long day, and by evening tempers would be ragged. She could only hope that Mrs Filby had slept well. If not, they would all suffer.

She let herself into Gideon's room, but it was too dark to see anything other than the shape of the bed.

'Good morning, Private Ellis.' When there was no response she placed his breakfast on a small side table and made her way to the window. With the curtains drawn back, daylight flooded in, but it was hot and stuffy and she opened the casement just wide enough to allow some air to circulate.

She hurried to the bedside where Gideon was beginning to stir, and she laid a hand on his forehead. His skin felt cool to the touch, and she sighed with relief. At least he was not running a fever. He opened his eyes and attempted to sit up, but fell back against the pillows with a groan.

'Where does it hurt?' Lottie asked anxiously. 'You might have broken some bones.'

He stared at her with a puzzled frown. 'What happened? I don't remember. Where am I?'

'You had a bad fall,' she said gently. 'Your mates brought you to us last night, but they've gone on to Chatham. Lieutenant Gillingham said you were to follow as soon as you were able.'

'Gillingham...' Gideon repeated dazedly. 'I can't place him.'

Lottie perched on the edge of the bed. 'He is your commanding officer, Gideon. I may call you that, mayn't I?'

'Gideon, yes. I think that's my name.'

35

'Don't you remember anything? Like what you were doing before you fell?'

He shook his head and winced, raising his hand to his temple. 'My head aches, miss.'

'Lottie,' she said firmly. 'I am Lottie, and you are in room fifteen at The Swan with Two Necks.' She waited for a moment to see if this meant anything to him, but his blank expression was answer enough. She tried again. 'You were brought here by Lieutenant Gillingham and Private Benson.'

He dashed his hand across his eyes. 'Nothing seems to make sense. Please leave me alone.'

'I will, but only after you've had some breakfast.' She went to retrieve the mug and bowl, and placed them on a chair by the side of the bed. 'Would you like a sip of tea?'

He nodded. 'I'm parched.' He struggled to a sitting position and Lottie plumped up the pillows behind him.

It took some time, but in the end she managed to persuade him to drink the tea. He took a few spoonfuls of gruel, but the effort exhausted him and he lay back, closing his eyes.

'I have to leave you now,' Lottie said in a low voice. 'I'll return as soon as I am able.' She was not sure if he heard or understood. She would have liked to stay longer, but the sound of the post horn announced the arrival of the mail coach and there was work to do. 'I'll come back when I have a spare moment.'

Mrs Filby was in the kitchen talking to Jezebel. They both turned to stare at Lottie.

'Well?' Mrs Filby fixed her with an enquiring

look. 'How is the soldier?'

'He seems to have lost his memory,' Lottie said carefully. 'I think he ought to be seen by a doctor.'

'Do you? And who are you to make decisions, I might ask?' Mrs Filby bristled angrily. 'I or my husband will decide whether or not to call in a physician. The lieutenant left money for the young man's keep, although not sufficient to pay a doctor's fees. You will look after him, Lottie, but only in your spare moments.'

'Yes, don't think you can wriggle out of your duties,' Jezebel added fiercely. 'Take the coffee and toast into the dining parlour, and be quick about it.'

'Don't stand there like a ninny, get on with your work.' Mrs Filby sailed out of the kitchen, leaving Lottie to struggle with the coffee pot and a plate piled high with toast.

Jezebel impaled a slice of bread on the toasting fork. 'Hurry, girl. There's another coach due any minute.'

Snatching odd moments of calm in between the frantic turnaround of coaches and private carriages, Lottie visited Gideon as often as possible. She gave him sips of laudanum diluted in water to ease the pain of his bruised ribs and his persistent headache, and at midday she helped him sup some broth. He remained dazed and confused, but she was pleased to see a little colour creep back into his previously ashen face.

Her frequent absences did not go unnoticed. Ruth was the first to comment when she passed

Lottie on the first-floor gallery. 'I dunno what makes you so special. Why were you given the job of nursing the soldier? I could have done it better.'

'I expect you could,' Lottie said calmly, 'but I happened to be there at the time, and you were off flirting with Lieutenant Gillingham. Didn't it go as you'd hoped?'

Ruth tossed her head. 'I ain't interested in military men. Here today and gone tomorrow, that's soldiers for you.'

'I thought you fancied him, Ruth.'

'To tell the truth I did, but then I discovered he was off to the Crimea. I ain't interested in someone what's going to get blown to bits. I think I'll stick to Trotter; at least he comes here twice a week and he's got the money to treat a girl now and then.'

'And a wife and family to support.'

'You don't know that for sure. Anyway, I'm up for a bit of a laugh now and then. I don't think I want to get hitched and end up like my ma with a new mouth to feed every year.'

Lottie smiled and hurried on to the sick room to check on Private Ellis.

Despite the Filbys' refusal to send for a physician, Gideon began to improve. His memory returned gradually, and his headaches lessened. On the third day he was able to get up and sit in a chair by the window that overlooked the stable yard.

Lottie was late bringing him his bowl of soup and a cup of tea, and she apologised as she set them on the small table in front of him. 'I couldn't get away sooner, Gideon. We've been even busier than usual.'

'I thought they worked us hard in the army,' he said with a wry smile. 'But you never seem to stop.'

'I've been doing this since I was twelve. I suppose I'm used to it.'

'This smells good.' He lifted the spoon to his lips, but the movement seemed to hurt him and he hesitated, pulling a face.

'Are your ribs still hurting?'

'Just a bit. Maybe you should stay and help me if I can't manage to feed myself.'

She hesitated, eyeing him suspiciously. 'Are you saying that to keep me here?'

'Of course I am. I get lonely, and you need to take a break every now and then.'

'Mrs Filby wouldn't agree with you, neither would Jezebel.' Lottie perched on the edge of the bed. 'I'll get shot if they catch me.'

'I'm a soldier. I'll protect you.'

'You can hardly stand,' she said, chuckling. 'But it's good to see you looking so much better. I was really worried when your mates brought you here.'

'I've got a hard head. It would take more than a tumble to put me out of action.'

'You won't get better if you don't eat. I should go and let you get on with your meal.'

'No, please stay. I'll finish this up if you'll stay and talk to me, Lottie. Tell me about yourself.' He picked up the spoon and held it poised. 'I'm waiting,' he said with a wry smile.

'You win, but I can't stay long.' Lottie frowned as she recalled the trials of her childhood. 'There's not much to tell. My pa is a soldier, like you. He's a sergeant in the Bombay Sappers and Miners stationed in Poona, or he was the last time he wrote to me. I used to get a letter from him every now and then, but I haven't heard from him for ages, and I haven't seen him since I was six.'

'So you come from a military family.'

'I was born in India, but I don't remember much of my time there, although I do recall a white house with a beautiful garden and sweet-smelling flowers. I often dream of walking up the path and knocking on the door, but I always wake up before it opens.'

'Why did you leave? It sounds too good to be true.'

'When Ma died of a fever, Pa sent me to England to be looked after by my Uncle Sefton. I'm sure I was a miserable little thing, and he didn't want to be saddled with me in the first place. Anyway, as soon as he could, he packed me off to boarding school.'

'So how did you end up slaving away in a coaching inn? It seems such a waste.'

'Uncle Sefton married late in life and his wife didn't want me around. I was just twelve when I was sent to work here. I didn't have any choice in the matter.'

'Didn't your father have anything to say about such a decision?'

'Of course I wrote to Pa, begging him to let me join him, but I had to wait months for a reply, and when it came he said he was stationed on the

40

North-West Frontier, and that I'd be safer in London – so here I stayed. That's my life in a nutshell. What about you?'

'My father died some years ago. He was a soldier, and it was taken for granted that I'd follow him into the army. My mother lives in Whitechapel, close to the Garrick Theatre. She takes in lodgers, and I help her as much as I can financially. That's me in a nutshell, too.'

Lottie jumped to her feet at the sound of someone bellowing her name. 'Oh Lord! That's Mrs Filby. She'll be furious if she knows I've been sitting here chatting to you. I have to go, Gideon, but I'll pop in later, when the rush is over.'

'Don't forget me, Lottie.'

She glanced over her shoulder, smiling. 'As if I would. Drink your tea.'

On the fourth day Gideon was dressed when she brought him his breakfast gruel and a cup of tea. He had shaved and, despite the bruise on his forehead, he looked dashing in his uniform.

'What are you doing, Private Ellis?' She placed the bowl and mug on the washstand. 'You mustn't overtax yourself.'

'I'm a fraud, Lottie. I can't stay here any longer, much as I would like to remain and be cosseted by you. I have to report to my unit.'

'Oh, well, I suppose you know best.'

He smiled and took both her hands in his. 'You've been wonderful. I owe my speedy recovery to you.'

'Nonsense. I didn't do much other than to bring you food and drink.'

41

'I won't have that, Lottie. A trained nurse couldn't have done better.'

She withdrew her hands, aware that she was blushing furiously. 'It's very kind of you to say so, but I know nothing about nursing. It was a matter of luck and Mother Nature was on your side.'

'Maybe, but you did your part, and I'm truly grateful.'

'You'd better eat your breakfast. You need all your strength if you're to ride all the way to Chatham.'

'This is one thing I won't miss.' He sat down and began spooning the thin sops into his mouth. 'I could do with a plate of bacon and eggs and a nice fat sausage.'

'You are better,' she said, smiling. 'I'm so glad to see you up and about. When they brought you here I thought you were going to die.'

'If the ladder hadn't given way I would never have met you, Lottie. I'm just sorry that I won't have the chance to get to know you better.'

'Do you think you'll be leaving for the Crimea very soon? They're talking about nothing else in the taproom.'

'I can't say for certain, but I don't think it will be long.' He dropped the spoon into the empty bowl. 'There, are you satisfied now? It's all gone.'

'I'm not your mother, Gideon,' she said, laughing. 'But I will be sorry to see you go.'

'Will you?' His smile faded and he reached out to clasp her hand. 'I wish I could say that we'll meet again, Lottie, but I'm afraid this really is goodbye.'

She was struck by a sudden and almost overwhelming desire to cry. She had known him for only a few days, but it seemed that he had become a part of her life, and now he was about to leave and she would never see him again.

'You'll be back, Gideon,' she said, forcing herself to sound more cheerful than she was feeling. 'You'll return covered in glory.'

'Will you be waiting for me?' He dropped his hand to his side and his expression was bleak. 'I'm sorry. That was wrong of me. I couldn't ask that of anyone, least of all you. I'll be going into battle, even if we're just digging saps or laying wires for the telegraph. The chances are I won't return.'

Acting on impulse, Lottie flung her arms around his neck and kissed him on the cheek. 'You will survive, Gideon. I know you will.' She backed away, blushing. 'I just wanted to wish you good luck.'

Gideon's cheeks flamed and his eyes were suspiciously bright. 'I'll take that kiss with me to the Crimea, and if I get downhearted I'll remember how it felt to be embraced by the beautiful girl who saved my life.'

Lottie was momentarily lost for words, but the door burst open and May erupted into the room. 'You're wanted in the kitchen, Lottie. Mrs Filby's been looking for you and she ain't best pleased.' She gave Gideon a cursory glance. 'There don't seem to be much wrong with you, mister. Anyway, there's someone waiting for you in the stable yard. He says he's come to take you to Chatham, and he's in a tearing hurry, so you'd better not keep him waiting.'

Gideon grabbed his cap and rammed it on his

head, wincing as it touched the tender part of his scalp. 'I'll be off then. Take care of yourself, Lottie.'

'You, too.' Lottie turned away, and began stripping the bed. Her first instinct had been to rush out onto the balcony and wave to Gideon, but May was already suspicious, and she was a terrible gossip.

'Give me a hand, May,' she said casually. 'I'd better get the room ready for the next occupant.'

'He's sweet on you.' May pursed her lips. 'I bet you'll miss him something chronic. You've spent every spare moment up here.'

'He was sick. I looked after him as best I could. That's all.'

'Maybe you think you're a touch above us chambermaids now. Perhaps you should sign up with Miss Nightingale and her nurses. You'd have lots of injured soldiers to look after then.'

Lottie recognised the signs of jealousy. May could be very mean when she thought someone was getting preferential treatment. 'Maybe I will. It would be better than slaving all day, and sometimes all night, in this place.'

Lottie stood outside the Institute for the Care of Sick Gentlewomen in Upper Harley Street, trying to pluck up courage to knock on the door. She had dressed in her Sunday best, which she realised now was sadly lacking in style, and was shabby compared to the attire of the well-dressed ladies who frequented this part of London. She had walked from Gresham Street and the hem of her skirt was caked with dirt and bits of straw, but

44

there was little she could do about that now. Taking a deep breath she knocked on the door, but she was seized by a moment of panic when she heard approaching footsteps and the turn of the key in the lock.

The door was opened by a parlourmaid wearing a neat black dress with a spotless white cap and apron. She looked Lottie up and down. 'The tradesmen's entrance is round the back, miss.'

'I came to see Miss Nightingale,' Lottie said boldly. 'I understand she is interviewing nurses to travel with her to the Crimea.'

'Miss Nightingale is at the Middlesex Hospital at present. She's nursing cholera victims from the East End. You might catch her there, although I doubt if she'll have time to see you.'

Lottie opened her mouth to speak, but the door was slammed in her face. She stood for a few moments, shocked by her reception, but not really surprised. She had not expected it to be easy, and she had not told anyone at The Swan where she was going. They would think her quite insane, and perhaps she was, but helping Gideon back to health and strength had given her a new purpose in life. It seemed quite natural to want to follow the young man who had made such an impression on her, and to be of service where it was desperately needed. She was now even more determined to see Miss Nightingale. She was familiar with the Middlesex Hospital, having been taken there with a suspected broken arm when she was much younger. It had turned out to be a bad sprain, needing no further treatment, but the grand building had made an indelible impression upon her. She set off for Mortimer Street.

It was a hot day and the stench from the Thames hung in a pall over the city. The river was said to be little more than an open sewer, and as London suffocated in the sweltering heat of August, the outbreak of cholera in Soho had caused many people to flee for safety. Lottie covered her nose and mouth with her hanky and quickened her pace.

The hospital waiting area was crowded, and the desk clerk was overworked and impatient. Despite Lottie's entreaties, she was told that Miss Nightingale was too busy to see anyone, and the wards were closed to visitors, but Lottie was not prepared to give up easily. Her one day off a month was too precious to waste in a futile exercise, and she decided to wait. She did not have a plan in mind, but she had not come this far to give in at the first setback, or even the second.

She took a seat at the end of a row where she had a good view of the comings and goings. She was hot and thirsty, and as the hours went by her stomach cramped with hunger pains, but she had set her mind on having a word with the illustrious lady, although whether she would be able to pick her out amongst the nurses who flitted around like so many pale moths, was another matter. Somehow, Lottie was convinced that she would know Miss Nightingale the moment she saw her.

It was getting late. Even so, the seats in the waiting room were crowded with victims of accidents and muggings, and anxious mothers holding small children who were limp with fever. She knew she ought to be getting back to Gresham Street, and yet she was reluctant to give up. Then, she saw her. The slight woman, pale-faced with exhaustion, walked with her head held high, looking neither to her left nor her right.

Lottie leaped to her feet. 'Miss Nightingale. It is you, isn't it?'

Chapter Three

'If you're unwell you must wait your turn. I'm off duty.' The voice was cultured, but the tone was clipped and impatient.

'No, I'm not ill.' Lottie hurried after her. 'Please could you spare me a moment of your time? I've waited here all day for a chance to speak to you.'

Florence stopped just short of the street door. She turned slowly, her face a pale oval in the light of a gas lamp. 'What do you want of me?'

'I'd dearly love to accompany you to the Crimea, Miss Nightingale.'

'Are you a trained nurse?'

'Not exactly.'

'I'm sorry. I can't help you.' Florence was about to leave the building, but Lottie caught her by the sleeve.

'Please give me a chance.'

Florence fixed Lottie with a piercing gaze, from which there was no escape. 'You're very young. How old are you?'

'I'm twenty, Miss Nightingale. I'll be twenty-one in January.'

'I don't consider anyone under twenty-three. If you want to be a nurse, you must train in a hospital here, at home. Now, allow me to go on my way.'

'Is this person bothering you, Miss Nightingale?' A uniformed porter hurried up to them, glaring at Lottie.

'No, she was just making enquiries.' Florence's stern expression lightened into what was almost a smile. 'What is your name, young lady?'

'Charlotte Lane, ma'am.'

'Good luck, Charlotte.' Florence nodded to the porter and he held the door open for her.

Lottie watched spellbound as the small figure climbed into a waiting carriage.

'You was lucky,' the porter said tersely. 'She could have had you thrown out.'

'Yes, but she turned me down. I just wanted to do something useful.'

'Go home, miss. It's getting late and a young person like yourself shouldn't be roaming the streets unaccompanied.'

Lottie was about to tell him she was quite capable of looking after herself, when she heard footsteps approaching. She turned to see Lieutenant Gillingham striding towards them.

'It's Lottie, isn't it?' He came to a halt beside her. 'I thought I recognised you.'

'Yes, sir.' She bobbed a curtsey, out of habit rather than necessity. Even this far from the inn she had a sneaking feeling that Mrs Filby might be hiding around the next corner, watching her.

'What are you doing here on your own?'

The porter cleared his throat noisily. 'I told her

it was late for a young lady to be wandering the streets, sir.'

'Yes, thank you. I know this lady and I'll see her safely home.'

The porter muttered something as he stalked off to deal with a drunk who was swearing and threatening to punch a young doctor.

A sudden thought occurred to Lottie and she shivered. 'It's not Private Ellis, is it, sir? He hasn't taken a turn for the worse?'

Gillingham smiled and shook his head. 'As far as I know, Ellis is already back on duty and doing well. I was visiting a patient: my old nanny, God bless her. She's very frail, but determined to make a full recovery, and she's the only family I have left now.' He proffered his arm. 'Anyway, you must allow me to escort you home.'

'I can find my own way back to Gresham Street, thank you all the same,' Lottie said with as much dignity as she could muster.

'I dare say you could, but I am headed that way, and we could share a cab.'

'You're going to The Swan?'

'My colonel's lady is arriving on the mail coach from Bath, and I've been detailed to meet her, which is why I took the opportunity to visit the hospital. I've booked two rooms for us at The Swan and we will travel on to Chatham in the morning.'

'Oh, well, in that case, thank you.' Lottie had been prepared to walk, but it was a hot night and there was a sense of unrest in the humid, foul-smelling air. A ride home would be more than welcome.

49

Gillingham ushered her outside onto the fore-court where a cab had just dropped off a fare. 'The Swan with Two Necks, Gresham Street, cabby.' He handed Lottie into the vehicle and climbed in after her. 'Were you visiting someone in the hospital? It's not the best place to be during a cholera epidemic.'

'I wanted to speak to Miss Nightingale.'

'By Jove, that's a worthy ambition. Did you succeed?'

'Yes, I spoke to her, although much good it did me.'

He settled back against the leather squabs. 'I don't understand.'

'I want to go to the Crimea. I wanted to join her team of nurses.'

'Really?' He eyed her speculatively. 'Did looking after Private Ellis have anything to do with your decision?'

'I suppose it did, in a way. I realised that I could do better than waiting hand and foot on travellers at the inn. I was born into an army family, and spent my first six years in India. Talking to Private Ellis brought it all back to me, and suddenly it seemed the most natural thing in the world to want to do something worthwhile. Does that sound silly?'

'No. It sounds like a brave move. It's a pity nothing came of it.'

'Yes, but I'm not giving up yet.'

They lapsed into silence as the cab tooled along the streets, which were much quieter now than they had been when Lottie set out that morning, and they arrived at the inn just as the mail coach from Bath was pulling into the stable yard.

Filby stepped out of the shadows and caught Lottie by the arm. 'What sort of time do you call this? You was supposed to be back by seven sharp.'

'I must take the blame for Lottie's late return, sir,' Gillingham said firmly. 'It was entirely my fault.'

'If you say so, sir.' Filby cringed visibly. He waited until Gillingham had walked off to greet the colonel's wife. 'No good will come of you mixing with the military, you stupid girl. Soldiers and sailors are all the same when it comes to women. D'you get my meaning, you stupid little bitch?'

She wrenched free from his tight grasp. 'It's not like that. I met the lieutenant by pure chance.'

Filby caught her a stinging blow on the side of her face. 'Don't cheek me, miss.'

'I say, was that really necessary?' A silvery voice rang out across the stable yard as a young, fashionably dressed woman descended from the mail coach.

'I'd leave it be, my lady,' Gillingham said in a low voice.

'No, Farrell, I won't.' She moved across the yard with the grace of a ballerina. 'You, fellow with the leather apron.' She addressed Filby, who stared at her, apparently dumbstruck by her beauty. 'What do you mean by slapping the poor girl's face? What could she have done to deserve such harsh treatment?'

'Who are you, ma'am?' Filby stuttered, puffing out his cheeks.

'I am Lady Aurelia Dashwood, sir. And who

51

may you be?'

Gillingham moved swiftly to her side. 'This is Filby, my lady. He is the landlord.'

'Landlord or no, what right have you to strike this young woman?' Aurelia demanded angrily.

'She is a maidservant, employed by me, my lady.' Filby dropped his voice to a mere whisper. 'Begging your pardon, ma'am.'

Lottie had an almost irresistible desire to giggle at the sight of Filby grovelling before the elegant lady. 'I'll get on with my work then, shall I, guv?'

'Yes,' Filby said with a vague wave of his hand, 'and don't let it happen again.'

Aurelia laid a gloved hand on Lottie's shoulder. 'What is your name?'

'Lottie, my lady.'

'Well, Lottie, my maid was taken ill at the start of the journey from Bath and I had to send her home. I need someone to help me with my toilette.' She turned to Filby with a smile that would have melted the hardest heart. 'I take it you have no objections, landlord?'

'No, my lady.' Filby bowed from the waist. 'Of course not. If there is anything you need, you have only to ask.'

Gillingham glanced at the luggage that was piling up on the cobblestones. 'Is this all yours, my lady?'

'Of course it is, Farrell. Have you ever known me to travel light?' Aurelia laughed and tossed her head. The feathers in her dashing straw bonnet waved and danced, and her golden ringlets bobbed with each movement of her head.

Lottie could only stare at her, entranced. She

had never seen anyone as lovely or as lively and spirited as the colonel's wife. 'I'll see that the lady's baggage is taken to her bedchamber,' she volunteered. 'Which room is hers, guv?'

'Why, you silly girl, the best in the house, of course.' Filby seemed to recover from his daze and he strode into the middle of the yard. 'Jem, where are you, boy? Take the lady's luggage to room ten.' He bowed to Aurelia, keeping his head bent low as if addressing royalty. 'Lottie will show you to your room, my lady. If there is anything we can do for you, please don't hesitate to ask.'

Lottie eyed him with distaste. If the silly man bowed any lower he would be in danger of falling flat on his face. She picked up a couple of band-boxes, leaving Jem to bring the heavy items. 'If you would come this way, my lady...'

'I'll see you at supper, Farrell.' Aurelia patted him on the cheek as she walked past. 'I'm extremely hungry, so I hope there is something tasty on the bill of fare.'

Gillingham clicked his heels together, staring straight ahead. 'Wouldn't you rather dine in the privacy of your room, my lady?' He lowered his voice. 'The clientele here might not be to your liking.'

'Nonsense, Farrell. I'm sure I'll find it most entertaining.' Aurelia moved on, pausing to give Jem the benefit of her sparkling smile. 'What is your name?'

He straightened up, shifting from one foot to the other. 'Jem, my lady.'

'Well, thank you for your services, Jem.'

Lottie watched in awe as Lady Aurelia charmed

the guard and the coachman who had brought her this far. It seemed she had a smile and a kind word for everyone; Lottie was impressed, and close to falling under her ladyship's spell. She led the way to number ten, which was the biggest and the best room they had to offer. Even so, as she opened the door and ushered Aurelia inside, Lottie had the feeling that the room, although reasonably clean and comfortable, was not what such a grand lady might expect. An apology tingled on the tip of her tongue as she lit the lamps, but Aurelia uttered a cry of delight.

'A four-poster bed, how delightful, and such a pretty coverlet.' She untied her bonnet and laid it on a chair, while she unbuttoned her silk mantle. 'Charming, utterly charming.'

'I'm afraid it's not what you're used to, my lady.'

Aurelia's violet-blue eyes danced with amusement. 'You obviously have no idea what sort of life a soldier's wife leads. I've slept in bivouacs in the most frightful conditions of rain, ice and snow, or blistering heat, not to mention vermin and wildlife of all sorts. There was even a bear who visited camp in Canada. So you see, Lottie, this is luxury indeed, but only for one night as we travel on tomorrow.' She breathed a sigh of relief as she laid her jacket on the chair. 'It's very hot. I think we might have a storm tonight.'

'It would clear the air.' Lottie moved to open the door and Jem struggled in, laden with cases, a valise and two carpetbags, which he set down on the floor. 'There's still a small trunk, my lady. Shall I bring that too?'

Aurelia cast an eye over the luggage. 'It would

54

be better stored somewhere until the morning, if you would be so kind, Jem?'

His cheeks flushed bright red and he grinned sheepishly. 'Of course, my lady. It's no trouble at all.'

'Wait a moment, please.' Aurelia opened her reticule and took out a coin, which she pressed into his hand. 'Thank you, Jem. That will be all for now.'

He backed out of the room, still grinning.

'What a charming young man.' Aurelia cast a curious glance at Lottie. 'And good-looking too – is he your sweetheart?'

'Certainly not.' Lottie had not meant to speak so sharply. 'I'm sorry, my lady, but Jem is more like a brother to me. You might say we grew up together.'

'Really? How interesting. You must have been very young when you began working here.'

'I was twelve, my lady.'

'And this is what you wanted to do, is it?'

'I didn't have any choice in the matter.'

'I suppose not. One is inclined to forget how hard life is for most people.' Aurelia sighed, shaking her head. 'I don't think I'll change for dinner, but I would like to wash the dust of the road off before I go down to dine.' She slanted a curious look in Lottie's direction. 'Can you dress hair, Lottie?'

'I've practised on May and Ruth; they're the other chambermaids. We do it for each other if and when we get a free moment, which isn't often. It's always busy here.'

'We'll see how good you are then, but I'd like

some hot water first.'

'Of course, my lady.' Lottie bobbed a curtsey. 'I'll fetch it right away.'

In the kitchen Lottie found Mrs Filby and Jezebel talking in loud whispers while Ruth rushed round taking food to the dining room. Mrs Filby turned on Lottie with a low growl. 'I blame you for this.'

'What have I done now?' Lottie looked from one to the other in astonishment. It was not uncommon to get the blame for anything that went wrong, but she had been out all day.

'I let you take a day off and you breeze in late on the arm of that lieutenant who brought the injured soldier to the inn,' Mrs Filby said angrily. 'I don't know what went on between you two, but it must have been something that pleased him or you wouldn't have been singled out by the lady. You're forgetting your place, Lottie Lane. You are a skivvy, little more than a slavey, so you can forget the airs and graces.'

'But that's not how it was,' Lottie protested. 'I bumped into the lieutenant by chance.'

'So you say.' Mrs Filby thrust a serving dish into Lottie's hands. 'Take this to the dining room and give Ruth a hand. We're full tonight and rushed off our feet.'

'Yes, rushed off our feet,' Jezebel repeated, scowling. 'You can carve the ham when you've finished in the dining room, Lottie. I've only got one pair of hands.'

'I have to take some hot water to her ladyship. She's getting ready to come down to dine, and she wants me to do her hair.'

'You're going to do her hair?' Mrs Filby and Jezebel exchanged wry glances. 'I'd like to see that, but she'll have to wait. Do as I tell you first, and see to the stuck-up bitch when you've finished in the dining room.'

There was little that Lottie could do other than to obey her mistress, and then she had to appease Jezebel by carving the ham, which she did to the best of her ability. It was almost an hour later by the time she was free to take the hot water to Lady Aurelia. She opened the door with an apology on her lips, but was met with a sunny smile as Aurelia sat up and swung her legs over the side of the bed.

'Ah, there you are, Lottie. I seized the opportunity for a quick nap, which is a trick I learned during my husband's last campaign. I find I can cope with staying up all night as long as I have plenty of naps in the day. You should try it sometime.' She moved to the washstand. 'I've been looking forward to this. There's nothing as comforting as dousing one's hands and face in clean, warm water, unless it's a long and luxurious bath.'

Lottie filled the washbowl with the rapidly cooling water. 'I'm sorry I took so long, my lady, but they are short-handed in the kitchen.'

Aurelia splashed her face with water and reached for the towel. 'How thoughtless of me. I shouldn't have commandeered your services, but I'm very glad I did. You seem to me to be an extraordinary young woman. Do you ever think about leaving this place and making a life for yourself in the outside world?'

'Sometimes I do, my lady.'

Aurelia moved to the dressing table and sat down, handing a silver-backed brush to Lottie. 'Let's see what you can do with my hair.' She met Lottie's curious gaze in the fly-spotted mirror. 'Tell me how you know Farrell. Did you have an assignation with him?'

Lottie smothered a sigh. Why did everyone jump to the wrong conclusion? 'No, my lady. It wasn't like that.'

'Go on. I've known Farrell for at least five years, and I'm very fond of him. Moreover, I trust his judgement: if he thinks you are worth his attention, then I must take note. Tell me how you came to meet him.'

Lottie launched into an explanation as to how she had come to know Lieutenant Gillingham, and how they had met again at the Middlesex Hospital. Aurelia was a good listener and she seemed genuinely interested.

'I've finished, my lady,' Lottie said, fastening the last curl with a hairpin. 'Is it satisfactory?'

Aurelia turned her head from side to side, examining her reflection from as many angles as possible. 'More than satisfactory, Lottie. You have a natural gift for dressing hair. My maid could not have done better.'

'I'm so glad you're happy with it, my lady.'

Aurelia twisted round on the stool. 'You know you're wasted in a place like this. I'm not certain about nursing as a career, but I would gladly take you on as lady's maid. You're quick and intelligent and you'd pick it up easily.'

'I hadn't even considered that prospect, my lady, but I would like to do something for the brave men who risk their lives to keep us all safe.'

'I applaud your sentiments, but you'll forgive me if I don't share your romantic notions of war and the battlefield. It's a beastly business, Lottie.'

'But you married a soldier, my lady.'

'My family, the de Morgans, have a long military history. My father, being the second son, naturally went into the army, but when his elder brother succumbed to typhus, Papa inherited the earldom. I knew what I was letting myself in for when I married Dashwood, but it's not the life for everyone.' She rose from the stool. 'I like you, Lottie, and I am in dire need of a maidservant. Unfortunately, Merriweather, who has been with me since I was a child, is not in the best of health and I think her days of following the drum are coming to an end. Would you be interested in taking her place?'

'Taking her place, my lady?' Lottie stared at her in disbelief. 'Are you offering me the position?'

Aurelia gave her a long look. 'Yes, I am. But you needn't give me an answer at this very moment. Think about it tonight, and if you decide to throw your lot in with me, be ready first thing in the morning.'

'Thank you, my lady.' Dazed and taken by surprise, Lottie could hardly believe her ears, but Aurelia had picked up her fan and was heading for the door.

'I'll need you to show me to the dining room, Lottie. I'm hungry and I intend to eat my fill, as I always do before we embark on a campaign.'

Lottie rushed to open the door for her. 'Are you planning to accompany your husband, my lady?'

'It goes without saying. I believe an army wife should support her husband, no matter what. We'll be leaving for the Crimea as soon as the order is given.' She stepped outside, pausing for a moment to glance over the balustrade. 'You would travel with me, of course.'

'Do you mean to say that I would be going to the Crimea?'

Aurelia shot her an amused glance. 'I thought that was what you wanted.'

'It was – I mean – it is.'

'Then you accept my offer?'

'I do, my lady. Yes, indeed I do.'

Aurelia clapped her hands, her eyes shining with delight. 'I am so pleased. I took to you at once, Lottie, and I know we will get on very well together. I'm not a demanding mistress, although I do like to have everything my own way.' Her cheeks dimpled prettily and her laughter echoed round the gallery, returning again and again in a merry chorus. 'You will dine with us tonight to celebrate.'

'Oh, no, my lady,' Lottie protested, horrified at the thought. 'That wouldn't do at all. What would Mrs Filby say?'

'Mrs Filby will do as I tell her, and you are now my personal maid and nothing to do with Mr or Mrs Filby. I have appropriated you, Lottie. Lead on.'

Lottie was not at all sure that this was a good idea. The thought of sitting in the dining room together with the other guests and travellers was alien to her. She could barely imagine how it must feel to be waited upon, let alone to have

Mrs Filby, Ruth and May at her beck and call. But Aurelia had spoken, and Lottie was coming to the conclusion that Lady Aurelia Dashwood was unused to having her wishes thwarted. She led the way to the dining room where Gillingham was already seated at a table by the window.

He rose to his feet and pulled up a chair. 'Lady Aurelia, I wondered whether you would be joining me.'

'Of course I am, Farrell, and so is Lottie.' Aurelia laughed at his dumbfounded expression. 'She has agreed to be my personal maid. Merriweather is too old and unwell to accompany me to the Crimea, and it seems that it's Lottie's ambition to go there, so we are all happy.'

'Begging your pardon, my lady.' Mrs Filby had come up behind them, and she was bristling. Lottie would not have been surprised to see the hairs standing to attention on her head like the hackles on a dog's back.

'Yes? What is it?'

Mrs Filby seemed oblivious to Aurelia's icy tone and haughty stare. 'Did I hear right, ma'am? You cannot take my servant without a by-your-leave.'

'Can I not?' Aurelia threw back her head and laughed. 'But I can, and I will. Lottie is not your property, and she is free to do as she pleases.'

Breathing heavily, Mrs Filby folded her arms across her chest. 'We'll see about that, your ladyship. Wait until Filby hears about this.'

Gillingham glared at her. 'You do not speak to Colonel Dashwood's wife in that tone of voice, ma'am. Lady Aurelia has explained the situation and you would do well to accept it with good grace. As far as I can see, you treat your staff abominably, and I'm surprised that any of them remain in your employ.'

'Well!' The word escaped in an explosion of indignation. 'I've never been spoken to like that in my whole life.'

'Then perhaps it's time someone put you in your place.' Aurelia sat down and signalled Lottie to follow suit. 'If you do not wish to serve us, please send someone who will.'

Mrs Filby cast a withering look in Lottie's direction and stomped off towards the kitchen.

Moments later May arrived at their table with a tureen of beef stew, followed by Ruth with a platter of bread and a dish of butter. Lottie was about to jump to her feet to serve the stew, but a frown from Aurelia made her sink back on her chair. She sent an apologetic look to Ruth, who served them, tight-lipped and unsmiling.

'Well then, Lottie,' Gillingham said cheerfully. 'So you're to get your wish after all. You'll be accompanying us when we embark for the Crimea.'

'Yes, sir.' Lottie waited for Lady Aurelia to start eating before picking up her spoon. For the first time in her life she was grateful for the strict rules of etiquette that had been drummed into her at school. At least she would not disgrace herself at table. She knew she was being scrutinised and she concentrated on her meal, barely tasting Jezebel's excellent stew.

Gillingham and Aurelia chatted amicably throughout the meal, and to Lottie's relief she was not expected to contribute to the conversation. She could feel Mrs Filby's eyes upon her and the curious stares of the other diners, but eventually the tables were cleared, and Mrs Filby was called away. Even so, Lottie was relieved when Lady Aurelia announced that she was going to retire to her room. They left Gillingham to his brandy and cigar, with Ruth hovering in the background, waiting to make the tables ready for breakfast next morning.

'You did well tonight,' Aurelia said as Lottie brushed her hair. 'You have a natural desire to look after people, and you'll make an excellent maid. I'm pleased with you already.' She shook her long golden hair so that it spread about her shoulders like a cloak. 'I can put myself to bed. I'm not entirely helpless, and you look tired. We need to be up early, so I want hot water and a cup of chocolate at six o'clock on the dot. Good night, Lottie.'

Still in a daze at the sudden turn of events, Lottie made her way to the attic. She felt that she ought to apologise, even though she had done nothing wrong, but Ruth was obviously in a bad mood.

'You must be off your head. I wouldn't go to war, even if you gave me a hundred quid.' Ruth gave her palliasse a shake. 'Blooming bed bugs. The little devils get everywhere.'

'I'm bitten all over,' May complained. 'I'd like just once to sleep in one of them four-posters we've got in the best bedchambers, with freshly laundered cotton sheets and an embroidered coverlet.'

'Lottie will be sleeping in a tent with nothing but a horse blanket between her and the damp earth,' Ruth said spitefully. 'You wouldn't find me camping on a battlefield.'

'You won't put me off.' Lottie lay down on top of the patchwork coverlet. It was hot beneath the eaves and her bedding had also become infested, which only added to her discomfort. 'Anything would be better than living like this.'

'Don't say things like that.' May covered her head with the grimy sheet. 'We got no choice.'

'Speak for yourself. I'm going to find meself a rich husband, or at least one what can pay the rent each week and put food on the table.' Ruth reached for a clay pipe and a poke of tobacco.

'Don't you dare light that pipe,' Lottie said angrily. 'You'll set the place on fire one night.'

'Yes, and the smoke makes me cough,' May added. 'Go to sleep, Ruth. We'll be up again in a few hours.'

Lottie lay back and closed her eyes. This would be her last night sleeping in the attic, which was stifling in summer, freezing in winter, and damp and draughty in the intervening months. She might not be able to fulfil her ambition to nurse the wounded, but she would serve her country in a different way. She had known Lady Aurelia Dashwood for only a few hours, but already she was her devoted servant. Morning could not come soon enough, and an added bonus – she might meet Gideon again.

Chapter Four

Jem was up and about, going through his seemingly endless set of chores before the first mail coach was due to arrive. Lottie could hear his cheery voice as she made her way down the wooden stairs to the yard, where the ostlers were preparing the horses and the young stable boy was adding to the already festering muck heap in the corner of the stable yard.

'Jem.' Lottie had to raise her voice in order to be heard above the clatter of horses' hoofs and the deep drone of men's voices. 'Jem, will you fetch her ladyship's luggage?'

He leaned the besom against the wall and came towards her, wiping his hands on the seat of his breeches. 'So it's true. You really are leaving us?'

'It's a wonderful opportunity, Jem. I'll get the chance to travel and see the world.'

'You'll see a lot of things you don't want to see,' he said grimly. 'I ain't been to war, but I've heard the soldiers talking, and it don't appeal to me. I'd rather slave away for Filby than risk my neck on the battlefield.'

'I'm a lady's maid now. Lady Aurelia has been on numerous campaigns with her husband, and she's come through without a scratch. I'll be with her, so I'll be safe, and I might be of service to some of the wounded soldiers.'

Jem's habitual grin faded into a frown. 'You'd

best watch out for them soldiers, or who knows how you might end up?'

'I'm not a fool,' Lottie said angrily. 'I know what I'm doing, and you might at least try to be happy for me. I don't want to spend the rest of my life working from dawn to dusk for a pittance.'

'Maybe you're right. I suppose joining the army would be a way out. It can't be worse than this. Anyway, Trotter was telling me that the railways will put an end to mail coaches, and it's already happening.'

'You don't have to be a soldier in order to get away from here. You could become an engine driver or a guard on the railway. You could do anything you set your mind to,' Lottie said thoughtfully. 'Anyway, you'd best fetch her ladyship's things. Lieutenant Gillingham ordered the carriage for half-past six, so it should be here soon.'

Jem gave her a peck on the cheek. 'Take care of yourself, Lottie. I'll miss you, girl.'

'I'll miss you too.' Lottie watched him as he loped off to take the outside stairs two at a time. She was sorry to leave Jem, who had been her true friend, but her spirit of adventure had been awakened and she was eager for new experiences. She waited, clutching the small valise that contained Lady Aurelia's valuables, and it occurred to her suddenly that she ought to inform Uncle Sefton of her change in circumstances. It would be several months until she attained her majority, and he was still her guardian, even though she had not had any contact with him since starting work at The Swan. She was still thinking about it when Lady Aurelia appeared on the balcony, with Jem close behind staggering beneath the weight of her various valises and carpetbags.

Lottie's stomach churned with excitement as she heard the sound of approaching horses' hoofs and the hired carriage was driven into the stable yard and came to a halt. Gillingham strolled out of the taproom and tossed a coin to Jem as he hefted the luggage into the growler.

'Good grief,' Aurelia said, laughing. 'I thought I was travelling lighter than this. I'm afraid you'll have to sit on the box with the driver, Farrell.'

He shook his head. 'Don't worry, my lady. I intend to ride and I've hired a hack for the purpose.'

'I would prefer to ride also but, as you see, I am not dressed for it.' Aurelia glanced down at her elegant travelling outfit. 'At least when I'm abroad I can get away with conduct that would be considered unseemly at home.' She turned to Lottie with a mischievous chuckle. 'Are you sure you want to be connected to a woman who breaks all the rules?'

'More than ever, my lady,' Lottie said firmly. 'I want to be just like you.'

'D'you hear that, Farrell? I have a staunch ally at last. Poor Merriweather was forever telling me that my actions were not those of a lady, and now I have *carte blanche* to do exactly as I please.'

Farrell helped Jem to place the trunk on end beside the driver. 'I doubt if the colonel will approve, my lady.'

'Dashwood adores me, as you very well know. He supports me in all that I do.' Aurelia allowed Jem to hand her into the carriage. 'Come along, Lottie. We've thirty or forty miles to go before we're in Chatham, and by the looks of that clear sky it's going to be another hot day.' She settled herself in the corner. 'You may sit beside me. I don't expect you to perch on the roof or run behind.'

Lottie climbed in and made herself as small as possible, not wanting to cramp her mistress or to crease the voluminous skirts of Aurelia's pale green poplin de laine gown. 'I learn quickly, my lady, but this is all very new to me.'

'Of course it is,' Aurelia agreed, smiling. 'You have had an extraordinary life for one so young, and I promise you it will be anything less than ordinary from now on.' Aurelia closed her eyes. 'I am going to have a nap. Wake me when we stop to change horses.' Her perky straw hat slipped over one eye as she leaned back against the squabs.

It was late afternoon by the time they arrived outside the house in Chatham. Set in a large garden, surrounded by trees, with well-kept lawns and neat flowerbeds, the three-storey building looked comfortable and solid. The white stucco gleamed in the afternoon sunshine and pink roses clambered over the stone portico. A maidservant rushed out, followed by a man wearing a leather apron, who hefted the trunk from the driver's seat as if it were filled with feathers instead of the weighty contents of Lady Aurelia's clothes press.

Farrell had ridden alongside them for most of the way, but had gone on ahead when they neared their destination, and was waiting to hand Aurelia from the carriage. Lottie was the first to alight and she stood on the path feeling shy and apprehensive. It was too late to change her mind, but she felt shabby and out of place in her new surroundings. The housemaid fixed her with a curious stare, but neither of them spoke.

Aurelia sailed into the house, leaving Lottie little alternative but to follow in her wake.

The interior was spacious, and cool air wafted in through open windows, adding the scent of roses to that of lavender and beeswax polish. The stark whiteness of the walls was relieved by large oil paintings, mostly scenes of victorious military battles, and a cocked hat had been left on a pier table as if to emphasise the fact that this was a soldier's residence. Aurelia took off her straw bonnet and tossed it in the air so that it landed on a marble bust of the Iron Duke.

Her merry laughter seemed to bring the silent house to life. 'A direct hit, every time.' She turned to Gillingham. 'I'll wager you couldn't do as well, Farrell.'

He tucked his shako under his arm. 'I'm sure you're right, my lady.'

'Don't be a spoilsport.' Aurelia snatched the hat from the duke, where it had hung over his sightless eyes at a rakish angle, and she placed it on Gillingham's head. 'Give me a smile, Farrell.' She seized his shako and put it on. 'How do I look?'

'Dashing, as always, my lady.'

'Lottie, remind me to order a shako from my milliner.' Aurelia peered at her reflection in one of the many gilt-framed mirrors. 'It is rather fetching.'

Lottie stood beside the housemaid, watching this piece of theatre wide-eyed. She had not imagined that titled ladies behaved with such frivolity, and there seemed to be little difference between Ruth's flirtatious behaviour and that of the colonel's wife. She glanced at the maid, expecting to see her looking shocked or at least a bit surprised by her mistress's antics, but she appeared to be unmoved and was staring straight ahead.

'Is it always like this?' Lottie whispered.

'This is nothing. Wait until they have a party, then you'll see some goings-on.' The maid jumped to attention at the sound of her name.

'Tilda.' Aurelia snapped her fingers. 'Stop gossiping and bring tea and cake to the drawing room. By the way,' she added casually, 'Merriweather is unwell and will be staying in Bath for the foreseeable future. Miss Lane is my new maid.'

Tilda bobbed a curtsey. 'Yes, my lady.'

'Is the master at home?' Aurelia demanded imperiously. 'He should have been here to greet me.'

'I believe he's with Lady Petunia, my lady.' Tilda curtseyed again before hurrying off.

'If I didn't know better I would be jealous of Lady Petunia.' Aurelia posed in front of the mirror, making a *moue* at her reflection as she tilted the shako at various angles.

Gillingham crossed the floor to stand behind her. 'You know, you do look splendid. In my hat.' He tweaked it off her head. 'But it's a trifle too large for you, my lady.'

'Spoilsport.' She turned to face him. 'Come and have some tea, Farrell, and stop calling me "my lady". Lottie is one of us now. She won't gossip if you call me Aurelia.' She shot a sideways glance at Lottie. 'You won't, will you? I'm sure I can trust you to be discreet.'

'Yes, my lady.' Lottie followed Tilda's example and curtseyed. 'I mean, no. I won't gossip. I saw things you wouldn't credit when I was at The Swan.'

'I'm sure you did.' Aurelia beckoned to the manservant who was standing by the entrance with the pile of baggage. 'Hansford, take my things to my room and show Lottie to her quarters. She will have Merriweather's room.'

Hansford bowed. 'Yes, my lady.'

'When you've done that I want you to find the colonel and inform him of my arrival.' She slipped her hand through the crook of Gillingham's arm. 'Dashwood simply adores Lady Petunia. I am definitely second best.'

'Never,' Gillingham said gallantly. 'You have never come second to anything or anyone in your whole life, Aurelia.'

She laughed and pinched his cheek as they strolled off, arm in arm.

Lottie turned to Hansford. She had thought him surly at first, but now she could see that a long scar on the right side of his face was the cause of his permanent scowl. She simply had to satisfy her curiosity. 'Who is Lady Petunia?'

'Ask no questions and you'll be told no lies.' He picked up as much of the luggage as he could carry. 'What happened to Merriweather? Why are you here instead of the old girl?'

'I don't know exactly. I think she was taken ill. That's what her ladyship told me.'

'Where did she find you?' Hansford demanded as he limped off, burdened by his heavy load.

'You smell like a taproom.'

Lottie sniffed her sleeve and her heart sank. He was right. Her clothes were impregnated with the smell of beer and tobacco smoke, but she had never noticed it until now. She followed him towards the back stairs. 'I worked in a London coaching inn.'

He said nothing, concentrating all his energy on mounting the narrow staircase. He came to a halt on the landing and dumped the baggage on the floor, flexing his fingers. 'I'd keep out of the servants' quarters if I was you; at least until you've got rid of that stink. Mrs Manners, the housekeeper, don't approve of public houses. If she thinks you've got loose morals you'll be out on the street afore you can say knife.'

'I am very respectable,' Lottie said stiffly. 'And Lady Aurelia hired me, so if Mrs Manners doesn't like it she knows what she can do.'

'Ho, like that is it? You're going to be trouble, I can see that. What's your name, girl?'

'It's Trouble with a capital T.' Lottie picked up one of the heavier carpetbags. 'But you may call me Lottie. Now, where do I take this?'

'Follow me, and less of the cheek. You'd best mind your manners in the servants' hall. You'll find it a bit different from working in a hostelry.' Hansford picked up the bags and led the way along a wide corridor, coming to a halt at the top of the main staircase. 'This is her ladyship's room. Open the door for me, there's a good girl.'

Despite his condescending tone, Lottie did as he asked without any argument. She could hold her own with ostlers, coachmen and male travellers who thought that inn servants were easy game, but for now she would bide her time. She opened the door and stepped inside to the room of her dreams. Furnished in the French style with ornate gilded furniture upholstered in blue toile de jouy fabric, the room was light and sunny. Aubusson rugs placed in appropriate places made pools of delicate colour on the highly polished oak floorboards, and the scent of flowers vied with the lingering fragrance of Aurelia's perfume. It was a heady mix and to Lottie it seemed a boudoir fit for a princess, let alone the wife of an army colonel.

Hansford dumped the baggage on the floor with a sigh of relief. 'I dunno how one woman could need to bring so much with her, but it's the same wherever we go, whether it's on a campaign abroad or moving between Bath and Chatham.'

'Do you always travel with them?' Lottie asked curiously. She had noticed that Hansford walked with a limp. 'Are you a soldier too?'

'I was, until I was wounded in Afghanistan. I was the colonel's batman in India when he was a captain seconded to the Bombay Sappers. He kept me on as his orderly, even when I was unfit for service.'

'I see,' Lottie said slowly. 'He sounds like a good man.'

'The best.' Hansford wiped his hands on his apron. 'You'll be expected to unpack and put everything in its place, but I expect you know that.'

Lottie stared at the pile of luggage. 'I'm used to working hard. This will seem easy by comparison.'

'Better you than me, that's all I can say.' Hansford made a move towards the doorway. 'Is there anything you want to know before I go?'

'There's just one thing,' Lottie said hesitantly. 'Who is Lady Petunia? Is she related to the colonel?'

Hansford's twisted lips curved into a semblance of a smile. 'You want to know who Lady Petunia is. You'd best follow me. I'm sure the unpacking can wait for five minutes.'

Lottie could not resist the opportunity to see more of the house and its grounds, and she was eager to discover who it was whose charms outdid those of the beautiful, spirited Lady Aurelia. She followed Hansford as he retraced his steps down the back stairs and through a maze of passages until they were outside in a large yard facing the stable block and coach house. He strode on, making surprising speed despite his uneven gait, and Lottie had to run in order to keep up with him. They passed through the kitchen garden where an aged gardener was tending to the rows of leafy vegetables, and at last they came to a low building surrounded by a brick wall. Lottie was used to the smell of horse dung, but the odour emanating from the pen was far worse. She covered her nose with her hand.

'You're having me on, Mr Hansford.'

He stopped with his hand on the gate. 'It's just Hansford, miss.'

'All right, Hansford. Then it's just Lottie from now on.'

He might have been grinning – it was hard to tell – but he unlatched the gate and ushered her into a straw-filled pen. 'Permission to enter, Colonel?'

'Permission granted, Hansford.' A straw hat

appeared from the depths of the sty, followed by a corpulent body, and then, as the colonel straightened up, a large black pig emerged.

Hansford closed the gate. 'Her ladyship has arrived, sir.'

'By Jove! Is it that time already?' Colonel Dashwood bent down to stroke the sow's head. 'Sorry, old girl. I'll have to leave you now.' He looked up and frowned. 'Who's this, Hansford? Lady Petunia doesn't usually like visitors, but she doesn't seem to mind this young person.'

Hansford pushed Lottie forward. 'This is Lady Aurelia's new maid, sir.'

'What happened to Merriweather? The old girl hasn't turned up her toes, has she?'

'I believe not, Colonel. Apparently she is unwell and has remained in Bath.'

'Sorry to hear that.' Colonel Dashwood looked Lottie up and down. 'Pretty girl. Best keep her away from the barracks, Hansford. What's her name?'

Lottie stepped forward. 'My name is Lottie Lane, sir.' She tickled the pig behind the ears.

'Well, well, Lady Petunia approves. You've got a way with animals, Lottie Lane.'

Lottie stared at the pig in wonder. So this was Lady Aurelia's rival. 'I worked in a coaching inn until yesterday, Colonel,' she said, controlling her desire to laugh with difficulty. 'I'm more used to horses, but she seems like a nice pig.'

'Lady Petunia is a Black Berkshire. She's more intelligent than a dog, and most people, if it comes to that.' Colonel Dashwood produced an apple from his jacket pocket and handed it to Lottie.

'Give her this. She's partial to an apple or two.'

Hansford cleared his throat. 'Lady Aurelia is in the drawing room, sir. Shall I tell her that you'll be with her as soon as you've changed your clothes?'

'Eh? What's wrong with the way I'm dressed?'

Lottie held the apple on the palm of her hand and Lady Petunia took it with surprising gentleness. 'She has very good manners, Colonel.'

'Of course she has. Lady Petunia is a thoroughbred, and better behaved than most of the nobility. I'd have her in the house, but Mrs Manners wouldn't approve.'

'I'd best get back to my work,' Lottie said, hoping that the smell of the pigsty was not clinging to her garments. It was bad enough to know that she stank of the alehouse, without adding animal odours as well.

Colonel Dashwood's blue eyes twinkled beneath his thick white eyebrows, which matched his bushy white moustache. He was obviously a good many years older than his wife – old enough, Lottie thought, to be her father – but despite his portly frame and weather-beaten features, he had a kindly expression. During her eight years at The Swan, Lottie had learned a great deal about human nature, and her instincts told her that here was a man she could trust. She even liked his pig.

'I've laid out your uniform, Colonel,' Hansford said tactfully. 'You have a regimental dinner to attend this evening, if you recall, sir?'

'Dash it, I'd quite forgotten.' Colonel Dashwood patted Lady Petunia's head. 'I'll see you tomorrow, old girl. I must leave you now.' He followed

Lottie from the sty. 'Make sure you fasten the gate securely, Hansford. She got into the vegetable garden yesterday. Figgis was very upset.'

'I will, don't worry, sir.' Hansford stayed back to make sure that Lady Petunia would not escape again, and Lottie followed the colonel into the house. To her surprise he retraced the route that Hansford had taken and entered through the scullery.

'Where's Hansford?' he demanded, lowering himself onto a wooden stool. 'I want him to help me off with my boots. Mrs Manners will have a fit of the vapours if I bring pig muck into the house.' He glanced over his shoulder. 'Hansford? Where is the fellow?'

Lottie hesitated, wondering what was expected of her. It would not be the first time she had helped a gentleman off with his boots, but she was not at the inn now. She glanced over her shoulder in time to see Hansford out in the yard, deep in conversation with Tilda. 'Can I help you, sir?'

Colonel Dashwood puffed out his cheeks and his moustache bristled. 'Where is Hansford? This isn't a task for a slip of a girl like you.'

'Let me try, sir. I see a lady in black bombazine coming this way. Could it be Mrs Manners?'

'Pull off me boots, girl. What are you waiting for?' Colonel Dashwood held up one chubby leg, turning red in the face with the effort.

Lottie grasped the toe and heel of the muddy boot, gave it a twist and a tweak and tugged hard. It slipped off as if the colonel's foot had been greased. She used the same technique to pull off the other boot.

'Well done,' Colonel Dashwood said, wheezing a sigh of relief. 'Hansford couldn't have made a better job of it.' He rose to his stockinged feet. 'Take them into the boot-room. Hansford will clean them up.'

'Yes, sir.' Lottie slipped out into the yard just as Mrs Manners entered the scullery. She did not want to meet the housekeeper until she had had a chance to change, and she loitered outside until the sound of voices died away. She tried hard not to stare at Hansford and Tilda, who made an unlikely pair, and she looked up into the blue sky, watching the swifts dart and dive about like airborne acrobats.

Hansford turned his head to look at her. He broke off the conversation and strolled across the cobblestones, followed by Tilda. 'I'll see to them.' He took the boots from Lottie. 'You'd best clean yourself up too.'

'You've got pig muck on your boots and the hem of your skirt.' Tilda put her head on one side. 'And your clothes smell something awful.'

'I know. You don't have to tell me.'

'She'll go mad,' Tilda said, shaking her head. 'Mrs Manners can't stand slovenliness.' She exchanged glances with Hansford. 'Tell you what, Lottie, as you're new here I'll help you out this once. Leave your boots with Hansford, and I'll find you a uniform to wear. You can sort your clothes out later.'

'We have to keep Mrs Manners happy,' Hansford added. 'She's a tartar when she's roused.'

'Why does the colonel keep her on?' Lottie asked curiously. 'Even he seems to be scared of her.'

78

'Who knows?' Hansford walked off towards the stables.

'Come on.' Tilda opened the scullery door. 'We'll get you something from the cupboard where Mrs Manners keeps the uniforms.'

The linen cupboard was situated at the end of a wide passage next to the housekeeper's office. It appeared to be locked, but Tilda jiggled the door and it opened. She glanced over her shoulder and grinned. 'Hansford was meant to fix this, but it's handy being able to get a clean uniform or apron without having to grovel to Mrs Manners.' She selected a black cotton dress and held it up against Lottie. 'That looks about your size. You can change in the broom cupboard. I'll keep a lookout for Mrs M.'

Minutes later Lottie emerged from the stuffy cupboard. 'It fits.'

'I knew it would,' Tilda said smugly. 'You can wash your duds in the scullery when we've finished clearing away the supper things. They'll dry overnight in the laundry room.'

'Thank you.' Lottie held out her hand, but Tilda ignored the friendly gesture.

'I only done it to please Herbie. He seems to think you'll be good for her ladyship. She led poor old Merriweather a real dance, I can tell you.'

'Herbie?' Lottie stared at her, confused.

'Hansford to you. We're stepping out together, in case you hadn't noticed, so hands off.'

'It's a promise,' Lottie said firmly. She could see that, Tilda thought she had won a great battle, although it was hard to understand the attraction. Hansford was a good twenty years Tilda's senior, and his best friend could not in all honesty call him good-looking, but Tilda seemed to think him a great prize.

'That's settled then, but don't expect me to keep getting you out of trouble, because I got better things to do.' Tilda stalked off towards the kitchen, leaving Lottie to find her own way back to Lady Aurelia's bedroom, but as luck would have it she turned a corner and came face to face with Mrs Manners.

'So you are the new lady's maid.' Ermintrude Manners looked her up and down. 'I wasn't consulted about your appointment.'

Lottie bobbed a curtsey, not knowing what to say or do in such circumstances. It was hardly her fault that the housekeeper had been overlooked.

'I suppose you understand your duties while you are in this house?'

'I think so, ma'am.'

'You address me as Mrs Manners.'

'Yes, Mrs Manners.'

'That's better.' Mrs Manners frowned thoughtfully. 'I suppose you will have Merriweather's old room, although I am loath to surrender it to someone like you.'

'I can sleep anywhere, Mrs Manners. I shared a room at The Swan; I don't mind doing so again.'

Mrs Manners flinched visibly. 'Yes, I heard that you'd been working in a common coaching inn. Well, we'll have none of your lewd behaviour and bad language in this house, so be warned.'

'I never swear and I don't allow men to take liberties,' Lottie said angrily. 'I'm a respectable young woman.'

'So you say, but what were you doing in such a place at all, I might ask?' Mrs Manners held up her hand. 'No, don't answer that. Come with me and I'll show you to your room. I just hope you will live up to your boast, Miss Lane.'

They climbed the back stairs to the top floor where Lottie discovered she was to have a room of her own. It was large enough for an iron bedstead, a deal chest of drawers, a washstand with a tiled top and. splashback, and a small cupboard. The floorboards were scrubbed to snowy whiteness and rag rugs gave the room a homely atmosphere. A dormer window looked out over the front garden, with glimpses of the road between the beech trees. It was not beautiful like Lady Aurelia's boudoir but it was airy and comfortable.

'It is not what you are used to?' Mrs Manners' sharp voice brought Lottie back from a delightful dream of sleeping on her own for the first time in her life.

'No, it's far better than anything I have had before. It's a delightful room.'

'Delightful? I'd hardly put it like that. Anyway, it's yours for the duration of your stay in Chatham, although I doubt if that will be for long.' Ermintrude Manners was about to leave the room, but Lottie barred her way.

'I don't understand. Why do you say that?'

'You don't look the type who could stand the life of a camp follower, or the sights and sounds of the battlefield, with gunfire, and mangled bodies lying on the ground and soldiers dying in agony and calling out for their mothers.'

81

'Have you ever been on a campaign, Mrs Manners?'

'Certainly not, but I've heard the soldiers' tales and I'm very glad that I live here, in this lovely house, where I am safe from such horrors. Think hard before you get involved with Lady Aurelia, Miss Lane. Think very hard.'

The mention of Lady Aurelia's name brought Lottie back to the present with a start. She had almost forgotten that she had duties to perform other than making herself comfortable in her new quarters. 'I should be unpacking Lady Aurelia's cases,' she said urgently.

'So you should. I was wondering when you were going to remember why you are here.' Mrs Manners moved a little closer to Lottie, sniffing the air. 'I suggest you purchase some cologne, Miss Lane. You have a very distinctive odour, and it is not pleasant.'

'Yes, Mrs Manners, I'll do that, of course.' Lottie backed out of the room. 'Excuse me, ma'am. I have a lot to do.'

Chapter Five

Lottie had barely finished unpacking the large trunk when Lady Aurelia breezed into the room. 'Heavens, did I bring all that luggage with me?' She sat down on the edge of the bed. 'I thought I brought only the bare essentials.'

'I'm sorry, my lady. I would have been quicker,

but I'm not entirely sure where everything goes.'

'Don't worry about that,' Aurelia said airily. 'I'm sure it will come in time, but for now I need you to find a suitable evening gown for me to wear. The regimental dinners are so tedious, but one must attend. I shall need you to accompany me, Lottie.'

'What do I have to do, my lady?'

'Very little. You take my cloak and wait for me in the anteroom. It's only a short walk to the officers' mess, and I usually make my escape from the proceedings when the ladies leave the gentlemen to their port and cigars. Between you and me I find the other wives a complete bore.' Aurelia kicked off her shoes and threw herself down on the satin coverlet.

Lottie gazed at the gowns she had unpacked and laid out over the back of a chair. 'I'm sorry, my lady, but I don't know which one to pick.'

'I feel crimson,' Aurelia said lazily. 'Magenta is my favourite colour. I intend to be a peacock amongst the dowdy hens.'

It was not hard to find the shimmering silk taffeta gown amongst the paler muslins and satins. Lottie held it up and the creases seemed to iron themselves out as if by magic. Bugle beads glistened on the bodice and she could imagine how it must look by candlelight. 'It's beautiful, my lady, but the waist is so small. I'm not sure I could fit into such a gown.'

'Then it's lucky you won't have to.' Aurelia snapped into a sitting position. 'You'll have to lace my stays tightly, or I might have a problem myself.' She yawned and reclined once again amongst the embroidered pillows. 'I won't be able to eat a thing, so you must ask Cook to send a tray to my room when we return. She knows what I like. Wake me up at half-past six, Lottie. I think I'll take a nap.'

When Lottie first arrived at the officers' mess, she had not realised that the Dashwoods' house was adjacent to the barracks. It was a warm evening and Aurelia refused to wear her cloak, leaving Lottie to carry it for her. Colonel Dashwood had changed into mess dress and applied a liberal amount of bay rum to his thinning hair and an additional splash of cologne, which left a perfumed trail in his wake as he escorted his beautiful wife into the building. Lady Aurelia had been less liberal with the scent bottle, but the sunlight played on her golden coronet of curls, and turned the beads on her bodice into molten glass. Her waist, accentuated by the swinging bell of her crimson skirts, was whittled away to a hand span, and her low décolletage was complemented by a ruby and diamond necklace with matching earrings. Lottie basked in her reflected glory. She felt a sense of pride, like an artist who had created a masterpiece for the rest of the world to admire and praise, and it did not matter that her own gown was plain and downright dowdy.

Lady Aurelia outshone all the other women present, and it amused Lottie to see them dragging their husbands into the mess hall in an attempt to keep them at a safe distance from temptation. The unattached officers paid their respects, bowing over Aurelia's gloved hand while keeping a wary eye on her husband. She greeted them with a pleasant smile and a nod of her head, but her attitude changed subtly when Gillingham approached. Lottie noted with some surprise that her ladyship's cheeks were flushed and her eyes sparkled as she held her hand out to him.

'Ah, Gillingham,' Colonel Dashwood said affably. 'Be so good as to escort my wife to the table while I have a word with the major-general.' He patted Aurelia on the arm. 'I'll join you in a moment, my dear. I need to speak to Fluffy.'

'Of course, Dashwood. Take as long as you like. I'm in good hands with Farrell.' Aurelia slipped her hand through the crook of Gillingham's arm, and they walked off, chatting like old friends.

'Fluffy?' Lottie murmured, gazing at the gentleman in question whose mess dress was heavy with gold braid and his chest emblazoned with medals.

'Major-General Frederick Fothergill, known to his friends as Fluffy.'

She turned to find herself looking into the smiling face of Private Ellis, although she barely recognised him in his smart uniform. His pallor had been replaced by a healthy glow and the ugly bruise on his forehead had already begun to fade.

'I didn't expect to see you so soon, although I hoped you might still be here.'

'I certainly didn't think I'd be lucky enough to see you again so soon, Lottie.' He glanced at the velvet cloak she was holding. 'How did you become involved with Lady Aurelia?'

'You make it sound like a crime,' she said, laughing. 'She has taken me on as her personal

85

maid. I've come up in the world from washing out chamber pots.'

He shook his head. 'You might think differently if her ladyship decides to follow her husband to the Crimea. It's no place for a woman.'

'Miss Nightingale doesn't think so.'

'Miss Nightingale has no experience of warfare.' Gideon glanced over his shoulder at the sound of a sharp command. 'I'm on duty, Lottie. Are you going to wait here for her ladyship? These affairs can go on well into the small hours.'

'I suppose so. She told me to wait, so I suppose I must.'

'Private Ellis.'

The staccato bark of his sergeant made Gideon snap to attention. 'I might see you in between courses.' He marched into the mess hall and the door closed behind him.

Silence echoed round the anteroom and for a moment Lottie thought that she was alone, but a muffled cough behind her made her turn her head to see a woman wearing the severe black uniform of a lady's maid. The woman crossed the floor to stand beside her. 'I'm Maggie Cole, Mrs Fothergill's maid. You must be standing in for Miss Merriweather.'

'I'm her replacement – Lottie Lane. Miss Merriweather is remaining in Bath, so I've been told.'

'Poor old thing. She struggled to keep up with her ladyship. Sometimes she'd look so tired you'd wonder how she managed to keep going, so I'm not surprised.' Maggie put her head on one side. 'Where did you work before this?'

Lottie hooked the cloak over one arm. 'I should

hang this up or it'll get creased.'

'Give it to me and I'll do it for you.' Maggie took the garment from Lottie and strolled over to a row of pegs hung with military caps and shakos. She took a couple down and draped them over the back of a chair. 'That'll do,' she said, hanging the cloak on the empty pegs before returning to Lottie's side. 'We have to look out for our ladies. Never mind the men, they can sort themselves out.'

'Do we have to stand here all evening?' Lottie asked anxiously. 'I haven't eaten yet and I'm starving.'

Maggie pulled up two stools, setting them close to the mess hall doors. 'Leave it to me. I'm used to this game.' She winked and nodded, turning her head as a door on the far side of the room opened and a procession of waiters marched towards the mess hall carrying silver serving dishes.

Maggie accosted the last one, a young fresh-faced private who looked pale and nervous. 'Bring us a plate of food, love,' she said, fluttering her lashes. 'You wouldn't see two lovely ladies go hungry, would you?'

He cleared his throat. 'I'll get into trouble, miss.'

'What's your name, Private?'

'Perks, miss.'

'Your first name, Perks.'

His blush deepened. 'I have to go, miss.'

Maggie clutched his sleeve. 'You can tell me, Perks.'

'Rodney, miss.'

'A very nice name, Rodney. I'll see that the major-general hears about it if anyone says anything untoward. Bring us a small plateful of something tasty, there's a good fellow.'

He nodded and hurried into the mess hall just as the doors were about to close. Maggie turned to Lottie with a smug smile. 'See! That's how you do it. We'll have the tastiest morsel he can find, bless him.'

'Poor boy,' Lottie said softly. 'You embarrassed him, Maggie.'

'He'll get over it, and I'll give him a kiss to reward him for his trouble.'

'I thought all ladies' maids were prim and proper. You're not a bit like that.'

Maggie threw back her head and laughed. 'I am when it's necessary. You'll learn the tricks of the trade, Lottie my girl. But my motto is to have as much fun as possible while I'm young enough to enjoy myself.'

'I suppose I can't argue with that.'

'My, you're the serious one, aren't you?' Maggie eyed her curiously. 'You never answered my question about your last position. Were you in service?'

'Not really. I was a maid of all work in a coaching inn.'

'Well, I never did. What with you speaking like the gentry and all that, I would have thought you were a convent girl. As for me, I was raised in the foundling hospital and sent into service when I was eleven. I don't know who my ma and pa were and I don't suppose I'll ever find out.'

Maggie broke off as the waiters teemed out of the mess hall with their empty dishes. She winked at Private Perks as he hurried past. 'Don't forget us, Rodney, love.'

'You shouldn't tease him,' Lottie said, trying not to giggle. 'He's just a boy.'

'They're all boys, but that doesn't stop the army sending them into battle. They'll grow up soon enough.'

'Have you seen military service, Maggie?'

'No, but I used to step out with a sapper. He'd seen conflict, and from what he told me it wasn't pretty. I'm glad that Mrs Fothergill isn't the sort of army wife who feels she has to follow her husband to war. She's happy to stay at home and so am I.'

'Lady Aurelia isn't like that.'

Maggie pulled a face. 'She's got quite a reputation, has that one. You'll find out, Lottie. I just hope you're up to the challenge.' She swivelled round on her stool as the waiters reappeared. This time they were empty-handed, except for Perks. He thrust a plate of food into Maggie's hands. 'That's all I could get, miss.'

She blew him a kiss. 'Thank you, Rodney. I'll love you for ever.'

He dashed into the mess hall, leaving them with bread, cheese and a slice or two of roast chicken.

'I do hope he doesn't get into trouble,' Lottie said through a mouthful of cheddar.

'This will do, but he'd better bring us some dessert, or I'll be very cross with that young man.' Maggie bit into a hunk of bread. 'He won't warrant a kiss unless I get a bowl of strawberries and cream or some fruit jelly.'

'Are we the only ladies' maids in the camp?' Lottie selected a piece of chicken.

'The wives of the more junior officers are more

likely to live in the town, and they'll have a servant or two, but not like us.' Maggie licked her fingers. 'We're far superior to most. Just remember that, my friend.' She slid off her stool. 'I'm going outside for a breath of air, but I'll be back in a few minutes.'

Maggie's idea of time seemed to be elastic and she was gone for such a long time that Lottie became worried and she went to open the door and look outside. Darkness was falling but she could just make out Maggie, who was sharing a cigarillo with the sentry. The end of the butt glowed in the dusk and puffs of smoke floated up into the sky.

'Maggie,' Lottie said as loudly as she dared. 'They've cleared away the main course.'

Maggie took a last drag on the cigarillo before handing it back to the man on duty. 'Ta, love. I needed that.' She sashayed towards Lottie, exhaling smoke. 'Don't look so shocked. I enjoy a smoke just as much as the men.'

'I was just thinking that you'd both be in trouble if you were caught,' Lottie said calmly.

'Life's no fun unless you take a chance or two.' Maggie opened the door. 'I don't know about you, but I'm ready for dessert.' She linked her hand through Lottie's arm. 'Come on, love.'

They arrived back to find Private Perks standing self-consciously by the door, clutching a plate of strawberries and cream. Maggie released Lottie and snatched it from him. 'You're a darling, Rodney. You must be your mother's pride and joy.'

He blushed to the roots of his blond hair. 'I

90

can't get you any more food, miss. That'll have to be the last.'

Maggie popped a strawberry into her mouth. 'I fancy one of those little cakes,' she said, eyeing a silver platter laid out with dainty pastries.

'Let him go,' Lottie said in a low voice. 'Don't tease the poor chap.'

Perks shot her a grateful look. 'No more, miss. You understand, don't you?'

'Of course. We won't bother you again.' Lottie stood aside to allow him to escape into the mess hall. 'Leave him alone, Maggie.'

'You're no fun.' Maggie shoved the plate under her nose. 'Have a strawberry. They're delicious.'

The words had barely left her mouth when the door opened and Gideon emerged from the dining room. He came to a halt, frowning. 'I might have guessed it was you, Miss Cole. Perks doesn't know if he's coming or going. He's just spilled a whole jug of cream on Mrs Fothergill's skirt.'

Maggie swallowed a mouthful of fruit. 'Oh dear Lord, she'll be in a state for days.' She thrust the plate into Lottie's hand. 'Take this, and don't let on.' She slid off the stool just as the doors flew open and an irate woman erupted into the ante-room.

'Oh Lord,' Maggie said again, sighing. 'It had to be her, didn't it?'

'Look at me, Cole. My best gown is ruined. I'll make sure that young private is dealt with severely.' Mrs Fothergill held out the skirts of her purple gown, which clashed horribly with her berry-red hair.

Maggie folded her hands in front of her. 'I'm so

sorry, madam.'

'This gown cost a small fortune.' Mrs Fothergill clutched her hands to her bosom. 'I feel faint. Send for my carriage, Cole. I want to go home.'

Maggie bobbed a curtsey. 'Yes, madam. Right away.' She snapped her fingers at Gideon, who had been standing to attention, keeping his eyes averted. 'You heard Mrs Fothergill, Private Ellis. See that her carriage is brought round immediately.'

Lottie noted the muscle twitching at the corner of Gideon's mouth and she could see that he was controlling himself with difficulty, but he nodded and strode out of the building.

Lottie herself had no such means of escape and she hid the plate behind her back. 'Is there anything I can do to help?'

Mrs Fothergill glared at her. 'Who are you, girl?'

'I'm Lady Aurelia Dashwood's new maid, ma'am.'

'Merriweather might have had a remedy, but I don't expect a girl like you to know how to care for expensive fabrics. I'm surprised that Lady Aurelia took you on.'

'Don't take your anger out on her, madam.' Aurelia's angry voice caused Mrs Fothergill to turn with a start.

'I didn't see you there, my lady.'

'Apparently not.' Aurelia closed the door to the mess hall, shutting out the burst of conversation and laughter. 'I saw what happened and it was entirely your fault. I hope you aren't going to pretend it was Private Perks who was to blame.'

Mrs Fothergill's cheeks puffed out as if she were about to explode. 'He was holding the cream jug. It was he who spilled it all over me. Just look at my gown – it's ruined.'

'You jogged his hand,' Aurelia said calmly. 'You weren't paying attention, Mrs Fothergill, and now the poor young man is in trouble because of your carelessness. It won't do, and I shall tell Dashwood so.'

Lottie held her breath, looking from one to the other, although she had no doubt who would win this contest of wills, and Mrs Fothergill seemed to have come to a similar conclusion. She tossed her head and marched towards the outer door. 'I think I heard the carriage approaching. Come along, Cole. Don't dawdle.'

Maggie snatched Mrs Fothergill's cape from its peg and followed her, pausing to turn her head and wink at Lottie before going outside.

'Well, then, you can put the plate down now, Lottie,' Aurelia said casually. 'Poor Perks was in a state of agitated nerves and I think I know whom to blame for that.' She held up her hand. 'It's all right, I'm well aware of Miss Cole's antics, and if her mistress knew the half of it she would sack the woman on the spot. Don't allow her to lead you astray.'

'No, my lady.' Lottie put the plate on one of the stools. 'Are we leaving now?'

'Yes, I've had enough chitchat for one evening, and Mrs Fothergill's unfortunate accident gave me the opportunity to slip away.' Aurelia beckoned to Gideon, who was standing by the door. 'Private Ellis, you may see us home.'

Gideon snapped to attention. 'Yes, my lady.'

'Miss Lane is new to army life and I shall charge you with the responsibility of showing her around.'

'Yes, my lady.' Gideon held the door open for them. 'It will be my pleasure.'

'Not too much pleasure, I hope.' Aurelia tapped him on the arm with her fan. 'You'll be leaving soon for the Crimea, Private Ellis. Just remember that.'

'I will, my lady.'

'Your cloak, my lady.' Lottie hurried after her, but Aurelia dismissed the offer with a wave of her hand.

'It's a lovely warm evening. I don't need it.' She walked on slowly, leaving Lottie and Gideon to follow at a discreet distance.

'Is it always like this?' Lottie whispered.

He nodded. 'Yes, and worse. This was a quiet evening compared to some.' He leaned closer, lowering his voice. 'Miss Cole has a certain reputation in camp, Lottie. I wouldn't get too friendly with her if I were you.'

'Thank you for your concern, but you are not me, and I am perfectly capable of choosing my own friends.' Lottie quickened her pace. 'I'm not a schoolgirl, Gideon. I've met all manner of people at the inn, and I can take care of myself.'

'If you say so.'

She knew she had offended him, and deep down she was grateful for his concern, but it was really none of his business. They walked on in silence and Gideon left them outside the Dashwoods' residence.

Tilda opened the door and Aurelia stepped into the entrance hall, acknowledging her with a smile. 'Tell Cook that I'm hungry. Miss Lane would also like some supper.'

'Yes, my lady.' Tilda sketched a curtsey and hurried off towards the baize door that separated upstairs from the servants' domain below stairs.

'Shall I go and help her?' Lottie asked anxiously.

'That's not necessary. The servants are well aware of your position in the household. You answer to me and me alone.' Aurelia took off her cloak and handed it to Lottie. 'You were hard on that young man. You've obviously met him before tonight. Is there something I should know?'

'Not really, my lady. Lieutenant Gillingham brought Private Ellis to the inn after he had an accident. He stayed with us for several days until he was well enough to return to duty.'

'Ah, I see. So you nursed him back to health – a sure way to win a young man's heart.' Aurelia mounted the stairs, pausing to glance over her shoulder. 'By the way, I'm inclined to agree with Private Ellis. Miss Cole has a reputation for being free with her favours, and is not the sort of person who would normally be employed as a lady's maid.'

'That might be said of me, my lady.'

'True, but you are a completely different proposition from Miss Cole, who lives by her wits and has somehow convinced Mrs Fothergill of her worth. Anyway, I'm tired of the subject now. I want to take off my stays and enjoy my supper. You may have yours when I am comfortably settled in my room.'

It was almost an hour before Lottie was free to sit down to her meal in the kitchen, which was deserted except for Cissy, a small slavey who was mopping the floor. The girl, who could not have been more than eleven or twelve, was heavy-eyed and kept stopping to lean on the mop handle. Lottie could remember her first weeks at the inn, when she had been about the same age as Cissy, and her heart went out to the exhausted child. She rose from the table, leaving the pie and pickles half eaten.

'Cissy, let me finish that for you.'

'What?' Cissy opened her eyes wide, and a look of fear crossed her small features. 'Don't tell Cook I wasn't doing this proper.'

'You are doing very well considering the fact that you're half asleep.' Lottie took the mop from her. 'I'm good at this and I can finish it in half the time. Why don't you take my place at the table and finish up the pie for me? I can't eat it and it would be a shame to leave it for Lady Petunia. I think she's fat enough already.'

Cissy hesitated, eyeing the pie and licking a dribble of spittle from the corner of her mouth. 'Are you sure, miss?'

'Certain sure.' Lottie worked the mop energetically. 'Eat up and then you can go to bed. Where do you sleep?'

Cissy had already crammed her mouth full of pie and rendered herself speechless. She jerked her head in the direction of a small corner at the far side of the range.

'Well, at least it's warm in winter, even if it's a

bit too cosy in summer.' Lottie wrung the mop out and took the bucket into the scullery where she emptied it into the stone sink. 'There you are, Cissy. If you've finished I'll wash the dishes while you get ready for bed.'

'No, really, miss. I can manage now. Ta for the grub.'

Lottie smiled. 'All right, if you're sure. Good night, Cissy. Sleep tight.'

'Don't let the bed bugs bite,' Cissy added, giggling.

Lottie gave her a hug. 'Get some sleep, nipper.' She lit a candle and made her way through the silent corridors and up the back stairs, but as she reached the first floor she heard the creak of a floorboard and the patter of footsteps. She blew out the candle. It was an automatic response and it left her in deep shadow, but moonlight filtered through a window at the far end of the landing, and as she peeped round the corner she saw Lady Aurelia heading down the main staircase. She had left her mistress ready for bed, but now it seemed that Lady Aurelia had dressed herself and, judging by the speed of her descent, she was in a hurry.

It was none of her business, but curiosity got the better of her and Lottie followed Aurelia at a safe distance. She wondered if her ladyship was sleepwalking, but she seemed to have a definite purpose, and she unlocked the front door as stealthily as a burglar. She slipped outside, closing it softly behind her.

Lottie hesitated, wondering whether she ought to leave well alone and retire to bed, but she knew she would get little sleep and she followed her mistress, keeping to the shadows as much as possible. A gap between the buildings left her nowhere to hide, and she came to a halt in time to see a tall male figure emerge from a doorway.

Lady Aurelia ran straight into his arms.

Chapter Six

Lottie clamped her hand to her mouth to stifle a gasp of surprise. She could not make out the identity of the man who was kissing her mistress, but he was an officer. Then the couple disappeared from view, leaving Lottie to come to terms with what she had just seen. She turned and retraced her steps. She had been dazzled by Lady Aurelia's charm and beauty, but having married a much older man maybe it was inevitable that she would take a lover. Lottie had certainly witnessed all manner of goings-on during her time at the inn, and perhaps she was being naïve, but she had imagined that officers and their ladies would behave with honour and chivalry, like the knights of old she had read about in school. She entered the house quietly and went straight to her room.

Next morning she awakened early, half expecting to hear the sound of a post horn announcing the arrival of a mail coach, but the house was eerily silent. She was used to sharing her room with Ruth and May, with all the attendant muddle and chaotic mess of discarded stockings and torn petticoats strewn on the floor or hanging from the rafters. The foul city smells had seeped through gaps in the roof tiles, and had mingled with smoke from Ruth's clay pipe and the cheap scent that May purchased in the market. It was all history now, but perhaps the strangest thing of all was the silence. There had never been a quiet moment at the inn; even in the middle of the night there would have been sounds coming from the stables, and from the street outside. Ruth snored and May often talked in her sleep, shouting out unintelligible words.

Lottie rose from her comfortable bed and had a wash in cold water. She dressed, put up her hair and went downstairs to the kitchen, where Cissy was only just waking up.

'Oh lawks,' she said, scrambling to her feet. 'Is it that late? I'll be in for a hiding if Cook comes down to find I ain't lit the fire.'

'I'm up early, so don't panic.' Lottie went to the range and riddled the ashes. 'We'll soon get this going.'

Cissy yawned and stretched. 'I'll fetch some water. I got to go outside and visit the privy anyway.' She snatched up two buckets and headed for the scullery.

Lottie was left to make up the fire, and when she was satisfied that the flames had taken hold she left it and went out into the yard. Cissy passed her, slopping water over the cobblestones as she hefted the buckets into the house. 'I'll put the kettle on, miss. We'll have a cup of tea.'

'That will be nice, thank you.' Lottie took deep breaths of the clean air, untainted by the stink of the Thames and the manufactories that lined its banks. She could hear the sound of a bugle call and the clatter of booted feet on the parade ground, but tall trees obscured the view of the barrack buildings. There was already a hint of approaching autumn in the air, with a faint blue mist caressing the treetops, and touches of gold and russet amongst the foliage. She had sensed feelings of tension mixed with excitement and apprehension in Gideon during his stay at The Swan, and it was hardly surprising. The men of the Corps of Royal Sappers and Miners were preparing to go to war, and some of them would not return. Perhaps that was why Lady Aurelia had risked her marriage and her reputation by a clandestine meeting with her lover…

'Ho, ho, young lady. I see you are an early riser like myself.' Colonel Dashwood emerged from the scullery carrying a bucket of vegetable peelings. 'My wife never rises before ten o'clock, and often it will be much later.'

'I didn't know, sir. I am new to the duties of a lady's maid.'

'Then you can offer your services to Lady Petunia, just this once, of course.' He uttered a deep belly laugh. 'Here, take the bucket, and I'll fetch the shovel. I don't trust the gardeners to muck out thoroughly. Come with me – er – what's your name? I forget.'

'Lottie, sir. Lottie Lane.'

'Well, Lane, you'll do nicely. I can't abide women who shrink at the sight of anything remotely agricultural. What d'you say to that?'

'I'm used to living above a stable, sir. I've

emptied countless chamber pots onto the dung heap in my time at the inn.'

'Splendid. You'll make an excellent trooper, Lane.'

'Trooper, sir?'

Colonel Dashwood strode on towards the pigsty. 'You'll accompany my wife when she travels to the Crimea.' He glanced over his shoulder. 'Did she mention it to you?'

'Yes, sir.'

He came to a halt at the gate. 'We'll be leaving for Southampton in six or eight weeks, not sure exactly when, and this mustn't go any further, Lane. D'you understand?'

Lottie nodded wordlessly. Lady Petunia poked her snout over the top of the gate, gazing at her with small beady eyes. 'Good piggy,' Lottie murmured automatically.

'Scratch behind her ears, the old girl loves that.' Colonel Dashwood opened the gate and slipped into the pen. 'Fill the trough, Lane, and fetch me the wheelbarrow. We'll soon have Lady Petunia's boudoir as clean and sweet-smelling as that of my dear wife.'

Lottie had much to think about as she made her way back to the house, having done all she could to help Colonel Dashwood make Lady Petunia's sty habitable for such a grand dame of the pig world. The knowledge that Lady Aurelia was having an affair with one of her husband's underlings had made her feel uncomfortable. Colonel Dashwood might be a hard taskmaster to his men, but he was like a loving father to his pig, and as they worked together he had treated Lottie as an equal. The news that they would be leaving so soon for the Crimea had come as something of a shock, but she was ready for anything.

She arrived back in the kitchen to find Cook in the middle of preparing breakfast. Tilda was rushing about taking cutlery and crockery upstairs to the dining room, and Cissy was at her usual place at the scullery sink, washing the pots and pans.

'Where've you been, Miss Lane?' Cook demanded angrily. 'Her ladyship's been ringing the bell for the last ten minutes.'

Lottie glanced at the large, white-faced clock on the wall above the mantelshelf. 'Oh dear, I didn't realise I'd been gone so long.'

'You got caught by the colonel,' Tilda said, chuckling. 'I can smell Lady Petunia.'

'Go on up. Never mind stopping to change. You'll have to explain to her ladyship.' Cook pointed to the stairs. 'You'll learn, miss.'

'I'm so sorry, my lady,' Lottie said breathlessly. 'I was up early and Colonel Dashwood asked me to help him clean out the pigsty.'

Aurelia's golden hair spilled over her shoulders as she sat in bed propped up against a small mountain of pillows. 'I might have guessed. Never go outside before eight o'clock or you'll suffer a similar fate. My husband adores that animal and he'll commandeer the first person he sees to help him.' She wrinkled her small nose. 'You'd best go and change before you help me dress. I can stand most things, but the smell of pig first thing in the morning is not one of them.'

'Yes, my lady.' Lottie hesitated in the doorway. 'I'm afraid I haven't got anything suitable to change into.'

Aurelia raised a delicate eyebrow. 'Good heavens! Why not? You must have brought clothes with you from your last place of employment.'

'They all reek of the taproom, my lady.' Lottie hung her head. 'I'm told they smell of tobacco and beer, but I was so accustomed to it that I never noticed.'

'Oh, is that all? I've been subjected to far worse during my travels abroad, but I do object to farmyard odours in my boudoir. Go and change immediately.'

'Yes, my lady.' Lottie opened the door, but again she hesitated. 'Is it true that we will be leaving for the Crimea in a few weeks?'

'Of course. I thought that was understood. Is there a problem, Lottie?'

'No, my lady. I'll be proud to follow you wherever you go.'

'Excellent. But I can see that we will have to get you outfitted for the journey. Can you ride a horse?'

'I don't know, my lady. I've never tried.'

'Then we must arrange for you to have lessons. We have so little time in which to prepare. Now, change your gown and then you can help me dress. I'm going riding with Lieutenant Gillingham this morning.' Aurelia threw back the coverlet and swung her legs over the side of the bed. She paused, frowning thoughtfully. 'This might be the ideal time for you to have your first lesson. I think I have an old habit packed away somewhere.

Merriweather would have known where to put her hands on it, but I want you to find it and try it on. We must be close enough in size.' She stood up and stretched. 'I'll ask Lieutenant Gillingham to detail a man to ride with you.'

Hansford had to be called upon to bring a brass-bound trunk down from the attic, which he placed in a spare bedroom for Lottie and Tilda to unpack. A strong smell of lavender filled the air as the sprigs were disturbed, sending showers of tiny blue flowers onto the polished floorboards. Lottie almost forgot the reason for their search as they lifted the delicate fabrics and shook out the creases of silk afternoon gowns, sprigged muslins, and cool cottons. At the very bottom they discovered the cream sateen riding habit. The lavender seemed to have kept the moths at bay and the gown was as good as new.

'I wonder if this will fit me.' Lottie held it up against her. 'Why would clothes like this have been put away and forgotten?'

'That's what the rich people do.' Tilda scrambled to her feet with a feather fan clutched in her hand. She strutted round the room, fanning herself and then stopping to peer over the top, fluttering her eyelashes. 'Look at me, I'm a titled lady at a ball and you're a handsome gentleman.'

'You are a silly-billy, Tilda,' Lottie said, laughing. She cocked her head on one side, listening. 'Someone's coming. Quick, put the rest away or we'll be in trouble.'

They had just folded the last gown and put it in place when Mrs Manners poked her head round the door. 'What are you doing in here, Tilda? Get back to the kitchen at once.'

Lottie closed the lid of the trunk with a snap. 'I'm sorry, Mrs Manners. It's my fault. Lady Aurelia wanted me to find her old riding habit and I asked Tilda to help.'

'It's not your place to give orders, Miss Lane. However, I'll overlook it this time as you were both doing something for her ladyship.' Mrs Manners shooed Tilda out of the door. 'Get along with you. Do I have to tell you everything twice?'

'No, Mrs Manners. Sorry, Mrs Manners.' Tilda's voice faded into the distance.

Left on her own, Lottie tried on the riding habit and was surprised to find that it fitted as if it had been made for her. She studied her reflection in the cheval mirror that stood in the corner of the room, and it seemed as though she was looking at a complete stranger. She lifted her hand and waved to make sure that her eyes were not playing tricks on her, and she smiled. The elegant young lady waved back and smiled. It seemed like a miracle – a maid of all work at the inn had suddenly been transformed into a lady. Her smile faded. She might be dressed up, but she was still Lottie Lane, a common girl from the tavern. She picked up the long, trailing skirts of the habit and made her way back to Lady Aurelia's room.

'You'll do.' Aurelia looked her up and down. 'But you cannot go riding without a hat. I'm sure I must have one that will go with that habit.' She moved gracefully to one of the cupboards, which lined an entire wall, and flung it open.

The sight of shelves filled with headwear of all

shapes and sizes made Lottie catch her breath. This was one cupboard that she had yet to explore, but the colourful assortment of hats and bonnets decorated with flowers, bows and feathers was dazzling. Aurelia selected a small straw hat with a half veil. She tossed it to Lottie. 'Try that one.'

Lottie attempted to balance it on top of her head, but it slid over one eye. 'It's too small, my lady.'

'Nonsense.' Aurelia snatched a pearl-headed hatpin from her dressing table and advanced purposefully on Lottie. With a deft movement she thrust the pin into the straw and secured it through a loop of hair. 'There you are. Perfect. Now come along, Lottie. I sent a note to Lieutenant Gillingham requesting him to find someone to give you a riding lesson. They'll be waiting for us.'

Lieutenant Gillingham leaped to attention when Aurelia approached, closely followed by Lottie. 'Good morning, my lady.' He bowed from the waist. 'A lovely day for a ride.'

'Yes, indeed,' Aurelia said primly.

Lottie caught her breath as she realised that the soldier holding the reins of her mount was none other than Private Ellis.

Aurelia greeted him with a curt nod. 'I take it that you will be instructing Miss Lane today, Private?'

'Yes, my lady.' Gideon stood stiffly to attention, staring straight ahead.

'Excellent.' Aurelia stepped onto the mounting block and arranged herself on the side-saddle.

'Lead on, Gillingham.' She glanced over her shoulder. 'There's no need to follow us, Private. Take Miss Lane on an easy route, as this is her first lesson.' She flicked the reins. 'Walk on.'

Gideon relaxed visibly as they rode off. 'Miss Lane, are you ready?'

Lottie was accustomed to the large coach horses, but the grey mare was comparatively small and dainty. She stroked the velvety nose and smiled into the animal's lustrous brown eyes. 'I hope you'll be patient with a beginner.'

'She will be,' Gideon said. 'She's a game little mare, but she knows when to be gentle. Is it true you've never ridden a horse?'

'Quite true.' Lottie climbed onto the mounting block. 'How hard can it be?'

After an hour of learning the rise and fall of a trot, Gideon slowed the pace so that his large black horse walked sedately alongside Lottie's smaller mount, and they found a shady avenue of trees.

'Why does her ladyship want you to have riding lessons, Lottie?'

The question came suddenly after a period of silence when Lottie was concentrating on keeping her seat. She glanced at Gideon, puzzled. 'Why do you want to know?'

'I never saw Merriweather riding a horse. It seems odd, unless she intends you to accompany her to the Crimea.'

'I only learned that this morning.'

'They can't force you to accompany them abroad. You could leave and find another position, you know.'

'Why would I do that?' Lottie shot him a curious glance. 'I've always wanted to travel and see more of the world. It might be my only chance.'

'War isn't pretty. You'd see things you wished you hadn't seen, and you might put yourself in harm's way.'

'You'll be going to the Crimea soon.'

'But I'm a soldier, Lottie. I'm paid to fight for my country. It's what I do.'

She drew her horse to a halt beneath the shade of a tall oak tree. 'I asked Miss Nightingale if I could go with her, Gideon. It was you who gave me the idea that I might do something more useful than wash dishes and make beds.'

He reined in beside her. 'Me? I don't understand. What have I got to do with all this?'

'When I was caring for you with your head wound it seemed the most natural thing in the world. Maybe I was destined to be a nurse.'

'Well, I don't know whether to be glad or sorry that I've brought you to this.'

'Why would you be sorry? It's my decision.'

A slow smile spread across his even features. 'You're right. I should be glad because now I've got the chance to get to know you better. Perhaps it was fate that brought us together.'

'It was a bump on the head,' she said, laughing. 'Come on, I'll race you to the stables.'

Lottie was stiff and sore after her first lesson, but Lady Aurelia insisted that she rode every day. After breakfast each morning, they walked the short distance to the stables, where their horses were saddled and waiting. Aurelia and Gillingham always led the way on these rides, breaking into a gallop when they were on open land, while Lottie and Gideon followed on at a slower speed. Sometimes they would be completely outpaced and find that they had been left far behind, only catching up with Aurelia and Gillingham when they returned to the barracks. Lottie looked forward to her riding lesson with Gideon, who was a good instructor and an entertaining companion. She was determined to become proficient in the saddle, although she doubted if she would ever be as good a horsewoman as her mistress, who had learned to ride when she was a small child.

The lessons were followed by frequent visits from Aurelia's dressmaker and her brother, who was a tailor. They had been commissioned to make a habit for Lottie suitable to the winter climate in the Crimea, and a couple of heavyweight woollen skirts, as well as a worsted jacket cut in military style to echo, but not to compete with, the dashing outfits that Aurelia had chosen for herself.

Lady Aurelia was not a demanding mistress, but she was impetuous and unpredictable. Sometimes she would choose to lie in bed all day, refusing to eat or to offer any explanation of her lassitude to her anxious husband. The servants would tiptoe around on these occasions, fearful of making a noise and disturbing her ladyship, and Lottie would find herself banished from the room and forbidden to return until summoned, which invariably occurred in the early evening. Sometimes Aurelia merely wanted a tray of food sent to her room; at other times she decided to dress for dinner.

At the end of the first month, Lottie was accustomed to such behaviour. She suspected that her mistress took to her bed out of boredom, but it was not her place to comment, and she filled her time by helping in the house or assisting the colonel to clean out Lady Petunia's sty. She had grown quite fond of the big Black Berkshire, and the pig seemed to know her, or perhaps it was the titbits that Lottie brought daily that she remembered more fondly.

One evening, after a day of relative inactivity, Lottie entered Aurelia's boudoir to find her mistress dressed in her chemise.

'Lace my stays, Lottie,' she said airily.

'Are you going down to dinner, my lady?'

'No, I think not. I'm dying of boredom and feel like a game of cards.' Aurelia held her breath while Lottie tugged at the laces.

'I'm sure the colonel would oblige, my lady.'

'I mean a proper game of cards. I want you to help me dress and put up my hair, then you must take a message to the officers' mess. Make sure that Lieutenant Gillingham receives it in person.'

'Yes, my lady.' Lottie had guessed almost from the start that Gillingham was Lady Aurelia's secret lover, and this seemed to confirm her suspicions. She helped her mistress to dress, and was about to embark on an elaborate coiffure when Aurelia held up her hand.

'I don't want it to look too formal, Lottie. I'm going for a private card game amongst friends. Just take my hair up at the sides and secure it with combs. I'll wear it loose tonight.'

'If you say so, my lady.'

Aurelia met Lottie's anxious gaze in the mirror, and her lips curved into a smile. 'You don't approve?'

'It's not for me to say, my lady.'

'Quite right.' Aurelia turned her head this way and that, surveying her hair with a critical eye. 'That's it exactly.' She took a note from her reticule and handed it to Lottie. 'You know what to do. Don't keep me waiting.'

It was a fine evening and still very warm. A faint breeze sighed in the trees and the aroma of onions and roast meat wafted from the cookhouse, mingling with the damp muddy smell of the River Medway. Lottie knew her way around by this time and she hurried to the officers' mess. To her relief it was Private Benson who answered her knock on the door. His eyebrows shot up in surprise.

'Can I help you, miss?'

'I have a message for Lieutenant Gillingham,' she said breathlessly. 'I need to give it to him personally.'

Benson frowned and shook his head. 'I can't let you in, miss. Officers only.'

'Then will you ask him to come to the door, please, Joe?'

'I dunno, Lottie. You shouldn't be running after an officer. It'll end up badly for you.'

'It's not from me, Joe. I can't say any more, but if you tell him I have a note for him I think he'll come.'

'Wait here. I'll do me best, love.' Joe disappeared into the building, leaving Lottie standing on the doorstep.

She glanced around, hoping that no one had seen her. Gossip flew around the barracks like summer lightning. She did not have long to wait.

Gillingham took Joe's place in the doorway. 'You have something for me, Lottie?'

She handed him the folded slip of paper and waited while he scanned its contents. 'Is there an answer, sir?'

'It won't do,' he said frowning. 'You must tell her ladyship that I'm very sorry but it's not possible.'

'Of course it is, Farrell. Anything is possible if one puts one's mind to it.'

Lottie turned with a start to see Lady Aurelia standing behind her.

'Aurelia, you can't do this,' Farrell said in a low voice. 'Allow me to see you home.'

She tossed her head. 'Is this the sort of greeting I am to expect? Why may I not visit my friends for a game of cards?'

'Because your husband is my commanding officer. Please keep your voice down.'

'I'll raise it to a shout if you don't let me in, and then the whole barracks will be aware of what is going on.' Aurelia moved closer, looking up into his handsome face with a persuasive smile. 'Just one or two hands of whist, my dear. I promise not to bankrupt you, for you know I always win.'

Lottie shifted from one foot to the other. 'Someone's coming, my lady.'

Farrell followed her gaze. 'It's all right, it's Private Ellis.' He seized Aurelia by the shoulders. 'Please, my love, allow one of us to take you home. I'll see you tomorrow.'

She slipped her arms around his neck and pulled

112

his head down so that their lips met in a brief kiss. 'No, Farrell. I will have that card game.'

He allowed her to slip into the building. 'Private Ellis.'

Gideon came to a standstill. 'Yes, sir.' He saluted but his gaze was fixed on Lottie.

'Come inside, Ellis. You too, Miss Lane.' Farrell held the door open. 'Lady Aurelia has decided to grace us with her company this evening. I want you both to sit in on the game.'

'I don't know how to play cards,' Lottie protested as she followed her mistress into the building. 'Perhaps I can persuade her ladyship to come home with me.'

'You don't know her very well, do you?' Farrell shook his head. 'Ellis, I want you to act as steward. Private Benson will make sure that we are not interrupted.'

'Really, Farrell, you're not getting ready for a rout. It's a simple game of cards, no more, no less.' Aurelia patted his cheek, smiling.

'There are only two of us, Aurelia,' Farrell said grimly. 'Wait for me. I'll get Lombard and Cheney, if you insist on carrying on with this idiotic plan.'

'Indeed I do.' Aurelia opened the door to the dining hall and sniffed the air. 'I haven't eaten all day. A tray of food and some wine would be wonderful, my dear.' She beckoned to Lottie. 'Come with me and leave the men to do their duty.' She glided into the room, leaving Lottie no alternative but to follow her.

Once inside, Aurelia glanced round at the trestle tables, which were bare of their white cloths. 'Another month or so and this will seem like the height of luxury. We must make the most of it.' She pulled up a chair and sat down, spreading her silk skirts around her. 'I suppose you disapprove of my behaviour, Lottie? It isn't what one would expect of the wife of a high-ranking officer.'

'I don't think it matters what I think, my lady. It seems to me that you do exactly what you want regardless of anyone or anything.' Lottie thought for a moment she had gone too far, but she was angry to think that her friends might get into trouble because of a bored military wife. Aurelia frowned and then she started to chuckle.

'You are a bold person, Lottie Lane. In fact you are a woman after my own heart. I despise toadies and lickspittles. You are right, of course, but I will make it up to Farrell and his friends.'

'What happens if the colonel finds out, my lady?'

'Dashwood is a darling man, and he wants me to be happy. The only person he loves more than me is that blessed pig. I thank the Lord for her porky personality, which keeps him amused.'

Lottie was struggling to think of an appropriate answer when the door burst open and Gideon entered the room. 'My lady, the colonel is at the door. He's looking for you.'

Chapter Seven

'Damn it!' Aurelia rose to her feet. 'Someone must have seen me leave the house.'

'What will you do, my lady?' Lottie asked anxiously.

'I don't know. I need time to think.'

Lottie had seen her mistress in many moods, but this was the first time she had seen her looking scared, and even then the impression was fleeting. As the door opened Aurelia's expression changed subtly.

Colonel Dashwood erupted into the mess hall. 'Aurelia, I was told you had come here alone, but I didn't believe it.'

She met his accusing look with a defiant lift of her chin. 'It's not like you to listen to common tittle-tattle, Dashwood darling.'

'You can't get away with it this time, Aurelia.' His colour deepened and his bushy white eyebrows knitted together in a frown. 'I can see the evidence with my own eyes. It isn't seemly for a senior officer's wife to behave like a camp follower.'

Lottie could bear it no longer. She stepped forward, forgetting her humble position in the need to defend her mistress. 'It was my fault, sir. I beg your pardon for speaking out, but Lady Aurelia put herself to a great deal of trouble on my behalf.'

There was a moment of stunned silence and

even though she cast her eyes down, she sensed that everyone was staring at her.

'What are you talking about, Lane?' Colonel Dashwood demanded angrily. 'Speak up.'

Lottie shot a sideways glance in Gideon's direction. She had intended to claim that it was she who had a romantic tryst and that the man in question was Private Ellis. Then, in a moment of near panic, she realised that such a claim might get him into trouble with his superiors. She shook her head. 'I can't say, sir.'

'What can't you say? What nonsense is this?' Colonel Dashwood's booming voice echoed round the room like cannon fire.

'I think we're well enough acquainted with the ways of the world to understand what she's saying, Dashwood.' Lady Aurelia moved to his side. 'It's true I came hotfoot here without a thought for propriety or what others might make of my actions, but there's no harm done.'

Lottie raised her head. 'It was because of me. I'm truly sorry, sir.'

Colonel Dashwood cleared his throat noisily. 'Perhaps I was hasty, Aurelia. But you know how people gossip, and you seemed to have forgotten that the Fothergills are our guests for dinner this evening. Cordelia saw you leave the house...'

'I might have guessed that she would be behind such an outrageous slur on my good name.' Aurelia smiled and laid her hand on his arm. 'We'll return home and show the awful woman that her mischief-making has not worked.'

Colonel Dashwood patted his wife's small hand. 'Quite right, my love. We'll show the enemy a united front. I never could stand that woman.' He made for the door, stopping for a moment to address Gillingham, who was standing rigidly to attention. 'Keep a tighter rein on your men, Lieutenant.'

'Yes, sir.' Gillingham snapped to attention.

'Come, Miss Lane. I think our business here is concluded.' Aurelia beckoned to Lottie. 'We understand young love,' she added with a wistful sigh. 'Don't be too hard on the person in question, Lieutenant Gillingham.'

'No, my lady.'

'Good evening, gentlemen.' Aurelia swept out of the room on the arm of her husband.

Lottie hesitated, turning to Gideon with a wary smile. 'I know you don't approve. I could feel you looking daggers at me, Private Ellis, but I did what I had to do.'

He stared ahead, saying nothing, confirming her worst fears.

'Well, that was a near thing.' Aurelia tossed her reticule onto the bed. 'You are to be congratulated for your quick thinking, Lottie. I couldn't have done better myself.'

'It was nothing, my lady.'

'Nevertheless, you saved me from an embarrassing situation. Of course I would have talked my way out of it eventually, but no harm was done.'

'No, my lady.'

'And now I'll have to go down to dinner and be nice to that wretched woman. I really could wring her neck. If she were a chicken I would happily roast her on a spit.'

'She might be a bit tough and stringy,' Lottie said, chuckling.

Aurelia dissolved into giggles. 'You are good for me, my dear. I was fond of dear old Merriweather, but she could be the most frightful bore at times and she had a nasty habit of reminding me what a brat I was as a child. You, on the other hand, are much more fun.' She sank down on the dressing-table stool. 'You'd better put my hair up or the old tabby will have something more to criticise.'

'Yes, my lady.' Lottie put her head on one side, frowning thoughtfully. 'Might I suggest that you wear your green taffeta gown, my lady?'

Aurelia glanced down at her décolletage and smiled. 'I know what you're thinking, but I refuse to alter my style of dress to satisfy Cordelia Fothergill's idea of what is proper. If her husband chooses to ogle my bosom, it's not my fault.'

'No, my lady.' Lottie realised that it was useless to argue. Lady Aurelia was hell bent on annoying Mrs Fothergill, and nothing she could say or do would stop her.

'I can see that you don't agree, Lottie. You are as transparent as a pane of glass, but I am shockingly prim compared to my grandmother, who wore gowns made of sheer muslin and dampened her petticoats in order to show off her figure. Even earlier family portraits show ladies with their bosoms barely covered, so you see I am quite modest compared to my ancestors.'

'Perhaps it would be best to keep that information from Mrs Fothergill at dinner,' Lottie said, smiling.

'Do you dare me to bring up the subject?'

'No, I do not, my lady. Think of the poor colonel's embarrassment if you did.'

'I suppose you're right, but it's going to be a deadly dull evening. I'm quite looking forward to getting away from here for a while when we leave for the Crimea. It's not long now before we'll be setting sail.' Aurelia twisted her head from side to side as she studied her reflection in the mirror. 'That's very nice, Lottie. You have a talent for dressing hair. Now I suppose I must go and face the enemy.'

'Yes, my lady.' Lottie waited until her mistress had finally left the room, and having tidied it to her satisfaction she slipped her shawl around her shoulders. Her conscience had been bothering her since she had taken the blame for Lady Aurelia's erratic behaviour. Now Gideon was enmeshed in the web of lies and deceit surrounding the relationship between his superior officer and the colonel's lady. The servants, she decided, would be fully occupied serving dinner that was almost an hour late, and tempers below stairs were likely to be frayed. They would be far too busy to notice her absence.

She let herself out of the house unseen and went in search of Gideon. She knew his roster off by heart and this was his off-duty time. It was not hard to imagine how he might be feeling at this moment, and she could hazard a guess as to where he might go should he wish to be alone. Their conversations during the morning rides had given her an insight into his likes and dislikes, and she knew that he had a particular fondness for a secluded spot by the river. There was enough daylight left for a quick sortie and she set off at a brisk pace.

A faint whiff of tobacco smoke gave him away, and she found him exactly where she had thought he might be. She picked her way down the muddy foreshore to the spot on the river bank, half hidden by a weeping willow. 'Gideon.'

He had been leaning against the tree trunk but he straightened up, staring at her in astonishment. 'Lottie. What on earth are you doing here?' He tossed the butt of the cigarillo into the oily waters of the Medway.

'I had to see you, Gideon. I wanted to apologise for making it seem as if you and I were involved in some way.'

'Lady Aurelia has us all entangled in her affairs.'

The bitterness in his tone made Lottie shiver. 'I believe she really does love him.'

'Who? Her husband or the man she teases and toys with and will probably toss aside the moment she becomes bored with him?'

'That's unfair, Gideon.'

'Is it? You don't know her. I've been with Farrell for four years now and I know he's a splendid fellow. He's genuinely in love with Lady Aurelia, even though he knows she will never leave her husband. She's had other lovers and the affairs always ended badly, if not for her, then for her poor victim.'

'You make her sound like a monster, but she's nice and she's kind.'

'She's a woman of the world and she knows what she's doing. It's all a game to her.'

'That's a bit harsh, Gideon. Lady Aurelia must have been very young when she married the colonel, and I dare say she was coerced into agreeing to such a match. I can't believe that she would have wanted a husband who was so much her senior.'

'Don't believe everything she tells you. The truth, as I heard it, is that she married against her family's wishes. She has a fortune of her own, which allows her to do exactly as she pleases, and that's what she's doing now, if you ask me.'

'I think that's very unfair. She can't have been a day older than seventeen when she married the colonel.'

'I think she knew exactly what she was after. Some girls seem to fall in love with the uniform and not the man, and I'd say that was the case with Lady Aurelia. She loves adventure and she lives for thrills and excitement. I would have thought that this evening's little performance demonstrated exactly what she's like.'

Shocked by his words, Lottie was silent for a moment, trying to compare the vision he had of Lady Aurelia with her own, and failing miserably. 'I think you're being very hard on her,' she said at last. 'Perhaps some of it is true, but that doesn't mean she's a bad person. Maybe she does love Gillingham.'

'The colonel is a decent chap, Lottie. He deserves better.'

'It's plain for anyone to see that he worships her.'

'Even more than Lady Petunia?' Gideon's lips twitched and his hazel eyes twinkled. 'Come, don't let us fight about them. It's their business when all is said and done. I just don't want you to get too involved in Lady Aurelia's schemes.'

'I can think for myself, and I can look after myself. Perhaps I made a mistake coming to look for you, but I just wanted to make sure that you hadn't got into trouble because of what I said.' She turned to leave, but he was too quick for her and he caught her by the hand.

'Don't go, Lottie. I'm sorry if I offended you.'

'It's all right. You're entitled to your opinions, as I am to mine.' She withdrew her hand gently. 'I'd better get back to the house before I'm missed.'

'I'll walk with you. It'll be dark soon.' He proffered his arm. 'There's no need for us to fall out.'

'Of course not.'

He helped her up the slippery bank. 'Your boots are muddy. How will you explain that to the ogress Mrs Manners?'

'That's easy. I'll just say I was visiting Lady Petunia.' Lottie glanced ruefully at the muddy hem of her skirt. 'I seem to spend half my time in the laundry room, thanks to that pig.'

'When it comes to his two ladies, I wonder who the colonel would miss more if Lady Aurelia decided to remain at home when we leave for the Crimea,' Gideon said, chuckling.

'I wouldn't like to say, but that won't happen. We are kitted out and ready to go.'

'I wish you would change your mind, Lottie. You don't know what you're letting yourself in for.'

'I'll face whatever comes.' She walked on but he caught up with her before she had gone more than a few steps.

'It's madness, Lottie. It will be winter when we arrive in the Crimea, and who knows what terrible conditions we'll have to face. If I were your husband I wouldn't think of putting you in such danger.'

'Well, we're not married, Gideon, and you have no say in my future.'

He grasped her hand, crushing her fingers in a tight grip. 'Then marry me, Lottie. Marry me and I'll look after you.'

'Let me go. You're hurting me.'

He released her instantly. 'I'm sorry, but I meant what I said. We could get married by special licence and I would see that you were well provided for while I'm away.'

'This is crazy talk. We hardly know each other.'

'I think a lot of you, and I believe you like me. The rest would follow, if you'll just allow me to keep you safe from harm.'

She shook her head. 'Stop it, Gideon. This is madness.'

'Is it madness to want to protect you from an experience that might scar you for life, or could prove fatal?'

'No, of course not. In fact it's a kindness I don't deserve, and one I cannot accept. Mutual liking isn't a firm basis for marriage, and I refuse to take advantage of your good nature.'

'I meant it, Lottie. I do care for you deeply, and there is no need for you to do this.'

'I've given you my answer, Gideon.'

He lengthened his step in order to keep up with her as she hurried homewards. 'All right, I won't say another word, but if you change your mind...'

The words hung in the night air and were wafted away on a cool breeze as they continued in silence. They parted outside the gates of the Dashwoods' residence.

'Good night, Gideon.' Lottie shot him a sideways glance. 'Thank you for walking me home.'

He opened the gate and stood back. 'Good night, Miss Lane.'

'This is ridiculous,' she said crossly. 'We've been friends until now. Don't be angry and spoil everything.'

'You made your feelings clear. I think it's better if we don't see so much of each other.'

She stiffened, chilled by the icy tone in his voice. 'If that's the way you want it.'

'You know it isn't.' His voice throbbed with emotion. 'I asked you to marry me, Lottie, and you turned me down. You brushed my offer aside and said it was madness. "Crazy" was a word you used.'

'And it would have been madness had I accepted you simply to get out of accompanying Lady Aurelia to the Crimea. You don't love me, Gideon. You were being a gentleman, and I think it was very kind of you–'

'Stop there. You don't need to go on. I'm sorry I mentioned it.' He turned and walked away.

She was tempted to call him back, but what would she say? They had argued and gone round in circles. He could not, or would not, see her point of view and she was at a loss to understand why he was being so stubborn. She had tried to make him understand why she could not accept a proposal made on the spur of the moment, even if it had been made with the best of intentions. She did not doubt his sincerity, but she was convinced that when he had had time to think it through he would wish it unsaid. She walked round to the servants' entrance and let herself in.

Hansford met her at the foot of the back stairs. 'Lady Aurelia has been ringing for you, Miss Lane.'

'I went for a walk,' Lottie said, glancing down at her muddy boots. 'I didn't realise how late it was.'

'If you'd like, to leave your shoes with me I'll give them a clean, miss. It's not a good idea to walk mud through the house. Mrs Manners gets a bit upset.'

'Of course. What was I thinking?' She leaned against the wall and took off the muddy footwear. 'Thank you, Hansford.'

'This is river mud, miss. It's not a good idea to walk that far at night.'

'I lost my way, Hansford, but I won't make that mistake again.'

'I don't doubt you, miss.'

Aurelia was seated at her dressing table when Lottie entered the room. She glanced at her in the mirror, but did not look round. 'Where were you? I've been ringing the bell for ages.'

'I'm sorry, my lady. I went for a walk and lost track of the time.'

'I suppose you went to meet your beau.'

'I haven't got a beau, my lady.'

'I'm not stupid, Lottie. I've seen the way you

and Ellis are with each other. There's only one reason why a young woman ventures out alone at night and I'll wager it wasn't to visit my husband's prize sow.'

'You're right, of course. I needed to apologise to Gideon for pretending that we had an assignation.'

'Which didn't go well, by the look on your face.' Aurelia twisted round on the stool, giving her a searching look. 'You can't fool me, Lottie. I'm well versed in affairs of the heart. Heaven knows I've had enough to last a lifetime. What happened?'

'We had a slight argument, my lady. I'm sure it will blow over.'

'You like him quite a lot, I think.'

'Quite a lot, my lady.'

'So what went wrong?'

'He didn't think it was a good idea for me to accompany you to the Crimea.'

'And he offered you marriage as a way out?'

Lottie stared at her in amazement. 'How did you know that?'

'My dear girl, he's a born gentleman. In his mind it would be the only way in which he could keep you from harm. I take it you turned him down.'

'Yes, of course. What else could I do?'

'You could have accepted and married him.'

'Which I'm sure we would both live to regret.'

'Good. I'm glad you have a mind of your own, Lottie. Now will you please take the pins out of my hair and help me to get ready for bed. I'm exhausted. I've spent the last part of the evening trying to be nice to that ghastly woman when all I wanted to do was to pull off her hideous red wig and throw it in the fire.'

'She wears a wig?'

'Of course it's a wig. Underneath that false thatch she's as grey as a badger, or maybe she's bald. I don't know, but I was sorely tempted to snatch it from her head. I'll take a few drops of laudanum when I'm in bed, or I'll never get to sleep.'

Whether or not it had anything to do with the unfortunate incident in the officers' mess, or if it was merely a coincidence, Lottie was disappointed to learn that there were to be no more riding lessons. Aurelia was furious, but the decision had been taken and an order given, and there was no chance of having it countermanded. She paced the drawing-room floor wringing her hands in frustration.

'Can you believe it, Lottie? Dashwood neglected to tell me that Gillingham and his men have to complete their training with the Telegraph Detachment as a matter of urgency.'

Lottie stood by the door, wondering why she had been summoned so urgently. 'Have they, my lady?'

'Do you understand what that means?'

'Not really,' Lottie admitted, eyeing her mistress warily. Lady Aurelia had been edgy and difficult for a whole week. She was, Lottie thought, like a saucepan of milk simmering and ready to boil over at any minute.

'It means that we won't see them again until we are on the ship bound for the Crimea,' Aurelia continued angrily. 'I had to find out from Hansford. Can you believe that, Lottie?'

'No, my lady.'

'My own husband kept the truth from me.'

'Begging you pardon, my lady, but what are we talking about?'

'We are leaving for Southampton tomorrow, and we'll remain there, kicking our heels, while we wait for orders.'

'But we aren't ready,' Lottie protested. 'I haven't even begun to pack your things.'

'Then you'd better begin right away. Ring the bell and I'll send for Hansford. He'll bring the rest of my trunks down from the attic.'

'I'm not sure what you want to take and what you want to leave.'

'Throw everything in, but not too many ball gowns.'

'Surely you won't need ball gowns in the Crimea, my lady.'

'Who knows how long we'll be stuck in Southampton. I'm not going to sit in our lodgings night after night.' Aurelia moved swiftly to the escritoire in the corner of the large room. 'I've written a note to Farrell, I mean Lieutenant Gillingham. I want you to make sure that he gets it, do you understand?' She snatched up a folded and sealed sheet of writing paper. 'Take it to him now.'

'I'll try, my lady.'

'It's too bad,' Aurelia cried, clutching her hands to her flushed cheeks. 'I'll never forgive Dashwood for this, never.'

Their lodgings in Southampton were luxurious by Lottie's standards, but Aurelia declared them fit only for pigs.

'Dashwood's wretched sow is housed better,' she said, throwing her smart new shako down on the sofa in disgust. 'I feel as if I'm being punished, like a naughty child sent to the nursery because of bad behaviour.'

'I'm sure that wasn't Colonel Dashwood's intention, my lady.' Lottie nodded to Hansford, who had spent the last half an hour unloading the cabin trunks and cases from the carrier's cart.

He stood in the doorway, clutching his cap in his hands. 'Will there be anything else for the moment, my lady? If not, I thought I'd walk down to the docks and take a look at the ships.'

'No, there's nothing else you can do for now, Hansford.' Aurelia's brow cleared and she managed a tight little smile. 'I trust your room is to your satisfaction.'

'I've no complaints, my lady. It's as tidy a billet as I could hope for.' He backed out of the room, closing the door behind him.

Aurelia slumped down on the sofa. 'This is so hard it feels as though it's been stuffed with the horse's bones as well as its hair. I'll have a few words to say to Dashwood when he decides to join us. Whenever that might be.'

'It can't be too long, my lady.'

'I will die of boredom if we have to spend weeks here.' Aurelia rose to her feet and went to stand in the bay window, which overlooked the busy street. 'I don't understand why Farrell didn't reply to my note. You did give it to him, didn't you, Lottie?'

Lottie smothered a sigh. Her ladyship had asked this question so many times that she had lost count, and her answer had always been the same. 'I wasn't allowed to see him, my lady. I gave it to Private Benson, who was on guard duty, and he promised he would pass it on.'

'I think that someone must have intercepted his response.'

'I suppose it's possible,' Lottie said reluctantly. She had come to that conclusion herself, but she had not dared to voice her concerns. 'Would you like me to ask the landlady to bring some refreshment? A pot of tea or some cordial?'

'At this moment I would like a tot of brandy or a glass of champagne to lift my spirits.' Aurelia ran her fingers up and down the heavy velvet curtain. 'Dust,' she said crossly. 'These curtains should be hung outside in the fresh air and beaten.'

'Yes, my lady.' Lottie was at a loss to know how to handle her mistress in this mood. 'Would you like me to go out and buy a bottle of brandy? For medicinal purposes, of course.'

'I should have sent Hansford, only it's too late now. Yes, take the money from my reticule. I think I'll lie down for a while. I have a headache coming on. You might purchase some laudanum while you're out. I doubt if I'll sleep a wink in this noisy town.'

Lottie put on her bonnet and wrapped her shawl around her shoulders. Their suite of rooms occupied the whole of the first floor of what had once been a smart town house, but was now divided into letting rooms. Lady Aurelia might have a poor opinion of the place, but it was clean and nicely decorated with well-proportioned rooms and decent, if slightly shabby furniture. Lottie left the building and walked along the street, which was lined with similar terraced houses, interspersed with older buildings and shops. She idled away some time, looking at hats in a milliner's window, and the items displayed in a haberdashery. Then, having purchased a bottle of cognac and a pennyworth of laudanum she walked back to the house, pausing for a moment as she saw a smart carriage draw to a halt on the far side of the road.

Her hand flew to her mouth as she recognised the occupants. How, she wondered, would she break the news to Lady Aurelia?

Chapter Eight

'Oh Lord, no.' Aurelia sipped the brandy that Lottie had had the forethought to give her before she broke the news. 'Not the dreaded Fothergill woman. You must have been mistaken, Lottie.'

'No, my lady. I've never seen anyone else with hair that colour. I'm quite certain that it was the major-general and his wife. Perhaps they were just visiting.'

Aurelia swallowed the last drop in her glass and held it out for a refill. 'That's nonsense and you know it. There's only one reason why Fluffy Fothergill would be here, and that is to oversee arrangements for our departure.'

'But that's good, isn't it?' Lottie added another small tot to the glass. 'It means that we won't have to stay here for any great length of time. The

colonel will join us and so will Lieutenant Gillingham.'

'Don't mention Gillingham's name again. It's
obvious that he cares little for me or he would
have found a way to communicate.'

'He's in a difficult position, my lady. You are the
wife of his commanding officer.'

'You don't have to remind me of that, Lottie.'
Aurelia stared into the glass, twirling it round
between her fingers. She set it down on the table
at her side. 'This isn't the answer. I'm behaving
like a lovelorn schoolgirl. Fetch my bonnet and
shawl. We're going out, and the devil take Cordelia
Fothergill.'

Next morning, Lottie had just finished unpacking the garments that Lady Aurelia considered
absolutely necessary for her immediate needs,
when there was a knock on the door.

'You've got a visitor, miss,' the landlady said,
breathing heavily. 'I ain't no parlour maid, you
can tell that to her ladyship. I don't do stairs if I
can help it.'

'Who is it, Mrs Kempson?'

'Look, dearie, I ain't no butler neither. I didn't
ask the old crow her name, but she's got hair that
ain't natural for a woman of her age. It's dyed or
it's a wig. You can take your pick.'

'Mrs Fothergill.' Lottie glanced over Mrs
Kempson's shoulder, half expecting to see the
major-general's wife at the top of the stairs. 'Did
you say that Lady Aurelia is at home?'

'What have I just said? I told you I ain't a
servant in this establishment. I'm the owner and

I lets rooms. If you want to go down and tell the woman you're not at home, it's up to you. I done me bit.' She stomped off along the landing, grumbling loudly.

Lottie went to give Lady Aurelia the bad news. 'You've got a visitor, my lady.'

Aurelia was still in bed, sipping a cup of chocolate. 'Oh, no. Not Cordelia?'

'I'm afraid so, my lady.'

'Tell her I'm out.'

'I'm afraid Mrs Kempson's already informed her that you're at home.'

'Then say I'm indisposed.'

'Very well, my lady. Although I doubt if she'll believe me.' Lottie left the room and came face to face with Cordelia Fothergill. 'I'm sorry, Mrs Fothergill, but Lady Aurelia is not feeling well and is not receiving visitors.'

Cordelia pushed past her. 'Nonsense, I saw you both out walking yesterday. I would have come across the road sooner, but I had to make sure that Cole put my things away tidily.'

'No, really, ma'am,' Lottie insisted, backing towards Aurelia's bedroom. 'My lady is still in bed.'

'That doesn't surprise me.' Cordelia brushed Lottie aside and thrust the door open. 'Good morning, Lady Aurelia. I'm sorry if you are not feeling up to snuff, but we'll soon put that right. Your dear husband has asked me to keep you company while we're waiting for him to join us.'

Aurelia pulled the coverlet up to her chin. 'How kind of Dashwood, but I mustn't detain you, Mrs Fothergill. I fear I might be going down with something catching.'

'I think we can be on more intimate terms now, Aurelia. You must think of me as your friend and call me Cordelia. After all, we are in the same boat, so to speak, or rather we soon will be.'

'You're accompanying your husband to the Crimea?' Aurelia said faintly.

'I feel it is my duty, my dear. For too long I have sat at home and waited for my husband to return from foreign parts, but now I've decided that he needs my womanly companionship and loving care while he's fighting for his country.'

Lottie had to use all her self-control in order to stifle a giggle. Lady Aurelia's expression of horror would have registered on anyone less full of herself, but Cordelia Fothergill seemed to have skin as thick as an elephant's. Lottie had never felt sorrier for her mistress than she did at this moment. With her hair loose around her shoulders she looked small and pale, and almost childlike as she lay in the large bed, but there was a glint in her eyes that did not bode well for Mrs Fothergill.

'Excuse me, ma'am,' Lottie said hastily. 'Might I offer you some refreshment in the drawing room? I could easily run downstairs and fetch you something from the kitchen.'

'I'm here for your mistress, girl. You may leave us.'

'No.' Aurelia pushed back the covers. 'I'll get up, despite my malaise. Kindly leave me to get dressed, Cordelia. I don't like entertaining in my boudoir.'

'That's not what I heard,' Cordelia said with an arch smile.

Aurelia leaped out of bed with her fingers clawed

as if ready to scratch Cordelia's smug face, but Lottie had been quick to spot the danger signals. She snatched a dressing robe from a chair and wrapped it around her mistress, pinning her arms to her sides.

'Let me go,' Aurelia hissed in Lottie's ear. 'I'll strangle the bitch.'

'I'll wait in the drawing room,' Cordelia said as she left the room, closing the door behind her. She seemed unperturbed by Aurelia's anger, although Lottie suspected that she was either hard of hearing or incredibly stupid.

'It's just as well she went when she did or I might have done something I would regret.' Aurelia slumped down on the stool in front of the dressing table. 'How dare she barge into my boudoir and insult me in such a manner?'

'She's a horrible woman,' Lottie said angrily. 'I can't believe that the colonel asked her to spy on you.'

'That's what it amounts to.' Aurelia picked up her hairbrush. 'But I have to agree, it's not the sort of thing that would enter Dashwood's head. However, if she wants to set herself up as my moral guardian I'll give her something to think about.'

'Are you sure that's wise, my lady?'

Aurelia smiled wickedly. 'Oh, yes, Lottie. And it will be fun. I'm beginning to enjoy myself already.'

Lady Aurelia Dashwood launched herself into Southampton society, starting that evening at a charity ball. The tickets were supplied, at considerable cost, by Mrs Kempson, who proved to have an endless knowledge of social events in the town, which she was pleased to share, for a price. Lottie would have been content to stay at home and read a book, but Aurelia insisted that she should accompany her on all occasions, some grander than others.

As the weeks went by invitations were showered upon Lady Aurelia Dashwood, who was fêted wherever she went, and her name was prominent in the social columns of the local newspapers. Hansford had to be sent to Chatham to bring a further selection of her afternoon and evening gowns, and her clothes now occupied a whole room in their lodgings. Gentlemen callers had to be turned away, a task that fell to Mrs Kempson, and seemed to give her a certain amount of grim satisfaction; it was obvious that she was revelling in the popularity of her aristocratic guest.

Undoubtedly the opposite was true of Cordelia. Lottie saw her pale face peering out of her window every time a carriage drew to a halt outside their lodging house. At first Cordelia had made an effort to attend the same social gatherings, but Aurelia was tireless and sometimes there were two or even three engagements on the same evening. No one, Lottie thought wearily, could keep up such a pace for ever – no one except Lady Aurelia Dashwood, the toast of the town.

Lottie herself was kept busy from the moment she woke up in the morning until she tumbled into her bed late at night, or in the early hours. She had to accompany her mistress everywhere and act as her chaperone as well as her maid. Her duties were not onerous but she had little time to rest, and even less time to think about her own problems.

Not that Gideon was a problem now, of course. She had pushed his proposal to the back of her mind, and yet his words still lingered. Sometimes, when she was least expecting it, she would see his face as clearly as if he were standing before her. It would have been foolish to accept his offer of marriage, but she wished she had rejected him with more tact and grace. He was a good man and a true friend, and to tell the truth she missed his company. She missed his lazy smile and his sharp sense of humour, and above all she missed the conversations they had shared during her riding lessons. She looked forward to seeing him again, even though it would not be under the best of circumstances, and she could only hope that he would have forgiven her for turning him down.

Despite Aurelia's frenetic social life, it was obvious to Lottie that her mistress was not happy. There was a brittle gaiety in her manner when in public, but when they were alone in the apartment Aurelia often lapsed into moody silences. She ate little and complained bitterly about the food that Mrs Kempson served, although Lottie could find no fault with their meals, which were plain but well cooked. Sometimes Aurelia was restless and at other times she could barely drag herself out of bed. Lottie was beginning to wish that the colonel would arrive and that their sea voyage would begin, and she tried not to think of the hardships they might endure or the dangers they would inevitably face. She could refuse to go, but that was not an option now. Her relationship with Lady Aurelia was a delicate balance between friend and confidante and servant, but

Lottie felt in some way responsible for her. She had caught glimpses of the fragile person hidden behind an outward display of bravado, and she sensed the depth of feeling concealed beneath Aurelia's blatant disregard for convention. They might be separated socially by accident of birth, but they suffered like sisters when it came to affairs of the heart.

When she had a few moments to herself Lottie had taken to walking down by the docks. She was watching some passengers disembarking from the mail ship *La Plata* one afternoon when she was aware of a sudden commotion. Shielding her eyes against the hazy autumn sunshine, she thought at first that she was witnessing the arrival of a noisy theatrical troupe.

Sunlight glinted on the gold braid worn by the army officers who accompanied a stout, dark-skinned woman wearing a bright blue gown, and a bonnet trimmed with scarlet and yellow ribbons. She was middle-aged and motherly, with a kindly expression and a loud laugh that echoed round the dockyard, causing heads to turn. Lottie stood aside as the small party strolled past, followed by a procession of sailors carrying an assortment of luggage.

Curiosity getting the better of her, Lottie way-laid one of the seamen. 'Who is she? Who is that lady?'

'That's Mother Seacole,' he said, grinning. 'You might not have heard of her yet, but soon she'll be a household name. She's come all the way from Navy Bay, Panama to join Miss Nightingale in the Crimea. That's what she told us on board. Excuse me, miss. I must hurry or I'll be left behind.'

Lottie watched them until they were out of sight, but the merry laughter of Mother Seacole floated in the air, competing with the mournful cries of the seagulls. Lottie hurried home to tell Aurelia, and found her lying on her bed, staring listlessly at the ceiling.

'Are you ill?' Lottie asked anxiously. 'You do look a bit pale.'

'Did you get the pot of rouge I asked for?'

'I did, but you don't need to put paint on your face, my lady.'

'You're my maid, not my mother. She died years ago.'

'I'm sorry, but you are a lovely woman. You really don't need anything to make you look prettier.'

'Stop preaching at me, Lottie. I'm perfectly all right.' Aurelia raised herself on one elbow. 'What did you have to tell me? I can see by your expression that something has excited you. Has Cordelia fallen down and broken her stringy neck?'

'No, nothing of the sort. I was walking down by the docks when this extraordinary woman disembarked from a mail ship in the company of several quite high-ranking army officers.'

'Really? How interesting.' Aurelia subsided onto the pillows. 'I'm hungry. I fancy some straw-berries.'

'They're not in season. What about a nice juicy apple?'

'No, Lottie. I said I want strawberries.' Aurelia closed her eyes. 'Never mind. Perhaps there'll be some at the ball this evening.'

'Do you think you ought to go out again tonight? I mean, you look exhausted. A rest might do you the world of good.'

Aurelia opened one eye. 'Are you a nurse now? I thought Miss Nightingale had turned you down. Go away and leave me in peace. Wake me up in time to get dressed. We're going to the ball and that is that.'

The charity ball was held in a large function room in the centre of town. They were late arriving as Aurelia's toilette had taken longer than usual and she had changed several times, having found fault with each of the gowns that Lottie had laid out for her.

'Are you sure you feel up to this, my lady?' Lottie asked anxiously as they crossed the foyer, heading for the ballroom.

Pale, but determined, Aurelia shot her a sideways glance. 'We won't stay late. I want you by my side, Lottie. Don't let that woman come near me or I might forget myself.'

'But I ought to stay in the anteroom with the other maidservants.'

'Tonight you are my companion and my chaperone. You will sit with the dowagers while I dance and enjoy myself, but if you see that dragon moving in my direction I want you to head her off. Do what you like, but keep her away from me.'

'I'll do my best.'

Aurelia treated her to a beaming smile. 'I know you will, dear Lottie.' She linked arms with her as the usher opened the double doors and they entered together. Aurelia paused on the threshold and Lottie moved aside. Heads turned to stare at the vision in shimmering emerald green with a diamond necklace flashing white fire around her slender throat, and earrings that reflected the light from the many chandeliers. The orchestra played on, but the dancing had stopped. Lottie held her breath. Her mistress had captured the hearts and imaginations of the illustrious gathering as if a queen had suddenly arrived in their midst. She made the staid matrons look dowdy and the young unmarried girls look gauche and plain.

There was a moment of silence as the orchestra finished their piece and it seemed to Lottie that the world had stopped spinning. There were many military uniforms amongst the guests, but she had spotted Colonel Dashwood, who was making his way through the crowd followed by Farrell Gillingham. She made a move towards Lady Aurelia intending to warn her, but Aurelia had spotted her husband and her lover. Her hand flew to her lips and she slid to the floor in a dead faint.

Lottie went down on her knees beside her but Gillingham was first to reach them and he lifted Aurelia in his arms. Colonel Dashwood followed more slowly, puffing and red in the face and to Lottie's horror she saw Cordelia bringing up the rear. Lottie sprang to her feet and signalled to the usher to open the door.

'There's an anteroom outside to the right,' she said in a low voice. 'I know because we've been here before.'

Gillingham nodded and carried his precious burden from the crowded ballroom.

'You'd better come with us, Lane.' Colonel

Dashwood followed Gillingham out into the comparative cool of the foyer. He stopped on the top step, turning to Cordelia with a frown. 'The fewer people around the better, madam. There's no need for you to trouble yourself.'

'Well, really! I only wanted to help. I've been keeping an eye on your wife, Colonel.'

'I don't think Lady Aurelia needs you to chaperone her, Mrs Fothergill. I suggest you return to your husband's side.' Dashwood closed the door on her. 'Send for a doctor, Miss Lane. My wife is obviously unwell.'

'I will, of course, if you think it necessary, sir. But it was probably the surprise on seeing you that overcame her,' Lottie said tactfully. 'We weren't aware that you were in town.' She followed the colonel into the anteroom where Gillingham had set Aurelia down on a sofa.

'Get some water, Miss Lane,' he said, looking up. 'Or some smelling salts, if you have them.'

'What happened?' Aurelia opened her eyes and attempted to sit up, but fell back again and covered her eyes with her gloved hand. 'Gillingham, is it really you?'

He shot a wary glance at the colonel. 'Yes, my lady. I am here with your husband, who is very concerned for your welfare.'

'Dash it, man. I can speak for myself.' Colonel Dashwood brushed him aside. 'Are you unwell, Aurelia? Shall I send for a doctor?'

Lottie stood by with the glass she had just filled from a jug on a side table. 'Perhaps a sip of water would help, my lady?'

Aurelia made another attempt to sit up. 'Yes,

please.' She drank thirstily. 'I was overcome by the heat in that room, and of course, the pleasure of seeing you, Dashwood.' She shook her head as Lottie offered her another drink. 'Thank you, I'm quite recovered now.'

'Why don't you lie back and rest a while, my lady?' Gillingham said softly. 'I could send for a cab to take you back to your lodgings.'

'Yes, my love,' Dashwood agreed, nodding. 'That sounds like a capital idea. We've been apart far too long and a quiet evening at home would be most welcome.'

Aurelia sat upright, staring at him with narrowed eyes. 'And yet you didn't apprise me of your arrival, Dashwood. You attended the ball without bothering to find out if I would care to accompany you.'

Lottie held her breath, looking from one to the other. She could see that Gillingham longed to take Aurelia's part, but could not without betraying his feelings, and she, for her part, was deliberately ignoring him.

'Well, my love, of course I would have come straight to you, but we arrived at the barracks just a few hours ago. I am on duty.'

'Of course you are.' Aurelia rose to her feet, leaning on Gillingham. She smiled. 'Duty must come first, Dashwood. I've been an army wife for long enough to know that. I wouldn't dream of asking you to disobey orders from above.'

'You are, as always, the perfect wife.' Dashwood raised her hand to his lips. 'Are you recovered enough to dance with your husband, Aurelia?'

'Yes, indeed.' Aurelia moved from Gillingham's

protective arm and laid her hand on her husband's sleeve. 'On one condition, Dashwood. Keep that red-haired termagant away from me for the rest of the evening. She has made my life a misery while I've been here waiting for your arrival.'

Colonel Dashwood's reply was lost as they left the room. Lottie was not sure whether she was supposed to remain where she was, or if she was expected to follow her mistress into the ballroom. Gillingham was about to follow his superior, but he hesitated, turning to Lottie with a grin.

'It looks as though you aren't needed for a while, Miss Lane. I think you might enjoy a breath of fresh air.'

She stared at him, puzzled. 'I don't feel faint, Lieutenant.'

'No, but there is someone outside whom you might like to see.' He left the room, giving her a wink and a smile.

'Gideon.' His name left her lips in an involuntary sigh, but she hesitated. They had not parted on the best of terms and she was unsure of her welcome, but the desire to see him overcame her misgivings.

The smells and sounds of the stable yard brought back memories of her years at The Swan. Horses stamped and pawed the ground in their stalls, while stable boys walked the more restive animals. A group of soldiers stood apart from the civilians, smoking and drinking ale, as they waited for orders. Lottie wrapped her cloak around her as the cool night air stung her cheeks. Summer was now a distant memory and autumn had brought in the long dark nights and the promise of colder weather to come. She hesitated, trying to make out the faces of the men who had gathered in the light of a flaming torch, but she could not see Gideon and she wondered if Gillingham had been teasing her. If so, it was a cruel jest and she could taste disappointment on her tongue as if she had swallowed a draught of bitter medicine. She turned to go and almost collided with a tall figure in uniform.

'Gideon?' It was too dark to see his face clearly, but she would have known him anywhere.

'Lottie. By God, it is you?' He seized her by the shoulders, drawing her into a pool of light that spilled from an uncurtained window. 'I didn't expect to see you tonight.'

'Gillingham told me that you were here.'

'This is a wonderful surprise. I hoped we'd meet again soon.'

'I am so happy to see you, Gideon.'

He met her gaze with a long look. 'Are you really, Lottie? Or are you just saying that?'

'I felt so bad after I turned you down, but you caught me unawares.'

'Would you have answered differently if I'd given you time to think?' His eager expression touched her to the core, but it made her think hard before she responded.

'I wouldn't have accepted an offer of marriage in order to get me out of a difficult situation,' she said slowly, 'but I might have admitted that I felt something more for you than mere friendship.'

He dropped his hands to his sides. 'And how do you feel now? For a moment just then I thought you had some tender feelings for me.'

'Oh, Gideon, I have, but it's confusing. I do care for you, very much, but I had to be sure.'

'Sure of what? I don't understand.'

'I had to be sure that you weren't just being a gentleman, and that you weren't offering me marriage because you felt responsible for me in some way. After all, we hardly know each other.'

He answered her with a kiss that robbed her of breath, reason and possibly sanity. The stable yard and the drunken grooms and soldiers melted into nothingness. The world about them ceased to exist and she was intoxicated with the heady masculine scent of his body, and the familiar aroma of Macassar oil and saddle leather. His lips were tender and yet demanding and she gave herself up to the pleasure and heart-stopping sweetness of the moment.

'Private Ellis, this won't do.'

The jovial sound of Joe Benson's voice shattered the dream, and Lottie gasped for air like a swimmer coming up from the deep.

'Leave us alone, Joe,' Gideon said, chuckling. 'You're just jealous because I've got the most beautiful girl in the world.'

'I won't argue with that, mate.' Joe turned to Lottie with a broad grin. 'Glad you sorted him out, miss. He's been a miserable devil since you left Chatham.'

'Thanks, mate.' Gideon slipped his arm around Lottie's waist. 'Now go away. Lottie and I have a lot to talk about.'

Joe shrugged and ambled off to join his fellow sappers.

'I've been miserable too,' Lottie said earnestly. 'I've had to put a brave face on it, but there wasn't a day went by when I didn't wish I could see you to make things right between us.'

He laid his finger on her lips. 'There's no need. I understand, and I love you all the more for being honest with me. Although,' he added smiling ruefully, 'I couldn't see it at the time.'

'You didn't tell me that you loved me, Gideon.'

'I thought you knew how I felt, Lottie. I thought women sensed that sort of thing without having to be told.'

'Maybe someone like Lady Aurelia has that intuitive power, but I didn't know how you felt. I needed to be told.'

'I'm telling you now, Charlotte Lane. I'm not a poet or even very good with words, but I've loved you from the first moment I saw you.'

A gurgle of laughter rose to her lips. 'You didn't even know your own name then, my boy.'

'I might not have known who I was, but I knew you. It was as if you'd always been there in my heart and in my head. I am your boy, Lottie. I am your man, and always will be, no matter what.'

A cold shiver ran down her spine and it was not just the cool breeze that wafted through the stable yard. 'And I am yours for ever, Gideon. I'm going to the Crimea with Lady Aurelia and I'll be close to you.'

He kissed her again, to the accompaniment of whistles and shouts of encouragement from his comrades.

Lottie pushed him away gently, holding him at a safe distance with her hands flat on his uniformed chest. 'I have to go. Lady Aurelia might be looking for me.'

He covered her hands with his. 'I don't know exactly when we'll be leaving, but I must see you again.'

'We're staying at Mrs Kempson's lodging house in the High Street. Anybody will be able to give you directions; she's well known in this town.'

'If I asked you to marry me now, would you accept? I would be far happier to know that you were safe in England than risking your life abroad.'

'No, Gideon. That wouldn't do at all. I want to be where you are, and I have a duty to Lady Aurelia. I have a feeling that she needs me more than she would ever admit. I'll follow you with a glad heart, and I'll share the danger with you. I'm not a meek and mild little woman who would ever be content to sit at home and wait.'

They parted with one last, lingering kiss, and then Lottie hurried back to the ballroom. Her joy on being reunited with Gideon and on hearing him declare his love for her was tinged with fear and sadness. They had been thrown together, but for how long?

Chapter Nine

Lottie lived for the brief moments she was able to spend with Gideon, although they were rarely alone. Colonel Dashwood had decided to remain at the barracks to oversee the important business

148

of getting the Telegraph Detachment and the telegraph wagons ready for embarkation at the beginning of November. His visits to the lodging house in the High Street were brief and infrequent, and it was Gillingham, accompanied by Gideon, who called at every available opportunity. Quite how he managed to arrange it was as much a mystery to Lottie as it was to Aurelia, who seemed to think it a huge joke. Lottie was not convinced that the colonel would be amused if he knew that the man he sent bearing messages of love and bouquets of flowers was a rival for his wife's affections. It was clear to Lottie that the colonel had lost the fight almost before it had begun.

Aurelia was a different woman now that she had been reunited with Gillingham. Her megrims were forgotten and the laudanum bottle put aside. She rarely expressed the desire for a glass of brandy, and she bloomed like a rare and delicate flower. Her skin glowed with health and her eyes sparkled. Lottie was happy in her own right, but it was a deep, serene calm that had taken hold of her spirit now that she knew Gideon loved her. Even so, she was afraid for her mistress and for Gillingham, whose whole future was at risk even before he had set foot on the battlefield.

Lottie confided her worries to Gideon on one of the rare occasions when they had time to themselves at Aurelia's lodgings. 'It will end badly,' she said, sighing. 'I can't believe that the colonel is so blind that he cannot see what's going on under his nose.'

Gideon held her close as they sat side by side on the uncomfortable sofa. 'There's nothing we can do about it, sweetheart. Gillingham knows the risks he's running, and he obviously thinks she's worth it.'

Lottie angled her head so that she could look him in the eye. 'You don't like her, do you?'

'It's not a question of like or dislike. She's my commanding officer's wife, and her father is an earl. She's so far above me that I get dizzy from looking up to her, but I don't approve of what she's doing.'

'And yet you don't disapprove of Gillingham. That doesn't seem fair.'

Gideon kissed her on the forehead. 'I think he's a fool, but he's besotted, and there's nothing that I or anyone else can do about it.'

'You think he's a fool to be so deeply in love that nothing else matters?'

He drew her into his arms and kissed her, but, from the street below, the sound of someone hammering on the door knocker made them draw apart.

'Mrs Kempson will see who it is.' Lottie slid her arms around his neck and parted her lips, waiting for him to take her to the point of desire when it was dangerous to go any further, but the sound of heavy footsteps on the stairs was followed by a sharp knock on the door.

'I've an urgent message for Lieutenant Gillingham.'

Gideon stiffened. 'That sounds ominous.' He rose to his feet, straightened his tunic and moved quickly to open the door.

He stepped outside, and Lottie sat very still, straining her ears in an attempt to hear what was being said. Moments later he reappeared. 'We've had the call to duty, my love. I'll rouse the lieutenant and then we'll have to leave you.'

She rose to her feet. 'What does it mean?'

'It looks like our ship has arrived in dock.' He seized both her hands and raised them to his lips in a brief salute. 'This is it, Lottie. It looks as if we'll be leaving very soon.' He released her and went to knock on Lady Aurelia's door.

'Sorry to disturb you, sir, but orders have come. We must leave right away.'

A muffled voice answered and then Gillingham appeared, smoothing his hair and adjusting the high collar of his jacket. 'I'm ready, Private Ellis.'

Aurelia appeared behind him. 'Does this mean we're all leaving for the Crimea? Why wasn't I told sooner?'

'I don't know, my love,' Gillingham said gently. 'Perhaps the colonel wants to tell you in person.'

She tossed her head. 'Heaven knows I'm used to his sudden departures, but it doesn't usually involve me. I need to know urgently, Farrell. I can't pack and be ready in a blink of an eye.'

He clasped her hand to his cheek. 'I can't tell you what I don't know, but Ellis and I have to leave immediately.' He kissed each of her fingers in turn. 'Always remember that I love you, Aurelia.' He turned to Gideon. 'Come along, Private. You've had plenty of time to say goodbye.'

Gideon blew a kiss to Lottie as he followed Gillingham out of the apartment. The door closed with a bang and they were gone.

Aurelia's bottom lip trembled. 'They can't leave without us. Start packing, Lottie.'

Lottie spent the rest of the afternoon filling the cabin trunk and the various cases and portmanteaux with little or no help from her mistress. Aurelia sat on the bed issuing instructions as to which ball gown she would take and those she would send home to Chatham. At any other time Lottie would have demanded to know what good a ball gown would be in camp, but she knew better than to ask questions of a woman teetering on the brink of losing self-control. Aurelia's blue eyes were red-rimmed and her fingers plucked nervously at the counterpane. 'I don't understand it,' she said angrily. 'Why hasn't Dashwood sent word to tell me what is happening?'

Lottie folded a shot silk gown carefully and laid it in the trunk. 'I don't know, my lady.'

'It's ridiculous.' Aurelia stood up and walked to the window. 'Heaven help us. There's that dreadful old hag and I do believe she's heading this way.' She crossed the floor and leaped back onto the bed. 'Tell her I'm ill. Tell her anything, but don't let her near me.'

'I'll do my best.' Lottie abandoned the packing and went into the next room, where she waited for the inevitable tap on the door. She went to open it and Cordelia Fothergill brushed past her.

'I want to see Lady Aurelia.'

'I'm afraid she is indisposed, ma'am.' It was a well-rehearsed sentence that tripped off Lottie's lips without her having to stop and think.

'Nonsense. I saw Lieutenant Gillingham leaving the building earlier. Anyway, she will see me as I have something important to impart. We've received orders and I need to pass them on. Kindly ask her to rise from her sick bed.'

Lottie could see that Mrs Fothergill's mind was made up, and it seemed useless to continue with the charade. 'Very well, ma'am. Please wait and I'll see if her ladyship is well enough to receive visitors.'

Aurelia climbed out of bed reluctantly and moved like a sleepwalker to the dressing table. 'I heard what she said. Hateful creature.' She smoothed a curl into place and reached for the rouge pot. 'I don't want the old bitch to see me looking pale and wan.'

'I think she might have news of our departure date, my lady.'

'I'll have something to say to Dashwood when I next see him. How dare he leave me to find out what's happening from that person.' Aurelia straightened up, braced her shoulders and marched into the drawing room.

'Cordelia, how kind of you to pay us a visit. What brings you here?'

'I see that your maid is packing,' Mrs Fothergill said, glancing through the open door. 'It is a little premature, my dear.'

'Really? How so?'

'We are not to travel on the troop ship. Orders have come from the top, so there is nothing that our respective husbands can do about it, although I myself am far from disappointed.'

'Are we not to accompany them to the Crimea?' Despite her outward show of calm, Aurelia's voice broke on a suppressed sob.

'You have not been well, my lady,' Lottie said

urgently. 'Won't you sit down?'

Mrs Fothergill's lip curled disdainfully. 'Your maid has a lot to say for herself, Lady Aurelia. I keep Cole well and truly in her place.'

'I think I know how to treat my servants, Cordelia. Please say whatever it was you came here to say.'

'The vessel taking our men to the Crimea has to pick up another contingent from Plymouth and there will be no room for civilians. We will travel at a later date, which has yet to be decided.'

'Of course I knew this was a possibility,' Aurelia said coldly. 'Dashwood keeps me informed of all such matters.'

'Then it seems it must have slipped his mind this time.' Mrs Fothergill's voice was silky smooth but her eyes flashed with malice.

Lottie had to curb the desire to throw the hateful woman out of the apartment, but Aurelia seemed to have no such reservations. She moved swiftly to the door and opened it. 'Thank you for calling, Cordelia. Let's hope the weather doesn't deteriorate too much before we eventually set sail. *Mal de mer* is a beastly affliction, so I hope you are a good sailor.'

This sudden change of topic seemed to throw Mrs Fothergill off track. Her startled expression was replaced by one of studied nonchalance. 'I come from a long line of seafarers,' she said icily. 'My great-grandfather was a vice admiral.'

'Really?' Aurelia uttered a mirthless laugh. 'One of my ancestors was a privateer, but he used his wealth to good effect and was granted lands and a title by Good Queen Bess.'

154

'Well, I must be going,' Mrs Fothergill said hastily. 'I'll keep you up to date with travel arrangements.' She whisked out of the room. 'I'll see myself out.'

Aurelia slammed the door. 'Good riddance, I say. Pour me a large brandy, Lottie. I'm in need of resuscitation after that ordeal by Fothergill.'

'I'm so sorry, my lady. That woman has no tact and no feeling.' Lottie measured a small tot of brandy into a glass and gave it to her mistress. 'Are you all right?'

Aurelia twirled the glass in her hand, staring into the amber liquid. 'I don't know why she hates me so much, Lottie. What have I ever done to her?'

'She's just jealous, my lady. You are everything she wishes to be but is not.'

'I don't know if that is true, but you are such a comfort to me, Lottie.'

'I am?' Lottie stared at her in amazement. 'But I'm just a servant.'

'You're more than that. You are probably the only true friend I have in the whole world, and I need you now, more than ever.'

'I don't understand.'

Aurelia raised her head to look Lottie in the eye. 'I will tell you now because it will soon become apparent to all, but I am, in common parlance, in the family way.'

'You are?' Lottie was at a loss for words. She did not know whether to congratulate her mistress or to commiserate as there was no joy in the announcement.

'I am.' Aurelia fixed her with a hard stare. 'Don't tell anyone, especially Gideon. If my husband finds out he'll forbid me to travel.'

'But is it wise to undertake such a journey, my lady? Wouldn't it be better for you and the child to remain here in England where you are safe from harm?'

Aurelia shrugged and shook her head. 'Childbirth is unsafe wherever the mother happens to be. I might easily die, and the baby too. I've no intention of being left behind. I will be close to the man I love, and that is more important to me than anything.'

'More important than the child you carry?'

'Yes it is, if I'm honest. Does that sound wicked and heartless?'

'I don't know, my lady. I can't imagine being in your position, so I couldn't say.'

'Well, I've made the decision and you are the only one who knows about it.'

'When is it due, my lady?'

'I'm not sure, but I think it will be February or March, but it will be winter when we finally arrive in the Crimea and I will be swaddled in fur, so I should be able to keep my condition hidden for quite some time.'

'But the colonel will have to know,' Lottie suggested tentatively. 'You won't be able to conceal your condition for much longer.'

'I'll tell him when the time is right, but until then it is our secret. I'm relying on you, Lottie. Don't fail me now.'

They were at supper that evening when Colonel Dashwood arrived. Lottie ushered him into the parlour, where Aurelia was just finishing her meal. She looked up, unsmiling.

'Dashwood, this is a surprise.'

He moved swiftly to her side. 'My dear, I must apologise for not coming sooner, but our orders came through just as the ship docked, and everything had to be organised in a hurry.'

'You could have written a note. I'm sure that wouldn't have taken up too much of your valuable time.'

He pulled up a chair and sat down beside her. 'Now, now, my love. I understand that you're angry and perhaps a little disappointed not to be travelling with me.'

'I am exceedingly upset, as you can see.' Aurelia pushed her plate away. 'What are you going to do about it?'

'The reason I'm so tardy in coming to see you is because I have been attempting to make alternative arrangements for you and your maid.'

Aurelia leaped to her feet. 'What are you saying? Are you going back on your word?'

'No, my dear. It's just that you will have to be patient and wait a while longer.'

'How long?' Aurelia demanded angrily. 'Or is this just an excuse, and I am to sit the war out in this horrible apartment?'

'No, of course not. Be reasonable, Aurelia. Our transport is overfull and is no place for a lady, or ladies, as the case may be. I've booked passage for you and Miss Lane on a vessel in three weeks' time.'

'Three weeks, Dashwood? Do you mean to say I have to kick my heels in this dreary town for another three weeks?'

'I'm afraid you have no choice, my love. Mrs Fothergill and her maid will be travelling on the same vessel, and I'm sending Hansford with you, so you will be quite safe.'

'Cordelia will hate life in camp,' Aurelia said crossly. 'She'll do nothing but complain.'

'That, my dear, is the major-general's problem, not mine. Now, if you'll forgive me, I have to return to the barracks. We leave on the morning tide and there is much to do.' He rose to his feet and looked down at her with an indulgent smile. 'As I've heard it, you have been the toast of the town. The society here will be rather dull, I fear, when you have left.'

'I expect it will, but I'm more than ready to depart.'

'I'll see to it that you have the best billet Balaklava has to offer, Aurelia.' He hurried from the room, acknowledging Lottie with a brief nod of his head.

'He's a good man,' Lottie said as the door closed on him, 'and he's devoted to you, my lady.'

Aurelia sighed and reached for her wineglass. 'Yes, he is. In some ways I wish the child was his. He would have loved to have a son to carry on the family name.'

Lottie stared at her, shocked. 'Are you sure he's not the father, my lady?'

'Oh, yes, I'm quite certain, but he must never know. I think he would kill Farrell if he were to discover the truth, or at the very least he would have him cashiered and made to suffer the ignominy of a dishonourable discharge.'

'Then why are we going to the Crimea, my

lady?' Lottie asked in desperation. 'Wouldn't it be better to remain at home? You could have the baby in safety and the colonel would return to find he was a father.'

'You don't understand, Lottie. Dashwood has never been demanding when it comes to conjugal rights, if you understand my meaning. It's going to be difficult enough to convince him that he fathered my child, but if he is there when it's born he might accept it as his own.'

Lottie felt the blood rush to her cheeks. The intimate side of Lady Aurelia's marriage was none of her business. 'I see,' she said vaguely.

'I know I have a reputation as a flirt, but Farrell was my first true love and nothing will ever change that. I just want to be close to him, and I don't care about the danger, but now I won't see him for weeks.'

Forgetting her lowly status, Lottie wrapped her arms around her mistress and held her while she sobbed.

Three weeks later they set sail for the Crimea. The new screw steamer was sleek and fast, and even though it was mid-November the weather was reasonably calm at the start. But the Bay of Biscay proved to be Cordelia's undoing and she took to her cabin with Cole looking after her. Lottie was surprised and pleased to find that she was an excellent sailor, and despite the cramped living conditions, she discovered a love of sailing and a deep respect for the ocean in all its moods. Leaning on the ship's rail, watching the white-crested waves was a constant source of pleasure mixed with awe at the power of the sea. The worries that beset her on shore seemed far away, and the war in the Crimea assumed the dimensions of something she might have read about in a book. Even though she knew that this period of calm could not last for ever, she was almost sorry when land came into sight.

Their first port of call was Malta and when they docked in Valletta they were able to disembark. The prospect of visiting a foreign country was exciting, but Mrs Fothergill made a miraculous recovery once she set foot on firm ground, and insisted on chaperoning Aurelia, even though she had Hansford to act as bodyguard.

Their stay was supposed to be a brief one for taking on water and supplies of fresh food, but engine trouble kept them in port. The captain informed his passengers that he had had to send to Gibraltar for a vital part of the machinery and that might take several weeks. Aurelia was angry at the delay and restive, but Lottie took it all in her stride and spent as much time ashore as possible. Mrs Fothergill made friends with the wife of the commander of the barracks in Valletta, and it was left to Hansford to chaperone Lady Aurelia and Lottie during their excursions on the island.

Lottie was surprised to find that there were a large number of British women and children in Valletta: army wives and camp followers who were waiting for permission to join their men in the Crimea. She discovered, talking to one young woman who had travelled far from home in her attempt to join her husband, that only a very few were given the small white card which read 'to go', and even then they were not allowed to take their children. The quota system was very strict, although some women got round it by offering their services as laundresses or cooks, and missing Gideon as she did, Lottie could understand their need to be close to their men. Aurelia was risking everything, including the life of her unborn child, in order to be with Gillingham, and with each passing week her condition was becoming more and more difficult to conceal. Her trips ashore became less frequent and she spent much of her time lying on the bunk in the cabin she shared with Lottie. She grew pale and listless and Lottie was worried about her health, but she had no one to turn to. It would have been pointless to confide in Cordelia, who had never gone through the experience of pregnancy and childbirth.

The captain was vague as to when they might expect the repairs to be completed, and it was becoming obvious that they would spend Christmas moored alongside. Aurelia was tearful and petulant, but to Lottie's surprise it was Cordelia who brought an end to Aurelia's self-imposed imprisonment.

She burst into their cabin on Christmas morning, dressed in her outdoor clothes. 'Just look at you, Lady Aurelia. What would your husband say if he could see you lounging about in bed? Stop moping, get up and get dressed. We're going to church.'

Aurelia turned her face to the bulkhead. 'I don't feel well, Cordelia. You'll have to go without me.'

'You don't feel well because you need fresh air and exercise.' Cordelia tugged at the coverlet.

'It's no wonder you're getting fat. Lying about all day and eating your head off isn't good for you. Colonel Dashwood will hardly recognise you by the time we reach Balaklava.'

'Go away, Cordelia. I'm unwell.'

Lottie had been hovering in the background, but she could see that Mrs Fothergill was not about to give up. 'Perhaps some fresh air would be good for you, my lady,' she suggested tentatively. 'I'll help you get dressed.'

'The girl is right. Get up, Aurelia. I command it as the wife of your husband's superior officer. I'll wait for you on deck, but if you're not ready in ten minutes I'll want to know the reason why.' She backed out of the small cabin, leaving Aurelia staring after her.

'I can't believe she had the temerity to tell me what to do,' she said tearfully. 'Follow the woman, Lottie. Tell her to go to hell.'

'No, my lady. I hate to say it, but Mrs Fothergill is right. You should get up and go ashore for a while. You're making yourself ill and you might be harming the baby.'

'Nonsense. It's the child that's making me like this. I don't want to be a mother. I hate being swollen and bloated like a whale, and if I go out looking like this everyone will know.'

Lottie helped her to a sitting position. 'We could raise your hoop a bit higher, and if you wear that smart fur-trimmed cape no one will be any the wiser.'

'I suppose so,' Aurelia said reluctantly. 'I must admit that I'm sick to death of being shut up in this cabin.'

162

'Then let me help you.' Lottie selected a grey silk morning gown from the cabin trunk. 'I moved the buttons on the bodice so this should fit well. You are still quite small, my lady. A touch of rouge and a smile will work wonders.'

A shadow of a smile flitted across Aurelia's pale features. 'You are a determined minx when you put your mind to it, Lottie. You win. I'll go to church and hope that God doesn't strike me down for the sinner that I am.'

The spare part needed to restore the ship's engine to working order arrived two days later and the vessel set sail for Constantinople on New Year's Day. Lottie encouraged her mistress to take daily walks on deck, and the weather improved as they approached the Greek archipelago. She put her worries for Gideon's safety aside in her attempt to keep Aurelia from fretting, and Hansford was an unexpected ally. He seemed to know instinctively if Aurelia needed a strong arm to cling to on days when the choppy sea made walking on deck hazardous, and his large presence kept their curious fellow passengers at bay. Mrs Fothergill was stricken with seasickness from the moment they left Valletta until they docked in the port of Pera on their arrival in Turkey. She revived enough to go sightseeing in Constantinople and this time Aurelia and Lottie accompanied her, with Hansford, as always, close at hand to protect them from danger, real or imagined.

During their stay in Constantinople they met officers who were convalescing from injuries received in the Crimea and others who were taking a few days' leave from the battlefields, and for the first time they had first-hand news. Lottie listened to accounts of the hurricane that had left a trail of damage and disaster when it had hit Balaklava in the middle of November, and the latest attack by the Russians on the port. Cholera, she was told, was rife, and many had succumbed to the terrible disease. Even so, she suspected that the war-weary men were not telling them the full extent of the horrors they had seen and endured.

It was agonising to be this close to Gideon and yet so far away, but the end of their journey was in sight. They had only to cross the Black Sea and they would be reunited with their loved ones. It was this thought that kept Lottie going, and gave her the patience to deal with Aurelia's changeable moods. Their sailing was delayed once again, but this time it was the weather that kept them in port until the end of January. To make matters worse Aurelia had started getting pains, but these were not consistent and she refused to consult a doctor.

'You know what a physician would say, Lottie,' she said, grimacing and holding her side. 'I would be confined to bed and told to rest until the baby arrived, and that is not for another month or so. I cannot remain here until the birth. I will not.'

'But what will happen if you go into labour on board ship?' Lottie asked anxiously. 'I wouldn't know what to do.'

'My child is the son of a soldier,' Aurelia said with a touch of her old spirit. 'He will obey orders and stay where he is. I'm sure it is nothing. Perhaps all women in my condition suffer this way.'

Lottie was about to answer when someone

rapped on the cabin door. She opened it to find Maggie Cole, looking agitated, although that was her natural expression. Lottie assumed it was working for Mrs Fothergill that had given her a permanent frown.

'Yes, Miss Cole. Is anything wrong?'

'Only that the engine has broken down again and we're going to have to transfer to another ship. Mrs Fothergill is having hysterics as we speak.'

'Come in and tell us what is happening.' Lottie held the door open.

Cole stepped inside. 'I can't stay because she'll have a fit if I don't go back immediately, but I believe we have been given a choice. We can either remain here for an indefinite period until the engine is once again repaired, or we can board a transport vessel carrying commissariat officers to the Crimea.'

Aurelia remained seated, clutching her filmy wrap around her body. 'I won't stay here a moment longer than necessary. We will go on the transport ship.'

'Are you sure about that, my lady?' Lottie asked anxiously. 'It won't be very comfortable.'

'I don't care,' Aurelia cried passionately. 'I'll swim if necessary.'

'You'd better tell Mrs Fothergill,' Lottie turned to Maggie, lowering her voice. 'I don't think Lady Aurelia will change her mind.'

Chapter Ten

In pouring rain and gale-force winds, they boarded the *Albatross*. Lottie had hoped that Mrs Fothergill might balk at the idea of transferring to a smaller, less comfortable vessel, but it seemed that she was as eager to bring the journey to an end as anyone. The dark sky and stormy sea might have put her off, but she insisted that her place was with her husband. Perhaps the tales of disease and suffering had reached her ears, but the moment the ship was under way, she retired to her tiny cabin, with Cole in attendance.

'Well, that's the last we'll see of her until we reach Balaklava,' Aurelia said smugly. She grasped Lottie's arm as the vessel pitched and tossed. 'Am I imagining things or do I hear cows lowing?'

'There are cattle in the hold, my lady,' Lottie said grimly. 'This isn't the sort of ship your husband had in mind for your journey.'

'Nothing has gone to plan.' Aurelia hesitated at the top of the companionway. 'I'm not sure I can manage ladders in my condition, Lottie. Perhaps this was a bad idea.'

'It's too late now. We've left port and there's no turning back.' She descended the steep ladder and held up her hand. 'It's not too bad. Don't look down.' She held her breath as she watched Aurelia's booted feet feeling for each slippery rung, but somehow she managed to get to the bottom. She leaned against the bulkhead, clutching her sides.

'The pains have returned. He mustn't come yet. I'm not ready.'

'Babies come when they're good and ready, child.'

The loud voice behind her was oddly familiar. Lottie spun round to find herself looking into the twinkling brown eyes of the gaudily dressed woman she had seen disembarking from the mail ship *La Plata* in Southampton. 'It's Mrs Seacole, isn't it?'

'That's me, child. I am Mary Seacole, late of Jamaica and now on my way to do what I can for our brave soldiers in their time of need.' Mary's throaty chuckle wrapped itself round Lottie like a warm breeze. There was something both trustworthy and endearing about this stout, black lady with a huge personality and an equally impressive presence.

Aurelia looked from one to the other in astonishment. 'Do you know each other?'

'My dear lady, I am known to many,' Mary said modestly, 'but I haven't had the pleasure of your acquaintance, nor that of this pretty young lady.'

Lottie felt the blood rush to her cheeks at the unexpected compliment. 'I saw you in Southampton, Mrs Seacole, but we didn't meet then. My name is Lottie and this is Lady Aurelia Dashwood. She is on her way to join her husband, Colonel Dashwood.'

'I am delighted to make your acquaintance, my lady.' Mary inclined her head graciously.

Aurelia eyed her suspiciously. 'What you said

just now – how did you know?'

'My dear lady, I've seen more women in your condition than I can remember. You should rest awhile. It's going to be a rough crossing.'

'I think we should find our cabin.' Lottie could see that her mistress was deeply offended by Mrs Seacole's motherly advice.

'And I have to check on my stores,' Mary said cheerfully, seemingly oblivious to the fact that she had upset anyone. 'I'm going to supply the gallant soldiers with comforts from home and give them the benefit of my extensive medical knowledge. You'll excuse me, ladies. I have much to do.' She shinned up the ladder with surprising agility for a large, middle-aged woman.

'Well, of course I've heard speak of her,' Aurelia said slowly, 'but I never expected to meet her under such circumstances, and she has no manners.'

'She was just speaking the truth, my lady.' Lottie staggered against the bulkhead as the ship crested a wave and dropped into a trough. 'You should take better care of yourself.'

'Don't tell me what I should or should not do, Lottie. You're forgetting your place.' Aurelia marched off, pausing to peer at the numbers on the cabin doors. 'Hurry up, do.'

That night, as the storm continued to rage, Aurelia's pains grew stronger and closer together. Lottie had been dozing in her bunk, but she had awakened to hear the suppressed groans from below. There was little she could do other than offer comfort and bathe Aurelia's brow with a cold flannel, but as the hours went by, and Aurelia's distress became more evident, she knew that her mistress needed help.

Aurelia's screams were drowned in the soughing of the wind and the vicious pounding of the waves against the hull of the ship, and as Lottie opened the cabin door she became aware of the pathetic lowing of the cattle in the hold. She had heard Mary Seacole laughing and joking with some of the officers as they headed for their accommodation after dinner that evening. They had sounded very jolly and Lottie suspected that they were all rather tipsy, but she needed someone with experience of childbirth, and Mary Seacole was the only other woman on board apart from Cole and Mrs Fothergill. She knocked on the cabin door where she thought she might find her, but the loud snoring sounded more like that of a man than a woman and she moved on. Eventually, a door opened and Mary Seacole emerged with her jet-black hair tucked into a frilled nightcap and a voluminous wrap hugged around her ample frame.

'She's started, I suppose.'

'Yes. I'm sorry to bother you, ma'am, but Lady Aurelia's in desperate need of your help. There's nothing more I can do for her.'

'Wait while I fetch my medical bag, child.'

Lottie stood outside the door and a moment later Mary reappeared. 'Lead the way. I'll soon have the little one delivered safe and sound.' She followed Lottie along the narrow corridor to the cabin where Aurelia lay, white-faced and writhing in agony.

Despite her protests, Mary gave her a thorough

examination. 'Hush now, lady. We women are all the same when it comes to birthing babies. There's no room for modesty or pride.' She turned her head to give Lottie an encouraging grin. 'You can make yourself useful, child. Go to the galley and fetch me a bowl of hot water and some clean towels. You might make a pot of tea while you're at it.'

Lottie cast a quick glance at Aurelia, but she had her eyes closed and her teeth bared as another pain racked her body. Lottie was halfway out of the door when she hesitated. 'Do you take sugar in your tea, Mrs Seacole?'

'Lord, no. I'll have a tot of rum in mine when this is over. The tea is for you. This will take a while, but don't worry. Everything will be just fine.'

Aurelia's baby was born as dawn broke. The storm had abated to a degree, but the sea was still rough and Lottie was exhausted but overjoyed to hold the tiny scrap of humanity in her arms. The little red face was wrinkled and lined, giving the baby girl the appearance of a small monkey, but to Lottie she was a thing of wonder and beauty. The infant opened her eyes and they were the deep blue of an English summer sky.

'It's a girl, my lady. You have a lovely daughter.'

Aurelia waved her away. 'I wanted a boy. What use is a girl except to sell into marriage?'

'But she's beautiful, like you, my lady.' Lottie looked to Mary, who was washing her hands.

'Let her rest, child. She'll come round to motherhood soon enough.'

'Don't talk about me as if I weren't here,' Aurelia said angrily. 'I don't want her. Dashwood won't want a girl child. He's always wanted a son.' Her voice broke on a sob and she closed her eyes.

'It affects some women this way,' Mary said in a low voice. 'Take no notice. She'll change her mind when she's had a sleep.'

'Thank you for everything,' Lottie said, rocking the baby in her arms. 'I know she'll love her little girl once she gets used to the idea.'

'Sure she will, but for now let's leave her. I want that cup of tea laced with rum, and you look as though a tot would do you good, too.'

Lottie glanced round the small cabin. 'We've nothing for a baby, Mrs Seacole. Not even a crib or any garments.'

Mary met her anxious gaze with a knowing look. 'I guessed as much, but a layette is one thing I haven't got on my list of necessities for the army.' She stroked the baby's downy head with the tip of her finger. 'A drawer will do for a cot, and I have some bolts of cloth. I guess you can sew, as can I. We could use the time we have on board to make a few little garments for her, and I have a lace shawl that I'll be proud to give the young lady as a christening present. We'll go to my cabin and I'll look it out now.'

'There's just one thing,' Lottie said when they were safely out of earshot. 'I think Lady Aurelia would rather that this birth was kept secret for now. It's a delicate matter...'

Mary laid her hand on Lottie's shoulder, that same knowing look in her dark eyes. 'I won't say a word. I've done my bit and I leave it to the

171

colonel's lady to introduce her child to the world, or not, as the case may be. In the meantime I'm darned hungry and very thirsty. Let's go and see if the cook has risen, and if not I'll take charge of the galley myself. I'm very good in the kitchen.'

'But I can't leave the baby unattended.'

'We'll make the little one comfortable in my cabin for the time being, but she'll need to suckle soon. Lady or not, Mrs Dashwood will have to look after the poor little mite.'

Later, having breakfasted on pancakes and bacon cooked on the galley stove by Mrs Seacole herself, Lottie carried the baby, swaddled in Mary's second-best shawl, to the cabin. Aurelia was awake and sitting up.

'I thought I'd been deserted,' she said, pouting. 'I'm hungry and thirsty.'

'I'll fetch you some breakfast, but I thought you'd like to hold your baby. She's a little poppet and she has the bluest eyes you've ever seen.'

'Dashwood's eyes are brown, and she looks nothing like him. I can't arrive with a baby in my arms. He'll never believe that she's his.'

'I'm sorry, my lady, but I don't see what's changed.'

'A daughter isn't the same as a son. Dashwood won't have any interest in a girl child.'

'But Lieutenant Gillingham will love her dearly.'

'He won't know. I've thought it through and I'm not going to tell him. The easiest way out is for me to pass her off as an orphan I've picked up on the way, or perhaps I can find a peasant woman who will take her.'

'My lady, that's terrible. You mustn't think like that.'

Aurelia's eyes flashed angrily. 'Who are you to tell me what I may or may not do? She's my child and I'll see that she's well cared for, but this gives me a way out. Can't you see that?'

'No, my lady. She's a helpless babe and she's your flesh and blood.'

'Stop talking like that. I've made up my mind. You must look after her and I won't even hold her, so there can be no chance of me developing an affection for the infant.'

'You're going to give her away?'

'Yes, and I want you to swear that you'll keep my secret.'

'I will, if that's what you really want, but she will need to be fed soon.'

'There are cows in the hold. I heard them last night. I don't want her near me.'

'Aren't you even going to give her a name?'

'Call her what you like, but take her away. I don't want to look at her.'

Lottie could see that this was going nowhere and she took the infant back to Mary's cabin.

'What will I do?' she asked anxiously. 'Lady Aurelia won't even hold her own baby. She's determined to give her away.'

Mary looked up from the bolt of cotton she was about to cut into. 'Leave it to me, child.' She put the scissors down and raised herself to her feet. 'Wait here and I'll have a word with her ladyship.'

'I'm afraid she won't listen to you, Mrs Seacole.'

Mary turned her head and grinned. 'There

ain't nothing that a determined Jamaican woman cannot do when she sets her mind to it.' She left the cabin with a purposeful toss of her head.

Lottie sat on the edge of the bunk, rocking the sleeping baby in her arms. 'I won't let her give you away, Molly,' she said out loud. The name had sprung to her lips bringing with it long-forgotten memories of her own mother. The once-familiar scent of her perfume came back to Lottie in a waft of fragrance, far different from the overpowering smell of smoke and oil that pervaded the ship, and the ever-present odours from the hold where the cattle existed in miserable conditions. 'Molly,' she said again, savouring the word. 'That was my mother's name, little Molly. She had beautiful blue eyes, just like yours. From now on you will always be Molly to me.' She looked up as the door opened and Mary beckoned to her.

'Give me the baby. I've managed to convince Lady Aurelia that she must suckle the babe for her own sake, let alone that of the child,' Mary said with a wink and a broad grin. 'I told her it's the best and quickest way to get her figure back.'

Lottie laid the sleeping infant in Mary's arms. 'Does that mean she'll keep Molly?'

'I like that name, but it might be best if we keep it to ourselves for now. And in answer to your question, I don't believe she's changed her mind, but we'll have to wait and see. According to the captain it's going to take a day or two more to reach Balaklava. Maybe the lady will learn to love her child, maybe not.'

Lottie stood on deck as the ship negotiated the

narrow inlet that forged its way between high cliffs and opened out into a small harbour, bristling with the masts of ships. The *Albatross* moved slowly through the channel between tightly packed vessels. It was dark in the shadow of the steeply rising land, and lowering clouds brushed the tops of the hills with a swirling white mist. A feeling of gloom and despondency was made worse by the stench of rotting animal carcasses, and the water was thick with driftwood and all kinds of detritus. The town itself looked to be damaged beyond repair by the November hurricane. Tumbledown wooden shacks fronted the wharf, and their broken windows gazed blindly at the scene of destruction of what had once been a thriving community. Pantile roofs were shattered and the stucco was peeling off the more substantial buildings in huge flakes.

It was not a welcoming sight. Lottie turned to Mary, who was at her side, gazing at the devastation with a determined set to her jaw.

'I can see there is work for me here,' Mary said firmly. 'My services will be much needed.'

'It's not the place for her ladyship.' Hansford had come up behind them and his expression was grim. 'She can't be expected to live here.'

'Nor I,' Mary said with a wry smile. 'I have to see to the unloading of my stores, but I've spoken to the captain, and the *Albatross* has to leave almost immediately. He suggests that I remove to the *Medora* for the duration of my stay here, but my intention is to build my British Hotel somewhere inland. It will be a haven where our brave soldiers will find comfort and enjoy some respite from the

175

horrors of war. It will be done, I promise you.'

Lottie had no doubt that Mary Seacole could do anything she set her mind to, but that was not her problem. She turned to Hansford. 'We have to send a message to Colonel Dashwood, informing him of our arrival.'

'I can see a soldier waiting on the wharf, miss,' Hansford said, pointing to a man wearing the familiar uniform. 'I believe they are expecting us.'

'I'd better go and tell her ladyship.' Lottie made a move towards the companionway. 'And Mrs Fothergill, of course,' she added with a wry smile.

Hansford nodded, his expression carefully controlled. 'Yes, miss. And I'll see about getting us ashore without getting our feet wet.'

Lottie went first to Mrs Fothergill's cabin and found her dressed in her best outfit with a plumed hat pinned to her elaborate coiffure. 'Yes, I was expecting to be met,' she said calmly. 'My husband will have organised our accommodation. I demand only the best, and I'm sure that Colonel Dashwood will have made suitable arrangements for Lady Aurelia.'

'Yes, ma'am.'

'By the way,' Mrs Fothergill said as Lottie was about to leave the cabin, 'I thought I heard a baby crying last night. Do you know anything about a child on board?'

'No, ma'am,' Lottie said, crossing her fingers behind her back as the lie tripped off her tongue. 'Perhaps it was seagulls. They sound much the same.'

'I suppose so.' Mrs Fothergill turned to Cole, who was hovering behind her. 'Get along with

176

you, woman. Make sure that all my luggage is transferred to the shore. I'll be very angry if anything goes missing.'

Lottie left them and hurried to the cabin she had been sharing with Aurelia. 'We've landed at last,' she said eagerly. 'But Mrs Fothergill is suspicious. She thought she heard a baby crying.'

Aurelia finished buttoning her blouse. 'The sooner we find a woman to take the child, the better.'

'Are you sure, my lady?' Lottie picked up the sleeping baby and hitched her over her shoulder, receiving a milky burp for her trouble. She smiled. 'She is a little poppet and hardly ever cries.'

'She's your responsibility now, Lottie. I've done my duty by her and I'm giving her to you.'

'You don't mean that, my lady. You'll change your mind once you've recovered your health and strength.'

'I am well enough and I won't relent. The child is yours.'

'But how am I to hide her? What do I do if she wakes up and cries? And she'll need another feed in a few short hours.'

'I don't know and I don't care. I'm a free woman now. The fact that she arrived early has liberated me and I don't have to lie to Dashwood. Find a wet nurse. There must be army wives in the town who will do almost anything for a few shillings.' Aurelia opened her valise and took out a small leather pouch. She tossed it at Lottie. 'That should be enough to pay a peasant to take the child.'

'Are you absolutely certain about this, my lady? Oughtn't you to tell Lieutenant Gillingham that

177

he is a father? Hasn't he the right to know?'

'Listen to me, Lottie. We have enjoyed a close relationship of necessity during our travels, but from now on you will concentrate on the duties for which you are paid. I am resuming my position in society, and in the army, and you have to know your place. Do I make myself understood?'

Lottie hugged the baby to her. 'Yes, my lady. Perfectly.'

Their disembarkation complete, their guide led them through the muddy streets. The filth and devastation shocked Lottie to the core. The worst places she had seen in the East End of London were as nothing compared to a town ravaged by the after-effects of war and the vicious destruction caused by the hurricane. The day was overcast and menacing clouds hugged the tops of the hills surrounding Balaklava. It seemed to her like the entrance to hell, and in the distance she could hear the continuous thunder of cannon fire. Their guide seemed oblivious to everything other than the need to take them to the residence of Major Stomati, the second-in-command of the local militia, where Lord Raglan had made his headquarters.

The substantial stone building had escaped damage and they were greeted by a young lieutenant who ushered them into a whitewashed entrance hall that echoed to the sound of their footsteps.

'If you would care to follow me, my lady...? The major-general's wife has already arrived.'

'My husband, Colonel Dashwood, should be

here very soon,' Aurelia said confidently. 'I trust that suitable accommodation has been arranged for us.'

'Come this way, my lady.' The lieutenant walked on, and with Molly concealed beneath her cloak, Lottie prayed silently that the baby would remain sleeping as she followed Aurelia, with Hansford bringing up the rear.

Mrs Fothergill and Cole were ensconced in the only two comfortable chairs in the sparsely furnished reception room. 'We've been offered accommodation in Lord Raglan's residence until my husband puts in an appearance,' Mrs Fothergill said proudly. 'Lord Raglan is most hospitable.'

Aurelia sat down heavily on a camp stool. 'Were we mentioned, Cordelia? Is there any news from Dashwood?'

Lottie kept in the background, clutching her cloak around her and hoping that Molly would not be woken by the babble of voices. She glanced at Hansford, who was watching her with his usual inscrutable expression, and she wondered if he had guessed the truth.

'No news,' Mrs Fothergill said smugly. 'No doubt he will send for you soon, although I'm not sure whether there is room here for you and your servants.' She turned to the lieutenant. 'Is there any suitable accommodation for a senior officer's wife, Lieutenant Bonney? I saw several rows of huts not too far from here.'

Bonney flushed uncomfortably. 'I will enquire, madam.'

'Where is my husband stationed?' Aurelia demanded. 'A messenger must be sent to apprise

179

him of my arrival.'

'The telegraph is installed and working at least as far as the monastery, my lady. The colonel has been informed, but this is the Crimea and roads are just tracks; getting from one place to another takes time.'

Molly stirred and made a little whimpering noise and Lottie covered her mouth, pretending to smother a cough. Aurelia shot her a meaningful glance. 'I have been unwell during our journey,' she said hastily. 'I would appreciate a private room while I await news from my husband.'

'You have been unwell?' Mrs Fothergill narrowed her eyes so that she looked like a cat getting ready to pounce. 'You were never unwell at sea, Aurelia. It is I who was struck down by seasickness during our voyages. I should have privacy, and if my room is ready I will retire until luncheon.'

Lottie could feel Molly stirring and she was afraid the poor child would suffocate beneath the heavy folds of the cloak. She coughed again. 'Might I go outside, my lady? I am in need of fresh air.'

'Yes, go.' Aurelia dismissed her with a wave of her hand, but her gaze was fixed on Mrs Fothergill and her lips were folded into a thin, angry line.

'I'll show you the way, miss.' Lieutenant Bonney escorted her through a series of rooms and out through the servants' quarters. It was a small house compared to similar residences at home, and the kitchen was little more than a lean-to. Lottie could see servants rushing around and a male cook was shouting orders. It reminded her of The Swan, and for the first time she had a pang of homesickness.

'I will ask the cook to make a pot of tea, miss.' Bonney gave her a searching look, and his pleasant features puckered into a look of concern. 'Take a seat in the courtyard and I'll have it sent out to you.'

'Thank you.' Lottie gave him a tired smile. 'Are you with the Telegraph Detachment?'

'I'm in charge of the commissary, miss.'

'I hoped you might know a friend of mine, Private Ellis.'

'I don't know him personally. There are many different units here.'

Another small whimper from Molly rapidly turned into a mewling cry and Lottie was forced to uncover the baby. She met Lieutenant Bonney's startled gaze with an attempt at a smile.

'Lady Aurelia saved the child,' she said, thinking quickly. 'The mother was trying to sell her to the highest bidder in Constantinople, and her ladyship took pity on the little mite.'

'I'm afraid children are not allowed in the barracks.'

'I know that, but she needs a wet nurse,' Lottie said, hopefully. 'Are there any army wives who have recently given birth and might be glad to earn some extra money? Lady Aurelia is very generous.'

'I do know of one such woman,' he said thoughtfully. 'She lost her husband and her infant within days of each other.'

'Is she available now? The baby is hungry.'

Molly began to cry in earnest and Lieutenant

Bonney backed towards one of the outbuildings. 'I'll make enquiries right away.' He disappeared into one of the wooden sheds.

Lottie rocked Molly in her arms, hoping that she would quieten down or go to sleep, but the baby was not to be comforted. After what seemed like an hour, but could not have been more than ten minutes, the sound of approaching footsteps made Lottie look up hopefully. A young woman came hurrying towards her with a tray of tea in her hands.

'Lieutenant Bonney sent me to see you, miss.' The woman moved a little closer, her gaze fixed longingly on Molly. 'He told me about the babe, poor mite.'

'She is an orphan.'

'It's a little girl.' The woman's eyes filled with tears and her bottom lip trembled. 'May I hold her, miss?'

Lottie laid the screaming infant in her outstretched arms. 'Of course you may.'

'I lost my little one two days ago.' Tears spurted from the woman's brown eyes as she held Molly close. 'My husband succumbed to cholera, along with many others, and my baby went to heaven in the night. I don't know why, but the angels must have taken her to join her pa.'

'I'm so sorry.' Lottie laid her hand on the woman's shoulder. 'My name is Lottie Lane and I'm Lady Aurelia Dashwood's maidservant.'

'I'm Ruby Wagg, and I'm waiting to be repatriated along with the other widows.' She rubbed her cheek against Molly's downy head. 'What's her name?'

'Molly. I named her for my mother, who died when I was a child.'

'My little one was called Iris. I was told it means rainbow.' Ruby shifted Molly to her other shoulder. 'I miss her so much, and I'm hoping my milk will dry up soon. I feel like one of them cows in yonder field.'

Lottie picked up the tin mug filled with rapidly cooling tea and took a sip. 'My mistress has taken an interest in the child's welfare and has asked me to find a wet nurse for Molly. Would you be willing to undertake such a task?'

Chapter Eleven

Lottie found Lady Aurelia where she had left her in the large reception room. Lieutenant Bonney was hovering in the background, but there was no sign of Mrs Fothergill or Cole, and Aurelia was visibly annoyed.

'Might I speak to you in private, my lady?' Lottie shot a wary glance at Lieutenant Bonney.

He smiled and inclined his head. 'I'll be in the next room, should you need me, Lady Aurelia. I'll check to see if we've received an answer to the telegraph I sent to the monastery.' He hurried off, leaving them alone in the echoing room.

'Well, what is it?' Aurelia demanded irritably. 'What have you done with the child?'

'That's what I came to tell you, my lady. It just so happens that I came across a soldier's widow,

Mrs Wagg, who has only recently lost both her husband and her baby. She is suckling your – I mean, the – infant as we speak, and glad to do so.'

Aurelia pulled a face. 'I understand how she feels. I myself am in considerable discomfort but the dark-skinned woman assured me that it will pass.'

'We were fortunate that Mrs Seacole was on board, my lady. I wouldn't have known what to do had she not been at hand.'

'Never mind that now. We won't speak of this again.'

'But the child needs a wet nurse, my lady. I know it's not my place to tell you what to do, but–'

'It most certainly is not. Tell the woman she can keep the infant and take it back to England. I'm giving it to her.'

Lottie took a deep breath. She could hardly tell Lady Aurelia that she was behaving like a spoiled brat, but her patience was wearing thin. 'She is a poor widow, recently bereaved. What sort of life could she offer little Molly?'

'I don't want to talk about it now, or ever.'

Lottie chose to ignore this petulant remark. Perhaps her ladyship was still suffering the aftereffects of the birth. She had heard Ruth and May chattering on about such matters, although it had gone over her head at the time. 'On a practical note, my lady, we need someone to cook for us, so perhaps you could employ Mrs Wagg and she can take care of the infant until we return home.'

'I suppose so,' Aurelia said carelessly.

'What shall I tell Ruby?'

'Ruby?' Aurelia raised a delicate eyebrow.

'Her name is Ruby Wagg, and she is taking care of Molly as we speak.'

'You may bring her to me. I'll decide whether or not to take her on. She will have to be sworn to secrecy, of course.'

'I'm sure we can trust her,' Lottie said confidently. 'But we need to find shelter before nightfall. Have we been assigned a billet, my lady?'

Aurelia stared out of the window overlooking a row of wooden huts and a forest of bell tents. 'Apparently we are to have one of those huts, which are little better than Lady Petunia's pigsty.'

'Will the colonel be expected to camp there too?'

'Certainly not. My husband is comfortably ensconced in the Monastery of St George, high on the cliffs with a splendid view of the sea, so Tom Bonney tells me. I am not happy, and I shall tell Dashwood so when I see him.'

Lottie knew better than to press the point. At least Molly was safe for the time being.

Colonel Dashwood did not arrive until early evening. He breezed into the hut as if he were returning home after a day's hunting expedition. He looked surprisingly well and had lost weight during his time in the Crimea. If he was pleased to see his wife it did not appear to be mutual.

Lottie was kneeling in front of the stone fireplace, trying to encourage the feeble flames licking round damp logs, but she rose hastily to her feet. 'Should I leave this for now, my lady?'

Aurelia turned her head away as her husband attempted to kiss her cheek. 'No, stay, Lottie. It's so cold in here that I can't feel my fingers and toes.' She shot a sideways glance at her husband. 'I suppose you have a cosy room in the monastery, Dashwood. Are you going to leave me here to die of cold and hunger?'

'Come, come, my love. You've been campaigning before. You knew what you were going to face.'

'I don't see why I have to live here when you have a comfortable billet,' Aurelia said sulkily. 'What sort of welcome is this, husband?'

'It's only temporary, Aurelia. But you cannot expect to be housed in the monastery. Women are not permitted to enter the living quarters, and it's far from cosy. You will be better off here until a house becomes available, though that is by no means certain.' His brow creased in a worried frown. 'This isn't like you, my dear. Are you unwell?'

She moved towards the fire, turning her back on him. 'I am quite well, thank you, Dashwood. It's been a long and tedious journey.'

'Of course it has, and you must be exhausted and in need of a good rest. We've been invited to dine with the major-general and Mrs Fothergill this evening. Tomorrow I'll ask Gillingham to procure a suitable mount for you and we'll ride up to the monastery so that you can view it for yourself. Visitors are welcome.'

'Is Gillingham billeted with you, Dashwood?' Aurelia asked casually.

'He is, my dear. I know I can rely on Farrell. Anyway, you'll see him tomorrow.' Colonel Dashwood shot a mischievous glance in Lottie's direction. 'There will be no secret assignations, miss. People sometimes behave differently in times like these, but I hope you will remember that your loyalty is to your mistress.'

Lottie bobbed a curtsey. 'Yes, Colonel.' She kept her eyes lowered. The memory of the humiliating scene in Chatham, when she had shouldered the blame for Lady Aurelia's ill-considered attempt to spend the evening with Gillingham, still lingered.

'You may unpack one of my evening gowns, Lane,' Aurelia said sharply. 'I see no reason to allow standards to slip merely because we are in this godforsaken wreck of a town.'

'Quite right, my love,' Colonel Dashwood said cheerfully. 'But when the sun shines and you ride out into the countryside I think you will find that there is some spectacular scenery, and I'm told that when the warmer weather comes the valleys are carpeted with wild flowers.'

'It's hard to believe, from what I've seen so far,' Aurelia said, shuddering. 'Now you must allow me to get dressed for dinner. There is barely room for myself and my maid, and absolutely no privacy.'

'Of course, my love. I'll leave you now, but I'll be back in an hour or so.' Colonel Dashwood paused in the doorway. 'By the way, I'm taking Hansford with me. There's little point him kicking his heels in Balaklava when he can be of more use as my batman. It will be like old times.'

'Yes, of course. Do as you please, Dashwood. I have no need of him at present.'

'Quite so. I'll say *au revoir*, my love.' He left the hut, closing the door behind him.

Aurelia sank down on the roughly constructed

187

wooden bed. 'Is the child safely out of sight, Lottie?'

'Yes, my lady. Ruby and I have been allocated a bell tent not far from here. We'll take good care of Molly.'

'I wish you wouldn't call the infant by name. Refer to her as "Ruby's child" from now on, otherwise I can see you making a terrible mistake.'

'I'm afraid it's too late for that, your ladyship,' Lottie said hastily. 'Everyone in camp knows that Ruby's baby died, and I told Lieutenant Bonney that you rescued the child from an uncertain fate in Constantinople.'

'Did you now?' Aurelia's frown was replaced by a smug smile. 'That's even better. It makes me out to be a benefactress, and I can place the child in an orphanage when we return to England. Well done, Lottie.'

It was bitterly cold in the tent and Lottie slept back to back with Ruby on a straw-filled palliasse. Molly awakened every two or three hours and Ruby suckled her, still half asleep, and then passed the small bundle to Lottie, who cradled her in her arms.

Next morning the ground outside sparkled with a hard frost and it seemed that winter had not yet lost its grip on the Crimean peninsula. Lottie was up early to light the fire in Lady Aurelia's hut. She drew water from the communal pump, acknowledging the salacious remarks from bleary-eyed, unshaven soldiers with a nod and a smile. She had grown used to handling such men while working at The Swan, and she felt pity for them in their dire living conditions. Without exception they looked half-starved, filthy and no doubt lice ridden. She made her way back to the hut, passing Ruby, who was outside their tent with Molly tied to her in a makeshift sling. She had made a campfire surrounded by stones over which she baked a rough kind of flatbread.

'Can you spare some for my lady?' Lottie had to raise her voice to make herself heard over the clatter of booted feet on the frozen mud and the sound of the bugle call.

'It's not what she's been used to,' Ruby said, frowning. 'No doubt she's as fussy about her food as she is about her looks.'

Lottie tucked a slab of hot bread into her apron pocket. 'If she's hungry, she'll eat anything. Thanks, Ruby.' She walked back to the hut to make breakfast for her mistress.

Eaten warm with a cup of sweet tea, the bread made a reasonable meal, although it did not tempt Lady Aurelia's delicate appetite. She sipped her hot drink and refused to get out of bed until the temperature in the hut rose to a little above freezing.

'I've lost my appetite for campaigning,' she said bitterly. 'I used to enjoy the challenge and nothing bothered me, but I'm beginning to think that this was a terrible mistake.'

'Well, we're here now, my lady.' Lottie laid out Aurelia's merino-wool riding habit. 'You're still getting over the birth. I've heard women say it takes almost a year to get back to normal.'

'Heaven help me,' Aurelia said with a touch of

189

her old spirit.

Gillingham arrived an hour later. He rode up to the hut leading a sturdy grey mare and announced his presence with a loud 'View halloo,' as if he were on the hunting field.

Aurelia leaped to her feet and ran to open the door. 'I might have guessed it was you, Gillingham,' she said, laughing. 'What a rowdy fellow you are, to be sure.'

He dismounted. 'Good morning, Lady Aurelia.'

'It's good to see you again, Lieutenant.'

He kissed her hand, holding it longer than was strictly necessary. 'I hope your billet is satisfactory, my lady?'

'As a matter of fact it is totally unacceptable that I am confined to a shed, while you and the colonel live in luxury at the monastery.'

'It isn't like that, my lady. You will see for yourself what monastic life is like and I think you might think you have the best of the bargain.' Gillingham turned to Lottie and smiled. 'There is someone who will be very pleased to know that you are here, Miss Lane.'

'Is Private Ellis stationed nearby, sir?' Lottie asked eagerly.

'He's only a few miles away. If I can procure a mount for you I would be pleased to take you there.'

'Never mind that now, Farrell,' Aurelia said without giving Lottie a chance to respond. 'You're here to escort me to the monastery. I'm impatient to get away from this dreary place and I want to see something of the countryside.' She hitched up the skirt of her riding habit and stepped outside. 'You'll have to help me into the saddle.'

'Of course, my lady.' Gillingham put his hands around her tightly corseted waist and lifted her into the saddle. He handed her the reins before mounting his horse.

'We'll ride slowly, Farrell,' Aurelia said with an arch smile. 'I don't care if it takes all day to reach the wretched monastery.'

Lottie watched them ride away with a feeling of foreboding. It was obvious that their feelings for each other were unchanged, but their affair would almost certainly bring heartache and disgrace. However, that was not her problem, and, safe in the knowledge that she would see Gideon again soon, she set about the task of tidying up the hut. Having satisfied herself that she could do no more, she went to find Ruby.

She was in the tent with Molly at her breast. 'Oh, it's you, Lottie,' Ruby said nervously. 'I don't know what to say to people if they ask me about the baby. Everyone here knows that I lost my child, so I can't pretend that Molly is mine.'

'I told Lieutenant Bonney that Molly's mother was trying to sell her to the highest bidder in Constantinople, and Lady Aurelia took pity on the poor little thing. No one must discover the truth, especially the colonel.'

'I understand.' Ruby shifted the baby to her other breast. 'But the poor mite must have proper clothing, and we need cloth to make nappies for her.'

'I know nothing about babies,' Lottie said, shaking her head. 'Mrs Seacole helped me to

191

make that tiny garment, but what else does she need?'

'Flannel is the best material to use. She'll need a little shirt, like the one I made for Iris, and a barracoat to go over the top. Then there's the petticoat and a dress.'

'That seems a lot of clothes for a tiny little thing like Molly.'

'The undergarments are the most important, and she needs one set for the day and another for nighttime. She must have a cap to keep her head warm, and she should by rights have a warm cape, but the shawl will do for now. It's flannel we need, Lottie. And some fine cotton for the petticoat, and diaper cloth for the nappies.'

'You seem to know a great deal about these things, Ruby.'

'I should do. I was employed as a nursemaid in a big house up West before I married Fletcher. If I'd stayed on I might have worked my way up to being a nanny, but I fell in love.' Ruby sighed and hitched Molly over her shoulder, patting the tiny back until the baby emitted a satisfactory burp. 'Now I've lost everything.'

'I'm so sorry. You've had a terrible time. I'll do anything I can to help you.'

'When I get back to England I've been told I'll have to apply to the Patriotic Fund for money, but at the moment I can't even afford to buy food.'

'Don't worry on that score. Lady Aurelia will pay you to cook for us as well as providing for the baby. She has a kind heart.'

Ruby's eyes brightened. 'She has, and I love Molly already. She isn't my little Iris, but we need each other and that is something of a comfort.'

Lottie smiled. 'We'll look after her together, and as far as the cloth is concerned, there is only one person I can ask, and I happen to have a few hours free.'

With Molly's desperate need for clothing on her mind, Lottie made her way to the harbour, negotiating the dirt roads with her skirts bunched up to prevent them trailing in the mud. The stench from the rotting animal carcasses and overflowing latrines was nauseating, and she found herself caught up in a long procession of wounded soldiers who were making their way painfully towards the wharf. Some could walk unaided, but others, having lost limbs, were carried on stretchers. Their uniforms were filthy and alive with fleas and lice. The smell of putrefaction from their bloodied dressings was even harder to bear than the foul odours from the docks, and she covered her mouth and nose, keeping her eyes averted when possible. It was a nightmare scenario, made worse by the dark cumulus clouds that squatted on top of the surrounding hills, and the steady drizzle that soaked through clothes in seconds and made them cling damply to the skin.

As luck would have it, when Lottie reached the wharf she found Mrs Seacole brewing tea for the soldiers while they waited to be helped onto the boats.

'Well then, I didn't expect to see you again, child,' Mary said, grinning. 'I thought they would find you a comfortable billet in the officers' quarters.'

'Not exactly.' Lottie stepped aside to allow a one-armed soldier to reach out for a mug of hot tea.

Mary hefted the large Brown Betty teapot and filled a tin mug. 'Would you like sugar in your tea, my darling?'

The soldier nodded and she added a lump, stirring it vigorously.

'Ta, Mother Seacole.' With an attempt at a grin, he ambled off to join the bedraggled line of men on the quayside.

'Mother Seacole, d'you remember me?' The next man in the queue was younger and had all his limbs, but had sustained a terrible injury to one side of his face, which was barely concealed beneath a grubby bandage. 'You tended me in Kingston when I near died of the cholera.'

She put her head on one side, studying him intently. 'It's never little Bertie, the drummer boy?'

'It most certainly is, Mother. I'm a corporal now, or I was until I near got half my face blowed off in the Redan.'

'I'm truly sorry, Bertie. But you was always a brave boy and I can see that you're a brave man. Are you off to Scutari now?'

'Yes, ma'am.'

'I know Miss Nightingale personally, and she'll take good care of you. Tell her Mrs Seacole sends her regards, and take care of yourself, sweetheart.'

'I will, Mother Seacole.' Bertie took the tea from her. 'God bless you.'

Lottie dashed tears from her eyes as she watched him move slowly away. 'I don't know how you keep so cheerful, Mrs Seacole. Doesn't it break your heart to see these poor men suffering so?'

'It does, but if I can bring them a little comfort then it's worth every tear I shed in private.' Mary handed out another mug of tea. 'Now, young lady, what can I do for you?'

Lottie returned to the camp with a bolt of flannel and one of calico, which would have to do in place of the diaper-woven cloth. Mary had also donated needles and thread and a pair of business-like scissors that would slice through the material with ease, and the rest of the day was spent in cutting out tiny garments and squares of calico to use as nappies. Lottie and Ruby worked together while Molly slept peacefully in a cocoon of blankets procured by Lieutenant Bonney. At midday he brought them half a pound of dry biscuits, which Lottie suspected were from his own daily ration, and he showed them how to grind the green coffee berries that were standard issue.

'If you dip the biscuits in the hot coffee they'll be easier to eat.' Bonney demonstrated by dunking one and handing it to Lottie. 'Sometimes this is all we have to keep us from starvation.'

'That's terrible,' Lottie said earnestly. 'How can men be expected to fight if they're half starved?'

'They keep going on their daily ration of spirits and coffee,' Bonney said with a wry smile. 'I've heard that the French are better organised than we are. Lord Raglan has done his best to improve our lot, but the meat that arrives is often inedible, and the shipments of fruit and vegetables are rotten and have to be tossed overboard.'

'My husband suffered from scurvy,' Ruby said,

wiping her eyes on the back of her hand. 'I didn't know it at the time, but he was giving me most of his rations, and I think it was that which left him too weak to fight off the cholera.'

'I'm truly sorry for your loss, Mrs Wagg.' Lieutenant Bonney lifted the tent flap. 'I have to leave you now, but I'll try to organise some supplies for you, although I can't promise anything.'

'Thank you for all your help.' Lottie scrambled to her feet, taking care not to spill a drop of the precious coffee. 'I don't know what we would have done without you, Lieutenant.'

'It's Tom, Miss Lane. If you'll take my advice you'll get away from here as soon as you can. I can't think that the colonel will allow his wife to suffer such privation for any length of time. Balaklava is no place for a woman.' He left them abruptly and the canvas flap fell back into place.

'He's right,' Ruby said sadly. 'I've lost all who were dear to me. It is a terrible war.'

'We'll get through it somehow.' Lottie gazed at the sleeping infant. 'She deserves better than this and so do we, but I must see Gideon. I have to make sure that he is all right. I hope Lieutenant Gillingham remembers his promise to take me to him.'

Gillingham and Aurelia returned just before dark. Their pleasure in each other's company was obvious, and it was also apparent that they had been drinking, although neither was drunk.

Aurelia greeted Lottie with a dazzling smile. 'We've had such a wonderful day. You won't believe how beautiful the monastery is, and in such a breathtaking setting. We dined on fish the monks had caught this morning, and we drank champagne. I haven't enjoyed myself so much for weeks.' She turned to Gillingham. 'Thank you for escorting me home, Farrell. Will you stay and share the bottle of wine that Dashwood gave me?'

He took her hand and raised it to his lips. 'I'd better get back. It looks like rain and when it comes down it does so in torrents and the roads turn to rivers. I'll return in the morning.'

Lottie had been standing quietly in the corner of the hut, praying silently that he would remember his promise to take her to see Gideon. She stepped forward to take Lady Aurelia's hat and gloves and Gillingham acknowledged her with a charming smile.

'I haven't forgotten, Miss Lane. I have my eye on a sturdy little pony that will carry you over the worst terrain, and I hope to bring it with me tomorrow morning. That's if Lady Aurelia has no objections.'

'None at all. Lottie has earned a little time to herself, and perhaps she will lose that disapproving expression if she spends an hour or two with Private Ellis.' Aurelia blew him a kiss. 'Off you go, Gillingham. I need my beauty sleep.'

'Thank you, my lady,' Lottie said, bobbing a curtsey. 'Thank you, sir. I will look forward to it immensely.'

'And it will be done. Good night, ladies.' Gillingham stepped outside and disappeared into the gloom. It was starting to rain and Lottie hurried to close the door.

Aurelia stood by the fire warming her hands.

'Help me to undress and then you can go to your quarters, Lottie. I'm exhausted, but in a good way. I've had such a wonderful day.'

'Did you, my lady?' Lottie had to bite back a sharp retort. Lady Aurelia might have been feasting, but they had been existing on hard tack and bitter green coffee, and that only because of Tom Bonney's thoughtfulness and generosity.

'Yes, indeed. My husband was called away to visit one of the telegraph stations, and so Farrell and I spent the whole day together. It was sheer bliss.'

Lottie kept her eyes downcast as she unbuttoned Aurelia's well-cut riding habit. 'I expect so, my lady.'

'And I trust you kept yourself gainfully employed. Not that there is much for you to do here, but the good news is that we will soon be on the move. Dashwood has promised to rent a house near Kadikoi. We'll be much more comfortable there.' Aurelia stepped out of the habit and yawned. 'Unlace me, and warm my nightgown by the fire. How I would love a cup of hot chocolate before I go to bed, but I suppose that is out of the question.'

'It is unless you have filled your saddlebags with luxury items, my lady.' Lottie bent down to retrieve the expensive habit from the dusty floor. No matter how many times she swept the bare boards the dust seemed to rise from the cracks and settle in a thick film.

'I was told that the black woman who delivered – I mean who attended me when I was unwell on board ship – that she intends to open a store sell-

198

ing all manner of produce. Who knows, she might even have a stock of cocoa?'

'It's quite possible, my lady. She is the most remarkable person I have ever met.'

'Possibly, but she's not the sort of person one would invite to dinner.' Aurelia sat on the edge of the bed and began to peel off her stockings. 'Wake me early, Lottie. I want to be ready when Gillingham arrives. And see if you can find me something better for breakfast than that burned offering you served this morning. You may go now. Good night.'

Lottie was up at dawn. The ground was iron hard and rimed with frost, and the hills were misty blue in the early morning light. Her breath formed clouds around her head as she went to fetch water, and she could hardly feel her fingers as she collected fuel for the campfire. Many of the tents were deserted, several units having been moved to the camp at Kadikoi, and the war seemed far away, like a bad dream from which she had just awakened. The scent of wood-smoke and the fragrance of hot coffee filled the air, and the thought of being reunited with Gideon made her pulse race. For once there was no echoing rumble of cannon fire or the fusillade of musket shots, and the world was once again a beautiful place. The horrors of disease and the suffering of the wounded soldiers were momentarily forgotten. Her buoyant mood survived even when Lady Aurelia complained about everything, from the bitterness of the coffee to the temperature of the rapidly cooling water in the enamel washbowl.

Gillingham arrived early, bringing their mounts with him, and for once Aurelia was ready and waiting. Her temper improved the moment she saw him, and she became her old self, laughing and joking. She was moved to give Lottie one of her straw bonnets to prevent the winter sun from ruining her fair complexion, and they set off soon after sunrise following the track at the side of the newly constructed railway line. They stopped briefly to allow the horses to drink from a stream when they reached the heights, and Balaklava stretched out below them. Plumes of smoke from dozens of campfires spiralled into the atmosphere, and from this vantage point everything seemed calm and peaceful. Birds soared overhead and the scent of wild flowers and herbs filled the air. Lottie could hardly contain her excitement at the thought of being reunited with Gideon, and, despite the beauty all around her, she was eager to be on the move again.

With their horses refreshed, they rode on until they came to the outskirts of the small village of Kadikoi. The entire plateau had been turned into an army camp, with regimented lines of white bell tents interspersed with wooden huts and stables. Gillingham rode ahead and came to a halt outside what appeared to be a ruin.

'Wait here, if you please. I won't be long.' He dismounted and walked slowly towards the gaping hole where the front entrance had been blown away by cannon fire.

'Private Ellis, are you there?'

Chapter Twelve

Lottie clutched her hands to her bosom. She could scarcely breathe and for a moment she felt as though she might faint from sheer excitement, but, even though the figure that shambled out of the near-derelict building was barely recognisable, she knew it was the man she loved with all her heart. She did not wait for Gillingham's approval and she slid from the saddle and ran.

'Gideon. I'm here. It's me.' The words tumbled from her lips as she raced towards him.

Gideon had grown a shaggy beard, as had many of the soldiers Lottie had seen in Balaklava. His tangled hair hung lankly over his brow, but his hazel eyes shone like beacons in his lean face. He took a step towards her, but came to a halt, holding his hands up as if to fend off her embrace. 'Lottie, I don't believe it – I must be dreaming.'

'I am here, Gideon. I came all this way to be with you.'

He held her at arm's length. 'I'm not fit company for anyone, least of all you. I can't remember the last time I had a bath and my uniform is filthy. I dare say I'm running with vermin, but I'm so used to them that I no longer feel their bites.'

'I don't care. It doesn't matter to me. I just wanted to see you again.' She turned with a start as Gillingham patted her on the shoulder. In her excitement she had almost forgotten his existence.

'I'll leave you here and come for you later, when I escort Lady Aurelia back to the barracks.'

'Yes, thank you.' Lottie was suddenly overcome with emotion. Laughter almost turned to tears of sheer relief on finding Gideon alive and well. Circumstances had forced her to hide her feelings, but now they bubbled close to the surface, threatening to overwhelm her.

'You'd best stable the pony, Private,' Gillingham added as he was about to walk away. 'We've lost hundreds of animals to thieves.'

'Yes, sir. I'll see to it.' Gideon slipped his arm around Lottie's shoulders. 'But first I must take care of you. Come inside, if you can bear it, my darling girl. It's not exactly home from home, but the two of us who man this station have grown used to living in squalor.'

'It doesn't matter. I'm here now and I don't care about anything else. We're together again.' Lottie followed him into the dingy building, stepping over rubble and broken glass. Fallen rafters formed archways in what must once have been the main room of the former village inn, but which was now an empty shell open to the sky.

'It's not all like this,' Gideon said, taking her by the hand. 'Be careful where you tread. We've tried to clear the floor but there are still small shards of glass stuck between the tiles.'

'It must have been even colder in the depths of winter,' she said, shivering at the thought, although in the sunshine it felt almost balmy.

'Freezing is the word. That's why there's nothing left in here. We burned all the wood we could get hold of without actually razing what was left of the old ruin to the ground.' He put his shoulder to a door, which hung from one rusty hinge, and it swung open to reveal a back room of similar size and shape. The ceiling was intact, apart from a few patches where the plaster had come down, but there was no glass in the window. At one end Lottie could make out a bench covered in instruments and coils of wire, tools and batteries, and at the other end a wooden ladder led up to the first floor.

Joe Benson had been intent on his work, but he rose to greet her. 'Miss Lane, by all that's wonderful. Good God, Ellis, you didn't tell me we were expecting company.' He grinned, exposing a gap where his front teeth should have been. He raised his hand to his face with a self-conscious grin. 'Got in the way of a bullet and fell flat on my face. It broke my leg and ruined my good looks somewhat. Anyway, I'm pleased to see you, but this ain't the place for a lady. No, it definitely is not.'

Gideon pulled up a chair that had been cobbled together from oddments of wood. 'Sit down, Lottie. Would you like a mug of tea? I'm afraid the leaves have been used more than once, but it's the best we can offer.'

'Yes, thank you.' Lottie watched him as he crossed the floor to take a battered kettle off the pot-bellied stove.

'We're more fortunate than the men living in tents.' Gideon filled three mugs with the steaming brew. 'They have to rely on campfires, which are all very well until the rains come down, and believe me when the heavens open we know all about it.'

'The snow is worse,' Benson added grimly. 'You

203

don't want to be here in mid-winter.'

'I hope the war will be over before then,' Lottie said quickly. 'Surely it can't go on much longer?'

Gideon handed her a chipped enamel mug filled with straw-coloured liquid. 'Who knows? Anyway, let's not talk about it now. You're here, and it's little short of a miracle.'

Benson left the bench to collect his tea. 'I'll take your shift, Gideon. Just pretend I'm not here.' He winked and limped back to his seat.

'Thanks, I'd do the same for you, mate, but we'll go outside. It's a sunny day and we won't be disturbing you.' Gideon held his hand out to Lottie. 'Careful how you go.'

She did not need any further encouragement to leave the dimly lit room that smelled of unwashed bodies, lamp oil and soot. It was a relief to step into the sunshine and breathe the sweet fresh air. 'On a day like this it's hard to believe that there's a war raging not far from here.'

'It's quiet at the moment, but it won't last.' Gideon led her to an old wooden settle, which had been placed against what remained of the kitchen wall. He took the mug from her and set it down. 'I can't believe that you're here, Lottie. It seems too good to be true.'

She slid her arms around his neck and closed her eyes. His beard and moustache tickled, but his kiss still had the power to make her forget everything other than her desperate need for him. He was the first to draw away. 'I'm sorry, my darling. I'm not in a fit state to be near you.'

She caressed his cheek with her fingertips. 'I don't care. Nothing matters now that we're together again and I know you are safe.'

'I'll make it up to you when this is all over.' He sat on the bench and pulled her down beside him. 'When the time is right I'm going to propose to you in style, Lottie Lane. I'll take you to the finest restaurant in London and ply you with champagne.'

She picked up her mug and raised it to him in a toast. 'I'll drink to that, Gideon.' She sipped the tea. It was tasteless, but it was warm and she was thirsty. 'It seems very quiet today. Normally we can hear the cannons and gunfire, but at least I know now that you aren't involved in the fighting.'

'Sometimes I wish we were,' Gideon said, sighing. 'We have to man the telegraph day and night, but we've been stuck here for months and seen very little progress. I know what we do is important, but it doesn't feel as though we are doing our bit. We're soldiers first and foremost.'

'Don't talk like that. I want you to come home safe and sound. I've seen the terrible injuries the men suffer, and I'm glad that you're here and not on the front line.' She moved closer. 'I love you, and I can't bear to think of you getting hurt or even worse.'

He took the mug from her and tossed it aside as he took her in his arms. 'You're even more beautiful than I remembered, Lottie. I was beginning to think I would never see you again, and yet here you are. I can hardly believe it.'

She slid her hands beneath his open jacket, and she could feel his heart beating in time to hers. Closing her eyes, she gave herself up to the sweet sensations of a passionate embrace when the world about them ceased to exist. She only dimly heard the shout from within the building, but Gideon was suddenly alert.

'Wait here. I'm sorry. I have to attend to this.' He hurried indoors and she was left on her own.

She blinked and raised her hand, touching her bruised lips with the tips of her fingers. The imprint of his kiss still lingered, but she had the feeling that their joyful reunion was at an end. Her fears were confirmed by Gideon's downcast expression when he reappeared.

'I'm so sorry, my darling girl. We usually have an orderly from one of the infantry regiments to do the running, but our chap hasn't turned up and this is urgent. I'll have to deliver a message because Benson isn't fit enough.'

'But you'll be back soon, won't you?'

'I'll be as quick as I can, but I have to find the officer concerned as the message is for his ears only, so it might take some time.'

'I'll be waiting for you, Gideon. I don't expect Gillingham to return until early evening, and there's so much I have to tell you.'

'And I you, sweetheart.' Gideon buttoned his uniform jacket and kissed her briefly on the lips. 'This is damnable bad luck.' He rammed his cap on his head, blew her a kiss and hurried on his way.

Tears of disappointment welled in Lottie's eyes, but she was determined not to cry. There was little she could do other than await his return. She sat on the wooden seat staring into the distance where the grassy plateau ended in a ridge of steep hills.

'Lottie, wake up.'

She opened her eyes and found herself looking up at Lady Aurelia. 'Is it time to go already?'

'Yes, come along, you're holding us up. We're leaving right away.'

Lottie stood up, wide wake now. 'But I can't leave without saying goodbye to Gideon.'

'Well, he seems to have abandoned you, so I wouldn't worry too much about him,' Aurelia said cheerfully. 'Where is your lover, anyway?'

'He's not my lover,' Lottie said angrily. 'He had to take an urgent message to someone important. I don't know who.'

'Oh, well, that's what happens in wartime.' Aurelia walked away to join Gillingham, who was waiting with the horses. He lifted her into the saddle and his hands lingered longer than was strictly necessary around her waist. Aurelia bent her head and said something that made him laugh. It was an intimate scene and one that confirmed Lottie's suspicion that her mistress and Gillingham were still deeply involved. It was a dangerous situation and one in which there could be no happy ending.

She hurried over to them. 'Might I leave a message for Private Ellis, my lady? He will wonder why I've left so suddenly.'

'Yes, but be quick. We're riding to the French camp at Kamiesch to watch the races. I've heard that Fanny Duberly will be there, and I confess that I'm curious to meet such an intrepid horse-woman and extraordinary army wife. Anyway, I'm bored to death with war and disaster, and

I'm longing for something more exciting.'

During the three-mile ride to Kamiesch Lottie's thoughts were with Gideon. She had left a message with Benson, explaining her sudden departure, but he had been intent on his work and she was not sure how much he had understood or would remember when he came to pass it on. It was early afternoon by the time they reached the makeshift racecourse, and the French officers were showing off their equestrian skills to the delight of the onlookers. Lottie had no choice other than to follow Lady Aurelia while she moved amongst the crowd, chatting to old friends and acquaintances. Gillingham was constantly by her side, and they might have been at a race meeting anywhere in France or England. The carnival atmosphere made it hard to believe that only a short distance away the town of Sebastopol was under siege, and the fighting continued unabated. The irony of the situation seemed to have escaped Aurelia, and she was obviously in her element as she basked in the attention of her many admirers.

Lottie had to smile inwardly when Gillingham introduced Mrs Duberly to Lady Aurelia. The two indomitable military wives were, in fact, quite alike in appearance; being of a similar height and slender build, with flaxen curls and blue eyes, but it was obvious to Lottie that they would never become bosom friends. The meeting was polite and compliments were exchanged, but Aurelia was quick to spot a familiar face in the crowd and made her excuses to move on, with Gillingham and Lottie following close behind.

'Fanny Duberly is a remarkable woman,' Gillingham said earnestly. 'She's accompanied her husband throughout the campaign, and I believe she's been keeping a journal of events that she intends to publish on her return to England.'

Aurelia stopped in her tracks, turning to him with a tight little smile. 'Is that so? I wanted to see this paragon of womanhood, and now I have.'

'Then you must agree that she is everything she is purported to be.'

Aurelia tossed her head. 'I've heard that she comes from quite an ordinary family who live in Weymouth, wherever that might be. I doubt if I would invite them to dine if we were at home in Bath or Chatham.'

'Really, Aurelia,' Gillingham said, sighing, 'sometimes I despair of you. I am not high born and yet you and I are soul mates. Fanny Duberly is a brave woman and deserves your praise and not your condemnation because of what you consider to be her inferior social status.'

Lottie held her breath, waiting for the storm to break over Gillingham's head. She could have warned him that he was on dangerous ground, but it seemed that he was oblivious to danger signs.

Lady Aurelia came to a halt by the refreshment tent. She glared at Gillingham, her eyes narrowed and her teeth bared like a lioness about to attack a predator that was threatening one of her cubs. Then, just as suddenly, she threw back her head and laughed. 'You put me nicely in my place, Farrell. You may buy me a glass of champagne to make up for being horrid to me.' She shot a sideways glance in Lottie's direction. 'You'd better go

209

and wait with the horses. We'll be leaving directly.'

'You are a perverse woman, Aurelia,' Gillingham said, chuckling. 'But I adore you anyway.'

'Of course you do.' Aurelia glided into the tent, acknowledging a dragoons officer who had attracted her attention.

Gillingham turned to Lottie. He put his hand in his pocket and took out some small coins. 'Buy yourself something to eat and drink. We'll be leaving soon, but I don't want you fainting from hunger and thirst during the ride back to Balaklava.'

Lottie took the money and bobbed a curtsey. 'Thank you, sir.'

He smiled. 'I'm sorry you had to leave without saying goodbye to Private Ellis. He's a good man.'

'Yes, sir,' Lottie said, nodding. 'He is.'

She hesitated outside the tent, suddenly alone amongst foreigners, and to her own countrymen, the high-ranking officers, she might as well have been invisible. She was both hungry and thirsty, and at a loss to know what to do in order to find something to eat and drink. It seemed that she would have to go without when, while walking back to where the horses were tethered, she came face to face with one of the French *cantinières*. It would have been difficult to miss the woman with her tight-fitting military jacket worn over a short, bell-like skirt and bloomers. Ruby had told her about these women, who were employed by the French army to run the canteens and do the laundry for the officers and NCOs. The fact that they received full pay for their services and the respect of the French military had been a sore point with Ruby, who, like the other army wives,

210

endured harsh conditions for very little reward. That aside, Lottie was hungry and the smiling *cantinière* was carrying a tray laden with pastries and a flask of wine. Although she did not know a word of French, Lottie was able to make herself understood and the woman was there to sell her wares. Having drunk a cup of rough red wine, Lottie handed over the money and walked away munching a sweet pastry.

The ride back to Balaklava was uneventful and the sure-footed horses coped with the rugged terrain with the skill of mountain goats. A full moon lit their way, turning the world to silver as the temperature dropped close to freezing. Spring might seem to have arrived earlier, but now winter returned and wrapped their small world in ice.

As she rode, allowing her mount its head, Lottie's thoughts were with Gideon, living in the draughty ruins of the old inn. At least she could picture him now, sitting at his bench and operating the instruments that kept vital communications open. When they passed through Kadikoi she had to curb the sudden impulse to break away and join him at his post, but that would be wrong and stupid. He had his job to do and she had hers, and even more important than attending Lady Aurelia's needs, she had taken on the responsibility for a young life. She hoped that her mistress might have a change of heart and acknowledge Molly as her child, but from what she had seen today, her ladyship was intent on enjoying herself and had no thought for anyone other than the man she loved.

Lottie yawned and shifted to a more comfortable position on the saddle. They were only a couple of miles from camp. It had been a very long day, but perhaps there would be another chance to visit Kadikoi tomorrow.

Next morning Lottie was up even earlier than usual. Molly was fretful, even though Ruby had just given her a feed, but she stopped crying when Lottie picked her up.

'You are a bad girl,' Lottie whispered, smiling. 'You just want attention, don't you? You are so like your mama.'

Molly gazed up at her with wide blue eyes.

'All right, miss,' Lottie said softly. 'I'll carry you round with me while I do my chores, but then you must promise to be a good girl for Ruby.' She knew that Molly did not understand a word of what she said, but the sound of her voice seemed to quieten the baby, and Lottie felt a wave of tenderness for the child whose mother had rejected her. She carried her round until Ruby awoke, refreshed and ready for the start of a new day.

'Did you mention the baby to her ladyship?' Ruby asked anxiously. 'Will she ever admit that Molly is her child?'

Lottie shook her head. 'I don't think she will. She can be very stubborn. Anyway, I have to leave you both now and go about my duties. Who knows what sort of mood her ladyship will be in?'

'I won't need you today.' Aurelia held up a silver hand mirror, turning her head this way and that in order to get a better view of her perky little hat.

'Gillingham is coming to collect me and we're riding to the monastery.'

'Are you sure, my lady?' Lottie tried not to sound too eager. 'I don't mind the ride.'

'You did well yesterday, considering you are relatively new to the saddle, but I think that my husband intends to take me to look over a house on the other side of Kadikoi, with a view to renting it for the duration. I won't need you.'

'Very well, my lady.' Lottie cast her eyes down and folded her hands meekly in front of her. It would not do to let her ladyship see that she was bitterly disappointed.

'Don't sulk, girl. It doesn't suit you.' Aurelia snatched up her riding crop. 'I know you want to visit your man again, but he has his work to do and you mustn't distract him.'

The unfairness of this remark almost made Lottie forget her place. It was on the tip of her tongue to tell Lady Aurelia Dashwood a thing or two. Surely a woman who was cheating so openly on her doting husband was not in a position to criticise someone who simply wanted to be with the man she loved? She remained silent. There was nothing to be gained and everything to lose if she lost the trust of her wayward employer.

Aurelia moved swiftly to open the door. 'Gillingham, I recognised your footsteps.' She stepped outside, leaving the door to swing on its hinges.

Lottie stood in the doorway, watching them ride off with a feeling of foreboding. Lady Aurelia was growing reckless and Gillingham seemed to be totally under her spell. She was about to close the door when she saw Mrs Fothergill coming towards the hut. As usual she was dressed as if she were about to promenade in the park on a Sunday afternoon, with a perky feathered hat perched on her red wig, and her long skirts trailing in the dust. She wafted a lace handkerchief in front of her face, which was screwed up as if she had been sucking a lemon.

'The stench in this camp is intolerable,' she grumbled as she entered the hut, pushing past Lottie. 'I wanted to see Lady Aurelia, but I see I am too late.'

'Her ladyship has gone riding,' Lottie said cautiously.

'Really?' Mrs Fothergill did not sound convinced.

'Yes, ma'am.'

'Then that was her ladyship I saw just now, and she was in the company of Lieutenant Gillingham.'

'Yes, ma'am. He came to escort her to the monastery.'

'Well, that is extremely odd because the colonel is attending a meeting here in Balaklava at Lord Raglan's residence. I came here at his request to ask Lady Aurelia to join us for luncheon.'

Lottie looked away. The triumphant gleam in Mrs Fothergill's eyes sent cold shivers down her spine. 'I know nothing about her ladyship's plans, ma'am.'

'Of course you do.' Mrs Fothergill tapped her foot impatiently. 'That innocent look doesn't work with me, Lane. You'll come with me and tell the colonel everything you know.' Her, hand shot out, catching Lottie by the ear. 'You may think

I'm a fool, but I know there's a baby in your tent and it doesn't belong to you or that other woman. Cole has been doing some checking on my behalf and I know all about Mrs Wagg.'

'She is a poor widow of a soldier who died of the cholera, Mrs Fothergill.'

'And she lost her baby too. It's on record, Lane, so there's no denying the fact. Who, then, is the mother of the child she is at present nursing?'

'I couldn't say, ma'am. Lady Aurelia took pity on an orphan baby in Constantinople.'

'Rubbish. Absolute nonsense. If that were true why did she hide the object of her charity while on board the *Albatross?* I suspected then that you and the Seacole woman were attempting to cover up something, and now I know what it was.'

'I don't know anything, ma'am.'

Mrs Fothergill opened the door and thrust Lottie outside. 'You can tell that to my husband and the colonel. Let's see if they believe you.'

Short of running away, with nowhere to go and nowhere to hide, there was nothing Lottie could do other than to accompany Mrs Fothergill to Lord Raglan's residence. The ensuing interview was not pleasant, but Lottie stuck to her story and refused to corroborate any of Mrs Fothergill's claims against Lady Aurelia. The colonel was visibly troubled and the major-general sat through the hearing with a grim expression on his weathered face.

'This is a nasty business, Dashwood,' he said gloomily. 'It could create one hell of a scandal if word of this got out.'

'It's just gossip, as far as I am concerned.'

215

Colonel Dashwood glared angrily at Mrs Fothergill. 'I'll thank you not to spread stories like this, ma'am. My wife is above suspicion.'

'No one is above suspicion, Colonel. Your wife at the very least is guilty of conduct that leaves her open to such gossip, as you call it. I hear that she was at the races at Kamiesch yesterday afternoon.'

Colonel Dashwood's florid complexion deepened to a rich shade of purple. He fixed his gaze on Lottie. 'Is this true, Lane?'

There seemed little point in lying. Lottie nodded. 'Yes, sir.'

'And you were in attendance?'

'I was, sir.'

'With Lieutenant Gillingham?'

'Yes, sir.'

'Then I am satisfied that my wife was adequately chaperoned.' Colonel Dashwood faced Mrs Fothergill with an ominous frown. 'Are you implying that there is anything untoward in their relationship, madam?'

'I'm implying nothing, Colonel. It's for you to decide, but questions are being asked as to the parentage of the infant in Lady Aurelia's care.'

Colonel Dashwood rose to his feet. 'If my wife said she took pity on a poor orphan then that is the case. I would expect you to refute any suggestion that this is not so.'

'Steady on, Dashwood.' The major-general slammed his hand down on the desk. 'My wife is not in the dock.'

'And neither is mine, sir.' Colonel Dashwood made for the door. 'Come along, Miss Lane. This conversation is at an end.'

Lottie hurried after him as he strode out of the room.

'Mrs Fothergill has had her knife into Lady Aurelia from the start, Colonel. She's a mean woman.'

Colonel Dashwood stopped to snatch his hat and cane from an orderly. 'I agree, but tittle-tattle like this can cause a great deal of trouble. Where is my wife? I need to see her urgently.'

'She said she was going to the monastery, sir.'

'I see. Thank you, Miss Lane. That will be all.' He placed his hat on his head and marched out of the building.

Lottie followed him more slowly. She needed time to think and she needed to speak to Mrs Seacole, who was the only witness to Molly's birth. One unguarded word from her would ruin Lady Aurelia's reputation and her marriage, if that was not already beyond saving.

Chapter Thirteen

Mary Seacole was on the wharf helping to care for the constant stream of sick and wounded soldiers who were waiting to embark on ships bound for Scutari. Lottie saw her wave the last man on board and then she turned her attention to a small drummer boy who had hurt his arm.

'Good day to you, Lottie Lane,' she said cheerfully. 'Just let me deal with this little chap's injury and I'll be with you.' The copper-headed child, who could not be more than ten or eleven, was trying hard not to cry as Mary examined his left arm. 'This will hurt a bit, soldier,' she said gently, 'but you'll soon be as good as new.' She kneeled at his side and with a quick movement set the bone. The boy uttered a sharp cry and fell into a dead faint. 'Pass me those bandages and the laths, please, Lottie.'

'The poor little fellow. He seems too young to be involved in this terrible war.'

'I agree, but that's the way they do things and they leave us women to fix their mess. This one is lucky because he'll be out of action for a long time. Maybe they'll send him home to his ma.' With impressive skill, Mary splinted the arm while Lottie cradled the boy's head in her lap.

'What was it you wanted with me, miss?' Mary's shrewd eyes twinkled merrily. 'I can see that you're troubled.'

'You're right, Mrs Seacole. I came to ask your advice.'

'Always happy to oblige. What is it?'

'You remember Mrs Fothergill?'

'I ain't likely to forget her, honey.'

'She's trying to ruin Lady Aurelia, and she's putting it about that Molly is her child.'

'Truth will out, as my dear old ma used to say.'

'I know, but it will be the ruin of Lady Aurelia and will do nothing for Molly.'

'If you're asking me to keep my mouth shut, you don't have to worry. I am a professional woman even though I didn't take no Hippocratic oath.' Mary held a vinaigrette under the boy's nose. 'Wake up, honey. It's all over.'

He coughed and spluttered and opened his eyes. 'It hurts.'

'Sure it does, and you're a brave soldier.' Mary produced a slab of sponge cake from her capacious black bag. 'You munch on that and Mary will mix you up a draught that will ease the pain.' She dug deep and took out a bottle of laudanum and a cup.

Lottie supported the boy while Mary mixed the potion. 'What's your name, soldier?'

'It's Edward, miss.' He nibbled the cake and a little colour tinged his waxen cheeks. 'They call me Teddy.'

Mary held the cup to his lips. 'Drink this down in one, honey. The pain will go away.'

He obeyed without question.

'There's a good boy.' Mary shook the drops from the cup and put it back in her bag. 'He should be taken care of, but there's no place for a boy his age in Scutari. As to the hospital here, I wouldn't trust them with a pet monkey.' She fixed Lottie with a knowing smile. 'I guess you might have a little room in that tent of yours, Miss Lane. Another poor child won't make much difference.'

'But he's in the army, young as he is, and I'm not a nurse.'

'I'm in the 97th Regiment of Foot,' Teddy said sleepily. 'I have to get back to duty, miss.'

Lottie and Mary exchanged weary glances.

'War involving children,' Lottie said angrily, 'should be banned.' She stroked a lock of sweat-darkened hair back from Teddy's brow. 'Can you stand, drummer boy?'

Mary shook her head. 'There's no need. My

man Johnny will carry him. I knew you'd want to help.'

'We have to look after each other at times like these.' Lottie hugged Teddy, who had fallen asleep against her shoulder. 'He's just a child. It's not right.'

'I'll give you some laudanum for him, and the rest of the cake. I bake them aboard the *Medora* in the evenings. Cooking is one of my talents, and medicine is another. The men don't call me Mother Seacole for nothing.' She patted Lottie on the shoulder. 'You're a kindred spirit, Lottie Lane. I have nothing but respect for you, but don't let that aristocratic woman run you ragged. She'll get what's coming to her.'

Lottie chose to ignore this last remark. People could think what they liked of Lady Aurelia Dashwood, but she had seen another side of her, one that was infinitely more likeable.

'I'll look after Teddy for now, but how long will it be before he can return to duty?'

'I wouldn't count on it, honey,' Mary said in a whisper. 'It's a bad break and I've done what I can, but it's going to take a mighty long time to heal.' She straightened up. 'Anyway, now I've got to collect more driftwood, iron sheeting and anything that will help me finish building my British Hotel. It'll be open soon, I swear to God it will.'

Mary's servant carried Teddy up the hill to the camp and laid him on the straw-filled palliasse in Lottie's tent.

'Thank you, Johnny,' Lottie said with a grateful smile. 'We'll take care of the boy from now on.'

'Pleased to help, miss.' Johnny backed out of the tent and strolled off whistling.

'Whatever next?' Ruby said, frowning. 'What's wrong with the boy, Lottie? It's not catching, is it? Think of the baby.'

Lottie kneeled beside Teddy, who was drifting off under the influence of laudanum. 'He suffered a broken arm, Ruby. There's nothing else wrong with him and I've agreed to look after him until he's fit enough to rejoin his unit.'

'That could take months, and the boy is a soldier. The army should be responsible for his welfare.'

'He has a mother somewhere in England, I'm sure, and a family who love him. If he were my son I would want someone to take care of him until his bones have knitted together.'

Ruby cradled the baby in her arms. 'We've barely enough food for ourselves, let alone a hungry boy.'

'Let me worry about that. I'll go to the colonel, if necessary, and ask for more rations.' Lottie sighed, shaking her head. 'Mrs Fothergill was out to cause trouble this morning, telling tales on Lady Aurelia, and the colonel was quite upset. I hope he's in a better mood now.'

'I should think he's got other things on his mind than that woman's tittle-tattle,' Ruby said angrily. 'But your lady is playing a dangerous game. What will happen if her husband discovers the truth?'

'I daren't think about that now. All I know is that the colonel is suspicious and Lady Aurelia rode off with Gillingham this morning, and I doubt if they've gone to the monastery. Gillingham would have known that the colonel was here in Balaklava.'

'Well, there's nothing you can do about it.' Ruby sat down as the baby began to cry. She unbuttoned her blouse. 'Molly is a hungry little thing. I just hope my milk doesn't dry up.'

Lottie rose to her feet, brushing dust from her skirt. 'As you're here I'll go and look for Tom Bonney. If I tell him we're taking care of the drummer boy he might let us have an extra ration of flour and some more blankets.'

'What should I do if the boy wakes?' Ruby asked anxiously.

'Talk to him. He's just a child and he's far from home. Treat him like you would your own son.'

Ruby's eyes filled with tears and she turned her head away. 'I'll never know what that's like now. I doubt if I'll have another child.'

'You don't know that,' Lottie said sympathetically. 'You can't be much older than I am.'

'I'm twenty-three. Living in camp ages a woman, unless you're an officer's wife, with servants at your beck and call, like Lady Aurelia. I was pretty once, so my dear husband used to say.'

'And you are still, Ruby. Anyone can see that, even in such dire circumstances as these.' Lottie opened the tent flap and a cool breeze brought with it the stench of the latrines. 'I won't be long and I'll see if I can beg some food from the kitchen.'

Leaving Ruby to cope with the baby and the injured boy, Lottie went in search of Lieutenant Bonney. She found him in the supply store.

He looked up from a list he was studying.

'Good morning, Miss Lane. What can I do for you?'

'Are you busy?'

'I'm trying to find enough food for the major-general's table this evening. I believe he's entertaining Colonel Dashwood and his lady, and there's a possibility that Lord Raglan himself might attend.' Tom Bonney's serious expression melted into a beaming smile. 'But I'm never too busy to talk to you, Miss Lane.'

'Thank you, Lieutenant. As a matter of fact I've come to beg a favour.'

'Of course, I'll do everything I can to help.'

'It's not for myself, but I'm looking after an injured drummer boy who was with the 97th Foot, and I've come to ask if we can have extra rations to feed the child. He's suffering from a broken arm and won't be able to rejoin his regiment until it heals.'

'I see. Perhaps that's a blessing in disguise, although I shouldn't say so, but the 97th are in the thick of things at Sebastopol. In my opinion it's no place for a child.' He glanced over his shoulder, smiling ruefully. 'Don't tell anyone I said so.'

'I won't, I promise. Can you help us? We could do with another couple of blankets, too.'

'I think that can be arranged. I'll have them sent over to your tent, and some extra rations. You can take some oats and sugar now, and I have a small supply of oranges and apples, which I'll be glad to let you have, only don't tell anyone or I'll be inundated with requests for fruit.'

'Thank you, Lieutenant. I'm forever in your debt.' Lottie was about to walk away when he called her back.

'It might not be important, but Mrs Fothergill's maid has been asking questions about Mrs Wagg. I thought you should know.'

'Yes, thank you, but I've already found that out. I hope you won't believe the rumours that might be flying around the camp.'

'I never listen to gossip, Miss Lane.' He took a step towards her, his smile fading. 'There's something else perhaps you ought to know.'

'What is it?'

'A telegraph message was sent to the station at Kadikoi regarding Private Ellis. You mentioned his name when you first arrived in Balaklava. I believe he's a friend of yours.'

Lottie shivered although it was hot and humid in the storeroom. 'Yes, I know him.'

'Ellis and Benson are being transferred to the most forward position.'

'Where is that? Is it far from here?'

'I can't tell you exactly because I'm not in possession of that information, but I would imagine it must be close to the front lines. I'm sorry if it's bad news.'

'Have they moved on already? Can you tell me that?'

'The message was sent last evening. They will have been relieved first thing this morning.'

'I see. Thank you for telling me.'

'Is Private Ellis a close friend, if you don't mind me asking?'

'Yes, he is a very good friend of mine.' She answered automatically, but the news of Gideon's transfer struck her like a blow. It seemed that she had found him only to be separated again in the cruellest possible manner. He had been relatively safe at Kadikoi, but being sent to the front meant one thing – danger. She left the store and was making her way back to the tent when she saw the colonel coming towards her. He stopped and beckoned.

'What exactly did my wife say this morning, Miss Lane?'

'She said that she was going to the monastery, sir.'

'And yet she has not returned, even though she would have found out that I am in fact here in Balaklava.'

Lottie could see that his distress was genuine. 'Perhaps they stopped to rest the horses, sir.'

'I dare say you're right.' Colonel Dashwood walked on, leaving Lottie staring after him. She walked slowly back to the tent, and only then she realised that she had left the fruit Lieutenant Bonney had given her in the stores.

Ruby had settled Molly down in her bed and she was sitting beside Teddy, holding his hand as he groaned in his drug-induced sleep. 'Did you have any luck with the lieutenant?'

'Yes, he's very kind, and he's sending over extra rations and some blankets. He was very understanding.'

'You don't look very pleased. What's wrong?'

'Everything.' Lottie sank down on the end of the palliasse where Teddy slept. 'Gideon has been moved on, to a telegraph station nearer the front, and Mrs Fothergill's attempt to cause mischief seems to have worked. The colonel's suspicions are aroused and I fear that Lady Aurelia and Gillingham will be found out.'

Ruby pursed her lips. 'I know you're fond of her, but she's been incredibly stupid and careless as to her reputation, and she's a bad mother.' She reached out to stroke the baby's head. 'How could she abandon this little poppet? I couldn't, could you?'

'No, of course not. I just keep hoping that Lady Aurelia will come to her senses and admit that the child is hers. You know, she's not such a bad person, Ruby. She can be kind and generous, and she was so full of fun and laughter when we were in England. I'm afraid this place will be the ruin of her, and Gillingham too.'

The sound of approaching footsteps made Lottie rise to her feet and she lifted the tent flap.

Lieutenant Bonney smiled apologetically. 'You forgot the supplies.' He held out a wooden box covered with a scrap of cloth. 'May I come in?'

'Yes, of course.'

He looked round their cramped quarters, frowning. 'This isn't suitable accommodation, especially with two children to care for. I'll have to see if anything can be done to make you more comfortable.' He placed the box on a camp stool beside Ruby. 'How are you today, Mrs Wagg?'

Ruby looked up and smiled. 'Tolerably well, sir.'

'I'm very glad to hear it.' He glanced at Teddy, who was still asleep. 'It was good of you to take the boy in.'

'It seemed the only thing to do,' Lottie said in a low voice. 'He's just a child.'

'If there's anything further I can do to make life a little easier, please let me know.'

'Thank you, Lieutenant. It's a relief to know we have one friend in camp.' Lottie extended her hand and he held it for a moment longer than was necessary.

'There are always people who choose to make life difficult for others, and I think you know to whom I'm referring. Anyway, I have to get back to the stores, but you must tell me if there's anything you need.' He stepped outside and Lottie followed him.

'I would dearly love to find out where Gideon, I mean Private Ellis, is now.'

He shook his head. 'That I can't tell you.'

'Can't, or won't?'

'Even if I knew, it would serve no purpose to pass on such information. You would both be in great danger if you attempted to see him.' His expression lightened and his generous lips curved into a smile. 'I'm sorry.'

Lottie sighed. 'I know you're right. I just wish this war would end.'

'You're not alone there. I'm thinking of selling my commission when this is all over. I've lost my taste for soldiering.'

Momentarily diverted, Lottie stared at him in surprise. 'Really? What would you do in civilian life?'

He was about to reply when a shout from a fellow officer made him snap to attention.

'Hey, Bonney. Colonel Dashwood is looking for you.'

'I have to go.' Tom hurried off in the direction

227

of Lord Raglan's headquarters.

Lottie watched him walk away with a feeling of regret. She would have liked to know more about the young officer who had shown them such kindness, but there were more pressing matters on hand and she realised that she was hungry. She entered the tent to find Ruby examining the contents of the box.

'He's a love,' she said, grinning. 'We'll eat well today. If you'll look after the nippers I'll make something tasty. That lovely fellow has given us some tea and sugar. What I wouldn't do for a nice cup of tea.'

The sight of food made Lottie's stomach rumble. 'I'm starving. What is there to eat?'

'He's given us two eggs. I can't remember the last time I had an egg. Anyway, I thought I'd make some pancakes and keep the other one for young Teddy when he wakes. He needs feeding up, poor kid.' Ruby picked up a bundle of dry kindling and hurried out of the tent.

Late that afternoon, Molly had been fed and was sleeping, as was Teddy, once again under the influence of laudanum. They had eaten well, and Lottie had enjoyed her first proper cup of tea since arriving in the Crimea. Ruby had picked up her sewing in an attempt to finish a tiny petticoat before the light faded, and Lottie took advantage of the quiet time to visit Lady Aurelia's hut. She made sure everything was clean and tidy before lighting a fire in readiness for her ladyship's return, although when that might be she had no idea. Having waited until the flames had taken

228

hold, she was about to leave when she heard someone tapping on the hut door. She went to open it and found Maggie Cole standing on the threshold.

'Can I come in?' Maggie stepped inside without waiting for an answer. Her normally tidy hair was windblown and there was mud on the hem of her black bombazine skirt.

'What's the matter?' Lottie pulled up the one and only chair. 'Won't you sit down?'

Maggie shook her head. 'No, ta. I can't stay. I just came to warn you that the old witch has been up to her tricks again.'

'I'm sorry? I don't understand.'

'Mrs Fothergill has it in for Lady Aurelia. You must know that.'

'Of course I do, but what's happened?'

'I accidentally had my ear to the door when she was ranting at her poor husband. I don't know how he's put up with her all these years. Anyway, that's not what I came to say. You must warn Lady Aurelia that the cat's out of the bag.'

Lottie reached for the brandy bottle and poured a stiff tot. She handed the glass to Maggie. 'You look as though you need this.'

'Ta. I do.' Maggie drank it in one greedy gulp. 'I don't normally interfere when the old bitch gets her knife into someone, but I'm sick and tired of her mischief-making. She told her old man that Lady Aurelia and Gillingham are lovers, and I'm almost certain that he's passed the good news on to Colonel Dashwood.' Maggie drained the last drop and handed the glass to Lottie. 'There, that's it in a nutshell. Make of it what you will, but be warned. There's trouble ahead.' She moved to the door and opened it. 'I've got to get back and comb her bloody wig before she wakes up from her after-noon nap. One day I'll set it on fire and she can go to dinner bald as an egg.' Maggie strode out into the pouring rain, leaving the door to shut of its own accord.

Lottie was about to close it properly when she heard the sound of a horse's hoofs and Lady Aurelia drew her mount to a halt. She flung herself from the saddle and tossed the reins to a passing soldier. 'Stable my horse,' she ordered, 'and see that she gets a good rub down.' Without waiting for his response she strode across the tussocky ground.

'Have you been telling tales to my husband, Miss Lane?'

'No, my lady,' Lottie protested, shocked by Lady Aurelia's angry tone. 'Of course not.'

Aurelia stormed into the hut and threw herself down on the bed. 'We had a wonderful day at Kamiesch, but as we rode into camp just now Gill-ingham was summoned to appear before Dash-wood and the major-general. Bonney wouldn't give me the details but apparently Gillingham has been posted to the front. Can you believe that?'

'I had nothing to do with it, my lady.'

'The only reason for such a move is if someone has been spreading malicious gossip. If it's not you, then who is it?'

'Do you really have to ask, my lady?' Lottie con-trolled her anger with difficulty. 'I would never do anything to hurt or betray you. Mrs Fothergill saw you ride off with the lieutenant this morning, and

I was questioned by the major-general and Colonel Dashwood. They already knew that you had attended the race at Kamiesch yesterday, but I gave nothing away.'

'I'm sorry, Lottie. I should have guessed she was at the bottom of this, but no one, other than yourself, knew that I planned to visit my husband at the monastery.'

'But the colonel was here at a meeting with the major-general.'

'I didn't know that. Dashwood should keep me better informed.'

'There is worse to come, my lady. Mrs Fothergill has been asking questions about Molly. She doesn't believe the story we put about, and she's been checking on Ruby's background. It's well known that her baby died within days of its birth, so it wouldn't be possible to pass Molly off as her child. Even worse, Miss Cole was here just now. Mrs Fothergill has openly accused you of having an affair with Lieutenant Gillingham.'

Aurelia took off her hat and threw it across the room. 'Damnable woman. I hate her with a passion.'

'She has done her best to ruin you, but you have the advantage still.'

'I do?' Aurelia looked up, a glimmer of hope in her stormy blue eyes. 'How so?'

'The colonel loves you, my lady. I don't have to tell you how to handle your husband.'

'You wouldn't dare,' Aurelia said with a reluctant smile. 'You're right, Lottie. I can wrap Dashwood round my little finger, and now is the time to exert all my feminine powers. Is he still with

Lord Raglan?'

'I believe they are having dinner, and that you were also invited.'

'Along with Mrs Fothergill, I suppose.' Aurelia rose to her feet. 'Unpack my magenta evening gown, Lottie. I'll wear my ruby necklace and earrings. This is not the time to be a shrinking violet. I'm going to outface that vicious bitch and make her look a liar and a fool.'

Lottie waited nervously for Lady Aurelia to return from Lord Raglan's residence. She could only hope that her ladyship's winning ways and quick wit would counteract Mrs Fothergill's spiteful accusations. She knew from past experience that these dinners were inclined to go on into the small hours, and was prepared to wait all night, if necessary, but shortly before ten o'clock Lady Aurelia burst into the hut.

'If I had a musket I'd shoot that woman.' She took off her necklace and dropped it onto the table together with her earrings. 'She's done her worst and the damage is complete. I've never been so humiliated in all my life. My God, I'm the daughter of an earl, and what is she but a jumped-up bourgeoise.'

'It didn't go well?' Lottie retrieved the jewels and dropped them into their small velvet bag.

'She used sly innuendo to try to trick me into saying something I would regret. I pride myself that I dealt with her insinuations promptly, but I could see that the major-general was on her side, and poor Dashwood was confused and embarrassed. It was a ghastly evening and I never want to live through anything like that again.'

'But surely it's what the colonel thinks and does that matters most, my lady. The major-general and his wife are of little consequence in your private life.'

'This is the army, Lottie. Men can get away with almost anything as long as it doesn't harm the honour of the regiment, but their wives have to live by a different set of rules. Cordelia Fothergill knows that full well and she's used it against me.' Aurelia held out her arms. 'Undo me. I'm going to bed.'

Lottie busied herself with the tiny buttons on the back of Lady Aurelia's gown. 'It will blow over, I'm sure.'

'I don't care.' Aurelia tossed her head. 'I only had a few minutes alone with my husband, but he made it plain that Gillingham's career will be in jeopardy if I try to see him again. I asked him for a divorce, but he refused point-blank. I am to remain here in this hellhole and pretend that nothing is amiss. Nothing must besmirch the honour of the regiment.' She stepped out of the gown and it fell to the floor, lying around her feet in a shimmering pool, the colour of blood.

The symbolism was not lost on Lottie and she hastily retrieved the garment, shaking out the creases and laying it over the back of the chair. 'I'm so sorry, my lady.'

'I refuse to be treated like a wayward child. Dashwood said I am not to leave camp unless he grants permission. You would have thought he would know me better after five years of marriage.' Aurelia took a deep breath as Lottie slackened the laces on her stays. 'That's better. Pour me a glass of brandy, and I'll take a few drops of laudanum to help me sleep. I'll think of a way out of this damnable impasse.' She caught Lottie by the hand. 'You are the only true friend I have in the whole world.' Her violet-blue eyes filled with tears, and she released Lottie with an attempt at a smile. 'You are worth more than wasting your youth on a spoiled woman like me. I couldn't love you more if we were sisters, always remember that, Lottie.'

'I – I don't know what to say, your ladyship.'

Aurelia's lips tightened and her eyes darkened. 'Life is very unfair. Whatever people say about me, you know that I am not a bad person.'

Lottie poured her drink and handed it to her. 'Of course not, my lady.'

'But I will not be beaten.' Aurelia raised the glass. 'To hell with Cordelia Fothergill and her ilk, and to hell with the army. Dashwood made the mistake of telling me where he's sent Farrell. He'll regret that until the day he dies.' She downed the brandy in one and tossed the glass into the stone fireplace where it shattered into shards. 'Pour me another and have one yourself, Lottie.'

'Don't you think you've had enough, my lady?'

Aurelia snatched the bottle from the table and half-filled a glass with brandy. 'Not yet, but I will triumph, Lottie. Just you wait and see.'

Chapter Fourteen

Lottie had tossed and turned all night, listening to the rain and the wind soughing round the camp like a soul in torment. She had not wanted to leave her mistress in such a state, but Aurelia had insisted that she wanted to be alone, leaving Lottie no alternative but to return to her sleeping quarters. The tent was not the most comfortable place to be when steady rainfall beat a tattoo on the canvas, and damp seeped up from the hard-packed soil beneath them. Teddy was restless and, despite a hefty dose of laudanum, even the slightest movement made him cry out, and this disturbed Molly, who needed to be fed every two or three hours.

At first light Lottie gave up all attempts to rest even though the others were now sleeping peacefully. She roused herself, dressed and went outside in the cool of a grey dawn. It had stopped raining, but as she went to fetch water she was faced with a sea of mud. Fires were being lit and wood-smoke formed a dense cloud above the encampment. The chill in the air made Lottie shiver as she picked her way towards Lady Aurelia's hut, avoiding the deep puddles as best she could in the hazy light. The kindling she had collected previously would be dry enough to get a decent fire going, and the prospect of a cup of tea made her quicken her steps, but as she approached the squat building she had a feeling that all was not well. The hairs on the back of her neck prickled with apprehension as she entered the hut, only to find it empty.

Even in the dim light she could see that the large cabin trunk was open and garments were spilled onto the floor. Gloves, hats and shoes were scattered around, and Lady Aurelia's jewel case lay empty and abandoned on the bed. Lottie's hands shook as she took in the scene. It looked as if a robbery had taken place, but she suspected that the truth was even more shocking. The bed had not been slept in and Lady Aurelia's portmanteau and valise were missing. There was no note to explain her ladyship's sudden departure, but, if her mood the previous evening was anything to go by, she had taken matters into her own hands and had gone to find Gillingham. There could be no other explanation, but what to do now? Lottie picked up a shoe and placed it in the smaller trunk. She found its match and put them together, working automatically as if tidying the room after a particularly trying session when Aurelia could not make up her mind what to wear. She folded the discarded garments and packed them away before sweeping up the fragments of glass.

When everything was put to rights she lit the fire and placed the kettle on the trivet. Perhaps Lady Aurelia would realise her mistake and return before anyone had missed her? It was a question that buzzed round in her head like a swarm of bluebottles on the dung heap at The Swan. But as the sun forced its way through a bank of clouds, and the ground outside steamed beneath its welcoming rays, Lottie's hopes began to fade. She was afraid, although not for herself; she would manage somehow, but Lady Aurelia had everything to lose. Wealthy she might be, but with her reputation in shreds she would find herself ostracised by polite society. She would be branded as an adulteress; a scarlet woman. Lottie had heard Ruth and May sharing titbits of gossip overheard in the taproom, and she knew that a reputation lost was difficult, if not impossible, to regain.

She made a pot of tea, and as she waited for it to brew she realised that she must do something. She picked up the pot and took it to the tent where Ruby was feeding the baby and Teddy was sitting up, looking pale, but determined not to cry.

Lottie filled their mugs and added some of the precious sugar that Tom Bonney had given them.

'Where've you been?' Ruby demanded crossly. 'I suppose her ladyship's whims and fancies are more important than seeing to the boy.'

Teddy glared at her. 'I got a name, missis. And I can take care of meself.'

'Of course you can, Teddy.' Lottie handed him a mug of sweet tea. 'I'm sorry there's no milk, but I suppose you're used to that.'

'I'm a soldier, miss. I've been with the 97th since I was nine.'

'Then you're an old campaigner.' Lottie placed Ruby's tea within reach. 'I'll make some porridge in a minute. We'll all feel better for some breakfast.'

'What is it you're not telling us?' Ruby demanded. 'It's obvious that there's something bothering you, so don't deny it.'

'Well, I've no doubt it will be common knowledge before the morning is out. Lady Aurelia has left.'

'What d'you mean?' Ruby shifted the baby to her shoulder and patted her tiny back. 'Has she gone to live at the monastery?'

'The truth is I don't know where she is, but I suspect the worst, if you get my meaning.' Lottie shot a warning glance in Teddy's direction.

'Oh Lord! That'll put the cat among the pigeons,' Ruby said, chuckling.

'What cat?' Teddy asked eagerly.

Lottie gazed at him, frowning thoughtfully. 'How do you feel this morning, Teddy? Do you think you could run an errand for me?'

'I should say so. I ain't a baby and I ain't sick. My arm hurts, but I'm a soldier and I got to learn to take pain.'

Lottie helped him to his feet. 'It's quite simple. I want you to take a message to Lieutenant Bonney. Do you know where to find him?'

'I knows this camp like the back of me hand, miss. What do I say?'

'Just ask him to meet me here. Can you do that?'

Teddy puffed out his chest. 'Yes, of course I can. Will you have the porridge ready when I come back? I'm blooming starving.'

Lottie brushed a stray curl of hair back from his forehead. 'I'll get the fire going and put the water on to boil. You'll get your breakfast, soldier.' She held the tent flap open to make it easier for him, but he marched off with his shoulders braced and a determined set to his jaw.

'You think she's gone to look for Gillingham, don't you?' Ruby cradled Molly in her arms, rocking her gently. 'That's why you want to speak to Bonney.'

'She knows where Gillingham has been sent, and I'm sure she's gone to find him.'

'Then she'll be safe, Lottie, or as safe as any of us are here.' Ruby swaddled the baby and laid her down on the bed. 'Stop worrying, there's nothing you can do.'

'That's easy to say, but she might be in terrible danger.'

'I'd say she knows what she's doing, and she can take care of herself.'

'She's not thinking straight, Ruby. You should have seen her last night. She was desperate.'

'She cuckolded her husband.' Ruby glanced down at the sleeping baby. 'And she abandoned this little moppet. What sort of woman does that?'

'I'm not defending her actions, but I can't help feeling sorry for her. She's besotted with Gillingham and that makes her behave as she does.'

'You're too soft on her, Lottie. Lady Aurelia is a selfish monster and she deserves all she gets. I'll say no more, because I know you care about her, but I know what I think, and it's what everyone else will think as well.'

'I'll see to the fire.' Lottie left the tent and set to work lighting the campfire. Arguing with Ruby was pointless. She was entitled to her opinion, and was undoubtedly correct in her assumption that the world would think badly of Lady Aurelia, but Lottie had seen beneath the outer façade. She knew that, for all her faults, Aurelia Dashwood was a woman deeply in love, willing to risk everything to be with the man she adored.

The sun had come out now, banishing the clouds and Lottie had just got the fire going, and had hung the kettle over the flames, when Teddy returned with Tom Bonney close on his heels.

'Well done, soldier.' Lottie smiled, but she was alarmed to see Teddy looking so pale and drawn. 'That's enough for now. If you'll keep an eye on the baby, Ruby will make breakfast for us all.'

Teddy's bottom lip trembled. 'I'm a drummer boy, miss. I ain't no nursemaid.'

'That sounded like an order, soldier,' Tom said, smiling. He put his hand in his pocket and took out an apple. 'Here's something for your trouble, but I expect you to look after the ladies. You're the only man in the tent, so it's your duty to protect them at all times.'

Teddy stood to attention and saluted. 'Yes, sir.' He accepted the apple with a pleased grin. 'Thank you, sir.' He hurried into the tent as if afraid that someone might steal his prize.

'I need to speak to you urgently, Lieutenant,' Lottie said in a low voice.

'Won't you call me Tom? I think we know each other well enough by now, don't you, Lottie?'

She shot him a wary glance. 'Yes, I suppose so, but we'd do best to go to Lady Aurelia's quarters. I don't want anyone to hear what I've got to say.'

He followed her as she sidestepped the puddles and made her way to the hut.

'It must be something important. What is it?'

'Come inside.' Lottie opened the door and entered.

He stood in the doorway, looking round. 'I can't see anything out of the way.'

'Her ladyship was very upset when I left her last night, and this morning she wasn't here. She's packed two bags and I think she's gone in search of Gillingham.'

'I don't know the whole story, Lottie, but could it be that you're reading too much into this? Might she not have decided to stay the night at Lord Raglan's residence? Or perhaps she accompanied her husband to the monastery?'

'I can't tell you everything without breaking a confidence, but it's very unlikely.'

'But it's possible,' he said gently. 'I have to report to the major-general and I'll make discreet enquiries.'

'Would you? I'd be so grateful. I'm sick with worry.'

'You really care about her, don't you?'

'Yes, I do.'

Tom gazed at her, frowning. 'I'm not sure she deserves such loyalty, but I'll do my best to discover her whereabouts. She can't have left the camp without someone seeing her. I'll make discreet enquiries.'

'I'm sorry to drag you into this, Tom, but you were the only person I could trust.'

'I'll let you know as soon as I have any news.'

There was nothing that Lottie could do other than await his return, but it was far from easy.

'For pity's sake, can't you find something to occupy yourself, other than pacing up and down?' Ruby put down her sewing and glared at Lottie, who had stepped outside in the hope of seeing Tom, and returned even more downcast than before. 'You won't help her ladyship by wearing yourself out like this.'

Lottie was about to defend her actions, but thought better of it. 'I don't know what else to do. I feel so helpless, and it's frustrating.'

'There's something you should do. Teddy ought to be seen by the medical officer,' Ruby said in a low voice. 'I know Mrs Seacole set his arm, but perhaps he should be checked by a real doctor.'

'You're right, of course, and we're running out of laudanum. I'll take him to the hospital.' Lottie beckoned to Teddy, who was hunched on his bed, staring gloomily out through the open tent flap. 'Come on, soldier. Let's make this official.'

He scrambled to his feet. 'Do you think that the doctor will let me go back on duty, miss? I've still got one good arm.'

Lottie ruffled his curls, smiling. 'We'll see what he says.'

Teddy was not a priority. Injured men arrived in droves, some walking but most of them carried on stretchers, bloodied and groaning horribly. The nauseous smell of infected wounds and gangrene filled the stuffy room, and the hard-pressed orderlies and nurses did their best to cope. Lottie was tempted to offer her services, but she was untrained and would probably get in the way, and she resigned herself to sitting with Teddy, endeavouring to keep his spirits up as they waited to be seen.

Eventually, after three long hours, a tired young surgeon examined Teddy's arm. 'Whoever did this made a good job of it,' he said, nodding. 'Where was he treated?'

'He was waiting to be shipped out to Scutari.' Lottie clasped Teddy's good hand in hers, giving it a comforting squeeze. 'Mrs Seacole set the bones and splinted his arm.'

Teddy nodded, biting his lip as the doctor examined the affected limb.

'Well, young man, that lady probably saved your arm from amputation,' the doctor said cheerfully. 'I'll leave well alone, but you must wear the splint until the bones knit together, which could take anything from four to eight weeks, maybe longer.'

'When can I return to duty, sir?'

The doctor gazed at him, frowning. 'I'm going to advise discharge from the army on medical grounds. Your arm will heal, but you will have a weakness there for a long time, and in my opinion you are not fit for military service.'

Teddy's green eyes filled with tears and his bottom lip trembled. 'But it's my job, sir.'

'You can join up when you're older, if that's what you really want, my boy.'

'I'm a soldier, sir.' Teddy's bottom lip stuck out ominously.

The doctor turned to Lottie. 'Are you related to the boy in any way, miss?'

'No, we're not related.'

'He should be sent home to the care of his family. I personally don't think boys of this age should be recruited, but that's just my opinion.'

'I ain't got no family, sir,' Teddy said hastily. 'I come to the army from the foundling home. The army is my family now, sir.'

Lottie slipped her arm around his shoulders.

'You've got me and Ruby, and little Molly too. You have a family, Teddy.'

The doctor wrote something on a printed form. 'That's settled then. I'll send this to his commanding officer. No doubt he will make arrangements for the boy to be sent back to England on the next transport available.'

Teddy opened his mouth to protest, but Lottie stilled him with a glance. 'Don't worry, Teddy. We'll look after you.' She turned to the doctor. 'Could you let me have some laudanum for him? The pain keeps him awake at night.'

'I'm sorry, but we're running low on supplies and there are seriously wounded soldiers who are in desperate need.' The doctor rose to his feet and shook her hand. 'You're a remarkable woman. The boy is lucky to have you taking care of him.'

Lottie managed a faint smile. 'I do what I can, Doctor.' She placed her arm around Teddy's shoulders and hurried him outside into the relatively fresh air.

'It'll be the workhouse for me if I goes back to London, miss.' Tears trickled unchecked down Teddy's freckled cheeks. 'They might as well have shot me dead on the battlefield.'

'I won't listen to talk like that,' Lottie said severely. 'You are with me now, Teddy Miller. We are a family and we will stick together. I know what it's like to be on your own at a young age, and I won't let that happen to you.'

'Why should you care about me?'

'I was only a year or so older than you when my uncle sent me to work as a slavey in a coaching inn. I've had to make my own way in the world.'

'But I want to be a soldier, miss.'

'When you're a bit older you can choose to do what you want, but for now I'm going to take care of you. We might not be related by blood, but that doesn't mean we can't be a family. What do you say?'

He nodded. 'I suppose so, miss.'

'And you must call me Lottie. I'm not your ma, but I can be like a big sister, if you'll have me?'

'I've always wanted a brother,' he said, attempting a grin and not quite succeeding.

'Well, you'll just have to put up with having an older sister and a baby sister, and Ruby can be an aunt. You'll be the man of the family, Teddy.' She took him by the hand and they made their way slowly back to the camp.

Lottie had almost forgotten Lady Aurelia, but everything came flooding back to her when she saw Maggie Cole standing outside their tent. She was smoking a cigarette and the smell of Turkish tobacco mingled with wood-smoke and the pungent odour of lye soap from the washhouse. Maggie tossed the butt into the fire and hurried towards her. She came to a halt, staring at Teddy.

'Who's this?'

'Miss Cole, may I introduce my young charge, Teddy Miller?'

Teddy eyed Maggie suspiciously and then looked away.

'Your charge? Are you mad? You seem to go round collecting waifs and strays, but to what end?'

'Go into the tent, Teddy,' Lottie said firmly. 'Tell Ruby I'm back.'

He hesitated, but it was an order and he obeyed, albeit reluctantly.

'Never mind. Don't tell me, I don't want to know.' Maggie caught Lottie by the sleeve as she was about to walk away. 'I didn't come here to give you a lecture. I came to pass on some information I happened to overhear, but don't tell anyone you had it from me.'

'What is it? Tell me, please.'

'First thing this morning, I heard the major-general telling his wife that he had received a telegraph from Kadikoi informing him that Lady Aurelia had been seen on the road to Sebastopol. She was on horseback and leading a mule laden with luggage, so it looks as though she was on her way to join Lieutenant Gillingham at the telegraph station.'

Lottie's hand flew to cover her mouth and stifle a gasp of dismay. 'Gideon is there, wherever it is, but if they're near Sebastopol they are all in terrible danger.'

Maggie took a pouch from her pocket and rolled another cigarette. She lit it with a burning twig from the campfire. 'Aren't we all, love? If a stray bullet doesn't get us then cholera or dysentery might finish us off. I've got a bottle of brandy hidden in my room. If you feel like a tot you're welcome to join me.' She walked off, leaving a wisp of blue tobacco smoke in her wake.

Ruby emerged from the tent. 'I heard what she said, but it just confirms what you thought, doesn't it?'

'Yes, but I didn't know where the telegraph station was situated. I've grown so accustomed to hearing gunfire that I hardly notice it at all, but they're so close to the fighting it scares me.'

Ruby laid a sympathetic hand on Lottie's shoulder. 'There's nothing you can do. It's up to the colonel now. She's still his wife.'

'Perhaps Gillingham will see sense and bring her to safety?' Lottie said hopefully, although somehow she could not believe that headstrong Lady Aurelia would listen to the voice of reason.

Later that day, Lottie was tending the campfire. A frisky wind sent the smoke spiralling up into the cloudy sky, and then changed direction, catching her unawares and making her cough. She stood up and stepped aside, but the breeze followed her as if playing a game of tag, and once again she had to move out of range of the suffocating fumes. The soot-blackened pot bubbled cheerfully, and the aroma of boiling onions whetted her appetite, but she knew that the soup would be thin and watery. The flatbread baked on a hot stone would be charred and hard to chew, but it was all they had. The small amount of rations Tom had given them would have to last, and Lottie was unsure how they stood now that Lady Aurelia had left the camp. Her eyes stung and she wiped them on her sleeve.

As the wind dropped and the smoke cleared, she saw Tom Bonney coming towards her and she ran to meet him.

'Any more news? Maggie told me that Lady Aurelia was seen on the road to Sebastopol.'

He put his hand in his pocket and pulled out a clean white handkerchief. 'Are you crying, Lottie?'

'No, it's the fire. The weather is playing tricks

247

on me.' She accepted the hanky with a grateful smile. 'Thank you.'

'Keep it. I bought half a dozen from Mother Seacole. She's doing a roaring trade down on the docks. We'll have to travel further to get such luxuries when she finally opens her British Hotel on the road to Sebastopol. I must admit I'm curious to see what the place will be like when it's built.'

'I'd love to see it myself.' Lottie dabbed her eyes. 'What happens now, Tom? Will the colonel order Gillingham back to camp?'

'That would seem to be the only answer. Lady Aurelia would be certain to accompany him, and Gillingham wouldn't refuse a direct order.'

'Has it been done?'

He shook his head. 'Not to my knowledge, but I'm not privy to the colonel's plans.'

'So what will happen? And perhaps more importantly, what will happen to us? Ruby is a soldier's widow and it looks as though her ladyship has no need of me. Will we be sent back to England?'

'I can't say, but I'll see to it that you still receive your rations. None of this is your fault.'

'Then there's Teddy. The army surgeon said he will be discharged on medical grounds. The poor child has nowhere to go and no family to support him. I've promised that I'll take care of him.'

Tom gazed at her, a frown creasing his brow. 'That won't be easy, especially if her ladyship has no need of your services. What will you do?'

'I've been asking myself that, Tom. To be honest, I don't know, but whatever happens Ruby and the infant will come with me, and so will Teddy. I won't let them down.'

'You are a remarkable woman. I'll do everything in my power to make life easier for you.' He glanced up at the sky. 'It looks like rain again. I suggest you and your charges use Lady Aurelia's hut for tonight at least. I'll give you fair warning if I get word that she's about to return, but there's no sense in leaving a perfectly good quarter empty in the meantime.'

'Do you really mean that? It'd be wonderful.'

'I do, and I'll send a man to help move your things. Unfortunately I have duties to perform at the residence, otherwise it would have been my pleasure to assist.' He glanced down at the simmering pot. 'Is that all you're having for supper?'

'It's more than we would have had if you hadn't come to the rescue. We can manage, Tom. I know that the men fare less well than we do.'

'The army are badly provisioned and the men suffer, but you are civilians and Ruby has a baby to care for. I'll see to it that Mother Seacole adds to your rations. She's a sutler who boasts that she can provide anything from a needle to an anchor, and I don't doubt it.'

'But she gives medical services and doles out refreshments to those who can't afford to pay,' Lottie protested. 'Teddy might have lost his arm were it not for her.'

Tom nodded and a smile lit his eyes. 'You are loyal to those you befriend, Lottie. I admire that quality in anyone.'

She turned away, conscious that she was blushing. 'I mustn't keep you, Tom. Thank you for everything.'

'I'd do more to make your life easier if it were in my power, but now I must go or I'll be in trouble with the colonel.' He leaned forward and brushed her cheek with a whisper of a kiss. 'Make yourselves comfortable for one night at least, maybe more.' He hurried off, leaving Lottie to rush into the tent and break the good news to Ruby.

That night and for many nights after, they lived in relative luxury in Lady Aurelia's quarters. Ruby and Lottie shared the bed, sleeping head to toe, while the cabin trunk made a cosy cot for Molly, and Teddy had two palliasses piled one on top of the other on the floor near the fire. They were dry and warm at night, and Tom saw to it that they had their usual rations, supplemented by little extras brought to them by Mother Seacole's servant.

The pounding of cannon fire continued day and night, and there was still no news of Lady Aurelia or Gillingham, although Tom said that telegraphs had been flying to and fro. The colonel was tight-lipped and even Maggie had nothing to add. Mrs Fothergill kept her distance and there was nothing that Lottie could do other than wait and hope that all would be well.

The army were getting ready for another major attack on Sebastopol. Lottie could feel the tension. The air buzzed with it as the men prepared to march. Teddy was restless and admitted that he was missing the soldiers who had become his surrogate uncles, although how many of them had survived the last encounter of the 97th was anybody's guess. There had been no word from

Lady Aurelia. Except for her belongings that remained in the hut, she might never have existed.

With the departure of several more companies the camp was eerily quiet. Rain fell like tears, as if the clouds were weeping for the men who would die during the assault on Sebastopol. With little to do, Lottie spent as much time as she could helping Mary Seacole. She made tea for the wounded and offered comfort where she could. There were times when she was left to hold the hand of a dying man, and these were the hardest of all, but Mary was always there to offer support. Lottie's respect for the larger-than-life black woman grew daily, and she understood now why the men called her Mother Seacole. Mary might be a shrewd businesswoman, as well as being skilled in treating all manner of ailments, but it was her generous nature and genuine compassion for the sick and dying that impressed Lottie the most. She would gladly have stayed in the Crimea to assist Mary in her British Hotel, which would soon be finished, but sadly this was not an option.

Lottie returned to the hut late one evening, tired and dirty, but she felt satisfied that at least she was doing something useful. She was about to follow Teddy into the hut when she saw Tom Bonney approaching at a run. She froze to the spot. The expression on his face said it all.

Chapter Fifteen

'What is it, Tom?'

He took off his shako and tucked it under his arm. 'It would be better if you went inside, Lottie.'

She clasped his arm, and her knuckles whitened. 'It's bad news. Tell me now.'

'There's no way of breaking this gently.' He opened the door, avoiding meeting her anxious gaze.

Lottie stepped inside. Her heart was pounding and she was finding it difficult to breathe. 'Go on. Tell me the truth.'

He cleared his throat. 'The telegraph station came under attack late yesterday. Reinforcements were sent, but the building had been razed to the ground.'

'But they escaped?'

'I'm sorry.' Tom held out his hand, but Lottie ignored the gesture and he dropped it to his side. 'I am truly sorry.'

'What's wrong?' Teddy demanded. 'What have you said to her?'

Ruby leaped to her feet. 'Is there no hope?'

'All were lost.'

'It can't be true,' Lottie said dazedly. 'They can't be dead. I'd know if anything had happened to Gideon. I'd feel it in here.' She clasped her hands to her bosom. 'It's a terrible mistake.'

Ruby pulled up a chair. 'Sit down, love. You've

had a terrible shock.'

'I don't believe it.' Lottie sank down on the hard wooden seat. 'I won't believe it.'

'Are you sure, Tom?' Ruby asked anxiously. 'Could there be a mistake?'

'There wasn't much left. I don't want to go into details, but there were the remains of cap badges and this.' Tom put his hand in his pocket and took out a blackened earring. The diamond winked in the sunlight, despite the coating of soot, and the ruby glowed darkly. 'Colonel Dashwood identified it as belonging to his wife. He'd received information that Lady Aurelia and Gillingham were hiding out at the telegraph station, despite the lieutenant having had orders to return to camp.'

'That's awful.' Ruby laid her hand on Lottie's shoulders. 'I don't know what to say.'

Lottie gazed up at Tom, desperate to see a glimmer of hope in his eyes, but there was no comfort in his desolate gaze. She shook her head. 'They can't be dead. They can't be.'

Next morning Lottie was summoned to the residence. The hope she had been harbouring had diminished during a sleepless night, and she felt as if her heart had been ripped from her body. She was an empty shell, going through the motions of living, but dead inside. Her feet were leaden as each step led her closer to a reality she had tried so hard to ignore, and the inevitable interview with the colonel.

Tom ushered her into a small office. 'Miss Lane to see you, sir.' He bowed out of the room and closed the door behind him.

Colonel Dashwood was staring out of the window. He turned slowly and she was shocked to see the change in him. His face was deathly pale and lines of suffering tugged at the corners of his mouth. 'You've heard the news, of course.'

'Yes, sir.'

'You will understand that your services are no long needed, Miss Lane. I've given orders for you to be sent back to England on the first transport available.'

Lottie had known this would be the case, but she could not take Molly without first telling him of her existence. A small voice in her head warned her not to say anything, but she owed it to Lady Aurelia to make sure that Molly had the best of everything.

She cleared her throat. 'Might I speak frankly, sir? I have something I feel I must tell you.'

He sank down on the chair behind the desk. 'What is it, Lane? Be quick, I'm a busy man.'

She gave an account of Molly's birth as briefly and succinctly as she could manage in the circumstances, although her voice broke occasionally as tears threatened to overcome her. She came to a halt, waiting nervously for his response.

He rose slowly to his feet. 'Get out.'

'But, sir, don't you want to see the child? She's a beautiful baby girl with blue eyes just like her mother's.'

'I was warned about this,' he said bitterly. 'Cordelia Fothergill told me of her suspicions, but I refused to believe her. You've just confirmed that what she said was true, and you aided my wife in the wicked deception. I'll have nothing to do with her little bastard, and you won't get a penny from me.'

Lottie drew herself up to her full height. 'That isn't why I told you about the child, sir. I don't want your money. I just thought you should know that you have a daughter.'

'Daughter!' He thumped the desk with his hand and stood up. Purple veins stood out in his neck and a pulse throbbed in his temple. His eyes narrowed. 'I have no daughter. The brat is an orphan, and as such should be put in a home. I want nothing to do with it. You will vacate my late wife's quarters immediately. Lieutenant Bonney will see that you have shelter until your passage home is arranged. Now get out and don't let me see your face again.'

Lottie left the office in a daze. She had not expected the colonel to be overjoyed, but she had hoped that his affection for his dead wife might lead him to feel something for her child.

'Are you all right, Lottie?' Tom's anxious voice broke into her thoughts.

'You must have heard what the colonel said.'

'He's very upset. Perhaps it was not the best time to break the news to him?'

'I thought I was doing the right thing by Molly.'

He opened the door leading into the courtyard. 'We'll go out this way. You won't have to face the rest of the staff.'

'I've done nothing to be ashamed of, Tom. I did what anyone would have done in the circumstances.'

'I know that, and I respect you for standing by Lady Aurelia. I won't speak ill of the dead, but things might have been different had she told her husband about the child in the first place.'

'I suppose you think she ought to have convinced him that he is the father,' Lottie said angrily. 'She was too honest to do that. People can say what they like, but she loved Lieutenant Gillingham and he loved her. It's just tragic that Molly has lost both her parents, but she's got me. I won't desert her.' She followed Tom across the walled courtyard. Outside she found herself on the brow of the hill overlooking the camp. Soldiers were mustering, horses were being saddled and sunlight glinted on buttons, badges and bayonets. She shivered. 'Thank goodness you're not going with them. At least I know I have one friend here.'

'There's very little I can do, but I'll make sure you have everything you need until you leave for England.'

'Thank you, Tom.' She started walking towards the camp and he fell into step beside her.

'Where will you go, and how will you manage when you return to London?'

'I can't think about that now. I suppose I could go to The Swan, where I used to work, but that would be the last resort. Anyway, I don't want to leave here in case Gideon is found. He might have been injured, or taken prisoner.'

'That's very unlikely,' Tom said gently. 'There's little doubt as to the fate of all those who were in the station when it was hit.'

'Then why do I feel like this?' She turned her head to look him in the eyes. 'If there is no hope, why can't I let him go?'

'Only you can answer that, Lottie. But you have

Molly to think of, and what will happen to the boy? Then there's Ruby. You two seem to have become good friends.'

'I don't know what she will do, but I'll take care of Molly and Teddy too.' She quickened her pace. 'I need to speak to Ruby.'

'Of course.' He lengthened his stride. 'Have you any family who might help?'

'No, not really.' She came to a halt outside the hut. 'I appreciate your concern, Tom, but you mustn't worry about us. We'll manage somehow.'

Ruby received the news with a shrug. 'It's what I would have expected, Lottie. You were a fool to tell him.'

'Maybe, but Molly comes from a titled family. She deserves more than the sort of life I can give her.'

Ruby threw the last of their possessions into a sack provided by Tom. 'A child needs love more than money. You'll be a better mother to her than Lady Aurelia would have been, and I don't know about the lieutenant, but I doubt if his family would want a little bastard thrust upon them.'

'Don't call her that. Molly is a love child, and I won't allow her to grow up thinking anything else.'

Ruby chuckled. 'She doesn't understand a word of what we're saying. She won't know any of this, unless you choose to tell her.'

'I can't see into the future, Ruby. All I can think of is Gideon.'

'He's gone, just like my husband, and they won't be coming back. We have to go on by ourselves, but you ain't alone. I'm with you, if you

257

want me. The only prospect I've got is to try and earn my living as a nursery maid when we get back to London. I've got no one waiting for me.'

'Neither have I.' Lottie glanced out of the window. Teddy was watching the last of the troops leaving for the next assault on Sebastopol. She knew that he wanted to return to his unit, but that was out of the question. He would be sad for a while, but he was young and would soon forget his former life as a drummer boy. She was about to turn away when she saw a familiar figure trudging towards the hut, the yellow and red streamers flying like pennants from her blue bonnet.

Momentarily forgetting her heartache, Lottie hurried to meet her. 'Mrs Seacole, this is a surprise.'

Mary stopped, bending over and holding her side and panting. 'I'm not as young as I used to be, honey. I just heard of your troubles. They sure don't need a telegraph in Balaklava. News travels quicker than a flash. Anyway, I'm on my way to the British Hotel, but I stopped to transact some business at Lord Raglan's residence and I heard that you would be leaving soon.'

'I wasn't given the choice, ma'am. You might say that my mind was made up for me.'

'Yes, I know that well enough, honey.' Mary enveloped her in a motherly hug. 'You take care of yourself and that little baby. I brought her into the world and I have a personal interest in the little mite.'

Lottie returned the embrace. 'You were wonderful, Mother Seacole. Molly will be safe with me and I'll see she has the best possible start in life.'

'I know you will, child.' Mary held her at arm's length, her shrewd eyes twinkling. 'You have it bad now, but you will win out in the end. I see it written in the stars.' She released Lottie and wrapped her colourful shawl around her shoulders as a chill wind whipped at her bonnet strings. 'I have to go now. My business partner, Mr Day, is waiting for me at the top of the hill. It's a pity you won't be around when I open my hotel where there will be good food, excellent wine and solace for the hard-pressed officers and men, but I hope to see you in England when the war is over.' She was about to leave but Lottie caught her by the hand.

'When Molly is christened I think one of her names should be Mary. She came before her time and may not have survived if you hadn't helped her mother give birth.'

Mary hesitated and her dark eyes were bright with unshed tears. 'I take that as the greatest compliment of all, honey. Thank you, kindly.' She continued up the hill, swaying from side to side like a ship in full sail.

Lottie turned to Teddy, who had been listening, open-mouthed. 'There goes a great lady.'

'Are we really going to leave here, Lottie?' he asked anxiously. 'I don't want to go back to England. I'm a soldier.'

'You are a soldier, Teddy. You're a brave one too, but for now you have to return to civilian life. We have no choice but to return to London.'

'I got no one, Lottie.'

'That's not true. You have me and Ruby and the baby. I told you, we're a family, and we'll do well together. Now I want you to help us move our things back to the tent, and we'll need kindling for the fire and fresh water. We're going to be very busy.'

He slipped his hand into hers. 'I'm sorry about the lady and your man. Maybe they ain't dead after all. I seen men left for dead on the battle-field who got up and walked off like nothing had happened.'

'There's always hope, Teddy,' Lottie said briskly. 'We won't give up, ever.'

Finally, after weeks of waiting for a ship to take them home, Lottie, Ruby and the children were on a screw steamer wending its way through the nar-row channel to the Black Sea, bound for England. Lottie was glad to leave Balaklava and all the pain and misery of war, but part of her refused to accept the fact that she would never see Gideon again. In her heart she was convinced that they would be reunited in life, if not in death, but she had two innocent children who needed her love and protection. She did not know how she was going to manage when they reached London, but she was determined that Lady Aurelia's daughter would not suffer from her mother's indifference.

During the long days at sea Lottie had plenty of time to work out a plan of action on her return to London. Her first mission, after finding them somewhere to live, would be to seek out Lady Aurelia's family. It would hardly be fair to raise a child in the East End, when that little girl was heir to her mother's fortune. Lottie was still smarting from Colonel Dashwood's reaction to the news that his wife had given birth to another man's

260

child, and she did not hold out much hope for a better outcome from the aristocratic de Morgan family, but Molly had much to gain if her wealthy and influential relatives chose to recognise her.

The ship was crowded with injured men and both Lottie and Ruby found themselves acting as unpaid nurses, helping the hard-pressed orderlies to cope with festering wounds and fevers. Teddy also did his bit to help in as much as he was able with one arm in a sling. He took food and water to the men who were confined to their bunks, and kept them amused with tales of his exploits in battle. Lottie overheard some of his stories and had to turn away with a smile. She could see that the injured soldiers were highly entertained, accepting Teddy's embroidered accounts of past events in good part. Working hard and helping to nurse the wounded men helped Lottie to get through each day, but the pain of losing Gideon was still as intense as at the moment she had learned of his death. She could not speak of it to Ruby, who had suffered a double loss, and Teddy was too young to understand. She buried the anguish deep inside, telling herself that no one died of a broken heart; they just ceased to live.

At night they shared a tiny, four-berth cabin, living in conditions that were worse than those they had endured in camp, but at the end of the day they were all too tired to care where they laid their heads. Molly was sleeping for longer in between feeds, which allowed Ruby more time to rest. It was not a pleasure cruise, and the conditions were quite shocking, but somehow they managed to get through each day and, apart from a rough passage across the Bay of Biscay, the weather was kind to them.

Lottie had hoped that the ship would dock in London, but they disembarked at Southampton and had to find their own way to the railway station, where they caught a train to Waterloo Bridge station. By this time Lottie's funds were running low and it was late in the evening. She could think of nowhere to go other than The Swan, and with two tired children and Ruby, who was flagging, she had little alternative but to hire a cab.

It seemed strange to be back in London. Her memories of Balaklava had faded a little during the sea voyage, but the city, with all its noxious smells and teeming streets, seemed to wrap itself around her like a warm blanket. This was her home and it felt good to be back on English soil, and away from the sounds of battle.

The cab stopped on the corner of Milk Street, and Ruby, who had fallen asleep soon after they left Waterloo Bridge, opened her eyes with a start.

'Where are we?' She sat up straight. 'Where's the baby?'

'I have her safe in my arms,' Lottie said, smiling. 'If you'll take her, I'll help Teddy with our bags.'

Laden with their luggage, they made their way into the courtyard of The Swan with Two Necks, and for once all was quiet, apart from the occasional whinny of a horse in the stable and the sound of raucous laughter as the door to the taproom opened and Jem emerged carrying two buckets. He came to a halt, and dumped them down, spilling dirty water on the cobblestones.

'By God, it can't be. Lottie, it is you. What are you doing here, girl?'

'We've come a long way, Jem, and we're all bone tired. We need a bed for the night.'

He ran his hand through his already tousled hair. 'We got plenty of rooms. Business ain't too good at the moment.'

'That's the trouble, Jem. I can pay, but not very much. One room will be fine and we'll make do. We just need to rest and recover from the long journey.'

'Ain't you going to introduce me, Lottie?' Jem asked, staring at Ruby. He ruffled Teddy's hair. 'And who might you be, young man?'

'I'm Drummer Miller, of the 97th, sir.' Teddy stood to attention.

'Teddy was wounded in battle,' Lottie said hastily. 'He is temporarily unfit for military service.'

Jem threw back his head and laughed. 'And I thought we had a deserter on our hands.' He slapped Teddy on the back. 'Well done, son.'

'I ain't your son, mate,' Teddy said, scowling. 'I'm a soldier and I've seen things that would make your hair stand on end more than it is now.'

Lottie could see the beginnings of an argument and she laid her hand on Jem's arm. 'We're very tired. Our ship docked earlier today and we've travelled all the way from Southampton. We need food and somewhere to sleep.' She turned her head, following Jem's anxious glance, and saw Mrs Filby heading towards them.

'What's all this? We don't take in gypsies.'

Lottie had not given it any thought until this moment, but she realised now that they must pre-

263

sent a sorry picture in their travel-stained clothes. Washing clothes had presented a real problem on board ship, and personal hygiene had been the least of their worries.

'It's me, Mrs Filby. Lottie Lane.'

'Lottie!' Mrs Filby peered at her and her expression changed subtly. 'You look a sorry sight. What happened? Did the fine lady get tired of you and send you packing?' She treated Ruby and the children to a cursory glance. 'And who are these people?'

Molly began to cry, and at the same time a carriage and pair clattered into the yard. The ostlers appeared as if from nowhere and Filby emerged from the taproom, followed by Ruth.

'We need a room for the night, Mrs Filby,' Lottie said urgently. 'I can pay.'

'Jem, get to work. Don't stand there like a half-wit.' Prudence Filby hesitated, glaring at Lottie and then she nodded. 'All right. You can have the top room, you know the one.'

Lottie did know the room she meant. It was the smallest and least comfortable in the whole building, but it was also the cheapest. She nodded. 'All right, I'll take it, and we need supper for that price too.'

'You can't come in the dining room looking like didicoys, and you don't smell too good either.'

'Then I'll collect our food from the kitchen, Mrs Filby.'

'All right. Tell Cook I said you might, but I'll add it to your bill.' Mrs Filby bustled off to help her husband greet the newcomers.

'Are you sure about this?' Ruby asked, hitching

Molly over her shoulder and rubbing her tiny back. 'She doesn't seem very pleased to see you.'

'Have you got any better ideas?'

Ruby shook her head.

'Then follow me.' Lottie beckoned to Teddy. 'Come on. I'll show you the way and then we'll go to the kitchen and get something to eat.'

'I'm bloody starving.' Teddy ducked as Lottie took a half-hearted swipe at him. 'Sorry. It slipped out. I ain't got used to being around ladies.'

'You'd better mind your manners, young man,' Lottie said severely. 'We're in London now, not the camp at Balaklava.'

The yard was bustling with activity and Lottie led them to the top floor. She opened the door and there was just enough light from the gas lamp on the far side of the building to make out a double bed, a chest of drawers and a wooden chair. She put the cases she had been carrying on the floor.

'Make yourself comfortable, Ruby. Teddy and I will get some food. I just hope that Jezebel isn't in one of her states.'

Ruby slumped down on the chair and unbuttoned her blouse to allow the baby to suckle. 'We can't all sleep in one bed. This is worse than the cabin on board ship.'

'I saw Ruth in the yard. I'll see if I can borrow a palliasse and one of us can sleep on the floor. We'll manage, and everything will look better in the morning.' Lottie tried to sound convincing. 'Come on, Teddy. Let's see if you can charm Cook into giving us something tasty.'

In the kitchen nothing seemed to have changed.

Jezebel was at the range, stirring a large pan of soup, and the table was littered with dirty crockery, dangerous-looking knives, wooden spoons and vegetable peelings. It was Lad who rushed over to greet them, barking ecstatically as he jumped up to lick Lottie's hand.

Jezebel turned round, scowling ominously. 'What d'you want? I'm busy.'

'It's me, Lottie.'

'I can see that. If you're not here to help you can get out of my kitchen. I haven't got time for idle gossip.'

'We're paying for our night's board and lodging,' Lottie said firmly. 'I came to get food.'

Teddy went down on his knees to pet the dog and Lad responded by licking his face. Jezebel stared at him in surprise. 'He hates nippers, especially little boys.'

'He seems to like Teddy.' Lottie went to the table and began to tidy up the mess. 'You need help, Cook. You should tell Mrs Filby.'

Jezebel put the spoon down and opened the oven door. 'I've told her that time and time again, but does she take any notice? No, she does not.' She took out a tray of pies. 'How many arrived just now? Did you see?'

Lottie piled the crockery onto a tray. 'No, but Teddy will take a look in the dining room, if you like. I'll put these in the scullery sink.'

'Through there, boy,' Jezebel said, pointing to the door. 'Turn right and the dining parlour is at the end of the corridor. Look in and count the people. You can count, I suppose.'

'Hold hard, lady. I'm a drummer boy in the

266

army. How d'you suppose I'd learn the beats if I couldn't count?' Teddy rose to his feet and stomped out of the kitchen with Lad following on his heels.

For once, Jezebel seemed at a loss for words.

Lottie deposited the crockery and came back to finish clearing the table. 'There, now you can work. It's all a question of being organised and keeping tidy.'

'When I want a lesson in kitchen management I'll ask for it,' Jezebel said crossly. 'Where is that boy?'

Teddy reappeared, holding up his hand. 'There's five in there, and the sergeant-major lady says there's another four that want food in the tap-room.'

'That's one name for her,' Jezebel said, curling her lip. 'I can think of a few more.'

'If I take the soup to the door, she can serve it.' Lottie was even more aware of her dishevelled appearance and her need to wash. She would not dare enter the dining room, but she could help out an old friend, just this once.

Jezebel served the soup and Lottie carried the laden tray to the door of the dining parlour where Mrs Filby snatched it off her.

'I don't know what you think you're playing at, but this won't make your bill any cheaper. Now get away from here. You look like something the cat dragged in.'

Lottie shrugged and returned to the kitchen. She had not expected any thanks, but at least Jezebel seemed grateful. She had placed two bowls of soup on the table with some slices of fresh bread and a dish of golden butter.

'Eat up before she comes in and catches you. There's meat pie too.'

'Thank you,' Lottie said with a grateful smile. 'I'm starving. In fact we all are. We'll have to take Ruby's up to her.'

'Who's she?' Jezebel demanded.

'Ruby is a friend, and she's in the room feeding the baby.'

'Baby? What baby? It can't be yours, Lottie.'

Teddy wiped his empty bowl with a chunk of bread. 'Molly's real ma don't want her,' he said in a matter-of-fact voice. He shot a sideways glance at Lottie, who was staring at him, open-mouthed. 'You think I don't know what goes on because I'm only eleven, but I got eyes and ears, and I ain't stupid. Little Molly is a b–'

'That's enough, Teddy,' Lottie said hastily. 'You're quite right, but we don't tell everyone.'

Jezebel pulled up a chair. 'Tell me more. I ain't heard a good story since I was in The Steel. Come on, Lottie. The boy's already let the cat out of the bag. I want to hear the rest. It's worth a slice of currant cake.'

The door opened just as Jezebel was about to sit down and Mrs Filby burst into the kitchen. 'What's all this? They've finished the soup and they're waiting for the pie. What d'you think you're doing, Cook?'

'The pies are there on the table. Take them in yourself,' Jezebel said curtly. 'I'm having five minutes to meself.'

'Mr Filby will hear about this. You'll be sacked without a character and you'll end up back in

268

prison.' Mrs Filby snatched up the tray of pies. 'I'll tell him what you just said.'

'Go on then, you miserable bitch.' Jezebel took a pipe out of her pocket and a pouch of tobacco. 'See if I care. You'll not find another cook who'll be willing to slave away for next to nothing.'

'You'll be sorry for this.' Mrs Filby struggled with the, door and Teddy jumped up to open it for her. She glared at him. 'I don't like boys. One word from you and I'll throw you out on the street with the feral dogs and cats.'

Lottie stood up. 'That's enough of that talk, Mrs Filby. No wonder your business is failing. You need to watch your tongue. Teddy is a brave soldier who's seen action in the Crimea. Shame on you for speaking to him like that.'

'You can stay here tonight, Lottie Lane,' Mrs Filby snapped, 'but I want you gone in the morning. You aren't welcome here.'

Chapter Sixteen

'Have a heart, missis,' Jezebel said angrily. 'You can't speak to a paying guest like that.'

'I can speak to her in any way I choose. Curb your tongue, Cook, or you'll be out on the street with her.'

Jezebel picked up a knife and stroked the steel lovingly. 'I've had enough of this. I ain't staying here to be bullied by the likes of you. If she's leaving in the morning, then so am I.'

'Good riddance, I say.' Mrs Filby flounced out of the room and Teddy slammed the door behind her.

'Bad-tempered old bat,' he said, grinning. 'You told her, missis.'

'Not before time.' Jezebel replaced the knife and sat down. She reached for her pipe and tobacco pouch. 'I'd rather live on the street than put up with her a minute longer.'

Lottie stared at her, frowning. 'I am so sorry, Jezebel. I didn't mean to cause trouble for you.'

'It's been coming for ages. I'd have walked out many a time, but it ain't easy for an old lag to find honest work or a decent place to live.' Jezebel lit her pipe with a spill from the fire, and Lad curled up at her feet.

'Come with us,' Lottie said impetuously. It grieved her to see the proud woman humiliated and left with no option other than to make herself homeless. Whatever her faults, Jezebel Pretty was a hard worker and a good plain cook. The Filbys would struggle to find someone to replace her.

'What did you say?' Jezebel clenched the clay pipe between her teeth, puffing smoke out of the corner of her mouth.

Teddy eyed her warily and his hand shot out to take another pie. Lottie waited for an explosion of wrath from Jezebel, but she chose to ignore Teddy's lapse in manners.

'We've got to find somewhere to live that's cheap, and I'll have to get a job,' Lottie said, thoughtfully. 'You know this part of London even better than I do, Jezebel. If you're determined to leave the Filbys, it would make sense for us to stick together.'

'I ain't sociable,' Jezebel growled. 'You'd soon get fed up with me.'

'Well, if you don't want to...'

'I didn't say that,' Jezebel said hastily. She took the pipe from her mouth and emptied the dottle into the fire. 'I ain't got much, but I'll pack me bag and be ready first thing. She can do the breakfasts herself, the old witch.' She rose to her feet and began piling food on a plate. 'Here, take this up to your friend, and keep out of Prudence's way or she might decide to throw us all out tonight.'

Teddy stuffed the last morsel of pie into his mouth. 'You make the best pies I've ever tasted, missis. We could win the war in the Crimea in a week if the troops was fed on such food.'

Lottie was not sure, but she thought she saw a blush rise to Jezebel's sallow cheeks. She took the plate and hurried Teddy from the kitchen. Lad was about to follow him, but Jezebel called him back and the dog obeyed instantly.

Ruby had taken the chair from the bedroom and was sitting outside on the gallery, rocking Molly in her arms. Lottie went out to join her, wondering how she was going to break the news that they would have to move on in the morning. It was a fine evening with a slight chill in the air. Starlings coming home to roost on window ledges and beneath the eaves filled the air with their raucous chatter, drowning out the sounds from the busy street. Down below in the courtyard the ostlers were attending to the horses as a private carriage made ready to leave. It was a comfortingly familiar scene and, despite the city smells, the crowds and the constant din, it was good to be back in London, far away from the battlefield, death and destruction.

Ruby looked up and smiled. 'Noisy blooming birds. Let's hope they settle down soon or we won't get a wink of sleep.'

'No fear of that,' Lottie said, stifling a yawn. 'I could sleep on a clothes line.' She leaned down, holding out her arms. 'Let me take Molly. There's food in the room. Jezebel was feeling generous.'

Ruby needed no second bidding. She stood up and passed the sleeping baby to Lottie. 'Have you eaten?'

'I have, but you'd best get in there before Teddy gobbles the lot. Jezebel makes delicious pies and he's already had two, maybe three.' Lottie followed Ruby into the room where Teddy was sitting cross-legged on the floor with the food spread out in front of him.

He greeted them with a guilty grin. 'I couldn't help meself, Lottie. I never ate nothing as tasty as them pies.'

'I hope you saved one for Ruby,' Lottie said, trying to keep a straight face and failing.

'Lucky you came in then or I'd have been sorely tempted, missis.' He wiped his mouth on his sleeve, watching Ruby enviously as she took a bite.

'You're right, Teddy. This is a good pie.' She ate it, frowning thoughtfully. 'It's not too bad here, Lottie. Can we afford to stay until we find ourselves somewhere more permanent?'

Holding Molly in her arms, Lottie perched on the edge of the bed. 'I'm afraid it's not good news. We have to move on tomorrow.'

'That's a pity. Is it too expensive?'

'It's not that,' Lottie said slowly. 'Mrs Filby's a difficult woman. We had a bit of an argument.'

Teddy leaped to his feet. 'And the big ugly woman had a knife. I think she wanted to stab the old bitch, and I wouldn't have blamed her. She's coming along too, and she can feed us on pie every day of the week.'

Ruby turned to Lottie, eyebrows raised. 'That would be Jezebel? The one who went to prison for injuring her lover?'

'She's not so bad when you get to know her,' Lottie said hurriedly. 'I felt sorry for her.'

'And her dog can come too,' Teddy added. 'He's called Lad and I've always wanted a dog, but I couldn't keep one in camp.'

'We'll need to find somewhere big enough for all of us.' Ruby stuffed the last piece of pie into her mouth. 'Somewhere with a range so that she can make pies like this. I don't care how dangerous she is. She cooks like an angel.'

An hour later everyone was settled in varying degrees of comfort. Molly had been tucked up in a drawer taken out of the chest, and Teddy lay on a palliasse provided by a reluctant Ruth, who had not been very welcoming when Lottie went to ask the favour. May had been friendlier, but it was clear that neither of them welcomed the prospect of having another servant to share the few perks they enjoyed. May warmed a little when Lottie assured her that she had no intention of returning to work at The Swan, and she admitted that both she and Ruth were worried for their jobs as the mail

273

coach trade was declining rapidly.

Lottie lay beside Ruby, who was snoring softly. It was hot and stuffy in the small room and she could not sleep for worrying about what they would do next. She had hoped for a day or two's respite while she looked for work and somewhere to live, but that was now out of the question. Memories came flooding in during the lonely night hours. The pain of losing Gideon was never far away, but now it was less acute and part of her stubbornly refused to let him go. If she closed her eyes she could see his face as clearly as if he were in the room with her, but when she opened them again she knew there would be just a darkness. There was perhaps only one other woman who felt the same sense of loss and that was Gideon's mother. She would be in as much need of comfort as Lottie herself, and Lottie knew then what she must do before anything else.

'I don't see why we've come here,' Jezebel grumbled. 'It would be cheaper if we went out Limehouse way.'

'This looks like a respectable lodging house,' Ruby said, glancing nervously over her shoulder. 'Whitechapel isn't as rough as Limehouse or Seven Dials.'

'We can't afford to be fussy.' Lottie took a deep breath and knocked on the door. She had not told the others the reason for coming to this place; if she mentioned Gideon's name she was afraid she would break down and cry, but this was not the time to show weakness. She must be positive, but as she heard approaching footsteps and the click of the key turning in the lock, she had to curb the sudden urge to run away. But it was too late. The door opened.

'Yes? Can I help you?' The woman facing her might once have been pretty, but she looked tired and drained of all colour.

'I was wondering if you had a couple of rooms to let.'

'I don't know. I haven't been very well recently and there aren't any rooms ready.'

Jezebel pushed forward. 'Look, lady, either you rent out rooms or you don't. If your rates are reasonable we don't mind a bit of mess.'

A group of ragged boys had gathered around them, pointing at Jezebel's ungainly figure. She was wearing her Sunday best, which might have been the height of fashion twenty or thirty years ago, but now looked tawdry and out of place. Jezebel turned on them, fists clenched. 'If you've got something to say, say it to me face.'

The boys backed away, their grins fading.

'Come in. They're a rough lot round here.' The woman stepped aside and Lottie entered the house, followed by the others, with Jezebel and Lad bringing up the rear.

'That's kind of you,' Lottie said hesitantly, 'but we don't know yet if we can afford to lodge here.'

'I know who you are, dear.'

Lottie stared at her in amazement. 'You do?'

'Gideon wrote to me, telling me all about you, and I would have known you from his description.' Mrs Ellis's voice broke on a sob and she wiped her eyes on her apron. 'You'll have to excuse me, Lottie. I'm still a bit upset.'

Lottie felt like crying too, and she would have given Gideon's mother a comforting hug, but everyone had crowded into the narrow entrance hall and Molly had begun to whimper. 'Of course you are, and so am I. I wanted to meet you anyway, but circumstances have forced us to come looking for accommodation. Gideon told me that you took in lodgers, and that's why we're here.'

'I don't think I can help you, but come into the parlour anyway.' Mrs Ellis backed into the dark corridor, almost disappearing in the gloom.

Cobwebs hung from the ceiling and the air was thick with dust. A basket of dirty washing had been abandoned at the foot of the stairs and it seemed as if the whole house had gone into deep mourning.

'That ain't the way to bargain,' Jezebel hissed in Lottie's ear. 'The place is a midden and she should pay us to stay here.'

Lottie shot her a warning glance. 'Hush, she'll hear you.'

'The place smells worse than the fish dock at low tide,' Jezebel grumbled.

'Do move on, Jezebel,' Ruby said impatiently. 'Baby is crying and I don't like the look of those street Arabs.'

Teddy pushed past them. 'It looks all right to me. I don't fancy sleeping rough in London.'

'You're right, Teddy. I agree entirely.' Lottie followed Mrs Ellis into the parlour, where an effort had been made to keep it reasonably clean and tidy. The well-worn furniture gave the shabby room a homely, lived-in look and a fire smouldered in the grate. Lottie was drawn to a daguerreotype in pride of place on the mantelshelf, and her eyes filled with tears.

'Yes, that's my boy.' Mrs Ellis's hazel eyes shone with pride.

For the first time Lottie could see a likeness between Gideon and his mother, and a wave of emotion threatened to get the better of her, momentarily robbing her of speech, but Teddy had spotted a military shako in the midst of a clutter of ornaments on a shelf and he pounced on it.

'I'm a soldier, missis,' he said proudly. 'I was a drummer boy with the 97th until me arm got broken, but I'm going back to the Crimea when it's healed.'

Mrs Ellis turned to him, her face contorted with pain. 'Don't throw your young life away, son. I lost my husband and my boy in battle. Haven't you got a ma somewhere who's waiting for you, as I waited for my Gideon?'

'No, ma'am. I'm an orphan, but I got family now.' Teddy slipped his hand into Lottie's. 'We're sticking together no matter what. Ain't that a fact, Lottie?'

She smiled down at him. 'It most certainly is.' She glanced at Ruby, who was cuddling Molly in a vain attempt to stop her crying. They needed a roof over their heads and Gideon's mother seemed lost and lonely. Perhaps they could help each other through this bleak time in their lives. 'We'll take what you have to offer, Mrs Ellis.'

'I stopped taking in lodgers when I received news of Gideon's demise.' Mrs Ellis sighed and she turned her head away. 'I let things go because I couldn't see the point of carrying on, but now you're here you might as well stay, although for how long I don't know. I'm thinking seriously of giving up my tenancy. I can't afford to live here unless I fill all the rooms. Gideon used to send me money...' She broke off, holding her hanky to her eyes.

'How much do you charge?' Jezebel demanded. 'It's all very well for you, missis, but we're looking for work and ain't too flush with the readies at the moment.'

Mrs Ellis sniffed and cleared her throat. 'I'm sure we can come to an agreement. I'm not much of a businesswoman, and I've had difficulty in getting my thoughts together since...'

Lottie laid her hand on Mrs Ellis's arm. 'We understand, and we'll try to help out.'

'Speak for yourself,' Jezebel said in an undertone, but just loud enough for all to hear.

'Lottie's right. It seems that we're all in a similar fix and we need to help each other.' Ruby sank down in a saggy, but comfortable-looking armchair by the hearth. 'If you don't mind I'll give Molly her feed?'

'No, dear, of course not. You must look after your baby.' Mrs Ellis seized a cushion and placed it behind Ruby's back. 'Are you a widow, too?'

Ruby nodded and her bottom lip trembled. 'I am, ma'am.'

'Please call me Grace, and you are...?'

'I'm Ruby and this is Molly, only she's not my child.'

'It's a long story, Grace,' Lottie said, making a move towards the door. 'Perhaps you could show us our rooms? I'm quite happy to share with

278

Ruby and the baby.'

'Well, I'm not sharing with anyone, except Lad.' Jezebel glared at Grace as if daring her to argue.

'I don't mind sharing with Lad,' Teddy said cheerfully. 'I'm used to bivouacking and sleeping under the stars, but that don't include dossing down on cold pavements.'

'I'm sure you are a brave soldier.' Grace beamed at him and for a moment she looked almost pretty. 'You're just like my Gideon was at your age. Come with me and we'll see what we can do.'

The building consisted of three storeys, and a basement. Lottie chose a room on the first floor, furnished with a single bed, a large oak chest of drawers and a washstand that had lost one caster and leaned at a precarious angle. The bare floorboards creaked beneath her feet and spiders' webs festooned the ceiling, but there were two tall windows overlooking the back yard and it would be reasonably quiet at night. Ruby and Molly were in the front room on the top floor and that left a small boxroom for Teddy, who was delighted to have his own space and a bed instead of a palliasse.

Jezebel took the front room. 'This'll do me nicely.'

Lottie noted the double bed and the mahogany dressing table with a triple mirror. 'Isn't this your room, Grace?'

'It was, dear, but when my husband died I moved down to the basement. It's warmer in winter and I'm close to the kitchen. It meant that I had more rooms to let, and I haven't seen the need to move upstairs.'

'How much?' Jezebel demanded as they descended the stairs.

Grace came to a halt when she reached the entrance hall. 'Shall we say sixpence a night, with extra for baths?'

'We could get lodgings for fourpence close by,' Jezebel said gruffly.

'And you'd have to share your room with several others, and your bed, too.' Grace glanced at Lottie with a hint of a smile. 'I'd have you to stay for nothing if I were a rich woman, but I'm as poor as a church mouse now, so I'm afraid I have to make a charge or I can't pay the rent and we'll all be out on the street.'

Lottie hurried to her side. 'Of course we must give you what you need. It's good of you to allow us to stay. I wasn't expecting such generosity; after all, you don't know me, or any of us, come to that.'

'But, my dear, I feel that I know you very well indeed. If Gideon loved you then so must I – there's nothing more to be said on the subject – and I feel better now than I have done for weeks, if not months. I'd sooner have you and your friends than complete strangers living in my house. I've had some odd lodgers, I can tell you, and some of them were more trouble than they were worth.'

'All this talk,' Jezebel grumbled. 'I'm hungry and thirsty. Where's the kitchen, missis? If you ain't prepared to turn your hand to feeding us, then I suppose it falls to me.'

Grace opened her mouth as if to speak and then closed it.

'Jezebel is an excellent cook,' Lottie said hastily. 'Her pies are unequalled and we're all prepared to help out. I have to find work, but I'll wash and clean and do anything I can to help.'

'Gideon said you were an angel, Lottie,' Grace said with a tremulous smile. 'I'm beginning to think he was right.'

Jezebel took over the kitchen, refusing to allow Grace into the room until she had reorganised everything to suit herself. The larder was bare, except for a sprinkling of dead flies that had probably died of starvation, and the mice had resorted to chewing the skirting boards. Jezebel sent Teddy out to purchase carbolic soap and washing soda, giving him money from her own purse. With strict instructions to purchase only the bare necessities, Ruby went to market to buy the ingredients for supper, and Lottie took on the task of sweeping floors, cleaning grates and removing the thick layers of dust and smuts that had accumulated over the past weeks. With all this activity going on around her, Grace was given the task of looking after the baby, and she sat in a chair cradling Molly in her arms.

She looked up as Lottie entered the room with a fresh supply of cleaning cloths and a bucket of lukewarm water. 'You never said whose child this is. She's not yours, by any chance?'

Lottie almost dropped the pail. 'Good heavens, no. She's not mine by birth, but she is my responsibility now.'

'Her mother is dead?'

'Sadly, yes. But from the start she wanted nothing to do with Molly.'

'I can't believe that.' Grace stared at her in horror. 'What sort of mother would abandon her baby?'

Lottie could see that nothing would satisfy Grace other than the truth. She put the bucket down and pulled up a chair. 'I'd better start at the beginning...'

Grace listened intently. 'Well,' she said when Lottie finished speaking, 'the poor little mite.'

'She'll never know that she was unwanted.' Lottie reached out to stroke Molly's downy head. 'She's much loved and she has a family who will take care of her.'

'Even so, you're not her flesh and blood, and Molly must have some relations living. From what you've told me they're rich and important – they could give her everything that you can't.'

'I hadn't thought about it like that,' Lottie said slowly. 'I suppose you're right.'

'I can see that you love her, but maybe you ought to seek out her mother's family and tell them what you've just told me. Do you know where to find them?'

'I only know that Lady Aurelia's maiden name was de Morgan.'

'There you are then,' Grace said triumphantly.

'I don't see how that helps. I wouldn't know where to start looking.'

'I could help you there, dear.' Grace's pale features became animated and her eyes sparkled. 'Before I married I was in service in a big house in Berkeley Square. One of the girls I worked with is now the housekeeper. We kept in touch until a year or so ago,' but there isn't much that Nancy doesn't know about the aristocracy.'

'Do you think she would know where to find the de Morgan family?'

'I'd be surprised if she did not.'

'Then could we go and see her? The longer I keep Molly, the harder it will be to give her up.'

'I haven't been far from the house for months, and I could do with a day out. What do you say we go tomorrow?'

Berkeley Square surpassed all Lottie's expectations of elegance and grandeur. The gated gardens were a green oasis, shaded by tall plane trees. Sparrows and pigeons wandered the lawns, pecking up minute pieces of food, and birds sang from the leafy branches, beneath which uniformed nannies sat and chatted while their small charges played around them. It was a scene far removed from the grim reality of Whitechapel, but Lottie did not have time to stand and admire the setting. Grace seemed to have thrown off the depression that dogged her at home and she marched up to the door of the servants' entrance.

'I had five years here, Lottie,' she said, smiling. 'It was hard work, but they were a good crowd, for the most part. Of course you always get one or two who spoil things.' She broke off as the door opened and a stern-faced footman gave them a stony stare.

'Good morning, James. I've come to see Mrs Dobson.'

'You'd better come in then, Mrs Ellis.' He stepped aside. 'You'll find her in her office or in the linen room.'

'Thank you.' Grace sailed past him. 'Come on, Lottie. This way.' She hurried along what seemed like a maze of passages. They were largely ignored by the servants who were going about their duties, although one or two of the older ones acknowledged Grace with a nod and a smile. 'Here we are.' She stopped and knocked on a door marked 'Housekeeper'.

'Come in.'

Grace entered with Lottie close on her heels. 'Nancy, how are you, love?'

Mrs Dobson, a plump woman in her mid-forties, took off her spectacles and her round face creased in a smile. 'Grace. This is a surprise.'

'I know. I've had little time for visiting, being busy with my lodgers, and then I didn't feel like seeing people after Gideon was taken from me.'

'Oh, my dear, I didn't know.' Mrs Dobson's smile faded. 'Do sit down.' She glanced at Lottie. 'I don't think we've met.'

'I'm sorry,' Grace said hastily. 'I'm forgetting my manners. This is Lottie Lane. She would have been my daughter-in-law if circumstances hadn't intervened.'

Lottie felt the blood rise to her cheeks. 'I don't know about that, Grace.'

'I'm certain of it, love. I know my son and he wasn't a ladies' man, but he thought highly of you.' Grace took her hanky from her reticule and blew her nose. 'I'm sorry, Nancy. You must think this very strange, but we came to ask your advice.' She turned to Lottie. 'Tell her what you told me yesterday.'

Lottie hesitated: it felt wrong to reveal Lady Aurelia's personal tragedy to a complete stranger, but Molly's future might be at stake, and she owed it to her to do everything in her power to make sure she had the best start in life. She took a deep breath and began at the beginning.

'Well, now,' Nancy said, when Lottie came to an end of her story. 'That's a tale, indeed.'

'But do you know of this family, Nancy?' Grace asked eagerly.

'As it happens, I do.' Nancy leaned her elbow on the desk, gazing intently at Lottie. 'Lord Aloysius de Morgan has an estate in Essex and a house in Grosvenor Square, not far from here. Lady Aurelia was a wild one, to be sure, although that would have been a little after your time, Grace. Her exploits were the talk of the servants' quarters some six or seven years ago. I think her father must have been relieved when she and the colonel were wed, even if he didn't approve of the match.'

'Give us the address, Nancy, and we'll go there directly.' Grace rose from her seat. 'This isn't going to be an easy thing for Lottie to do, so it must be done quickly, before she changes her mind.'

An hour later, Lottie emerged from the house in Grosvenor Square with Lord Aloysius de Morgan's words ringing in her ears.

Grace hurried up to her. 'What did he say?'

Lottie leaned against the iron railings, fanning her hot cheeks with her hand. 'I don't wonder that Lady Aurelia wanted to leave home. He's a horrible man.'

'Wasn't he interested in his granddaughter?'

'He just didn't believe me, Grace. He accused me of trying to extort money from him under false pretences. He even threatened to call a constable and have me arrested.'

'But surely you explained the circumstances of Molly's birth?'

'He simply didn't want to know. He said if it were even partly true it was Colonel Dashwood's responsibility, not his. If you ask me, Molly is better off living in the East End with us than she would be in that mansion with a hateful grandfather.'

'You tried, love,' Grace said softly. 'You did your best and it's his loss.'

'Maybe one day, when Molly is older and he can see the likeness to Lady Aurelia, he'll change his mind.'

'And maybe that pig you told me about, Lady Petunia, will fly.' Grace proffered her arm. 'Come on, Lottie. Let's go home.'

Chapter Seventeen

The house in Leman Street seemed to have come back to life after dying slowly from misery and neglect. Grace herself flowered amongst the company of women and children, and helping to care for Molly seemed to have given her a new purpose in life, but after a few weeks it was becoming clear to Lottie that their finances were in a desperate state. Grace received some money from the newly formed Patriotic Fund, but Ruby had only just applied for assistance, and the small amount of her husband's back wages paid by the army had all but run out. Lottie had gone through most of the money she had earned, and Teddy had spent the last of his pay on mint humbugs and toffee. Jezebel had saved as much as she could from the meagre amount she received from the Filbys, but that too was running low, and they had to find money for the rent.

Grace had been only too willing to give up some of her responsibility in the running of the house, and Lottie had been put in charge of the housekeeping. With the rent collector due in two days, she was only too well aware that they could not go on as they were. She raised the subject at breakfast. 'We're two shillings short. Grace says that the rent collector isn't sympathetic to those who can't pay in full. We have to find the money somewhere.'

'I've sold most of my valuables,' Grace said sadly. 'It will be the furniture next, and it's not worth much.'

Jezebel rose to her feet. 'I ain't related to any of you, so I'm the odd one out. I should leave and look for work as a cook.'

'You are as much a part of the family as any of us,' Lottie said stoutly. 'And Lad, too. We're all in this together. Don't you agree, Grace? It's your house, after all.'

'Having you all here has meant so much to me.' Grace's bottom lip trembled and her eyes brimmed with tears. 'You'll never know what a difference it's made. You are all connected in one way or another with my boy, and I feel as though he's still with me when you're here. I don't want to go back to living with strangers.'

'There must be a way to earn money quickly–' Ruby broke off as she caught Lottie's eye and her cheeks reddened.

'That would definitely be a last resort,' Lottie said, chuckling.

'I didn't mean that sort of thing. Shame on you, Lottie.'

'What are you talking about?' Teddy demanded, looking from one to the other. 'What's funny?'

'Nothing, boy. Little pitchers have big ears.' Jezebel sent a warning look in Lottie's direction. She pushed her untouched bowl of gruel across the table. 'I ain't hungry, but it's a shame to put good food to waste.'

Teddy grabbed the bowl and spooned the gruel into his mouth, curiosity apparently forgotten.

'You are a splendid cook, Jezebel,' Lottie said slowly. 'We always said your pies were the best in London. You could work anywhere.'

'I'll second that.' Ruby rose from the table and went to lift Molly from the wooden crate which served as a makeshift cradle. 'I never tasted the like of the eel pie and mash you cooked for us last week.'

'I would gladly go out and sell your pies in the street, if you could make enough,' Lottie said eagerly. 'If we could raise two shillings it would give us another month to find work.'

'I can't make pies without the ingredients.' Jezebel reached for her pipe and tobacco pouch. 'This is the last of my baccy. You'd all best watch out for me when I goes without a smoke. I get bad-tempered and likely to swipe anyone who crosses me.'

Grace stared at her in surprise. 'You don't mean it, Jezebel.'

'Indeed I do. Find me the makings and I'll bake pies until I drop. All I want in return is a pouch filled with baccy, and I'll be a happy woman.'

Teddy licked his spoon clean. 'If you want eels, I'm your man.'

Everyone turned to stare at him and even Molly was quiet.

'What are you saying, Teddy?' Lottie snatched the spoon from him. 'Can you really help?'

'I can catch eels, although I might need a bit of help until the splint comes off me arm.'

'Are you making it up, boy?' Jezebel demanded, scowling.

'No, miss. Honest, I ain't. Me and some of the boys from the foundling home used to sneak out at night and set a trap to catch eels, and if we was lucky we could get a few pennies for them in the market next day.'

'How did you manage that?' Lottie asked.

'We filled a sack with straw and put in some bait. Weighted it with a brick and tethered it so that the tide wouldn't take it away, and at first light we was down there hauling it in filled with eels.'

'You're not making this up, are you, Teddy?' Lottie gave him a stern look. Teddy had a vivid imagination and she wanted to be sure that this was not one of his tales.

'No, Lottie. As if I would.'

'I believe you,' Ruby said gently.

'It's worth a try.' Lottie turned to Jezebel. 'If Teddy could catch enough eels, what else would you need?'

Jezebel abandoned her pipe and did a quick calculation. 'Flour, lard, parsley and salt. I should be able to get what I need for about a shilling. How much have we got?'

Lottie emptied the contents of her purse onto the table. 'Tenpence ha'penny.'

'That will have to do then.' Jezebel's hand shot out to take the coins. 'Get me the eels, boy, and leave the rest to me.' She stood up and went to the door, snatching up her shawl and a wicker basket on her way out.

'Are you sure you can do this, Teddy?' Lottie turned her purse upside down to make sure there were no farthings caught up in the lining. 'That was the last of our money.'

He puffed out his chest. 'I'm an expert, but it's going to be difficult with one arm. I'll need someone to help me.'

'I will,' Lottie said firmly.

Teddy stared at her, frowning. 'I dunno about that. Your long skirts would hamper you, Lottie. Sometimes I had to climb down ladders and wade in the mud, and we had to make a run for it.'

'But it's not against the law to fish for eels, is it?'

'No, but we might be mistaken for river pirates.'

This made Lottie laugh. 'Do I look like a pirate?'

'No, Lottie, but there's all sorts roaming round the docks at night, and you wouldn't be safe. I couldn't do much to help with one arm out of action.'

Lottie was about to say that she could look after herself when Grace forestalled her.

'I kept some of the clothes that Gideon wore when he was a lad not much older than you, Teddy. I'd forgotten all about them until I was looking for extra blankets for all of you.'

'Are you suggesting that I dress up as a boy?' Lottie demanded, torn between dismay and laughter.

'It will be dark.' Grace rose to her feet. 'If you want to try them on I've got them in my room.'

It was a moonless night and rain had been falling steadily for hours. Lottie felt self-conscious but strangely comfortable in the clothes that Gideon had worn ten or more years ago. She felt closer to him now than at any time since the tragic news of his death. Besides which, the freedom that trousers gave when walking was quite astonishing and almost indecent, when compared to layers of petticoats and long skirts. Her hair was crammed into a peaked cap and she wore a pair of old boots that would have benefited from the attention of a cobbler, and would almost certainly leak. Teddy walked on ahead with a sack filled with straw and offal picked up from the gutter, which he said was the ideal bait. Lottie was certain that people would see through her disguise, but to her surprise she did not receive a second glance. It was as if she had suddenly become invisible, and she began to feel more confident.

It was not a pleasant walk to the docks. Huge puddles glistened like lakes and the cobblestones were slippery with mud and the filth washed up from overflowing gutters, but they reached the Hermitage Basin eventually, and Teddy found what he considered to be a good spot. With Lottie's help he tied the sack tightly and they weighted it with a brick he had collected on the way, and dropped it over the wall. Lottie watched it sink into the murky blackness, and Teddy secured his end of the rope.

'There now,' he said triumphantly. 'We'll come back first thing and see what we've caught.'

'Are you sure that was a good place?' Lottie asked as they hurried homeward. 'We'll be in desperate trouble if there are no eels.'

'Trust me, Lottie. I know what I'm doing.' He gave her a cheeky grin and swaggered along the street, hands in pockets.

Lottie barely slept that night. She had not laboured the point to Teddy, but their future depended on their catch. She was up before dawn and dressed when she went to wake Teddy. He grumbled, but raised himself from his warm bed and followed her downstairs.

It was still dark, although a thin pale line in the east heralded an early dawn. They walked quickly and in silence. Lottie tried to be positive, but the thought of returning home empty-handed was too terrible to contemplate. Eel pie was the only thing that stood between them and penury. Teddy did not seem to share her anxiety and he bounded along with Lad trotting at his side. The small mongrel followed Teddy everywhere, although Lottie suspected that Jezebel was slightly jealous of her dog's obvious affection for the boy, but it was good to see Teddy cheerful again. Leaving the army had hit him hard, and living in an all-female household must seem strange to a boy who had been raised in an orphanage and sent into the army at such a young age. Lottie picked up her skirts and ran in an attempt to keep up with him.

It was just getting light when they reached Hermitage Basin. 'The rope is still tethered,' Teddy called over his shoulder. 'It's heavy. I'll need a hand to pull it up.'

Lottie was at his side and they worked together, heaving the waterlogged sack from the depths. As the water drained away the sack began to move of its own accord.

'We've got some,' Teddy cried triumphantly. 'Pull harder, Lottie. Let's see what we've caught.'

Eventually the writhing sack lay on the ground at their feet. Teddy kneeled down and traced the shapes with his fingers. 'I can't say exactly, but there's several big ones in there. Help me get it onto my back, Lottie, and we'll get them home before daylight.'

Jezebel took on the task of dispatching the eels, which she did in the back yard, out of the view of sensitive souls like Grace and Ruby. Lottie built up the fire in the range, and within an hour the eels were simmering in parsley liquor and Jezebel was making the pastry. The aroma of cooking filled the house, but the family had to make do with tea and dry toast for their breakfast.

Lottie was eager to go out selling the pies, and as soon as the first batch came out of the oven she placed them on a wooden tray and set off to hawk them round the streets. It was almost noon and by the time she reached the Sailors' Home in Dock Street she had sold everything. She hurried back to the house to collect the next batch, and went out again. This time she was accompanied by Teddy and Lad, and again she sold out quickly. She returned home with a purse filled with pennies and an empty tray.

'How many pies were there, Jezebel?' Lottie asked as she spilled the coins onto the kitchen table. 'I lost count.'

'I made three dozen, and I've kept the liquor,' Jezebel said proudly. 'It will set into jelly and that always sells well. A cup of eel liquor jelly will fetch a penny.'

Lottie counted out the money. 'Six shillings. We've enough for the rent and we can fill the larder.' She turned to hug Teddy. 'And all because of you, soldier. You are a great eel catcher.'

Teddy blushed scarlet and hung his head. 'It were nothing. I could catch more tonight.'

'That's the spirit, mate.' Jezebel slapped him on the back. 'I never had much use for boys but I'll make an exception in your case.'

'Yes, well done, both of you,' Grace said, smiling. 'I can't thank you enough.'

'And we can eat now,' Ruby added with a sigh of relief. 'I didn't want to grumble, but I am starving.'

Lottie picked up some of the coins and put them back in her purse. 'Come with me, Ruby. We'll go to market and get what we need to keep us going until tomorrow.'

'Don't forget the flour, parsley and lard.' Jezebel reached for her pipe and pouch. 'I work better if I have baccy. Can we run to half an ounce, just to keep me going?'

'I think you've earned it several times over,' Lottie said, smiling.

'I can make twice as many tomorrow if the boy catches more eels.' Jezebel slumped down on the chair by the open window.

'It looks as though I'll be wearing Gideon's old clothes again tonight,' Lottie said, chuckling.

Over the next few weeks they slipped into a routine: laying the trap for the eels, moving it from the docks to a different wharf each night, and retrieving the squirming sack filled with eels at dawn. Jezebel baked the pies and Lottie sold them with Teddy and Lad at her side, ready to protect her should the need arise. Business boomed and customers flocked to purchase the hot pies and cups of eel liquor and jellied stock. Teddy found an old handcart abandoned on the foreshore that was about to be dragged off by a couple of mudlarks, who said they were going to chop it up for firewood. Teddy gave them sixpence and trundled it back to Leman Street where he set about repairing the damage, but it proved beyond his capabilities and he was on the point of giving up despite encouragement from Lottie.

She found him in the back yard with an axe raised above the broken wheel. 'Don't,' she cried. 'You've done so well until now, Teddy.'

He dropped his arm to his side. 'I can't fix it, Lottie. It's a waste of time.'

'Nonsense. I think you've done a splendid job so

far.' She took the axe from his hand and placed it on the chopping block. 'I know someone who might be able to help.'

'Really?'

'You met my friend Jem at the place where I used to work. He might be able to show you what to do. As I recall, he did most of the odd jobs and he could turn his hand to anything. Will you come with me?'

'I suppose we could do with another man around the house,' Teddy said warily.

Lottie smiled. 'I wasn't going to ask him to move in, but he's a useful chap to know.'

Jem greeted Lottie with a wide grin. 'I didn't expect to see you back so soon, girl. Are you looking for work?'

'No, I'm not.' Lottie slipped her arm around Teddy's shoulders. 'You'll recall meeting this wounded soldier?'

Jem pushed his cap to the back of his head. 'I most certainly do.'

'Teddy was a drummer boy with the 97th regiment,' Lottie said proudly. 'He was injured in battle and he's a very brave young man.'

Jem shook Teddy's hand. 'What can I do for you, Teddy?'

'Can you mend a broken wheel?'

'I can mend anything,' Jem said laughing. 'What's in it for me?'

Teddy put his head on one side, eyeing him thoughtfully. 'Do you like eel pie?'

'I'm very partial to an eel pie, but I ain't had a decent one for a long time.'

'Jezebel makes the best pies in London,' Teddy said proudly. 'And I catch the eels.'

'So I get paid in eel pies. That seems a fair exchange for doing a bit of carpentry.' Jem glanced over his shoulder at the sound of Mrs Filby's shrill voice.

'Get on with your work, Jem Barker, you lazy good-for-nothing.'

Lottie did not look round. A clash with her former employer was to be avoided at all costs. 'I see nothing has changed here, Jem,' she said in a low voice. 'I don't know how you stand it.'

At that moment Ruth emerged from the scullery and raced across the yard, head down.

'It gets worse,' Jem said, sighing. 'I can see the mail coach trade disappearing before long. We aren't nearly as busy as we used to be.'

'Does that mean you could spare some time to come home with us?' Lottie asked eagerly. 'I'm sure we'd all be grateful if you could give Teddy some assistance. He's trying to mend a handcart to make things easier for me when I go out selling pies.'

'I dare say I can get off for an hour or two without her ladyship throwing a fit. Where are you living, girl?'

'Whitechapel.'

He frowned. 'That's not a good place.'

'It's all we can afford, and we're lucky to have a roof over our heads. I'm not complaining.'

'No,' Jem said with a wry grin, 'you never do.' He took off his leather apron. 'All right then, let's go to Whitechapel and I'll see what I can do for you, soldier.'

Teddy snapped to attention and saluted. 'Thank you, sir.'

'That's the first time anyone has called me sir,' Jem said, laughing. 'I like you, Teddy. I can see that the two of us are going to be good mates.' He tossed his apron to one of the ostlers who had just come from the taproom. 'Tell the old man that I'm taking an hour or two off. It's only what I'm owed, and I'll be back before the mail coach from Bath arrives.' He proffered his arm to Lottie. 'This is like old times, girl. Let's go.'

Between them, Jem and Teddy managed to get the cart roadworthy, and during the next few months Jem became a regular visitor to the house in Leman Street. He treated Teddy like a younger brother, and it was obvious to Lottie that he provided the boy with much-needed male influence and encouragement. Jem came on his half-day off, and on these occasions he joined Teddy in his nightly trip to the foreshore to set his eel trap. Sometimes, when trade was slack at The Swan, Jem stayed the night. He slept in the attic room, once the domain of a maid of all work, and he was always up before anyone else, ready to accompany Teddy to the river to haul in the catch. Lottie had never seen her old friend looking happier or more relaxed than he was when he joined them round the table at mealtimes. He was Teddy's idol and Grace's pet, and Lottie suspected that Ruby was developing tender feelings for Jem, despite her blushing protests that she was still in mourning for her late husband. But Lottie was not easily fooled, and although Jem treated Ruby with his usual good humour, she thought she detected something more than friendliness in his manner when he spoke to Ruby. There was a gentler tone to his voice, and he tried his best to bring a smile to her face and worked even harder to make her laugh.

Jezebel had always had a soft spot for Jem, and he praised her cooking and ate her food with obvious relish. His only complaint was that he would grow fat and lazy if she continued to give him extra helpings of pie and mash, and her new speciality – jellied eels. He was, she said, her official taster, and his approval meant that the dish would go down well with the public. Lottie was content with her adopted family around her, but there was a void in her heart that she knew would remain there for the rest of her life. Her brief time with Gideon was a precious memory, and no one could take his place.

On a chilly November evening, when the city streets had been blotted out by a peasouper, Jem had little option but to stay, although he needed hardly any persuasion. They were all seated around the kitchen table having just finished their meal, and Jem was polishing off a second helping of eel pie and mash drenched in liquor.

'This is good grub, Jezebel,' he said, licking his lips. 'The Filbys were stupid to let you go.'

Jezebel shrugged. 'There weren't nothing they could say or do that would make me stay there a minute longer.' She bent down to stroke Lad, who had momentarily abandoned Teddy to sit at her side. 'It was lucky for me that I ended up here.'

'Lucky for us, too,' Grace said earnestly, 'and for me in particular. Having the girls here has made my life as complete as it can be without my son.' She smiled mistily. 'Gideon would have been so proud of you, Lottie.'

'I don't know where I would have been without you either, Lottie,' Ruby agreed wholeheartedly. 'I might have ended up in the workhouse, but for you. As for little Molly,' she shuddered dramatically, 'the poor baby would have been left in an orphanage somewhere in the Crimea. As it is, she's sitting up and taking notice, and before we know it she'll be starting to crawl.'

'I just wish that her real family would acknowledge her existence. She ought to be brought up as a lady with all the advantages that wealth and position would have given her.' Lottie picked up the teapot. 'More tea, Grace?'

Grace shook her head. 'You're talking nonsense,' she said sharply. 'That child has got people who love her and want the best for her. That's all that matters in this life, and it's due mainly to you.'

Lottie turned away to hide her blushes. 'Thank you, but that's not true. It's been a joint effort. We've all put everything we've got into making a home for us and we've all worked hard to earn a living.'

Jem scraped the last of the mashed potato and parsley sauce into his mouth. 'This food should be available to all the people in the East End and beyond. You ought to open a pie and mash shop.' He looked up and met Lottie's sceptical glance with a serious face. 'I mean it. You'd make a fortune with food like this.'

'That's all very well, Jem, but it would take money to start up in business,' Lottie said slowly.

'It's a good idea but where would we find the wherewithal?'

'We make a tidy living the way we are,' Jezebel added. 'I work all hours now; I couldn't do much more.'

'You would have to run it in a different way.' Jem raised his cup to his lips and sipped the tea. 'We're open day and night at The Swan, and we manage somehow.'

Lottie pulled a face. 'That's true, but it isn't much of a life. You're always saying that you'd like to get away from the Filbys.'

He put down his cup, his expression serious for once. 'I've been thinking, and this concerns all of you, so I'd like to say it now before I lose courage.'

'Good heavens, what can it be?' Grace asked, laughing. 'You're never serious, Jem.'

Jezebel blew a stream of smoke into the air. 'Spit it out, boy.'

'All right, I will.' Jem cleared his throat. 'I've got some money saved. It's not a fortune but it's always been my plan to leave the Filbys when I could afford to start a business of my own. I don't intend to be a potboy all my life. I'm twenty-four now and not getting any younger.'

'You ain't leaving us, are you, Jem?' Teddy jumped to his feet. 'You can't do that. We're partners, you said so.'

Jem reached out to ruffle Teddy's curly mop. 'That's not what I had in mind, soldier.'

'We wouldn't want you to stop visiting us.' Ruby's cheeks flamed and she bit her lip. 'I mean, it would be hard on Teddy, and we'd all miss you.'

'Would you, Ruby?' Jem's smile faded and he

met her flustered gaze with a questioning look.

Lottie could see that her friend was overcome and she laid her hand on Ruby's shoulder. 'Of course she would, Jem. You're one of us, so what's this all about? What are you trying to say?'

Chapter Eighteen

Jem looked round at their expectant faces and a wide grin almost split his face in two. 'I was walking along Aldgate High Street when I saw a likely-looking premises. I made enquiries and I think it's just the place for a pie and mash shop. There's a kitchen of sorts, and living accommodation above.'

There was a moment of silence. Lottie was the first to speak. 'What exactly are you suggesting, Jem?'

'I have enough saved to pay the rent for the first month, and the cost of setting up the business in a modest way. I could do most of the work,' he winked at Teddy, 'with the help of my mate.'

'I say yes,' Teddy said excitedly. 'Me and Jem can do anything we set our minds to.'

'But you wouldn't leave me alone here, would you?' Grace looked from one to the other. 'You wouldn't desert me?'

'Of course not,' Jem said firmly. 'This is just an idea at the moment. We would have to take a look at the place and it would be up to Jezebel to say if it was a good proposition, or not.'

Jezebel puffed on her pipe, frowning thought-fully. 'I'd need to have a look at the kitchen. I've got all my things round me here and I know what I'm doing.'

'I could help, if Grace would look after Molly,' Ruby said eagerly.

Lottie did not want to crush Jem's hopes, but she could see problems with his plan. 'Who would live above the shop?'

'I was thinking it would be my home. I've learned a lot about running a business during my time at The Swan, and I won't always be single,' Jem shot a sideways glance at Ruby. 'There's room to bring up a family.'

'I'm sure I don't know why you're looking at me, Jem Barker,' Ruby said primly.

'I meant no offence, but it is a simple truth.'

'I'll have to catch more eels,' Teddy said enthusiastically. 'But I don't fancy dragging a sack of wriggling creatures all the way to the High Street.'

Lottie could see that Ruby was discomforted by Jem's casual remark. It had been obvious from the start that they were attracted to each other, but this was not the time to bare personal feelings. 'It's a good idea, Jem,' she said slowly, 'but it wouldn't serve us all. You're thinking in a grand manner, but we all have to live off the profits and I doubt if enough could be earned to keep two establishments going. Your money would dwindle and you'd be investing in nothing.'

'But I'd share everything out equally.' Jem slumped down on his seat. 'I thought it was a splendid plan.'

'It is, Jem.' Ruby leaped to her feet and went to

stand beside him. 'I say we should think it over properly. If Jem is generous enough to put his own money into the venture, what have we got to lose?'

'So that's the way of it.' Jezebel pointed the stem of her clay pipe at them. 'You want to set up house together and we're to provide the means to pay for it.'

Lottie shook her head. 'We mustn't allow this to turn into a battle. I think Jem's idea is a good one, but maybe this isn't the right time. Or perhaps you could do it on your own, Jem?'

'He wouldn't be on his own,' Ruby faced them all with a defiant lift of her chin. 'I'd help him. I believe in him.'

'You're moonstruck, girl,' Grace said angrily. 'Lottie is right. We can't split the business in two. Jezebel would have to choose one or the other of us, and it's not fair to put her in that position.'

Jezebel nodded. 'I don't fancy living above no shop. I done it for years when I worked for other people, and all due respect to you, Jem, you're a good chap, but I don't fancy playing gooseberry with you and her.' She jerked her head in Ruby's direction. 'Don't deny it, the pair of you. We've all seen it coming and good luck to you, but I'm content to stay here and work with my mates. We've got a good little business here and we don't want for nothing.'

'I thought I had the answer to everything. I really did.' Jem managed an apologetic smile. 'I'm sorry if it came out wrong, but I meant to share the profits with all of you.'

'I know you did, Lottie said hastily. 'But I doubt if there would be enough to give you a profit on your investment. You might even end up losing money.'

'Then I might as well stay on at The Swan.' Jem patted Ruby's hand as it lay on his shoulder. 'I was going to ask you to step out with me if things had worked out, girl, but I'm not in a position to pay court to you at the moment.'

'See what you've all done now.' Ruby's eyes filled with tears and she fled from the room. Jem was about to follow her but Lottie rose swiftly to her feet and barred his way.

'Wait a moment. I think I might have the solution.'

'She's very upset,' Jem said anxiously. 'I shouldn't have spoken out of turn.'

'Sit down, please, and hear me out.'

'Spit it out,' Jezebel emptied her pipe and refilled it from her pouch. 'I'm going to me room for a rest.'

'What I suggest is quite simple. I think Jem's idea of an eel pie and mash shop is a good one, so why don't we start in a small way and turn the front parlour into the eating area? If you'd like to invest some of your money in fitting it out, Jem, you could give up your job at The Swan and come and live here. If you and Teddy could provide and prepare the eels then Ruby and I will help Jezebel and serve in the shop. I need not go out peddling pies in the streets and you could use my barrow to transport the eels.' Lottie turned to Grace. 'All this would depend on whether or not you agree. This is your house, after all.'

Grace clapped her hands. 'I say yes. I don't know how I would manage without you here, and

I'm happy to continue taking care of Molly. I love her as if she was my own.'

'Jezebel?' Lottie eyed her warily. 'What do you say?'

'It suits me fine, especially the part where someone else prepares the eels. It's men's work anyway. I say yes.'

Lottie turned her attention to Teddy. 'You are the eel catcher. Do you agree to all this?'

'I'll say I do. I want Jem to come and live with us, so I say yes.'

'You are very important in this, Jem.' Lottie held her hand out to him. 'We can't do it without you, and it might prove a better investment than risking your money by taking on another property.'

Jem nodded. 'Maybe I jumped the gun a bit, Lottie. I get carried away with my ideas at times, but I think this is more practical. There's just one other person to ask.'

'And you're the man to do it,' Lottie said, smiling. 'Go to her, Jem. See what she has to say, although I'd be very surprised if she didn't agree.'

Later, when Lottie was about to get into bed, Ruby burst into the room without knocking. Her cheeks were flushed and her eyes sparkling. 'I'm sorry, but I had to speak to you.'

Lottie wrapped her shawl around her shoulders and climbed into bed. 'Come in and close the door. We don't want to wake Molly.'

'No, indeed, especially now she's started sleeping through the night.' Ruby perched on the edge of the bed. 'Jem and me had a long chat.'

'Thank goodness for that,' Lottie said, smiling.

'You don't think it's too soon, do you, Lottie?'

Ruby asked anxiously. 'It's not yet a year since Fletcher died, but maybe I should wait longer before I think of remarrying.'

'Really? Did Jem propose?'

Ruby looked away, blushing rosily. 'Not in so many words, but we've come to an understanding. Jem is very kind and patient.'

'I'm glad for your sake.'

'And you don't think it's a bad idea?'

Lottie reached out to grasp Ruby's hand. 'No, I don't. You know in your own heart if you're ready to let go of the past and move on. I just wish that I could do the same.'

'I'm so sorry. I keep forgetting that you've suffered a loss too.' Ruby raised Lottie's hand to her cheek. 'Here am I, going on about myself, quite forgetting you have your problems too.'

'We have to deal with things in our own way,' Lottie said, sighing. 'I still can't believe that Gideon is dead. I don't speak about it because it would upset Grace, but deep down I feel that he hasn't gone for ever.'

Ruby enveloped her in a hug. 'You're so brave, Lottie. We would all have been lost but for you.'

'Nonsense,' Lottie said briskly. 'You must stop worrying about me and grab happiness with both hands. I've known Jem since I was twelve and he was fifteen. He helped me through the difficult times and he's a good man. You couldn't do better.'

'Thank you. I know that in my heart, but I didn't want to do anything that might upset you. We've been through a lot together, you and me.'

'And the good times are to come.'

Ruby gave her a final hug before rising and going to the door. 'Good night, Lottie. You are such a comfort to me.'

She left the room and Lottie blew out the candle, but when she closed her eyes it was Gideon's face she could see, and he was smiling. 'You are still close to me,' she said in a whisper. 'I don't know where you are, but you are still in my heart and always will be.'

Jem left the Filbys and moved into the attic room in Leman Street. He began work straight away and within a fortnight the front parlour had been transformed into a pie shop with two long trestle tables and benches that could seat six aside. Crockery and cutlery were purchased and, in order to add cups of tea to the menu, a second-hand tin water boiler was installed in the wash-house at the back of the building. Jem and Ruby were now officially engaged and the banns were read, enabling them to name the date of their marriage. Grace was doubtful about their hurried wedding, but Lottie defended their decision.

'Why wait?' she said calmly when Grace brought up the subject one morning while they were helping Jezebel in the kitchen. 'Jem and Ruby are old enough to know their own minds, and living and working together as they are, it seems the sensible thing to do.'

'But people will think it's a knobstick wedding.'

'Let them tittle-tattle all they want,' Jezebel added. 'Life's too short to bother about what other people think.'

'I suppose you're right,' Grace said sadly. 'If my

boy had lived we might be celebrating your wedding, Lottie.'

Jezebel glared at her. 'Trust you to put your foot in it, old woman.'

'This is my house, you're just the cook,' Grace countered, bristling.

Lottie held her hands up, trying not to laugh at their verbal sparring. 'Grace is right, Jezebel. It could have been my wedding, but it isn't, so we must be happy for Ruby and Jem. I think they'll make a lovely couple.'

On Friday 28 December 1855, Jem and Ruby were married in St Mark's Church, Whitechapel, with their small family in attendance. Molly was vocal in her appreciation of the echo her cooing noises made in the vast building, and she wriggled so much that Lottie was in danger of dropping her. Jezebel came to the rescue and Molly quietened instantly, turning her attention instead to tugging at the strings of Jezebel's best bonnet.

It was a short service, but as the newly married couple walked out into the winter sunshine they encountered a street fight between a group of Irishmen and some Polish immigrants. Jem and Jezebel formed an impressive spearhead and led the party to the relative safety of Leman Street and the Brown Bear pub, but by this time Molly had begun to whimper.

'Let me take her home, Lottie,' Grace said, holding out her arms to take the crying child. 'The poor little thing is tired and hungry.'

Lottie relinquished her reluctantly. 'I should look after her, not you, Grace.'

'I could do with a sit-down in my own back parlour,' Grace said firmly. 'I'll give the baby some sops and put her down to sleep. You go and enjoy yourself with the young people, dear.'

'I won't be long, Grace. We'll share a glass of port after supper tonight.'

'I'll hold you to that, Lottie. I'm partial to a drop of port, and we can afford it now so I don't feel guilty.' She walked off, carrying Molly, who was protesting with loud howls.

Lottie followed the others into the Brown Bear and they took a table by the fire. Jem fetched their drinks and Jezebel raised her glass of porter.

'Here's to Jem and Ruby and long may they live in harmony.'

Lottie sipped the warm beer. 'This time next year we might be drinking a toast in champagne,' she said, smiling. 'Here's to you both, and to the success of the eel pie and mash shop.'

Jem slipped his arm around Ruby's shoulders and gave her a hug. 'I'm the luckiest man alive. Not only do I have a wonderful wife, but I've got a new family to love and protect.' He reached out to slap Teddy on the back. 'And a good mate. What d'you say, soldier?'

Teddy raised his glass. 'Here's to–' He broke off, staring at a group of military men who were standing at the bar. 'Lottie, look over there. Do you recognise that officer?'

Lottie peered through the haze of tobacco smoke, and her breath hitched in her throat. 'I do, Teddy. It's Tom Bonney.' She rose to her feet, emboldened by the alcohol, and made her way through the crowd. She tapped him on the shoulder. 'Lieutenant Bonney?'

He turned to face her and his startled expression melted into a smile. 'Miss Lane! I mean, Lottie, this is a pleasant surprise.'

'What are you doing here? I didn't think you were allowed leave from the battlefront.'

'Won't you introduce us to the lovely lady?' A moustachioed officer stepped in between them. 'You've kept this little beauty quiet, Tom.'

'That's enough, Sanderson. This lady is a friend of mine from the Crimea. She's a very brave woman,' Tom said coldly.

'I apologise, ma'am.' Sanderson acknowledged Lottie with a bow, and resumed his conversation with his comrades.

'I'm sorry, Lottie,' Tom said hastily. 'He meant no offence.'

'I don't suppose the ladies of his acquaintance frequent pubs in Whitechapel, and I wouldn't be here but for my friends' wedding. It's just a remarkable coincidence that you happened to be here at the same time.'

'I'm sorry to say that I'm in London on a sad mission. Colonel Dashwood was thrown from his horse and killed. I was charged with the duty of bringing his body home for burial.'

'I'm sorry,' Lottie said softly. 'Both of them dead now. That's very sad.'

He drew her aside. 'That's not exactly true, and the reason I'm here in Whitechapel is that I came to find you.'

'I don't understand.'

'Lady Aurelia wasn't killed as was previously thought, although she was badly injured in the

311

attack on the telegraph station. Part of my mission was to escort Lady Aurelia on her journey home.'

'She's alive?'

'Very much so, although sadly altered in appearance.'

'And the others?' Lottie clutched his arm. 'What happened to them?'

He shook his head. 'I think it best if you let her ladyship give you that information. She sent me to find you with that in mind.'

'Then I must see her as soon as possible.' Lottie held her hand to her forehead as a wave of dizziness threatened to overcome her. 'I'm sorry, Tom. I feel a bit faint.'

He guided her to a seat by the door. 'I should have broken the news more gently.'

'No, you did the right thing.' She sank down on the hard wooden seat and a gust of cold air blew in from the street as a patron staggered outside. She took a deep breath. 'I'm all right now, but I have so many questions.'

'Might I suggest a tot of brandy? You've had quite a shock.'

'No, thank you. Sit down and tell me everything. How did you know where to find me?'

He pulled up a chair. 'Lady Aurelia sent me to the inn where you used to work, and one of the ostlers told me to seek you out in this area. I was about to make enquiries from the barman when you tapped me on the arm. I could hardly believe my eyes.'

'As I just said, we came in here to celebrate a wedding. You remember Ruby Wagg? You introduced us back in the camp at Balaklava.'

'Yes, of course I do, and Drummer Miller as well. You seem to have taken the waifs and strays under your wing.'

'Not at all. We're a family and we take care of each other.' Lottie glanced at the wedding party and she smiled. 'We started with nothing, but we've worked hard and now we're in business and doing very well.'

'Really? You amaze me. What is it you do?'

'We began by selling pies in the streets round here, which were so popular that we opened an eel pie and mash shop. We're closed today, of course, but while you're in London you must come and taste Jezebel's famous pie and mash with lots of lovely liquor.'

'I've never tasted eel pie, but I can see I'll have to remedy that very soon. In the meantime I have to fulfil my obligation to Lady Aurelia. Will you come with me now?'

'It's Jem and Ruby's special day, but I'm sure they can do without me for an hour or two. Where is Lady Aurelia?'

'She's at home in Chatham, supervising the packing of her belongings.'

'Is she moving back to Bath?'

'I'm not sure what she has in mind. Anyway, it's for her to tell you, Lottie. She really wants to see you as soon as possible.'

'If she's in Chatham it will mean an overnight stay.' Lottie rose to her feet. The thought of seeing Aurelia again and being able to talk freely about Gideon without upsetting those around her had given her a sudden burst of energy and a flicker of hope that Gideon might somehow have survived the attack on the telegraph station. 'I'll just tell my family what's happening and then I'll go home and pack a few things.'

It was late afternoon when they arrived in Chatham, having travelled as far as they could by train, and completed the journey by road. The sight of the white house gleaming palely in the early dusk brought back a flood of memories, and Lottie's eyes smarted with unshed tears as she walked up the garden path. Tom knocked on the door and it was opened moments later by Hansford. Lottie was shocked to see that Colonel Dashwood's devoted servant seemed to have aged ten years in the months since they'd last met. Streaks of grey at his temples accentuated the lines of sorrow on his weather-beaten face. He stood to attention and saluted Lieutenant Bonney, but Tom waved the formality aside.

'There's no need for that, Hansford. This is a strictly informal visit.'

'Thank you, sir.' He held his hand out to take Lottie's valise. 'Welcome back, Miss Lane.'

'I was very sorry to hear of the colonel's tragic accident,' Lottie said gently. 'We did not part on the best of terms, but he was a good man.'

Hansford nodded and backed away, head bent. 'Lady Aurelia is in the drawing room, miss.'

'Thank you, Hansford.' Lottie followed Tom through the silent house that had once been her home. Now the atmosphere was heavy with sorrow as if even the bricks and mortar had gone into mourning.

The drawing room was in semi-darkness with

the curtains not yet drawn against the fading light, but it felt cold, despite the fire that blazed in the hearth. Aurelia had her back to them as she stood looking out of the window.

Lottie hesitated, not knowing what to say.

Tom cleared his throat. 'We're here, my lady.'

'I know that. I can see your reflection in the windowpanes,' Aurelia said slowly. 'Will you leave us, please, Tom?'

'Of course, my lady.' He gave Lottie an encouraging smile as he left the room.

'I was so happy to know that you were saved, my lady.' Lottie stood very still, unsure what was expected of her. 'I was very sorry to hear of the colonel's demise.'

'Were you?' Aurelia turned slowly to face her. 'I wasn't. Does that shock you?'

'No, my lady.'

'Perhaps it should. You are too used to my tempers and tantrums, Lottie. You know all there is to know about me.' Moving slowly and painfully she made her way to the sofa and eased herself onto the cushions.

'Not everything, my lady.' Emboldened, Lottie took a step closer, but Aurelia held up her hand.

'Look at me, Lottie. This is what war has done to me.' She turned to face Lottie and with the tip of her forefinger outlined the livid scar on her right cheek. 'I'm no longer a beauty. I am hideous to behold.'

Lottie went down on her knees in front of her. 'No, that's not true. You have suffered greatly, I can see that, but you will always be beautiful, my lady. The scar will fade in time.'

'This is the injury you can see, but the shrapnel tore into my flesh. We were left for dead and would have been so within hours had we not been found by the French, who took us to their own hospital.'

'You were saved, but what happened to those who were with you?' Lottie could not bring herself to mention Gideon by name. If she did so she might be condemning him to death all over again. Surely Lady Aurelia would put her out of her misery and tell her if Gideon were alive or dead?

Chapter Nineteen

'We were in the telegraph station,' Aurelia said, closing her eyes as if to shut out the horrific memories. 'We were laughing and talking and drinking wine when the mortar hit. I remember nothing until I came back to consciousness. I had no recollection of my illness, but they told me I had suffered a fever that almost finished what the bomb had failed to do.'

'The army informed us that you and everyone in the telegraph station had been killed, my lady.'

Aurelia reached for a small green bottle that looked very familiar. 'Laudanum,' she said, pouring a few drops into a glass of water. She took a sip. 'I need it for the pain.' She drank deeply. 'What was it that you asked?'

'What happened to the others?'

'Farrell and your man, Private Ellis, survived, but Private Benson was killed outright, or so I was told.'

Lottie rose to her feet, momentarily bereft of speech. Moving like a sleepwalker she made her way to the window and rested her forehead against the cool glass. Her senses were reeling. She wanted to shout for joy and yet tears flowed freely down her cheeks. 'You say that they are alive?'

'They were not so badly injured as I. They were sent back to camp.'

Lottie turned to face her. 'But if Gideon lives why wasn't I told? Why hasn't he written to me?'

'Pour me a tot of brandy, Lottie. My head hurts and my whole body aches. The memories are as painful as my wounds.'

'I'm sorry. I was forgetting your suffering, but I have endured agonies that you cannot imagine.' Lottie went to the table and poured a generous measure of brandy. She pressed the glass into Lady Aurelia's hand. 'I can see that you are in pain, but please tell me what happened to Gideon.'

'My husband saw to it that Farrell was punished and humiliated, which is why I cannot mourn Dashwood's passing. There was a hearing of sorts, and Farrell was given the choice of facing court-martial and dishonourable discharge or being dispatched to India. He was led to believe that I had died in the French hospital, and he accepted his punishment without question, or so Dashwood told me with obvious enjoyment.'

'But what happened to Gideon? He'd done nothing wrong.'

'He was deemed guilty by association. He and his comrade had given us shelter in the telegraph

317

station, although they had no choice in the matter. Farrell was the superior officer and they had to obey his orders. Farrell left for India three months ago and your man went with him.'

Lottie sank down on the nearest chair. It was too much to take in all at once. 'That seems so unfair, my lady.'

'If anyone was at fault it was I for encouraging Farrell to break the rules.'

'He loves you, my lady. He would have done anything for you.'

'And look where it led him. Disgrace and dishonour, and banishment from England for as long as the powers that be consider the suitable punishment for his crime of loving too much.'

'They will come home eventually, my lady.'

'I cannot wait for that, which is why I sent for you.'

'You're surely not thinking about travelling to India, are you?'

'That's exactly what I plan to do, and I want you to accompany me.' Aurelia turned her head so that Lottie could see the full extent of her injury. 'Do you think he will still love me when he sees this disfigured countenance?'

'If you doubt him, why put yourself through such an ordeal? Why not wait until you are stronger and more able to stand the long voyage?'

'You see, even you have your doubts. I need to test Farrell's love for me. I want to know if it's me he wants, or my money.'

'How can you doubt him, my lady? He risked everything to be with you.'

'I am doubly wealthy now. My husband left me

properties and a small fortune, as well as his wretched pig. I was in half a mind to have her sent to join him in the afterlife. We could dine for weeks on salt pork and bacon.'

'You wouldn't do that, my lady.'

A hint of a smile curved Aurelia's full lips. 'No, the poor thing is not to blame for his obsession. Hansford is going to take her to my estate on the outskirts of Bath where she will no doubt breed piglets by the dozen, and live out her days in comfort.' Aurelia held out her empty glass. 'Pour me another, Lottie. Brandy and laudanum help take the pain away.'

Lottie did as she asked, only this time she was not so generous with the brandy. 'When were you thinking of travelling, my lady?'

'The ship bound for Bombay sails on Monday, New Year's Eve.' Aurelia snatched the glass from Lottie's hand, and drank deeply.

'But that doesn't give me time to go home and see my family. I need to explain my sudden departure and I have to collect my things.'

'You can put it all in a letter and I'll have it delivered by a messenger. As to clothes, I have trunks filled with gowns of every colour and style more suitable to your position as my companion. You are welcome to pick and choose.'

Lottie sat down again, staring at Aurelia in surprise. 'Are you saying that you want me to be your travelling companion, and not your maid?'

'I have no women friends. You and I have been through too much together to be servant and mistress, and I trust you. Didn't I hand my child over to you?'

'You did, indeed.'

'Is she well?'

'Molly is much-loved and thriving, my lady.'

'She must be nearly a year old by now.'

'She will have her first birthday in two months' time,' Lottie said, smiling proudly. 'She has several teeth and she's crawling and trying to pull herself up to stand. I don't think it will be long before she can talk.'

Aurelia sipped her drink. 'She will call someone else Mama. It won't be me.'

'We can rectify that, my lady. You have only to say the word and I'll fetch her from Whitechapel. It will break our hearts to lose her, but you are her mother and she should be with you.'

'I have no maternal feelings. I don't want to be burdened with a child, but I will send money to support her. You and your friends should not suffer for my mistakes.'

Lottie jumped to her feet. 'She was not a mistake. Molly is a beautiful little girl and she deserves to know her own mother.'

'Sit down, Lottie, please. I am not strong enough to face an argument about the child. Suffice it to say that I am happy to know that she is well cared for and loved. Before we leave I will instruct my lawyer to make funds available for her upkeep.'

'She has a name,' Lottie said angrily. 'She is a person in her own right, and she is your flesh and blood.'

'So you keep telling me, but motherhood is not for me. If you are truly my friend you will do as I ask, and stop questioning my motives.'

'I am your friend, and I do want to see Gideon

again, but I would like to tell my family in person.'

'Impossible. If you go back to Whitechapel you might be persuaded to stay there, and then what would I do? I cannot travel all that way on my own, and I need you with me. If you love Ellis, you will agree to my terms.' Aurelia put her head on one side, eyeing Lottie thoughtfully. 'Didn't you tell me once that you were born in India, and that your father served with the Bombay Sappers and Miners? You must surely want to see him again.'

Lottie was silent for a moment, torn between loyalty to her adopted family and her desire to see Gideon. Her father was a shadowy figure from the past and she could hardly remember what he looked like, but the mention of him brought back happy memories from long ago, making it almost impossible to refuse, and she nodded slowly. 'All right. I will come with you, and I accept your offer to support Molly while I am away. I think they can manage the eel pie and mash shop without me.'

'An eel pie and mash shop? What is that exactly?' Suddenly alert, Aurelia stared at her, eyebrows raised. 'It sounds disgusting.'

'Eels are the food of the poor, my lady. I wouldn't expect you to know about such things.'

'I can see that you and I will have many lively conversations now that you are to be my companion. I didn't think you had it in you to stand up to me.'

Lottie reached out and took the empty glass from Aurelia's hand. 'If you really want us to be equals you'll find out all sorts of things about me that you didn't know.'

'I think I need another drink.' Aurelia eased herself back against the cushions. 'My head aches.'

'An excess of brandy is bad for you. Why don't I ring for Tilda and order a tray of tea and some bread and butter or cake? I doubt if you've eaten today.'

'I said I wanted a friend and companion, not a governess. I am grown up enough to know what I want.'

Lottie moved to the mantelshelf and tugged at the bell pull. 'Tea it is, then.'

Once again they were at sea, only this time the ship was bound for India. Tom Bonney accompanied them as far as Gibraltar, where he disembarked and joined a screw steamer bound for Balaklava. Lottie did not envy him his return to the battlefield, although he assured her that the war was virtually at an end and it was only a matter of time before a treaty was signed. She had enjoyed Tom's company but now he had gone she was left to face the rest of the voyage with Aurelia, who kept mainly to her cabin, insisting on having her meals brought to her and refusing steadfastly to join their fellow passengers in the dining saloon. If she did venture out on deck she was heavily veiled, despite Lottie's assurance that the scar on her face was barely noticeable.

'Are you going to be like this when we reach Bombay?' Lottie demanded one day when Aurelia tried her patience to the limit. 'Lieutenant Gillingham risked everything for you. His career is ruined and he is in exile because of his love for you. Do you really think him so shallow that a scar will make a difference to the way he feels?'

'Don't nag me, Lottie. I will know by the way he looks at me. If I am repulsive to him I will see it in his eyes. Farrell cannot keep anything from me.'

Lottie snatched up a silver-backed hand mirror and held it in front of Aurelia's face. 'Look at yourself. What do you see?'

'Don't be cruel.' Aurelia raised her hand to shield her eyes. 'You know very well that I am not the woman I was.'

Lottie pulled her hand away. 'The scar is only a tiny part of you. Where is the spirited woman I served a year ago? Where is the smile that captured men's hearts? You are still the same person, Aurelia de Morgan Dashwood. The attraction you exuded was not simply due to a pretty face.'

Reluctantly, Aurelia took the mirror and gazed at her reflection. 'I fear that woman is gone.'

Lottie grabbed her shoulders and shook her. 'Stop it. Stop behaving like a spoiled six-year-old. You are hiding behind that scar, and if you don't find the old Aurelia you will lose Gillingham. Show him that miserable expression and self-pitying attitude and he'll run a mile, or he will if he's got any sense. Who would want to live with a woman who was permanently wallowing in misery?'

Tears ran unchecked down Aurelia's pale cheeks. 'Why are you being so cruel? I thought you were my friend.'

'It's because I care for you that I'm saying these things.' Lottie sank down on the bunk, shaking her head. 'I can't help you if you won't help yourself. You have to take control of your life again. Stop dulling your senses with laudanum and brandy and be as you were before all this happened.'

Aurelia held her hand to her head. 'I know you're right, Lottie. The woman you speak of is buried inside me, afraid to show herself.'

'The woman I knew wasn't afraid of anything,' Lottie said softly. 'She is still here. You are still the same, if only you could make yourself believe it. Don't wait until we reach Bombay to find yourself.'

'I don't know how.'

'You can start by joining me for dinner in the saloon.'

'I can't face meeting strangers.'

'I sit at a table with two elderly missionary ladies who are joining their brother in Delhi, and three clerks who work for the East India Company and their extremely plain wives, and also there are a couple of very dull government officials. You have nothing to fear from any of them.'

'But I've been confined to my cabin for three weeks. What do I say to them?'

'I told them you were a martyr to *mal de mer*. They understood perfectly, and I took the liberty of telling them that you had suffered terrible injuries in the Crimea, where you were bravely supporting your husband.'

'So they're expecting to see a disfigured hag.'

'No, they'll welcome you into their midst as a heroine, and, anyway, what does it matter? We'll be in their company for the next few weeks and after that we'll never see them again. Consider this as practice for when you take your place in society, whether it's in Bombay, Poona or London. You are Lady Aurelia Dashwood, an earl's daughter, as you used to keep telling me.'

A faint smile lit Aurelia's blue eyes. 'I wasn't a very nice person, was I?'

'You had your moments, but you were good to me and your smile could light up a room. I won't allow you to dwindle away like a guttering candle.'

'You make me ashamed of myself, Lottie. I will accompany you to the dining saloon and be damned to those who look at me askance.'

'I think you underestimate your fellow human beings. People are much kinder than you imagine.'

'Help me dress, Lottie. You've put me in a fighting mood, and I'll test out your theory this evening at dinner. We'll see how these colonial worthies react to me.'

Aurelia's reintroduction into society was not seamless, but gradually, day by day, she became easier in company and by the time they reached Bombay she was the queen of the dining saloon and the darling of the crew. She had the sympathy of all who came into contact with her and they listened avidly to her accounts of war in the Crimea, but Lottie knew that Aurelia's outward show of confidence was a façade to hide the fears that beset her. It was one thing to travel hopefully, but as they stepped ashore in Bombay, Lottie was conscious that this was just the start of what might prove to be a triumph or a terrible disaster.

Aurelia stood on the dock, heavily veiled and seemingly at a loss as to what to do next. Her former ability to command had deserted her and Lottie realised that she would have to take charge.

She hailed a coolie, giving him instructions in the few Hindi words that she remembered from her childhood, and he piled their luggage onto a trolley, beckoning to them to follow him. They edged their way through the throngs of newly arrived visitors, seamen and dockyard workers to where a line of tongas were waiting to transport passengers to their final destination.

'Railway station – we want to go to Poona.' Lottie spoke slowly, enunciating each word.

The coolie repeated their destination and the tonga wallah responded. 'Bori Bunder station,' he said proudly.

In the end they had to hire two tongas, one for themselves and the other to take the amount of baggage that Aurelia considered the bare minimum. She sat stiffly beside Lottie as they drove at a snail's pace through the packed, dusty streets where cows wandered freely, as if they were in an English meadow, and elephants carrying howdahs lumbered amongst them. The smells of animal dung and human excrement mingled oddly with the more fragrant scent of exotic spices. Baskets of bright-yellow marigolds spilled petals into the dust, and the vibrant colours of the women's saris glowed like jewels in the sunlight. All this was in startling contrast to the drabness of London streets in winter. Memories came flooding back to Lottie with a wave of sadness as she thought of her mother and her small brother and sister, taken from her too soon.

Aurelia held her handkerchief to her nose. 'This place is worse than Balaklava,' she said in a low voice as the tonga jolted over ruts in the road. 'I hope Poona proves to be more salubrious.'

'Are you certain that's where they were posted? I know it's a bit late to worry about it now, but India is a big country.'

'That was the information Tom gave me, and he should know. I'm acquainted with the camp commandant at Poona, Major Tressillian; we met once in London and he was very taken with me. His wife, however, did not approve. No doubt she will take great pleasure in my misfortune.'

Lottie sighed. 'There you go again, Aurelia. You must stop thinking like that. Mrs Tressillian would have to be a very mean woman to take pleasure in your misfortune, as you call it. Remember how popular you were on board ship. You charmed everyone.'

'That may be the problem. I was a flirt, I admit it, and I dislike most of my sex, apart from you, of course.'

'Perhaps you didn't give other women the chance to befriend you. I think you'll find things will be different from now on.'

'You mean that the army wives will pity me.'

'Not at all. I think they will admire your bravery, and if you are a little less charming when in the company of their husbands, the women will warm to you.'

'It's going to be hard,' Aurelia said, sighing, 'but I'll try.'

'I think we're approaching the station.' Lottie leaned forward, peering through the cloud of dust thrown up by the horse's hoofs. 'I can smell smoke and engine oil. It reminds me of London.'

The tonga wallah drew his horse to a halt and

they were immediately surrounded by coolies offering their services. Lottie paid the fare, and their luggage was seized by willing hands. The clerk in the ticket office spoke English and he announced proudly that the line to Poona had only recently been opened by the Great Indian Peninsular Railway Company. There would be a train in an hour and if the memsahibs would like to pass the time in the newly built 'Ladies Only' waiting room, they would be more comfortable.

'The local people are very polite and helpful,' Lottie whispered as they followed the coolies to a wooden building adjacent to the platform.

'They only want our money,' Aurelia said tersely.

Lottie sighed, shaking her head. 'I thought you had turned over a new leaf.'

'I have,' Aurelia said hurriedly. 'Of course you're right. He was being very polite and helpful.' She swept into the tiny room and sank down on the wooden bench. 'Are you going to keep pulling me up every time I slip back into my old ways?'

Lottie dismissed the coolies with a smile and a generous tip. 'Yes,' she said, smiling. 'One day it will come naturally to you.'

'A year ago I would have dismissed you without a character for your impertinence.'

'Yes, you would, but I'm not in your employ now.'

'Oh Lord! I never thought to offer you a wage for being my companion.'

'You can't put a price on friendship,' Lottie said, chuckling. 'Don't even think about it, Aurelia. You've brought me home. My family are here, as well as the man I hope one day to marry. What more could I ask?'

Aurelia pushed her veil back from her face, fanning herself with her hand. 'Oh, well, if you're happy to go on as we are I shan't argue with you. This place is like an oven. For heaven's sake open the door.' She hesitated, eyeing Lottie warily. 'Please.'

They waited for over an hour in the heat of midday, refreshed by cups of tea from the chai wallah, who fortuitously turned up when he was most needed. The platform remained empty until the rumble of the approaching engine made the wooden building shake to its foundations, and suddenly people appeared seemingly from nowhere, pushing and crowding round the carriage doors as the train came to a screeching halt. Lottie and Aurelia stepped into the seething mass, which parted instantly on the arrival of the coolies with their luggage. Within minutes they were ensconced in the first-class compartment, which was basic but clean and moderately comfortable.

Aurelia lapsed into silence and Lottie settled down to appreciate the view of a country she had left more than fourteen years ago. It was almost impossible to believe that in a few short hours she might be reunited with Gideon, and she was determined to find out what had happened to her father. His letters had been infrequent and then had ceased altogether. He might be dead, for all she knew, but she could still hope. The train trundled on and Aurelia slept, but Lottie was drinking in the scenes that flashed past at an alarming rate, and with each passing mile she became more and more excited at the prospect of what lay ahead.

Several hours later the train pulled into Poona station and the doors were flung open, crashing against the woodwork as the passengers alighted, pushing and shoving in their hurry to go about their business. Lottie and Aurelia followed a line of coolies to the street. Their luggage was piled onto an ox cart, and a tonga, drawn by an aged horse that looked fit to drop at any moment, transported them to the barracks. Aurelia had lapsed into silence, her face concealed by the thick veil, but she perked up at the sight of the sentry at the gates. She allowed Lottie to help her from the vehicle, but as soon as her feet touched the ground she became Lady Aurelia Dashwood, the colonel's wife. She demanded to see Major Tressillian in such a manner that it would have been a brave soldier who denied her access.

Lottie stood back. It was good to see Aurelia regaining her self-confidence, despite the fact that she had retreated behind her veil, but her brief conversation with the sentry had the desired effect and they were led across the dusty parade ground and escorted to the major's office. The punkah wallah sat cross-legged on the veranda, working the fan that kept the temperature inside bearable. Everything Lottie saw brought back bittersweet memories of childhood and the years seemed to melt away. Her throat constricted with unshed tears as a vision of her mother's gentle face flashed before her eyes, but an exasperated sigh brought Lottie back to the present.

Aurelia threw back her veil and began pacing

the floor. 'Why do we have to wait so long for things to happen in this country?'

'You get used to it,' Lottie said, sinking down on a hard wooden chair. 'The pace of life is different here.'

Aurelia came to a halt as the door opened and Major Tressillian entered the room.

'Lady Aurelia, it really is you. I could hardly believe it when the sentry relayed the message.'

'It's a pleasure to see you again, Major.' Aurelia held out her hand.

He touched the tips of her fingers and bowed. 'The pleasure is all mine. Won't you take a seat and I'll send for some refreshments?' He pulled up a chair.

'Thank you, but first may I introduce my travelling companion, Miss Charlotte Lane?'

Major Tressillian turned to Lottie with a nod and a smile. 'How do you do, Miss Lane? Welcome to Poona. Is this your first visit to India?'

'No, sir. I was born here. My father served with the Bombay Sappers and Miners. I was raised in England but I'm hoping to get in touch with him again.'

'Indeed? Well, I'm sure that could be done without too much effort.' Major Tressillian picked up a bell and rang it. Almost immediately the door opened and a servant hurried into the room.

'Tea for the ladies, and cake.'

'Yes, Major-sahib.' The man bowed out of the office.

Major Tressillian moved behind the desk and sat down. 'And what brings you all this way, Lady Aurelia? I heard about your husband's demise, and I must offer you my sincere condolences.'

'How fast news travels these days,' Aurelia said calmly. 'Thank you, Major. In fact we are on a mission to find Lieutenant Gillingham and Private Gideon Ellis.'

'Ah, yes. I know those names.' Major Tressillian avoided meeting her anxious gaze.

'I'm sure you are aware of the reason for their transfers to Poona,' Aurelia said coldly. 'No doubt it is common knowledge here.'

'I can assure you that such matters are strictly confidential, known only to myself and my aide.'

'Are they here?' Lottie demanded. She had intended to keep calm and quiet, but there was a reluctance in the major's tone of voice that made her think he was keeping something from them.

'We've come a long way.' Aurelia leaned towards him, her lips trembling. 'Where is Lieutenant Gillingham?'

'I'm afraid you've had a wasted journey, Lady Aurelia. I cannot, for reasons of security, give you the details of their mission, but suffice it to say that there has been an ongoing dispute between the British Government and the Persians over the province of Herat in Afghanistan, and an expeditionary party has been sent north, led by Lieutenant Gillingham.'

Aurelia sank down on the nearest chair, but Lottie leaped to her feet. 'Private Ellis – has he gone there too? Please tell me, sir. I must know.'

Chapter Twenty

'Yes, Miss Lane, Sapper Ellis accompanied Lieutenant Gillingham on that mission.'

Lottie sank back on her seat. 'Will they be gone for long, sir?'

'Impossible to say.' Major Tressillian glanced anxiously at Aurelia. 'Are you all right, Lady Aurelia?'

'I'm not about to faint, if that's what worries you.' Aurelia rose to her feet. 'I have no intention of returning to England until I've seen Lieutenant Gillingham.'

'Lady Aurelia, I don't think you understand the situation.' Major Tressillian leaned forward, fixing her with a piercing stare. 'I have some sympathy with your predicament, but there is every possibility that the situation will escalate into war with Persia. The best advice I can give you is that you go home and await events.'

'We've come too far to give up so easily, Major Tressillian,' Lottie said before Aurelia had a chance to say something she might later regret. 'I know I speak for Lady Aurelia when I say that we will stay here for as long as necessary.'

Aurelia nodded. 'I've no intention of leaving without Lieutenant Gillingham, but we'll need to find suitable accommodation. Would you be able to assist us in that respect?'

A look of admiration, or perhaps it was relief,

relaxed the major's aquiline features into a semblance of a smile. 'I'll make enquiries, my lady. In the meantime I hope you will both be our guests tonight. I know that my wife would be delighted to meet you.'

'Thank you, Major,' Aurelia said meekly.

'I'll go and tell Esther the good news, if you would like to wait here.' Major Tressillian rose swiftly to his feet and crossed the floor in two strides.

'I get the feeling he can't wait to be rid of us,' Lottie said as the door closed on him.

'I don't care what he or anyone else thinks.' Aurelia tossed her head. 'I will stay here until Gillingham returns. I don't care how long it takes.'

They were made welcome at the major's house. Esther Tressillian was obviously flustered by the sudden arrival of such an illustrious guest as Lady Aurelia Dashwood, and also a little embarrassed, if Lottie was not mistaken. It was obvious that the scandalous affair between her ladyship and the lieutenant was common knowledge in the camp, although Esther tried valiantly to hide her curiosity. She was helped in this by her brood of young children, who escaped from their ayah at every opportunity and crowded around Lottie, although they were wary of Aurelia. Whether it was her patent dislike of youngsters or her scarred face that made them shy in her presence was something known only to them, but Lottie felt more at home in their company than she did with the adults or the Indian servants.

When the children were in bed and dinner had been served in the panelled dining room, Esther rose from the table and led them into the parlour. Both rooms were furnished in a style reminiscent of home and more suitable to the English climate than the tropics. Esther was eager for news from England, and she wanted to learn about the current London fashions in clothes and hairstyles, as well as any titbits of gossip concerning the rich and famous. Lottie realised that these questions were a result of homesickness, but Aurelia's answers were short, and it was obvious that she was bored with the topic. Lottie had only a vague idea about the latest modes, but she did her best to entertain Esther with descriptions of life at The Swan, and her experiences selling eel pies on the city streets.

Esther listened avidly and there was little doubt that she would have kept them up until the small hours, but Aurelia was pale and although she would not admit it, Lottie suspected that her injuries were giving her pain.

'Thank you so much for a wonderful evening, Mrs Tressillian,' Lottie said, rising to her feet. 'But we've had a very long and tiring day.'

Esther jumped up from her chair, her face contorted with anxiety. 'I am so sorry. Of course you must both be exhausted. I'll show you to your room, but I must apologise because we only have one guest room. Do you mind sharing?'

'Madam, we are old campaigners,' Aurelia said stiffly. 'Not so long ago we were in the Crimea, bivouacking beneath the stars. A bed and clean linen is a luxury.'

'Oh, of course. How silly of me. I should have realised.' Esther's bottom lip trembled ominously.

'We are most grateful to you for putting us up at such short notice,' Lottie said hastily.

'Yes, of course.' Aurelia raised herself from the depths of the armchair. 'You are very kind, ma'am.'

Esther's face lit up and her hands fluttered nervously. 'No, indeed. It's the least we could do. I am only too happy to–'

'Might we go to bed now?' Aurelia limped towards the door. 'I would like to lie down.'

In the small, white-painted bedroom, containing a brass bedstead, a washstand and a single chair, Aurelia slumped down on the bed. 'I hoped at least there might be two single beds, but it looks as though we will have to share. I hope you don't snore, Lottie.'

'I could say the same of you, Aurelia. You wanted us to be equal and now we are. I hope you're satisfied.' Lottie sat on the chair and began unlacing her boots. 'You could have been kinder to poor Esther. She was bending over backwards to make us feel welcome.'

'I told you that I don't get on with women. Fluttery little things who make gods of their husbands only serve to annoy me. I can't help it.'

'You could try to hide it while we're guests here. We must be putting them to considerable trouble.'

'Unlace me, Lottie. I'm dead on my feet.'

That night Lottie dreamed again of the white stucco house, shaded by a peepal tree. Oleander and frangipani grew in wild profusion, filling the garden with fragrant perfume, and the flame-coloured blossom of a gulmohar tree was just coming into bloom. She walked up the path and was about to knock on the door when she woke up. A feeling of intense loss and sadness made her feel like weeping, but the sound of Aurelia's voice brought her abruptly back to the present.

'I've been awake for hours.' Aurelia eased herself to a sitting position. 'You were mumbling in your sleep.'

'I'm sorry. I've had the same dream ever since I can remember. I find this lovely house set in the most beautiful garden, and I know that inside there is something wonderful, but I never get further than the front door.'

'Sounds deadly dull to me, Lottie. My dreams are far more exciting. Help me up, please. I'm stiff as a board from sleeping on this lumpy mattress.'

Still drugged with sleep and disturbed by her recurring dream, Lottie climbed out of bed to help Aurelia to her feet. 'What are you going to do today?'

'I'm going to have another word with the major. There must be an army bungalow that we could rent for the time being. I doubt if he'll want us to remain in his home for too long.'

Lottie smiled as she heard the sounds of childish laughter and the scampering of small feet coming from the nursery. 'I think Esther has more than enough to do without having to cope with house guests. Do you want me to come with you?'

'I think I can handle it on my own, thank you, Lottie,' Aurelia said with a wry smile. 'I told you before, I need neither a nanny nor a duenna. I am quite capable of handling a man like Major Tressillian by myself.'

Breakfast was a hurried meal. Esther was pale with dark shadows underlining her grey eyes and their meal of bread rolls, quince jelly, fruit and coffee was interrupted several times by urgent messages delivered by an anxious servant, all of which seemed to concern the children. In the end, Esther rose from the table with an apology.

'I am so sorry, your ladyship, but I have to go to the nursery. The baby is teething and Vickie is suffering from croup. Their ayah is at her wits' end.'

'I understand,' Aurelia said graciously. 'Of course you must go to them.'

Esther hesitated in the doorway. 'But how will you entertain yourselves today? I am failing in my duties as your hostess.'

'Not at all. I am going to pursue the possibility of renting a bungalow and I want to hire servants for the duration of our stay in Poona.' Aurelia reached for the quince jelly. 'I'm sure Lottie will be only too pleased to help with the children.'

Esther's hand flew to her mouth and her eyes widened with distress. 'Oh, I couldn't ask such a thing. Perhaps you would like to see some of the countryside, Miss Lane? Do you ride?'

'Yes, I do.' The memory of riding lessons with Gideon brought a smile to Lottie's face. 'I seem to remember a place called Kirkee. I think we lived there for a while when I was very young.'

A look of sheer relief crossed Esther's mobile features. 'There is a barracks there, so it's quite possible. It's about four miles from here. If you leave soon, before it gets too hot, it would be a pleasant ride.'

'There, that's settled.' Aurelia spread the jelly liberally on a piece of bread roll. 'I will go about my business, and you may borrow my riding habit. I shan't be needing it today, but take care you don't get it dirty.'

'We have a very good dhobi wallah,' Esther said defensively. 'We are quite civilised here, my lady, despite what you may think of us.'

Lottie shot a warning look at Aurelia. She could see that their hostess was exhausted, anxious and close to tears.

'I apologise if I've offended you in any way.' Aurelia abandoned her meal and stood up. 'You have been most kind, and I am very much obliged to you.'

'There's no need to apologise.' Esther's cheeks flamed and she bowed her head. 'It's just that I didn't get much sleep last night, my lady.'

Aurelia moved swiftly to her side and laid her hand on Esther's shoulder. 'I am a mother myself, so I do understand, and I would take it very kindly if you were to call me Aurelia.'

'Th-thank you – Aurelia.' Esther burst into tears and fled from the room.

Aurelia turned to Lottie, hands outspread. 'There – you see what being kind does to people? Now the poor woman is confused and humbled by my graciousness.'

Lottie threw back her head and laughed. 'Never mind, you did extremely well. She'll get over it and I'm proud of you.'

An hour later Lottie was on her way to Kirkee accompanied by a sapper who had been selected as her guide. It was still early morning and the sun was low in the sky, but already the heat was intense and dust rose in clouds around them. It was the end of winter, but even so, by midday the heat was searing, and Lottie was obliged to dismount and rest beneath a stand of trees close to the barracks. Her guide was not very communicative although he did go to find a water carrier and returned with their canteens refilled, and pani puri purchased from a street seller. The spicy fried dough-balls spread with tamarind chutney were delicious and Lottie enjoyed every tasty mouthful. She thanked the sapper, who nodded in return and suggested that it was time to move on. He helped her to mount and then sprang lightly onto his horse, urging it to walk on towards the cantonment. Lottie had hoped that she might see something that would be a link with her childhood in India – something that would ease the ache in her heart and give her a feeling of belonging – but it was just another military establishment and she was bitterly disappointed. The cherished images of her mother and younger brother and sister were fading fast, and she was left with a feeling of deep sadness as they started back for Poona. Quite what she had hoped to find she did not know, but now her greatest need was to discover what had happened to her father, and why he had ceased to correspond. Had he remarried and forgotten her? Or, even worse, had he died in a foreign land and was buried far from home and all but forgotten?

That evening, after dinner, she waylaid Major Tressillian as he was about to go outside on the veranda to smoke a cigar. 'I know you're a busy man, Major, but did you manage to find out anything about my father?'

He hesitated in the doorway. 'I did check the records, Miss Lane. It seems that Sergeant Lane was invalided out of the army some six years ago.'

'He was ill?' Lottie stared at him in horror. 'Why didn't he come home? I would have looked after him.'

'I'm afraid only he could answer that.'

'But what was wrong with him?'

'His company were sent on a mission to the North-West Frontier seven years ago, which is where he received a near-fatal injury.'

'But he survived?'

'Yes, it seems so. All this was before my time here, but unfortunately the records don't reveal his current whereabouts. He would have received an army pension, and it would be reasonable to assume that a man in his delicate state of health might have returned home to England.'

'If that was so I don't understand why he didn't contact me.'

'I'm sorry I can't be of more help. Now, if you will excuse me, I am going outside to smoke my cigar. It's the one time in the day when I can relax and be assured of quiet.'

'Of course, thank you anyway, Major.' Lottie stood aside to allow him to pass.

'By the way,' he said casually, 'I've found a small bungalow that you and her ladyship can move into straight away. It's quite basic but you are here for

341

only a short while, so I hope it will suit.'

'Thank you, Major.' The information barely registered as she struggled to come to terms with the news that her father had been badly wounded and discharged from the service. He had been a shadowy figure in her early years. All she could recall was the tickle of his moustache when he kissed her good night, and the smell of boot polish and bay rum that lingered even after he had left the room. A mixture of emotions threatened to overcome her – she was relieved to think that he had survived, and angered by the fact that he had made no effort to seek her out. Perhaps it would be best to allow him to slide into obscurity. She went to find Aurelia to pass on the news that they would soon have somewhere to call their own, even if it was only temporary.

The bungalow was small, but there were two bedrooms, a living room and a cooking area built on at the back. A veranda at the front overlooked a small garden bounded by a picket fence; and shaded by a rain tree. Esther said she would be sorry to see them go, but Lottie noticed with some amusement that their hostess set about finding them servants with surprising zeal. One morning a stream of applicants arrived at the Tressillians' bungalow, and Lottie was allowed to sit in while Esther interviewed them in a mixture of Hindi and English. By lunchtime they had a housemaid, a cook and a gardener, or as Lottie said airily when she told Aurelia, 'We have an ayah, a bobajee and a mali, and the bheesti will bring us fresh water twice a day.'

'Stop showing off,' Aurelia said impatiently. 'I refuse to learn their language because we won't be here much longer.'

'Really?' Lottie asked eagerly. 'Have you found out where Gideon is?'

'Not exactly,' Aurelia said, frowning. 'But I will soon. I've made friends with the officer in charge of the telegraph. It doesn't cover the whole country, as yet, but as soon as I know where Gillingham is stationed we'll set off.'

'Do you really mean to travel all the way to the frontier?'

'I'll brave the Khyber Pass and travel into Afghanistan, if necessary. I'm a military wife, or I was, and will be again if I have any say in the matter.'

'But you're not married to the lieutenant. Will the army allow you to follow the drum?'

'I don't care whether they will or not. I'll be a camp follower if it means that I can be with the man I love. Don't you feel the same?'

'Yes, but I'm not a lady like you.'

'You are more a lady than I will ever be, Lottie Lane. Now, let's stop talking and set about moving into the bungalow. It's going to be a week or two before we travel north, and there's a lot of planning to be done in the meantime.'

Aurelia threw herself into making arrangements for the journey that would take them to the North-West Frontier, but this left Lottie with little to do. The servants looked after their every need, and with no other outlet for her energy, Lottie spent each morning keeping Esther's children entertained, giving their exhausted mother a well-earned rest. Even so, the afternoons were long and the weather was getting warmer with each passing day. It was then that time dragged and Lottie was frustrated by the inactivity. She had not accustomed herself to the way the army wives retired to their rooms during the hottest part of the day, leaving the children to be cared for by their ayahs, and surfacing when it was cooler towards evening in time to change and dine with their husbands. Taking to her bed after luncheon was alien to Lottie's nature and she often chose to brave the heat, taking walks in the town or going for rides, accompanied by the Tressillians' syce.

One of her favourite walks took her through the bazaar where stalls were set up in front of the rickety buildings, displaying everything from bolts of cloth to rush baskets filled with colourful aromatic spices. Lottie was not interested in purchasing anything, even though the traders shouted their wares and did their best to entice her into sampling their goods. She smiled and walked on, holding her parasol at an angle to shield her from the ferocious heat of the sun. Flies buzzed around her head and monkeys skittered across the road in front of her, leaping onto stalls and stealing fruit despite the attempts of the traders to keep them at bay. Lottie headed for the shady area beneath the neem trees that lined the street. She turned a corner and came to a sudden halt. For a moment she thought that it was a mirage caused by the shimmering heat, or a touch of the sun, and she closed her eyes. When she opened them it would be gone, and she would know that it was just her imagination playing tricks on her.

She opened her eyes and it was still there – the house that had haunted her dreams for as long as she could remember. She moved slowly towards it, hardly daring to believe that it was real, and, as if still in her dream, she walked up the path and knocked on the door. This was when she always awakened, frustrated and feeling cheated of what lay behind that green door.

It opened and she found herself looking into a face that was at once strange and yet achingly familiar.

'Can I help you, miss-sahib?'

'Mala?' Lottie said slowly. 'Mala, is it you? Don't you remember me?'

The woman took a step backwards, her dark eyes wide with shock. 'No, it can't be.'

'But it is. I am Lottie, you used to call me your little rose.' Close to tears, Lottie threw her arms around the woman's neck. 'You were my ayah. I've come home.' She breathed in the scent of curry spices and patchouli, aromas that took her back fourteen years to a time of trust and innocence.

Mala returned the hug. 'Lottie-ji, my little rose.' She held her at arm's length. 'You are so like your dear mama that I thought you were a ghost. Come inside and let me look at you.'

Halfway between tears and laughter, Lottie stepped into the room. Memories came flooding back as she glanced round at the colourful hangings, the low sofa with its gaudy cushions, and the brass-topped table where Mala used to keep a bowl of sugar candy just for her.

'I used to come here and you would give me

lemonade and let me play in the garden, but it's so much smaller than I remembered,' Lottie said.

'You were just a baba-log when you were sent away.' Mala dashed her hand across her eyes, but she was smiling through her tears. 'The little ones were taken from us and then your mama. I had hoped that you would be allowed to stay with me here, but your papa said your only hope was to go to England. I felt my heart breaking when I kissed you goodbye.'

'I know I wanted to live here with you, and I didn't want to go back to our bungalow after Mama died.' Lottie enveloped the small, plump woman in a warm embrace. 'You were so big then. Now I am taller than you.'

Mala drew away, gazing at Lottie. 'You have grown into a beautiful lady.' She fingered the material of Lottie's borrowed riding habit. 'A fine lady, too.'

'I am little more than a servant. I came to India as companion to a rich lady.'

'I don't understand. Your father said you had gone to a good school. His brother in England told him so.' Mala shook her head, frowning. 'He wanted you to have the best of everything.'

'Never mind me. I am here now and I hope to find my father. Do you know where he is, Mala? His letters stopped coming many years ago and I feared he was dead. Then Major Tressillian told me that Papa had been injured and had left the army. That's all I know.'

'It is true, Lottie-ji. At first we thought he might die, but your papa is a strong man and he survived.'

346

'Where is he now?' Lottie asked, hardly daring to breathe.

Mala moved towards the bead curtain that separated the living room from the lean-to where she prepared her food. 'Where are my manners? Sit down, and I'll bring you refreshments.'

Lottie sank onto the sofa. 'If you know anything, however bad it may be, please tell me.'

'Let me serve you first, and then we will talk.' Mala slipped behind the curtain.

Lottie could hear her moving about and she closed her eyes, savouring the scent of sandalwood from the carved chest where Mala kept her linen, and the zesty aroma of lemons as Mala prepared the drink that Lottie had loved as a child. It was all so familiar and comforting. Lottie felt more relaxed than she had done for months. She opened her eyes and smiled. She had come full circle.

Mala bustled into the room carrying two glasses of lemonade. She placed them on the table. 'Take a sip, and then I would like you to see my garden.'

Lottie picked up a glass and drank deeply. The lemon juice, sweetened with sugar and diluted with water, was delicious. 'I remember your garden, Mala. We used to sit beneath the big tree with the yellow flowers and you would read to me.'

'There is someone sitting beneath that same laburnum right now. Someone you would very much like to see.' Mala moved swiftly to hold up the curtain. 'Come.'

Chapter Twenty-One

The garden simmered in the afternoon sunshine, but it was not quite the same as the idyllic setting of Lottie's dreams. The green lawn she had envisaged was little more than a dusty yard where hens pecked in the dirt and a goat was tethered in one corner, well away from the small vegetable patch. The laburnum, however, was even more beautiful than she remembered, and the jacaranda tree was just coming into bloom with a haze of deep blue. Rose-ringed parakeets and mynas vied with each other in a noisy clamour as they claimed the branches as their own.

Mala went on ahead, shooing hens out of their path by flapping her hands and scolding them in Hindi. Then as they approached the water tank, half hidden from view by a large hibiscus, Lottie saw someone sitting beneath the golden shower of the laburnum. Mala came to a halt.

'Wait one moment, Lottie-ji.' She disappeared behind the flowering hibiscus.

Lottie strained her ears in an attempt to overhear the conversation, but she could not make out the words, and then Mala reappeared, smiling broadly.

'Come. There is someone most eager to see you.'

Lottie's pulse was racing and she knew the answer even before she came face to face with a man she barely recognised. 'Papa!' The father she

348

remembered was tall and well built, but this man was a pale shadow of his former self. He was thin and frail; his dark hair and moustache were now snow white, his skin lined and sallow. She was deeply shocked by his appearance.

Harold Lane held out his hand. 'Lottie, my dear girl. I can't believe it's really you.'

'It was pure chance that I came this way,' Lottie said slowly. 'I didn't know where to find you, Pa.' She sank to her knees in front of him, clutching his hands like a drowning woman.

'My little girl.' His voice shook with suppressed emotion. 'How you've grown, Lottie.'

She lifted her head and tears ran unchecked down her cheeks. 'Papa, I thought I'd never see you again. It must have been fate that led me here today. I knew this house the moment I saw it, because it has haunted my dreams since I was a child.'

'It's truly a miracle,' he said slowly. 'But I am a wreck of a man, and no use to you or anyone else.'

'Don't say things like that, Lane-sahib.' Mala wagged her finger at him. 'That's no way to greet your long-lost daughter. She has come all this way from England to see you.'

'Is that true?' Harold met her gaze with an attempt at a smile. 'Did you travel all this way to find me?'

'Not exactly, Pa. There were other reasons for my journey, but I hoped I might have news of you. For years now I've thought that you were dead. Why didn't you let me know that you had suffered like this?'

'I did write to you, my dear girl. I wrote to you

at least twice a month, and I sent the letters to Sefton, asking him to pass them on, but I never received a reply.'

'But you didn't tell her that you were a cripple, sahib,' Mala interjected angrily. 'You made believe that you were fit and well.' She shot a sideways glance at Lottie. 'I didn't pry, Lottie-ji. I was given the task of sealing the letters and taking them to the barracks to be sent to England. I couldn't help but see some of what your papa had written.'

Lottie held her father's thin hand to her cheek. 'Uncle Sefton must have destroyed them, Papa. I never received anything from you after I left school more than eight years ago.' She rose to her feet, still holding his hand. 'We have so much to talk about. I can't believe that I've found you alive and well.'

'Reasonably well, given the circumstances,' Harold said with a wry smile. 'But better for seeing you, my dear girl. I would have known you anywhere; you are so like your mother.'

'That's what I said.' Mala folded her hands in front of her, nodding in agreement. 'Shall I call for the mali to carry you indoors, Lane-sahib? You must be getting tired.'

Harold shook his head. 'No, Mala, I am fine, but I would like some tea, and I expect my daughter would, too.'

'Perhaps we should go into the house, Papa.' Lottie gazed at him anxiously. It was clear that the shock of seeing her had exhausted him. His eyes were bright, but his face was pale, with a greyish tinge, and the skin of his hand felt dry and paper thin. 'I cannot stay too long or they will send out a search party for me.'

'I'll fetch the mali to carry you indoors.' Mala hurried off in the direction of the vegetable patch.

'Where are you staying, Lottie my love?'

'In the cantonment, Papa. I came to India as companion to Lady Aurelia Dashwood. Her husband, Colonel Dashwood, died in the Crimea, and she has come to find the man she hopes to marry.'

'Is he a soldier also?'

'He's a lieutenant, Papa. His name is Farrell Gillingham and he served in the Crimea with the Sappers and Miners. It's a long story, and I'd have to start at the beginning or it wouldn't make sense.'

'I heard that the corps had changed its name recently. My body might be crippled but my mind is as sharp as ever and I try to keep up to date. Mala brings me news from the village and, every so often, I get a copy of *The Times*.'

Lottie swallowed hard. It was painful to see the man who had once been tall and strong reduced to a helpless state physically, although mentally still alert. 'Yes, Pa. I believe they are now known as the Royal Engineers.'

Harold put his head on one side, eyeing his daughter with a faint smile. 'You seem to know a lot about the subject, Lottie. You are true to your military background, or is there some other reason?'

'I fell in love with a soldier, Pa. It must be in the blood.'

'And this soldier is here in India? Has he a name, and how did you meet him? I may be crippled, Lottie, but I am still your father and I need to know these things. Now that we've found each other I don't want to lose you to just anyone, even if he does wear a uniform. He might be quite unsuitable.'

Lottie raised his hand to her cheek. 'We will never be parted in such a way again, Papa, and I want you to meet Gideon. He's a fine man, just like you, and I love him.'

'That's good enough for me, Lottie. But where is he now?'

'He's with Lieutenant Gillingham on a mission to the North-West Frontier.'

'There is always trouble in that area. I can't see it ever coming to an end.'

Lottie rose to her feet at the sound of footsteps. She turned to see Mala accompanied by the gardener.

'We've come to take you indoors, Lane-sahib,' Mala said firmly.

'You see,' Harold said, twisting his lips into a grimace as the mali lifted him bodily from the chair. 'I am at the mercy of others.'

'Lane-sahib! Do not speak in such a way.' Mala glanced anxiously at Lottie. 'Do not believe him, Lottie-ji. Your papa is treated with the utmost respect.'

'He's teasing you,' Lottie said, smiling. 'I can see that you take great care of him, and I'm truly grateful to you.' She watched her father being carried into the bungalow and her heart ached for him, despite her brave words. 'Is there nothing that can be done for him, Mala?'

'They say his back was broken,' Mala said sadly. 'He will never walk again.'

Lottie followed her into the bungalow. Her joy on being reunited with her father was tinged with sadness for the once strong man, who was now broken and reliant on others. She could only admire the spirit that had sustained him throughout his ordeal, and she made a silent vow to do everything in her power to make his life more bearable.

Lottie arrived back at the cantonment to find Aurelia pacing the veranda of their bungalow in a state of agitation.

'Where on earth have you been?' she demanded angrily. 'I was about to send a search party to look for you. Don't you know it's unsafe to venture out alone? It will be dark soon.'

'I'm sorry,' Lottie said lamely. 'But I wasn't alone. I had an escort.'

Aurelia slumped down on one of the rattan chairs and reached for a glass. She took a sip, glaring at Lottie over the rim. 'It's lucky I purchased a bottle of brandy from the commissariat or I would have gone to the major an hour ago. Where have you been?'

Lottie was about to explain but Aurelia held up her hand. 'On second thoughts, I don't care. I needed you here when the news came through. I was in the telegraph room and had it first-hand from Sapper Smith.'

'What news? It can't be more momentous than mine.'

Aurelia drained the glass in one mouthful. 'Really? I suppose you don't care that both Farrell and your man Ellis have been wounded in a skirmish on the border.'

Lottie sank down on the chair next to her. 'No! Are they badly hurt?'

'Oh, so you do care then? Well, the truth is I don't know. The message was brief but this must have happened some time ago as they've been treated in a field hospital, and are being sent back to Poona to be repatriated. That doesn't happen unless the injury is serious. Heaven knows what they've suffered.' Aurelia reached for the bottle and poured herself another stiff drink. She offered it to Lottie. 'Here, you'd better have a snifter. Don't you dare faint. I can't carry you indoors and the mali has gone home. There's only Romila and she's busy preparing dinner, although I doubt if I can eat a morsel.'

Lottie poured a tot of brandy into a glass and took a sip. The fiery spirit went straight to her head, giving her a pleasant feeling of euphoria, which vanished as quickly as it had come.

'When will they arrive?'

'I don't know but they will be admitted to the hospital as a matter of urgency. I refuse to be widowed twice.'

'You aren't married to Lieutenant Gillingham,' Lottie said angrily. 'Why do you always think only of yourself?'

'You're right, of course.' Aurelia toyed with her glass, staring into the amber liquid with tears in her eyes. 'I am selfish. I was born that way, but I do love Farrell and we are man and wife in the eyes of God.' She shot a sideways glance at Lottie. 'I'm sorry, what was it you were going to tell me?'

'Just that I've found my father. He's living in a tiny bungalow with my old ayah and has been for the last six or seven years.'

Aurelia reached out to lay her hand on Lottie's. 'But that's wonderful, isn't it? Why do you look so sad?'

'He broke his back and now he cannot walk. He's crippled for life.'

'But is there nothing that can be done?'

'Apparently not.'

'Maybe not here, but we must get him back to London. There must be someone in the medical profession who could help him.'

'Even if there were, I couldn't afford to pay for his treatment.'

'I'm a wealthy woman, Lottie. You and I have been through much together, and if I can help you in any way, I will.'

Lottie smiled and shook her head. 'In any way? I can't see you working in our little pie and mash shop, Aurelia.'

'Dammit, I'll set you up in your own premises if that's what you want. You can have a string of pie and mash shops, on condition that you never expect me to put a foot in any of them.' Aurelia drained the last of the brandy from her glass. 'We'd better go in for dinner. I'm afraid it will be goat curry yet again, because Romila doesn't seem to know how to cook anything else.'

'Be thankful that it isn't eel pie,' Lottie said, chuckling. 'I'm sorry, but I refuse to be miserable. I've found my pa, and Gideon has survived this far and is on his way here. I learned a lot from Mother Seacole and I'll take care of him and Pa.'

Aurelia rose somewhat unsteadily to her feet. 'I wish I were as brave as you, Lottie. You put me to shame, you really do.'

'If you were a coward you wouldn't be here now, fighting for your man. We women have to be strong in a different way from men, but that doesn't mean our lot is easier or less painful. We have to pick up the pieces and try to put them back together. If that isn't courage, I don't know what is.'

Aurelia rose to her feet. 'I feel better now, even if I am a bit tipsy.' She held out her hand. 'Come on, Lottie. Let's face the goat curry together, and tomorrow we'll work out a plan to get us all home to England.'

It was a full week before they received the news that Farrell and Gideon had been admitted to the military hospital in Poona. In the meantime Lottie had taken the opportunity to visit her father every day and the slow process of getting to know each other after so many years of separation had begun. As a small child she had been in awe of the big man with the booming voice, but now he seemed so small. She was deeply moved by his helplessness, although she knew better than to show him pity. They shared reminiscences from the past, and Harold listened in rapt silence while Lottie told him about life at The Swan and her experiences in the Crimea. The only subject that he assiduously avoided was what would happen when Lottie returned to England. Any suggestions she had made about taking him home to London were skilfully side-tracked so that he avoided giving her a firm answer. Although Lottie understood her father's reluctance to be a burden, the thought of abandoning him to the care of others was insupportable. She knew that they would clash and it would be a contest of wills, but leaving him in India was not an option.

With her father's future settled in her own mind, at least, Lottie prepared to visit the military hospital for the first time. She was excited at the prospect of seeing Gideon again, but also anxious as to the extent of the injuries that were serious enough to allow him to be repatriated. One thing was clear in her mind – she would stand by him and look after him. There was nothing she could not face as long as they were together.

Aurelia emerged from her room, dressed in black from head to foot with her veil covering her face.

'Good Lord!' Lottie stared at her in horror. 'You look as though you're going to a funeral. What will Farrell think?'

'My white muslin is soiled and the veil on my straw hat has been eaten by something. I can't let him see my face; not yet anyway.'

'We've had this out before,' Lottie said, sighing. 'If he truly loves you he won't allow something like a scar to come between you.'

'It ruins my looks. You're used to seeing me like this, but he's in a bad way and the shock might be too much for him. Men place such importance on physical beauty.'

Lottie stepped outside onto the veranda. 'The gharry is waiting to take us to the hospital. Are you coming, or not?'

'A little sympathy would go a long way,' Aurelia muttered. 'This might be the end of everything for me.'

Lottie took her place in the rickety vehicle. 'I know it's hard, but you should have more faith in him.'

Reluctantly, Aurelia climbed in beside her. 'I don't think I can do this, Lottie.'

'Of course you can.' Lottie sat back as the driver flicked his whip and the gharry lurched forward.

Lottie had hoped that Gideon and Farrell might be keeping each other company in one of the wards, but Aurelia was taken one way and Lottie was led in the opposite direction to an open ward. A punkah at each end of the long room moved rhythmically, fanning the air just enough to provide a little relief from the summer heat. Beds on either side were occupied by men in varying degrees of consciousness. Some were clearly in a bad way, while others were sitting up and taking notice. Lottie received some cheeky comments from those who were on the mend, and weak smiles from others who were not so well. She moved quickly to the end of the ward where the nurse told her she could find Sapper Ellis.

'Did you give him the letter I wrote, telling him that I was coming?' Lottie asked anxiously.

The prim nurse's face creased into a smile. 'He's been counting the hours, miss.'

'Thank you.' Lottie's heart was thudding and her mouth was dry as she approached his bed, and it was a shock to see it empty and neatly made. For a wild moment she thought the worst, but then she realised he was seated in a chair on the far side and he was waving to attract her attention.

Forgetting everything else, she broke into a run, receiving a faint cheer from a man in the next bed. 'Go to it, girl. He's a lucky chap.'

Lottie rounded the bed, coming to a sudden halt when she saw the extent of Gideon's injuries. He seemed to be encased in bandages from his chest and right arm to his splinted right leg, which was raised and resting on a chair in front of him.

His lips twisted into a grimace. 'Not very romantic, I'm afraid, Lottie. As you can see I'm in a bit of a state.'

She hurried to his side and, taking his face between her hands, she answered him with a kiss. 'You're alive, and that's all that matters.'

'I can't believe that you came all this way to find me.' Gideon's voice shook and his hand trembled as he reached out to stroke her cheek. 'You are a wonderful woman, Lottie. I don't deserve you.'

'I thought at first that you'd died in the Crimea,' Lottie whispered 'When Tom Bonney told me that you'd been sent to India with Lieutenant Gillingham I was overjoyed to know you were alive, but you were even further away and I was afraid I might never see you again. When Lady Aurelia offered me the position of companion I jumped at the chance to come here.'

'Has she come with you today?' Gideon's fingers tightened around Lottie's hand. 'Gillingham pleaded in vain with his superiors for news of her, and he was convinced that she had succumbed to her injuries in the French hospital, which is why he didn't defend his actions. I think he came here hoping to die.'

'She is well now, but her face is badly scarred. She is terrified that he won't love her now.'

Gideon raised her hand to his lips. 'Gillingham isn't like that, Lottie. He risked everything for the woman he loved and he's paid the price.'

'What do you mean by that?' Lottie asked anxiously. 'How bad is he?'

'We were caught in a rock fall. I suffered cracked ribs, and broke my arm and leg, but Gillingham sustained head injuries.' Gideon looked away. 'It's not good news, I'm afraid.'

Lottie could see that talking about his experiences was upsetting him, but she needed to know what to expect, if only for Aurelia's sake. 'Go on,' she said gently. 'What is it that you aren't telling me?'

Gideon turned his head to look her in the eye, his expression desolate. 'My bones will heal in time, but Gillingham's condition will affect him for the rest of his life.'

'Tell me, please.'

'He lost his sight, Lottie. He's blind.'

Lottie digested this in silence. It was a shock, and for Gillingham it must be a terrible affliction, but all she could think about was how it would affect Aurelia. For two people who had suffered so much it seemed an unfair blow, and their love for each other would be tested to the limit. Lottie leaned over to kiss Gideon on the forehead. 'You've been through hell, Gideon. I'm sorry for Lieutenant Gillingham, but at least he is alive and Aurelia loves him, as I love you. We will be all right, Gideon. I promise you that.'

Before he had a chance to reply the nurse,

bristling with authority, came to stand at the foot of the bed. 'Visiting time is over, miss. We mustn't overtire our patient, must we?'

Lottie was tempted to argue, but she could see that the nurse was determined to have her way. 'I'm leaving now.' She kissed Gideon, on the lips this time, much to the delight of the patient in the next bed, who clapped enthusiastically, but was quelled by a withering glance from the nurse.

'I'll see you tomorrow,' Lottie whispered.

'Until then, my love,' Gideon said, smiling.

It was an image that Lottie knew would carry her through until the next day when she would visit the hospital again. She left the ward and went to the vestibule, expecting to have to sit and wait for Aurelia, but she was already there. Lottie hurried up to her. 'Gideon told me about the lieutenant's injuries. I am so sorry, Aurelia. I don't know what else to say.'

Aurelia threw back her veil. 'Well, I won't need to worry about this any longer, will I?'

'You're not abandoning him, are you?'

'Don't be silly. Of course not. Farrell is mine until death do us part, and I won't allow anything to come between us again. I'll take him back to London and he'll receive the best possible treatment. Whatever happens, I'll take care of him and we'll be married at the first possible opportunity.'

'Is he aware of all this?'

Aurelia tossed her head. 'You know what men are like, Lottie. He said all the usual things: that it wouldn't be fair to tie me to a blind man, and I deserve better. All very noble, but complete

361

twaddle, and I told him so in no uncertain terms. As soon as he and your man are fit to travel we're going home.'

Chapter Twenty-Two

London was bathed in golden September sunshine, but even so Lottie was conscious of the uniform greyness of the streets and buildings, and the drabness of the clothing worn by the passersby. As she stepped down from the hackney carriage in Leman Street she felt the chill of autumn in the air and she shivered. After the heat of India it would take some time to get acclimatised, although the change in the weather had been gradual during the long sea voyage. Their return to England had been delayed until both Gideon and Farrell were fit enough to undertake the journey, but now they were here and Lottie breathed in the familiar smoky air, tinged with the odours from the river and the dung and detritus that blanketed the cobblestones. The milling crowds and the babble of voices, combined with the clatter of horses' hoofs and the rumble of cartwheels, was in sharp contrast to the much slower pace of life in Poona. But this was where she belonged and she was home at last.

She turned to Gideon, who was having difficulty lifting her father. 'I'll get Jem,' she said, taking some coins from her reticule to pay their fare from the docks. 'If you would just wait a while, please, cabby, I'll get help.' She crossed the pavement and mounted the steps. The door was open and a familiar smell of hot pies wafted out to greet her. 'Jem. Are you there?'

He emerged from the front parlour, wiping his hands on his apron and enveloped her in a bear-like hug. 'You've arrived. We got your letter, but we didn't know exactly when you were coming. Teddy's been down at the shipping office every day, making enquiries as to when your ship was due.'

'I can't wait to see him and everyone, but I need your help to get my pa from the cab. Gideon can't manage him on his own.'

'We've made up a bed for your pa in the back parlour.'

Lottie stood on tiptoe to kiss him on the cheek. 'Thank you, Jem. I knew I could rely on you. It's only temporary until we can find somewhere to live.'

He shook his head. 'This is more your home than mine, Lottie. The missis and me are the ones who should find a place we can call our own.'

He was out of the door before Lottie had a chance to argue. She waited, watching anxiously as Jem lifted her father from the cab and carried him effortlessly into the house. Gideon followed more slowly. His arm had healed and he had abandoned his crutches, but he still walked with the aid of a stick. 'It's a long time since I was here.'

'Your mother will be so happy to see you again,' Lottie said, smiling. 'I expect they're all downstairs in the kitchen. I'll make sure that Pa is comfortable and I'll join you.'

Gideon brushed her cheek with a kiss. 'It's not exactly the homecoming I dreamed of, but I can't wait to see the old girl again.'

Lottie chuckled. 'Don't let her hear you calling her old, she'll never forgive you. Your ma is still a handsome woman. I could see at once where you got your looks.'

'You always make me feel good about myself, Lottie. You kept us all sane during the weeks at sea. I don't know how you did it, but you have a gift for making people happy.'

'Stop saying things like that. You'll have me in tears in a minute. Now go and give your ma a hug and a kiss, and don't forget to be nice to Jezebel. I don't know how we would have survived without her eel pies.'

'As I recall, she was a terrifying creature at The Swan. I don't think Frank Jenkins ever forgave you for telling him she was pretty. He was lucky to get away with his life when he went up behind her and tried to put his arms around her.'

'That seems such a long time ago,' Lottie said, sighing. 'So much has happened since then.'

Gideon leaned over to kiss her on the forehead. 'Don't be sad, sweetheart. I might not be fit enough for active service, but I'll make you proud of me yet.'

'I am proud of you, Gideon. Never doubt it. Now go downstairs and put your poor mother's mind at ease, and remember to pat Jezebel's dog. She dotes on Lad as if he were her child.'

'I'll kiss everyone, including the dog, if it makes you happy.'

'One more thing,' Lottie said urgently. 'I

haven't even told Pa that Molly is Aurelia's child. Grace and Jem know, of course, and I confided in you, but it mustn't go any further.'

'I don't understand how a mother could turn her back on her own flesh and blood, but for your sake I'll keep my mouth shut, although I don't like keeping it from Farrell.'

'It's not our decision,' Lottie said sadly. 'I keep hoping that Aurelia will come to her senses and realise what a terrible mistake she's making.'

Gideon kissed her on the cheek. 'If she had a heart, she hides it well.' He headed for the stairs.

Lottie was about to follow Jem and her father to the back parlour, but she paused for a moment. It was good to be home, even if the house looked even shabbier than before. The wallpaper was peeling and the paintwork was chipped, but the floorboards were scrubbed clean and the smell of lye soap mingled with beeswax polish. She suspected that Grace had worked hard to keep her home neat and tidy, even if it was in desperate need of redecoration. Lottie had been making plans during the journey from India, but she knew that things were not going to be easy. A small pie shop was not likely to bring in enough money to support them all, and money was tight. She jumped at the sound of the parlour door opening and she forced her lips into a smile as Jem came to meet her.

'Don't worry about your pa,' he said cheerfully. 'Harold will be fine and we're already good mates. I gave him a bell and told him to ring it if he needs anything.'

'Thank you, Jem. I knew I could rely on you.'

Lottie entered the room to find her father seated by the fire in Grace's favourite armchair.

He was pale and looked exhausted, but he managed a smile. 'He's a good chap, that Jem. He was telling me how he's known you since you were twelve. I didn't realise that you were sent out to work so young, Lottie. I trusted Sefton to bring you up as a lady, and he let me down. I'll have something to say to him next time we meet.'

'Don't upset yourself, Pa,' Lottie said gently. 'It's all in the past and we're together again now, which is all that matters.'

Harold stared moodily at the flames licking round the coal. 'At what cost, my love? I am a cripple, unable to do anything for myself, let alone to provide for you, and Gideon's leg injury makes it impossible for him to re-enlist. We're both dependent on you, and it's not right.'

Lottie pulled up a chair and sat down beside him, taking his hand in hers. 'It's early days yet, Pa. We have a roof over our heads and a good business in the pie shop. We won't starve, and I have plans for the future.'

'I don't deserve you, Lottie. If your dear mother had not succumbed to the fever things would have been different.'

'I know, Pa.' Lottie leaned over to kiss his thin cheek. 'There's one thing that's been puzzling me. I never told you, but when I first arrived at Poona I wanted to visit Kirkee. I don't know why, but I thought I'd been there before.'

'You have been there, Lottie. Your mother and the little ones are buried in the cemetery at Kirkee. You were only six years old at the time,

366

but it must have made a deep impression on you.'

'I understand now. I'm only sorry I didn't have time to go back there and visit their graves.'

'Do as I have done all these years, my love. Carry them in your heart and they'll never be forgotten.' Harold leaned back in the chair and closed his eyes. 'I'd like to have a nap, if you don't mind, dear girl.'

'You must be tired. I'll bring you some tea and something to eat in a while.' She waited for an answer but he had drifted off to sleep.

'Sweet dreams, Pa.' Lottie rose slowly to her feet. It hurt to see her pa suffering. He would have been in his prime, but for the injury that almost cost him his life. His mind was still sharp and there must be something he could do that would make him feel like a man again. She knew she would not rest until she had found the answer, but for now there were more pressing matters.

Lad was the first to spot Lottie as she entered the kitchen. He raced across the flagstone floor, slipping and sliding in his eagerness to greet her, and she bent down to stroke him. Ruby pushed him out of the way. 'Get down, you silly dog. It's my turn to make a fuss of Lottie.' She gave her a hug. 'It's good to have you home at last. We've all missed you.'

Lottie held her at arm's length. 'Jem didn't tell me that you were expecting an addition to the family.'

Ruby blushed and giggled. 'Isn't it wonderful? I never imagined I could be so happy.'

'It's due fairly soon, isn't it?'

'It's what they call a honeymoon baby,' Grace

367

said, clutching Gideon's arm as if she would never let him go. 'That's what you were, my boy. Nine months almost to the day and you came into the world, red-faced and angry and yelling at the top of your lungs.'

'Ma, don't embarrass me.' Gideon kissed his mother on the forehead. 'It's good to be home safe and sound.'

Jezebel put down the wooden spoon she was using to stir the eel liquor and she crossed the floor to grab Lottie by the hand. 'It's a happy day, Lottie. We've done all right while you were away, but I've a feeling we'll do even better now.'

Lottie smiled at the big woman. 'I've missed you all.' She glanced round. 'Where's Molly? And I haven't seen Teddy yet.'

'Molly's having a nap,' Ruby said hastily. 'But you'll hardly recognise her. She's walking and into everything. She says a few words too, and she's a beautiful little girl, just like...'

'Just like her mother,' Lottie finished the sentence for her with a wry smile. 'Lady Aurelia still refuses to have anything to do with her daughter, although she is going to help out financially.'

'She has her hands full, you must admit,' Gideon said mildly. 'She's devoted all her time and attention to Farrell.'

'He was blinded in a terrible accident,' Lottie added by way of an explanation. 'Perhaps, when they're married, she might feel differently towards Molly, although it will break my heart to let her go.'

'And mine.' Ruby clutched her belly. 'Ouch, he kicked me hard then. I'll swear your son is going to be a young ruffian, Jem.'

'I'll teach him to be a gentleman,' Jem said, grinning, 'and if it's a pretty little girl, just like her ma, I'll spoil her and treat her like a princess.'

Lottie was about to remind Jezebel to make a pot of tea, intending to take it upstairs to her father, when the street door burst open and Teddy rushed into the kitchen.

'I knew it,' he said gleefully. 'You've come home, Lottie.' He ran to her and wrapped his arms around her waist. 'Why did you stay away so long? I thought you was never coming home.'

'I've missed you too, Teddy.' Lottie ruffled his copper curls. 'I'll swear you've grown a couple of inches since I went away.'

He looked up at her with tears in his eyes. 'Promise me you won't go away again. The sun went in when you left, but it's come out again. Everything will be all right now.'

Jem moved to the door at the sound of the footsteps overhead. 'That sounds like customers. It's dinner time so we'd best get to our places ready to serve the pies and mash.' He took the stairs two at a time.

Suddenly the kitchen became a place of business. Grace abandoned her son and moved to the range where she started filling jugs with the parsley-flavoured liquor, and Teddy followed Jem upstairs to collect the orders for food.

Lottie stood at Gideon's side, watching with a feeling of pride as Jezebel opened the oven door and a blast of heat filled the room with the savoury aroma of hot pies. She shot a sideway glance in Lottie's direction. 'Don't just stand there, girl.

Fetch the plates from the dresser and get ready to serve the mash.'

'I'd better get out of your way?' Gideon took a step towards the door.

'We all have to work here, Sapper Ellis,' Jezebel said firmly. 'Take a cup of tea and a pie upstairs to Lottie's pa. You might not be in the army now, but you have to take orders when you're in my kitchen.'

'Yes, ma'am.' Gideon snapped to attention and saluted. 'You would make a very good sergeant-major, Miss Pretty.'

'Less of the cheek, sapper, and it's Jezebel to you.'

'You won't win a battle of words with Jezebel,' Lottie said, laughing. 'I know we keep saying it, but it's good to be home. I've missed you all so much.'

Teddy appeared at the top of the stairs. 'Four pie and mash,' he said importantly. 'And there's a queue outside the door.'

At first Lottie was delighted to find that business was brisk, but after a week at home she realised that there was very little profit to be made from such a small business. Gideon went out each morning, looking for work without success, and although he said nothing, Lottie could see that he was anxious and dispirited. What worried her even more was the fact that the rent was due at the end of the month, and unless a miracle happened they would be unable to find the money.

The evening before the rent collector was due to call Lottie sat at the kitchen table poring over

Jem's attempt at book-keeping, while Jezebel sat by the range smoking her clay pipe. Grace and Ruby had retired to the parlour to sit with Harold for a while before they went to bed, and Jem, Teddy and Gideon, accompanied by Lad, had gone to the river to lay traps for the eels that would be in tomorrow's pies. Despite helping in the pie shop, Lottie had been able to spend an hour or two each day with Molly, and had fallen in love with her all over again. She was a beautiful child, and already showed some of the wilfulness and spirit that characterised her mother, but her sunny smile would break many hearts in years to come, and it was obvious that everyone adored her. The thought of giving her up, even to Aurelia, was too hard to bear.

Lottie sighed and went back to the scrawled figures in the ledger, some of them virtually obscured by blots, which made it almost impossible to check their accuracy. What leaped out of the pages was confirmation of her worst fears: they were not making enough money to live on.

'Judging by your expression it don't look too good.' Jezebel relit her pipe with a spill from the fire. 'We're working ourselves into the ground for nothing. Ain't that the truth?'

Lottie stared at her, startled by Jezebel's grasp of the situation. 'That's just about it, as far as I can see, anyway.'

'There's too many of us. I can do me sums, and you don't have to be clever to work that out.'

'No one seems to have realised it but you.'

'I had to tot up the books for her ladyship at The Swan, so I got a rough idea how much things cost and how much profit there is to be made on certain things. Old Prudie weren't too bright, although she wouldn't admit it.'

'You're right, Jezebel. The pie shop is too small to make enough profit to keep us all and pay the rent, and we're in arrears as it is.'

Jezebel sucked on the stem of her pipe and smoke trickled out of the sides of her mouth. 'I didn't know that.'

'It looks as if Jem has been keeping it secret. I don't suppose he wants to worry Grace and Ruby, especially with her baby due in a few weeks.'

'Well, I won't be able to get me old job back. Neither will you, for that matter.'

'What do you mean?'

'I heard that The Swan is up for sale. The railways have finally done for the mail coaches, and the Filbys have been struggling for months. I had it from Ned Potts, the head ostler.'

'He had a soft spot for you, as I recall.'

'He's soft in the head, if you ask me.' Jezebel sniffed and rose to her feet at the sound of voices outside. 'I'm going to me bed.'

Lottie closed the ledger as the door opened. Lad bounded into the kitchen, followed by Teddy, Jem and Gideon.

'We should get a good catch tonight,' Teddy said excitedly.

'Eels are about the only thing tough enough to live in that filth.' Gideon sank down on Jezebel's recently vacated chair. 'The stench down on the foreshore is disgusting.'

Jem snatched a jug from the dresser and thrust it into Teddy's hands. 'Pop over to the pub and get them to fill it with ale, there's a good chap.' He took a coin from his pocket and gave it to him. 'We've earned a nightcap.'

Teddy grinned and saluted. 'Yes, sir.' He let himself out into the street, allowing the door to swing on its hinges.

'I see you've been checking me figures, Lottie.' Jem pulled up a chair and sat down beside her. 'You'll have seen that things ain't too good.'

'It's obvious that we can't pay the rent, let alone the arrears.'

'Is that true?' Gideon asked anxiously. 'Why didn't you tell us, Jem?'

'I done me best, honest I did.' Jem turned a worried face to Lottie. 'We worked really hard, girl, but people round here have barely enough to live on. If we charged more for our pie and mash we'd have no customers at all.'

'But we aren't a charity,' Lottie said wearily. 'All the hard work has been in vain, and I'm afraid your ma will lose her home, Gideon.'

'I've got some of my back pay,' he said, frowning. 'But when that's gone I'm broke until I can find work, which I fully intend to do, although no one wants to employ a man with a gammy leg, and the army won't have me now.'

'I don't want you to go back into active service, Gideon. We talked about this during the voyage home. We planned a life together.'

Jem cleared his throat. 'Would you like me to take myself off? This isn't my business.'

'And this isn't a conversation we should be having now,' Gideon said firmly. 'I'll find work, Lottie. I learned a lot when I was operating the electric telegraph, and the work we did installing cables and transmitting information in the Crimea should count for something. There must be something similar I can do; it just takes time to find it. I want to be able to support my wife and family, and I won't settle for second best.'

Lottie laid her hand on his. 'I understand, but we still have to face the fact that we can't pay the rent this month.'

Gideon's jaw set in a stubborn line. 'I'll raise the money somehow.'

Lottie knew better than to argue with him in this mood and she could feel his pain as if it were her own. She rose to her feet. 'I'm tired and I'm going to bed.' She leaned over to kiss Gideon on the forehead. 'Things will look better in the morning. They always do.'

Lottie rose early next day and left the house before anyone else stirred. A plan had formulated in her mind before she went to sleep, and she took a cab to Lord de Morgan's mansion in Grosvenor Square. She was still wearing clothes that Aurelia had given her and she presented herself at the front entrance, knowing that at least she was dressed like a lady, even if she lived over a pie and mash shop in Whitechapel. When the door was opened by a livened footman with a supercilious expression Lottie adopted the confident attitude displayed by Aurelia and her contemporaries.

'Please inform Lady Aurelia that Miss Lane has called to see her. She's expecting me.'

This time she had no difficulty in gaining admittance and the footman ushered her into a small but elegantly furnished room overlooking the square. Minutes later a maid came to take her to Lady Aurelia's boudoir.

Lottie was not surprised to find her ladyship sitting up in bed, sipping a cup of chocolate.

'You're bright and early,' Aurelia said, yawning. 'What's so urgent that you had to wake me from my beauty sleep?'

Lottie perched on the edge of the bed, taking in her surroundings with an admiring glance. The room was furnished with taste and elegance and no expense had been spared. The curtains and carpet were in delicate shades of silvery blue and crystal chandeliers hung from the ornate plasterwork on the high ceiling. It was a bedchamber fit for a princess, let alone an earl's daughter.

'This is a change from our rooms in the bungalow at Poona.'

'You didn't come all this way to compliment me on my bedchamber.' Aurelia replaced her cup on its saucer. 'Why are you here at crack of dawn? It must be urgent.'

'I need to know what you intend to do about your daughter.'

'I thought we'd settled that question, Lottie.'

'Molly isn't an object. She's beautiful and intelligent and altogether delightful. We all love her dearly, but she's your child. I can't believe that you could give her up so easily.'

'My dear friend, we've been through such a lot together, I thought you would know me better by now. I regret it, but I have no maternal feelings. I can't help it, Lottie. I'm not like you. I'm prepared to pay handsomely for the child's needs,

375

and maybe when she's older I'll want to get to know her, but only as a kind aunt or some distant relation. I gave her to you the moment she was born and nothing has changed.'

'I thought so, but I needed to hear it again.'

'Good, I'm glad that's settled. I'll always be your friend, even though our lives will take us in different directions. At the moment all I care about is getting Farrell the best possible treatment for his condition. I refuse to believe that he will never see again.'

'I understand, and I sympathise, but now I have a business proposition to put to you. Can we talk?'

Two hours later Lord de Morgan's carriage drew to a halt in the yard of The Swan with Two Necks. Ned Potts rushed forward to hold the horses' heads, and a lackey leaped to the ground to open the door and help Lottie alight. She could just imagine the sensation it would create in Leman Street if she turned up at the pie and mash shop in such style, and she sent the carriage back to Grosvenor Square. It was fun being treated like a lady of quality, but it was not really her style.

'Lottie, is it really you?' Ned stared at her, his pale melt-water eyes popping out of his head.

'Yes, Ned. I've come to see Mr Filby.'

'He's in the taproom, miss. Shall I get him for you?'

'Yes, please. Tell him that Miss Lane is here with an offer that he will not be able to refuse.' Enjoying herself hugely, Lottie stood aside and Ned bumbled past her on his way to the bar. She looked round, recalling the long years of servitude she had endured at the hands of the Filbys, half expecting to see May and Ruth leaning over the balustrade on the upper gallery, but the doors and windows were closed and a general air of dilapidation seemed to have taken over a once-thriving business. There were one or two sorry-looking nags in the stables, but no sign of carriage trade, and the cobblestones were ankle-deep in straw and dung.

Filby emerged from the taproom at the same moment as his wife waddled out of the scullery.

'Lottie Lane, is that you, girl?' Prudence's strident tones echoed off the walls and the horses whinnied in alarm. 'Come for a job, have you?' she added, smirking as she waded towards Lottie, but her face fell as she took in the cut of Lottie's fashionable gown and her expensive hat and shoes. She was not to know that they were Lady Aurelia's cast-offs. Lottie wanted to laugh, but somehow she managed to keep a straight face.

'What d'you want?' Filby demanded angrily. 'Have you come to gloat?'

'Shut your trap, Shem.' Prudence glared at her husband. 'She don't know nothing.'

'Oh, but I do.' Lottie faced her with her head held high. 'As a matter of fact I know that you're virtually bankrupt and likely to end up in the debtors' prison.'

'Who told you that? It's a rotten lie.' Prudence balled her hands into the fists that Lottie had seen her use on several occasions.

'She come in a toff's carriage,' Ned volunteered. 'I seen her get out of it.'

'Sold yerself to a rich cove, have you?' Prudence moved a step closer. 'I always knew you'd end up a wrong 'un.'

'You are mistaken, ma'am.' Lottie had begun to enjoy herself. For the first time she had the upper hand. Years of ill treatment, beatings and verbal abuse had left their mark and she could not bring herself to feel sorry for either of the people who had made her life a misery.

'Enough of this,' Filby said impatiently. 'What have you come for?'

'I've come to buy you out.'

There was a stunned silence. Prudence's jaw dropped and her mouth hung open. Her husband appeared to be dumbstruck.

Ned guffawed loudly. 'That's a good 'un.'

'This is a poor joke,' Filby said, breathing deeply. 'Very bad taste. I'm asking you politely to leave, but if you're not gone in ten seconds I'm throwing you out. Fine clothes and all.'

'If you touch me I'll have the law on you,' Lottie said coldly. 'I'm not joking, Mr Filby. I've come to make you an offer you would be mad to refuse. Now, do you want to hear me out, or not?'

Chapter Twenty-Three

Lottie arrived home to find the house in an uproar. Everyone had crowded into the front parlour, including Ruby with Molly in her arms. In the midst of them a tall, thin man wearing an illfitting black suit, tinged with green and frayed at the cuffs, was standing firm.

'If you don't pay up now I'll send the bailiffs in.' He had to raise his voice in order to be heard above the arguments put forward by Grace and Jem. Harold added his support from a chair by the window, emphasising his words by banging his fist on the trestle table. To add to the din, Lad was jumping up and down and barking and Teddy was bellowing insults in language fit only for the barrack room.

Jezebel advanced on the rent collector, white-faced and breathing heavily. 'Say the word and I'll throw this little worm out of the window.'

'What's going on?' Lottie demanded.

Everyone turned to look at her and there was a moment of silence. She was quick to notice that Gideon was missing, but she did not have time to wonder. Jezebel moved aside as Lottie advanced on the rent collector.

'It's Mr Clench, isn't it?' Lottie forced herself to sound calm, although inwardly she was seething. 'I seem to remember you from when we first came to Leman Street.'

'I am that man, miss.' He looked her up and down as if totting up the worth of her costly clothing. 'I've come to collect what is owing to the landlord.'

'I told him we can't pay it off in one go,' Jem said gloomily. 'He won't listen to reason.'

Clench shot him an angry glance. 'The landlord has been more than patient, sir.'

'No matter.' Lottie opened her reticule. 'There isn't a problem, Mr Clench. I have the wherewithal to settle the debt.'

A gasp of surprise was followed by a barrage of questions.

'I ain't sure you understand how much is due, miss.' Clench licked his thin lips. 'An amount I should think it unlikely that a young woman like yourself could lay her hands on with ease.'

Jem grabbed him by the collar. 'What are you suggesting, mate?'

'Nothing,' Clench said hastily. 'Just that it's a lot of money.'

'I know exactly how much it is.' Lottie dropped the coins into his outstretched hand. 'Good day, sir.'

'Out you go, cully. Don't come back too soon.' Jem marched him to the door.

'Where did you get so much money?' Ruby struggled to hold Molly, who was wriggling and waving in an attempt to attract Lottie's attention.

'I'll take her,' Lottie said, holding out her arms. 'You look done in, Ruby. Why don't you go upstairs and have a rest?'

'I'm not going anywhere until you tell me where you've been and how you came by all that cash.'

'Yes, dear,' Grace added. 'It is a great deal of money to come by.'

'Did you rob a bank?' Teddy asked, grinning.

'No, I didn't.' Lottie glanced at the eager faces. She wanted to wait until Gideon was there to share the news, but it was obvious that nothing would satisfy everyone other than the truth. 'I went to see Lady Aurelia.'

Ruby's expression darkened. 'So you borrowed the money. That means we have another debt to pay off.'

'Not exactly.' Lottie placed Molly on the floor and she headed for Lad, crawling at surprising speed.

The dog fled and Molly turned her attention to Teddy.

'So what did you do, Lottie?' Gideon's voice from the doorway made them all turn to look at him. He took off his hat and strolled into the room. 'Tell them what you've done.'

'I bought an inn,' Lottie said gleefully. 'Lady Aurelia put up the money, and I intend to bring The Swan back to prosperity. I hope it will be a joint venture, as I need all of you to help me make it work.'

Grace took a seat beside Ruby. 'My heavens. How do you propose to do that?'

'The days of the coaching inn are almost over,' Gideon said coldly. 'What made you decide to risk everything on such a wild venture?'

'You don't seem surprised. It's almost as if you knew what I was going to say.'

'I thought you were up to something, and I followed you this morning. When you walked into the house in Grosvenor Square I guessed that it was where Lady Aurelia lived. You and she were as close as sisters and I knew it wouldn't be long before you went to her for help.'

Lottie was conscious of the hurt in his eyes and the icy tone of his voice made her shiver. She could feel everyone staring at them and her feeling of elation was replaced by anger. 'How dare you spy on me, Gideon? Why didn't you ask me what I intended to do? I would have told you.'

'You prefer to rely on that rich woman than to

come to me. We aren't officially engaged so I suppose I haven't any right to criticise your actions, but I thought we had an understanding.'

'All I understand is that you were injured in the service of your country, and you're finding it difficult to find employment. That won't always be the case, but for now I have the means to provide us with a decent living. Jem and I grew up working at The Swan. Who better than us to run it?'

'And I am to be a kept man, I suppose?'

'Don't speak to her like that,' Harold said angrily. 'My daughter is a woman who should command your respect. It's not for you to lay down the law to her. Lottie has had a hard life, but she forgave me for abandoning her to my worthless brother, and you might still be in India, waiting to be repatriated by an uncaring military, had it not been for Lottie and Lady Aurelia.'

'Yes, you're being a bit hard, mate,' Jem said mildly. 'Lottie's just saved your ma from being evicted from her home, and she's offered us a future.'

'Which is more than you have at the moment, Gideon.' Ruby moved to Lottie's side. 'I think you owe her an apology.'

'I do too.' Grace nodded in agreement. 'You're just like your pa when it comes to false pride, my boy. Mr Clench has had it in for us since the day we opened the pie shop. He'll find a way to shut us down, unless I'm very much mistaken.'

Gideon's jaw tightened and his eyes flashed angrily. 'I can see that I'm outnumbered.' He turned to Lottie. 'It's obvious that you can manage very well without me, and I'm just a hindrance.' He turned on his heel and left them staring after him.

Lottie was about to follow, but Grace leaped to her feet and caught her by the arm. 'Let him go, love. He'll cool off in time and come to his senses. If you go after him now you'll only make things worse.'

Lottie shook her head. 'I hate to admit it, but he's right. I should have talked it over with him, but the idea came to me and I knew I had to act on it.'

'You were right to do so,' Harold said firmly. 'That fellow Clench would have taken pleasure in sending in the bailiffs. I've met his sort before.'

Teddy ran to the window and peered out. 'There's a queue. Shall I let them in?'

'It's dinner time.' Jezebel headed for the door. 'Come on, ladies. It's business as usual. We've got pies to dish up.'

Grace picked up Molly and followed Jezebel from the room, with Ruby and Teddy close behind, leaving Jem to lift Harold and carry him to a seat behind the counter. 'Are you all right to take the money today, Harry?'

Harold grinned and nodded. 'I never thought I'd end up working in a pie shop, but I'm glad to be useful.'

'I'll open up.' Jem hurried into the hall and a wave of sound wafted in as he opened the door to the waiting customers.

Lottie was about to take Lad downstairs when her father called her back. 'What is it, Pa?'

He leaned his arms on the counter. 'Don't be too hard on Gideon, love. It's difficult for a man to admit that he's not in control of his life. Gideon

383

was a soldier, and now he's nothing – in his own eyes at least. I know how that feels.'

'But I don't see either of you like that. You are still my pa and I love you, and Gideon is the same man he ever was. I don't understand why he is so upset.'

'Give him back his pride, Lottie. That's all I can say.'

'What can I do?'

'That I don't know.' Harold sat back as a crowd of hungry customers filled the room, taking their seats at the tables and demanding service.

Gideon remained distant, but Lottie was kept busy with her plans to take over the failing coaching inn. The others were behind her and eager to move from the house in Leman Street. Jezebel declared that she never wanted to see another eel, let alone skin one, and Teddy was tiring of the nightly trek to the foreshore and the early morning visit to the dock to haul in his catch. Lately, with eel supplies dwindling due to the excessive pollution, they had had to purchase extra supplies from Billingsgate Market, and this had eaten into their profits. Lottie had tried to talk to Gideon, but he had simply shrugged and wished her good luck with her venture.

Disappointed and angry, Lottie confided her worries in Aurelia when they met one afternoon over tea at Gunter's to discuss her ladyship's part in the business.

'You might say I'm a sleeping partner,' Aurelia said airily. 'Anyway, I think it's a very clever idea.'

Lottie toyed with a cream cake. 'I've tried to talk

to Gideon, but he's simply not interested. I've given the matter a lot of thought and I want to establish a business as a carrier for the railways. We've got ample stabling and room for storage. If I succeed in gaining contracts to deliver goods transported by rail it will provide work for all of us.'

'Does Gideon know what you're planning?' Aurelia put her cup down on its saucer, meeting Lottie's eyes with a stern look. 'You haven't told him, have you?'

'No, he's still very angry with me, and hurt because he thinks I went over his head and didn't consider his feelings. I don't know what to do to make things better.'

Aurelia sighed and reached for a pastry. 'Farrell is a problem, too. The physicians have little hope of him regaining full vision, although he has some sight now. He also frets because he doesn't want to be dependent upon me, which is patently ridiculous when we will never need to worry about money. It's not my fault that I inherited a fortune.'

'Poor Farrell. I remember how he was when he brought Gideon to The Swan. He was so charming and good-looking and he didn't seem to have a care in the world.'

'I want him to be that man again,' Aurelia said passionately. 'More than anything in the world I want him to be happy and fulfilled but, like you, I don't know how to set about it.'

Lottie stirred her tea, staring into the swirling liquid. 'The first time I saw Gideon he was unconscious and being cared for by Benson and Jenkins. They'd been laying cables under the

Strand for the Electric Telegraph Company, but the ladder had given way and he'd fallen into the trench.'

'If only it had stopped there.' Aurelia toyed with her pastry, breaking it into flakes. 'But for the telegraph I would still have my looks and Farrell would have his sight.'

Lottie dropped her teaspoon with a clatter and it landed on the floor. A waiter rushed up to retrieve it. 'I'll fetch you another, miss.'

'Thank you,' she said automatically. 'Aurelia, what did you say just now?'

'I said that but for the telegraph Farrell would still be able to see.'

'A blind man could send Morse code.'

'Are you suggesting that my intended should become a telegraph operator?'

'Not exactly, but both Farrell and Gideon know all there is to know about the telegraph system, from laying cables to sending messages. Soon the whole world will be connected by the electric telegraph. With your backing, Farrell could buy into the company, and Gideon could be at his side to offer help and advice. They would be doing what they were trained to do.'

'Go into business?' Aurelia frowned. 'I'm not sure about that. Farrell is a gentleman.'

'The world is changing and we have to keep up with the times. You said yourself that he's frustrated by his condition and doesn't know what to do with himself. This could be the answer for both of them.'

'It's certainly worth considering. As you say, they've had experience of setting up the telegraph system in the Crimea. Perhaps they could continue their involvement as civilians.'

'Yes,' Lottie said eagerly. 'I know that money means little to you, Aurelia, but for us ordinary mortals it's the means to keep us from the workhouse.'

Aurelia shuddered visibly. 'All right, you've made your point. I'll contact my man of business. He manages my investments, and I've the highest regard for his abilities.'

'But Gideon must never find out that I suggested it. He would never forgive me.'

'The same applies to Farrell. And they say we women have delicate sensibilities. For myself I think we are more hard-headed and less romantic than men. We see the world far more clearly than they do, poor dears.' Aurelia took a bite of the pastry. 'Delicious.'

'I will be so glad to get away from the smell of eel pie, tasty though it might be.' Lottie raised her teacup in a toast. 'Here's to the future.'

'The future.' Aurelia drained her teacup. 'I could do with a tot of brandy, although I am being very abstemious these days. Farrell knows instantly if I've been having a quiet tipple. He gets very perturbed if he thinks I am reaching for the bottle. We are already like an old married couple and we are yet to tie the knot. I am quite a reformed character.'

'Do you miss your old life and the balls and assemblies?'

'It's very odd, but I don't. I think our time in the Crimea and India has changed me for ever. I am not the rebel I used to be, in fact I am getting quite staid. I really must insist that Farrell makes an honest woman of me, although I think I'll wait until he's gainfully employed and feeling more like his old self.'

'We'll have to be careful that they don't discover our involvement,' Lottie said, chuckling. 'Gideon is so stubborn.'

'Let's do it now.' Aurelia summoned the waiter with an imperious wave of her hand. 'We'll visit my man Barnard together and put our case to him. His office is not far from Gresham Street and my carriage is outside. We'll go there right away.'

Barnard Coker's office in Cannon Street was situated at the top of a four-storey building. His clerk ushered them in with a deferential bow, and Barnard rose from his desk. 'This is an unexpected pleasure, Lady Aurelia. Please take a seat.' He pulled up a chair for Aurelia and another for Lottie.

'Miss Lane and I have come for some business advice, Barnard.' Aurelia sat down in a swirl of lavender silk skirts and starched white petticoats.

Lottie was not sure about Mr Coker. His smile was affable, but there was a shrewd, calculating gleam in his dark eyes that reminded Lottie of a bird of prey and made her feel nervous. She perched on the edge of the chair he hurried to provide for her.

'I'll come straight to the point, Barnard,' Aurelia said in a no-nonsense tone. 'I want some information and advice on a business project I have in mind.'

'That's what I'm here for, dear lady.' He resumed his seat.

'...So you see,' Aurelia concluded, having described her intention in detail, 'we need to act quickly but my name and that of Miss Lane must be kept out of negotiations. I don't know how you will go about it, but I trust your judgement and your diplomacy to see that Mr Gillingham and Mr Ellis have no notion that we are involved.'

Barnard was silent for a moment, his beady eyes shifting from Aurelia's composed features to give Lottie a hard stare. 'This won't be easy, but I think I can see a way forward. You say that both the gentlemen in question were trained by the Electric Telegraph Company under the aegis of the Royal Engineers.'

'That's right.' Aurelia nodded. 'My late husband's regiment.'

'Ah, yes. Of course I should have offered my condolences, Lady Aurelia.'

'I am out of mourning, as you can see,' Aurelia said calmly. 'I don't hold with the tradition that widows have to walk round looking like crows for a year, and I detest mauve. I am a modern woman, Barnard. Miss Lane and I have already entered the business world in a small way.'

Barnard's brow creased so that his eyebrows met in the middle. 'This is the first I've heard of it, my lady.'

'I am a sleeping partner and Miss Lane is in sole charge of the company, but that is neither here nor there. What do you think of our chances to buy into the Electric and International Telegraph Company? I want Mr Gillingham and Mr Ellis to be approached separately with regard to their proposed involvement.'

'It's a delicate matter, but I understand per-fectly.' Barnard sat back in his chair, looking from one to the other. 'Might I say that I think both gentlemen are extremely fortunate to have two such staunch supporters?'

Lottie chose to ignore his last remark. 'They must never know that we are behind this, sir.'

'I promise you complete confidentiality, Miss Lane. Leave everything to me.'

The Filbys were not going to go without putting up a fight, but the threat of the bailiffs and the debtors' prison finally persuaded them to move out at the end of the month. Lottie and Jem de-cided to keep the ostlers on for a while. Even though the mail coach trade had virtually ceased there were still enough private carriages to keep the business going until they signed contracts with the railway companies.

Lottie had tackled Aurelia on the subject of repaying the loan, but Aurelia had insisted that The Swan was Molly's inheritance. She would support her daughter and pay for her schooling on the condition that her relationship to the child remained a secret. Lottie did not approve, but she was not in a position to argue. She loved the little girl as if she were her own, and Ruby doted on her too. Grace was her surrogate grandmother and Jem and Gideon took the place of loving uncles. Teddy was like a big brother, and al-though Jezebel pretended to be immune to the baby's charms, Lottie had seen her making a fuss of Molly whenever she thought no one was looking. Jezebel had a heart, but she hid it well.

Gideon's attitude had mellowed, although he remained aloof from the preparations for the move, and even though Lottie tried to interest him in the project it was obvious that he still considered it was a mistake. She was disappointed, but determined to carry on. The Swan had become a personal journey. It had been her home since the age of twelve, and despite the hard work and the ill treatment meted out by the Filbys, the memories were not all bad. She would never have met Gideon had she not been working there. There might have been a cooling in their relationship but she still loved him, and she knew deep in her heart that his feelings for her had not changed. It was male pride that stood in their way, but everything would be different if Barnard Coker could make a deal with the telegraph company, of that she was certain.

The day for the move arrived and Grace's furniture was being laden onto carts, much to the delight of a crowd of young street Arabs, who had gathered outside and were poised, ready to snatch anything they could sell for a few farthings. The carters retaliated with threats of dire punishments, and if all else failed they resorted to their horse whips. Lottie was in the front parlour, checking that nothing had been left behind, and was about to leave the room when Gideon entered, grinning and looking so much like his old self that her heart missed a beat.

'You look very pleased with yourself,' she said cautiously.

'You'll never guess what's happened. I can hardly believe it myself.' He took a letter from his pocket and handed it to her.

She tried to look surprised as she read the contents. 'The Electric and International Telegraph Company want you and Farrell to join them on the board. That's wonderful, Gideon. I'm so pleased for you.'

'I can't imagine how they got my name, unless it was Farrell who put me up for it. I'm going to visit him in Grosvenor Square to find out.' He hesitated, his elation dimming visibly. 'I should be helping you with the move, Lottie. I'll go later when we're all settled in Gresham Street.'

'It's all right. There are plenty of us, after all, and the carters are doing most of the work. You go and see Farrell.'

'I've been visiting him every other day. I suppose I should have told you, but I feel responsible for the poor fellow. He can see a bit better these days, but I know how much he suffers.'

'You've been a good friend to him,' Lottie said earnestly. 'I'm glad that you two are close, and I'm sorry if my actions have made a rift between us.'

Gideon made a move towards her but at that moment Teddy burst into the room. 'Come quick, Lottie. Lad has bitten one of the street kids and his ma is threatening to wring Lad's neck.'

'I'll sort it out.' Gideon moved to the door. 'I'll see you later – at The Swan.'

'Hurry up, do.' Teddy stood in the doorway, his eyes wide with fright. 'She's going to kill Lad and if Jezebel gets wind of it there'll be hell to pay.'

A loud yell from the front steps made Lottie run

to the window in time to see Jezebel flying at the woman, who had Lad by the scruff of the neck. The carters stood back in amazement at the sight of the tall woman with muscular forearms, who swung a punch a boxer would have been proud of. The boy's mother crumpled to the ground, but Gideon arrived just in time to prevent Jezebel from kicking the woman as she writhed on the filth-encrusted cobblestones. Teddy snatched up Lad and leaped onto the cart as it was about to pull away from the kerb. He cocked a snook at the street urchins, who followed, throwing handfuls of dung and rotten vegetables.

'Oh Lord, what a day.' Ruby waddled into the room. 'I hope I don't give birth before we get to The Swan. I'm overdue as it is.'

Lottie hurried to her side. 'Have your pains started?' Memories of Aurelia giving birth to Molly on board the *Albatross* came flooding back. 'Perhaps we ought to leave right away. There's not much left to go on the carts. I'll come with you.'

Ruby held her hand to her side. 'Perhaps that would be best.'

'Stay here. I'll go and tell Jem and get my reticule and we'll hail a cab.'

Ruby's pains started in earnest as the cab pulled away from the kerb. It was not far to Gresham Street but the traffic was chaotic and horse-drawn vehicles vied with costermongers' barrows and pedestrians for right of way in the crowded streets. The journey took twice as long as it would have done normally and Ruby's pains were coming in quick succession.

'Me first labour was short, so they told me,' Ruby said, grimacing and clutching Lottie's hand until she thought her fingers would break. 'Although it seemed to go on for ever.' She paled and bit her lip.

'Just hold on until we get there.' Lottie glanced anxiously out of the window. 'It's not too far now, Ruby.'

'They say the second one is always quicker.' Ruby let out a howl of pain that startled the horse, causing it to rear in its shafts.

'Nearly there,' Lottie said, flexing her fingers.

Ruby closed her eyes and bared her teeth. 'I think it's coming.'

'Just a few more minutes and we'll be there.' Lottie clutched Ruby's hands. 'Hold on, please.'

They had come to a halt and the cabby was shouting at a costermonger who had blocked the street as he tried to turn his barrow laden with apples and pears. 'Get out of me way. I got a woman giving birth in me cab, you bloody numbskull.'

The costermonger replied in kind, but he managed to manoeuvre his cart just enough for the cab to pass just as the barrow tilted and fruit spilled onto the road; apples bounced over the cobblestones and pears were crushed underfoot as children scrambled to pick them up.

'I ain't giving birth in a cab for all to see,' Ruby groaned, clutching her belly as if trying to keep her baby from coming too soon.

'We are so nearly there,' Lottie said urgently. 'Just a few more minutes, Ruby.'

They reached the entrance of The Swan with

Two Necks and the cab trundled into the yard. Ruby had been screaming as if she was being murdered, but was suddenly silent. Lottie jumped to the ground calling for Ned Potts. 'Ned, come quick.'

He was helping the carter to unload the first wagon, and he turned his head, squinting into the sunlight. 'What's up, miss?'

Teddy dropped the box he had been carrying and hurried towards them. 'Is she having her baby?'

Lottie nodded, beckoning furiously. 'We've got to get Ruby inside.'

Ned lumbered towards them. 'There's a strange woman been asking for you, miss.'

'I can't deal with that now,' Lottie said hastily. 'We must get Mrs Barker indoors.'

'But the black woman is in the taproom, drinking rum. She's been here every day this week, looking for you. I didn't like to give her your address in Leman Street.'

'Did she give you a name?'

'I dunno, can't remember exactly. Mary Seacow, or something.'

Ruby opened her eyes. 'Mrs Seacole. It can't be.' Her face contorted with pain and she writhed in agony. 'Help me, Lottie.'

'It's a miracle if it is her.' Lottie turned to Teddy. 'Run to the taproom and ask the lady to come quickly. Tell her that her services are needed.' She turned back to Ruby, stroking her hair from her damp forehead. 'Don't worry. Everything will be all right now.'

'Put your arm round my neck, missis.' With surprising gentleness, Ned lifted Ruby from the cab.

'You'd better take her to the Filbys' apartment. I'll pay the cabby and I'll be with you as quick as I can.'

'Aye, miss. I know where to go.' Ned lumbered off with Ruby in his arms, leaving Lottie to pay the disgruntled cabby, who drove off muttering beneath his breath.

Lottie was about to follow Ned and Ruby when Mary Seacole came bustling from the taproom, her scarlet and blue skirts billowing like the sails of a tea clipper, and the ribbons on her bonnet waving like flags.

'Lottie, my darling, it's good to see you. I was hoping to find you here.'

'I can't believe it's really you, and you couldn't have turned up at a more opportune moment. There's a lady in desperate need of your services.'

'I heard her yelling. It's all in a day's work for Mother Seacole. Lead on.' Brandishing her umbrella Mary surged forward as if she were leading a cavalry charge.

Ned passed them in the doorway. 'I laid her on the bed, miss.'

'Thank you, Ned.' Lottie led the way to the Filbys' former bedroom.

'Mother Seacole,' Ruby whispered, 'I am so glad to see you.'

'I'm here to look after you now, girl.' Mary took off her bonnet and rolled up her sleeves. 'Fetch clean towels and hot water, Lottie. You can leave the rest to me.'

Chapter Twenty-Four

Lottie was only too pleased to hand over to such an experienced nurse and midwife, and she had complete trust in Mary's abilities. She went to the kitchen and was horrified to find it in complete chaos. The Filbys had left the remains of several meals to moulder on the table, and in the scullery dirty crockery was piled high in the stone sink. The fire in the range had long since turned to ash and it spilled onto the flagstone floor. The smell of rotting food and rancid fat turned Lottie's stomach, but she set to work to clean the grate and get a fire going. She fetched water from the pump in the yard and put a pan to heat on the top of the range.

Keeping busy by sorting out the mess in the kitchen kept her mind off Ruby's labour, and she enlisted Teddy's help, although he protested and said he was a drummer boy and washing pots and pans was not his job. Lad curled up in his old place by the fire and, still grumbling, Teddy attacked the dirty crockery.

It seemed that the Filbys had taken everything they could lay their hands on, but Lottie found a couple of clean towels that had been overlooked and took them, together with a pan of hot water, to the room where Ruby was in labour. She hesitated outside the door, head on one side, listening, but the sound of a baby crying filled her with

397

relief. She entered to find Mary about to wrap the squirming infant in a pillowcase. 'Ah, just in time.'

Lottie placed the pan on a table. 'How are you, Ruby?'

'It's a boy,' Ruby said, smiling sleepily. 'A beautiful little boy.'

Mary swaddled the baby in the towel and laid him in his mother's arms. 'There, that's my good deed for the day. Well done, honey.'

'I don't know how to thank you,' Lottie said, giving her a hug. 'I can't believe that you turned up out of the blue. It seems too good to be true.'

Mary drew her aside. 'To tell you the truth, honey, I need your help, which is why I've been here every day hoping to see you.'

'Of course I'll do anything I can. What is it, Mary?'

'Things aren't so good financially for me and my partner, Mr Day. You might say we overstretched ourselves in our business ventures.'

'I am so sorry to hear that.'

Mary shrugged and heaved a sigh. 'Oh well, that's the way things go, I guess. It looks like we'll be declared bankrupt very soon.'

'But that's so unfair. You put everything you had into nursing the sick and injured in the Crimea, and yet Miss Nightingale has come back to national acclaim. I can't understand why you're being treated so harshly.'

'Maybe I'm not such a good businesswoman as I thought I was.'

'Where are you living now? Have you got somewhere to go?'

'I'm not complaining, honey. I rent a pretty little room in Tavistock Street, on the corner of Drury Lane. I love Covent Garden and everything that goes on there, and Mr Day is in lodging in Goswell Road. We ain't homeless, but we might be in need of a little help from our friends in the military. To put it plain, child, I might soon be destitute.'

'That's awful, Mary. I'll do anything I can to help, and I'm sure that Lady Aurelia will also.'

Mary tapped the side of her nose and grinned. 'That's what I was hoping. I heard about her narrow escape and the fact that she ain't such a beauty now, but her ladyship is rich and influential and maybe she could remind some of my friends what I did for them in the Crimea, and help me get back on my feet. It ain't charity I want, you must understand that.'

'Of course I do, and I'll do anything I can to make things better for you. But how did you know where to find me?'

Mary threw back her head and laughed. 'You mentioned the name of the inn once and Mother Seacole never forgets a thing, so I sought you out because I didn't want to embarrass Lady Aurelia by turning up on her doorstep. I know how sniffy people can be about an old yellow woman like me, and I am fond of you, honey. I wanted to see you again and find out if things went well for you.'

'You aren't yellow and you aren't old, Mother Seacole,' Lottie said passionately. 'You are a wonderful woman and I'm proud to be your friend.'

'And I'm a proud Creole woman, Lottie. I have Scottish blood in my veins and I can hold my head up high amongst the best.' She kissed her on the cheek. 'I will survive, honey. I always have and I always will.'

The baby started to cry and Lottie hurried to the bedside. 'I'm sorry, Ruby. We're neglecting you. Shall I take the baby so that you can rest?'

'No, thank you. I want to show him to Jem. Has he come yet?'

'What you need, young lady, is a cup of tea brewed by Mother Seacole.' Mary moved towards the door. 'I can find the kitchen, Lottie. I have a second sense when it comes to culinary matters, as you well know.' She let herself out, closing the door behind her.

Lottie leaned over to drop a kiss on Ruby's forehead. 'You have a beautiful baby. Have you chosen a name for him?'

'I'll wait for Jem,' Ruby said, smiling. 'He must have the final say, but I wanted to call my boy Joseph, in memory of my pa.'

'Joseph is a fine name. He looks like a Joe, strong and brave, a son to be proud of.'

'Thanks to Mary.' Ruby lowered her voice. 'I heard what she said about being bankrupt. We must help her.'

'Don't worry, we will. I'll have a word with Aurelia, who owes Mary her life. She might have died on that ship in the Black Sea had it not been for Mary Seacole. I'll make sure she puts the word round amongst her wealthy friends.' Lottie straightened up, head on one side, listening. 'That sounds like a cart. I'll go and see if Jem has arrived and I'll send him in to see you and Joe.'

Lottie left Ruby cradling her tiny son and made her way to the stable yard. As she had hoped, Jem was seated on the box beside the carter. 'Jem, wonderful news. You're a father.'

He leaped to the ground, his face creased with anxiety. 'Is Ruby all right? She didn't tell me that her pains had started. I'd never have left her side if I'd known.'

'She's fine, Jem. I'll take you to her.' Lottie had to curb the desire to tell him that he had a son, but that was something for Ruby to share with her husband. She led the way to the Filbys' bedchamber and retired discreetly.

Lottie waited for the others to arrive, eager to share the good news with them, but there was little time for celebration. The furniture and their belongings had to be unloaded, and Lottie settled her father in the Filbys' parlour to be entertained by Mary. Molly had curled up in a chair and had fallen asleep, worn out by the excitement of moving day.

Jezebel took over the kitchen, and when she had stopped swearing and cursing the Filbys for leaving her kitchen in such a state, she started singing. Lottie breathed a sigh of relief: when Jezebel sang all was well and they would have a decent meal. There was nothing in the larder and Grace went to market to purchase necessities, accompanied by Teddy with Lad, as always, following close on his heels.

Mary stayed to have supper with them and Jem put her in a hansom cab with her fare back to Drury Lane, giving her a kiss and telling her it was the least he could do after she had brought his son into the world.

Gideon arrived soon afterwards, and Lottie

401

could tell by his expression that he had had a successful day. For once they were alone in the kitchen, Jezebel having gone to inspect the new arrival, even though she was adamant that she disliked children, and babies in particular.

'Farrell and I had our first meeting with the board,' Gideon said, taking a seat at the table.

'That sounds interesting.' Lottie set the plate of food she had saved in front of him. 'What was the outcome?'

'They said they'd discuss our ideas, although I think they were impressed with what Farrell and I put forward. I'm not interested in the financial side of things, but I'd love to get down to work planning and supervising the laying of cables to connect far-flung places.'

Lottie sat down beside him. 'And what of Farrell? Is there anything a blind man can do?'

'He knows the theory even better than I do, and he can see enough to get around. The doctors are hopeful that he might regain even more of his sight, but in the meantime we would work together as before, only this time we'll be equals.' He cut into a slice of roast pork. 'I hope this isn't Lady Petunia.'

'It might be a distant relation, but Aurelia told me she had sent the colonel's pet pig to her estate in Bath, where she'll live out her days in comfort.'

'I didn't think Aurelia cared about anyone other than herself.'

'That's not fair, Gideon. She's been more than generous setting me up in business.'

He raised an eyebrow. 'I'd say it was to salve her

conscience for abandoning Molly.'

'I know we'll never agree on that, but I think it's better for Molly to be here, with people who genuinely love her, than hidden away in a nursery, cared for by a succession of nannies and nursery maids.'

'Farrell loves Aurelia, and you do too, so the woman must have some qualities that I don't see.' Gideon reached out to hold Lottie's hand. 'I respect your judgement, sweetheart. But you really must curb your instinct to protect every lame dog you meet, or we'll have half the population of London living with us.'

'Now you're being ridiculous,' Lottie said, chuckling. 'Eat your supper before it gets cold.'

'It's good to have something other than eel pie and mash.'

'It kept us going during the hard times.'

'I know, and I hate to think of everything you've been through.'

'It was my choice to follow you to the Crimea, and I chose to accompany Aurelia to India.'

'I'm sorry I didn't support your plan to move here, Lottie. I felt that I should take the lead in everything because I'm the head of the family, or I will be once we're married.'

'We aren't even engaged, Gideon. You've never proposed to me, not in so many words.'

His eyes darkened. 'I wanted to have something better to offer you. I didn't want to be a kept man. I suppose it was foolish pride on my part.'

She was about to reply when Teddy burst into the room. He stood by the door, holding it open for Jezebel and Grace to enter followed by Jem, who was staggering beneath Harold's weight.

'We've come to celebrate the birth of Joseph James Barker,' Jezebel said, placing a bottle of wine on the table. 'There are a few of these left in the cellar and we have to wet the baby's head.'

Grace glanced anxiously at her son. 'Have we come at a bad time?' She turned to Jezebel, scowling. 'I said we should leave it until tomorrow, when Ruby can join in.'

'Put me down, Jem,' Harold said firmly.

Jem lowered him onto a chair beside Lottie. 'There you go, guv.'

'I'd prefer ale, if there's any left in the taproom.' Harold turned to Teddy with a persuasive smile. 'Why don't you go and see what you can find, young man? If you're old enough to be a soldier, you're old enough to sup a pint of ale.'

'Yes, sir.' Teddy needed no second bidding. He was out of the door before either Grace or Jezebel could stop him.

'You're leading the boy into bad ways,' Grace said, tempering her words with a smile.

'Teddy took on a man's job catching the eels for us.' Lottie met her father's amused gaze with a nod of approval. 'The boy is growing up fast.'

'Well, I'm going to have some wine.' Jezebel fished in a drawer and produced a corkscrew. 'Have we got to drink it out of tin mugs?'

'I'll go and see if there are any glasses left in the dining room,' Lottie said, stifling a yawn.

'You look done in, love.' Harold gave her a searching look. 'You should sit down and rest. I'd give anything to be able to help you. I hate being half a man.'

Gideon patted him on the shoulder. 'A Bath chair would make things easier for you, Harry. I'll do my best to track one down.'

'I'm sorry, I shouldn't grumble when you've all gone out of your way to look after me.' Harold's eyes reddened as if he was fighting back tears. 'You're a good chap, Gideon.'

'You mustn't talk that way, Pa,' Lottie said earnestly. 'I'm just glad to have you home.'

'Ta, love.' Harold wiped his eyes on his sleeve. 'I don't know what I've done to deserve such a splendid daughter.'

Gideon nodded emphatically. 'I'll second that. You and I would still be in Poona, waiting for a ship to bring us home if it hadn't been for Lottie's efforts.' He turned to Lottie with an apologetic smile. 'I was wrong about this place, and you were right to go ahead. The most important thing is for us all to be together, and, heaven knows, there's plenty of room here. I'm sorry I didn't support you when you needed me.'

'Well said, my boy.' Grace gave him a warm look.

'It takes a man to admit that he's in the wrong.'

Overwhelmed by the unexpected apology, Lottie met Gideon's intense gaze with an attempt at a smile. 'It's all right. I understand.'

'Get them glasses, girl,' Jezebel said impatiently. 'There'll be plenty of time for making sheep's eyes at each other later. Although, come to think of it, I could do with something stronger than that red stuff. Where's the gin?'

Lottie went to find the glasses. There was so much that she wanted to say to Gideon, but that would have to wait, although, as things were, she wondered if they would ever have a moment to themselves. It seemed even more unlikely as the evening wore on and the wine flowed, not to mention the gin. Jezebel became quite maudlin and had to be put to bed with the combined efforts of Lottie and Grace, and, having drunk a pint of ale, Teddy fell flat on his face in the stable yard, giggling and threshing about with Lad jumping up and down, yapping. This time it was Ned Potts who came to the rescue and he slung the drunken drummer boy over his shoulder.

'I'll put him in the room next to mine above the stables, miss. Don't worry, I'll keep an eye on the young 'un.' He snapped his fingers and Lad followed meekly as Ned carried his still chuckling burden across the yard.

'What a night,' Gideon murmured when he returned from helping Jem to settle Harold in a room on the ground floor, where Filby had cat-napped when awaiting the arrival of a late mail coach. Jem had gone to join Ruby and their small son, and Grace had retired to her bedchamber, pale and exhausted, but still smiling.

'What a day,' Lottie said, yawning. 'I don't know how we managed when the inn was at its busiest. I wouldn't have dreamed of taking this place on if the mail coaches had still been running.'

Gideon slipped his arms around her waist, twisting her round to face him. His hazel eyes were in shadow but his lips curved into a tender smile. 'We are alone. I can't believe it.' He bent his head to kiss her, but just as their lips were about to meet the sound of carriage wheels and the clatter of horses' hoofs made them draw apart. 'No,' he said angrily. 'It can't be.'

'It's the first consignment from the railway company. I'd almost forgotten it was due tonight. They've agreed to give us a trial to see if we can deliver goods quickly and efficiently.' She ran to the stable block and rang the bell. 'Ned. Come down, please. You're needed.'

'What has to be done?'

She spun round to find Gideon taking off his jacket. 'I don't expect you to be involved. It's up to me to make this work. I'll get Jem. This is his job, not yours.'

He rolled up his sleeves. 'Nonsense, Lottie. We're together now and I'm not afraid of hard work. Jem will have a disturbed night with a new baby wanting attention every few hours, so he should get some rest while he can. What do you want me to do?'

Ned emerged from the stables, shrugging on his waistcoat, just as the wagon drew to a halt. He joined Gideon in unloading the crates, boxes and packages while Lottie ticked the checklist and signed the delivery note. It took an hour to stow everything safely in the storehouse next to the stables, and by that time Lottie was almost too exhausted to think. She said good night to Gideon and Ned, leaving them to lock up, and went to her room, tired but happy.

She was up early next morning, supervising the loading of the cart to deliver the most urgently needed goods, but she had not forgotten her promise to Mary Seacole, and at the first opportunity she took a cab to Grosvenor Square. The butler greeted her with due respect and she was shown to the blue saloon like an honoured guest. She had to smile to herself, recalling the first time she had visited the de Morgan mansion and had been advised to use the servants' entrance. The butler announced her but as she walked into the room she came to a sudden halt.

'Tom Bonney.' His name escaped her lips on a cry of delight. 'I hardly recognised you out of uniform.'

He clasped her outstretched hands in a firm grasp. 'Lottie, I could say the same for you. You look wonderful.'

She knew she was blushing, but somehow it did not matter. Tom was an old and valued friend who had stood by her when times were hard, and seeing him unexpectedly had taken her breath away. She glanced at Aurelia, who was seated by the fire with a smug smile on her face.

'How fortunate you chose this moment to call, Lottie. Tom called in on the off chance of finding me at home, and he was just enquiring about you.'

It was Tom's turn to redden. 'Of course I wanted to know how you both had fared. I heard about your exploits in India, and I wanted to see Gillingham.' He shot an apologetic look in Aurelia's direction. 'I didn't realise that the poor fellow had suffered such a terrible injury.'

'He is on the road to recovery, as I told you just now. In fact he's embarked on a business venture with Sapper Ellis,' Aurelia said with a dismissive sigh. 'It seems that once an engineer, always an engineer. What do you think, Tom?'

'I don't know about that, your ladyship. I'm in

the process of selling my commission.'

Lottie moved to the damask-covered sofa and sat down. 'What will you do then? Have you made plans?'

'I've inherited the family estate in Shropshire. I intend to live the life of a country gentleman. You will all be very welcome to visit me, should you wish to rusticate.'

'That sounds wonderful,' Lottie said enthusiastically, 'but I'm afraid we won't be able to accept for a while. I have also gone into business. I've taken over The Swan in Gresham Street, but it's no longer a coaching inn. I've started a carrier business, collecting and delivering goods for the railway companies.'

'You are an incredible woman.' Tom gazed at her admiringly. 'I thought so when we were in Balaklava and I'm doubly impressed now.' He hesitated, twisting his top hat between his fingers. 'Are you spoken for? I mean, I know that you and Sapper Ellis...' He tailed off, glancing at Aurelia.

'Lottie is still a free woman, Tom. Gideon takes Lottie for granted and in my opinion he doesn't deserve her.'

'That's not true, Aurelia,' Lottie said angrily. 'I don't know why you say that.'

'After everything you've been through on his behalf, he still hasn't done the right thing.'

'I could say the same for Lieutenant Gillingham.'

'Ah, but there you would be wrong,' Aurelia said, holding up her left hand where a large solitaire diamond winked in the firelight. 'Farrell asked me to marry him last evening. We're to be married by special licence as soon as arrangements can be made. You, of course, will be my bridesmaid.'

'I'd be honoured, but what you said about Gideon is not true. He's had a lot on his mind since we returned from India.'

'That I can understand. It's not easy to adjust to life as a civilian. I'm only just starting and I find myself quite lost at times.' Tom sat beside Lottie on the sofa. 'Gideon is a good chap. I'd like to see him again and, more than that, I'd like to visit your new home.'

'Let's go there now,' Aurelia said impulsively. 'I must confess I'm curious to see The Swan with Two Necks under new management.'

'If you wish.' At any other time Lottie would have been pleased and flattered to think that Aurelia was taking an interest in her business venture, but the critical remark about Gideon had hurt, and even more so as it contained an element of truth. Despite his protestations of love and devotion he had seemed more interested in his new project with the telegraph company than in planning for their future together.

'That's settled then.' Aurelia rose from her seat and tugged at the bell pull. 'I'll send for the carriage.'

The de Morgan landau pulled into the stable yard, and the footman leaped down to open the door and hand Aurelia and Lottie from the carriage. Tom alighted, taking stock of his surroundings with obvious interest, but Lottie was surprised to find Gideon in his shirtsleeves

410

helping Jem to refurbish a Bath chair that looked as though it had been rescued from a dust yard. Ned was busy loading the cart with another consignment of goods, and the sound of a baby crying made Aurelia turn to give Lottie a questioning look.

'Ruby gave birth last evening. A fine baby boy.'

'Splendid,' Tom said enthusiastically. 'Mrs Wagg is a wonderful mother–' He broke off, frowning. 'What have I said?'

Jem rose slowly to his feet. 'Mrs Wagg is now Mrs Barker, sir. I am her husband.'

'Congratulations to you both.' Tom shook Jem's hand. 'She is a fine woman, as of course you know. We are surrounded by remarkable ladies, don't you agree, Ellis?'

Gideon stood up, wiping sweat from his brow. 'I'm not in the army now, and neither are you, if your appearance is anything to go by.'

'Gideon.' Lottie moved to his side, speaking in a low voice. 'That wasn't necessary.'

'It's all right, Lottie,' Tom said quickly. 'I'm the one who should apologise. Old habits die hard, I'm afraid. Let's start again, Gideon, civilian to civilian.'

Gideon answered with a curt nod, and Lottie slipped her hand through the crook of his arm. 'Aurelia has some wonderful news.'

'Indeed I have,' Aurelia said, smiling. 'Farrell and I are to be married very soon, by special licence. I imagine he'll tell you himself, Gideon.'

'As a matter of fact he confided in me yesterday afternoon. I took him to the jeweller to purchase the ring.' Gideon smiled ruefully. 'I'm sorry, Lottie. I was sworn to secrecy. I couldn't even tell you.'

'It's splendid news anyway,' Tom said hastily. 'It makes me feel like a staid old bachelor.'

'I'm sure the young ladies in Shropshire will be falling over themselves in their attempts to attract your attention.' Lottie felt Gideon stiffen, but she was unrepentant. Tom was handsome, charming and kind. He deserved to find someone who would make him happy, but she was aware of an awkward lapse in the conversation and hastily changed the subject. 'I almost forgot to tell you, Aurelia. Mary Seacole turned up unexpectedly and it was she who delivered Ruby's baby. Apparently the poor woman is in financial straits and in dire need of help and support–' She broke off as Grace chose that moment to emerge from the inn with Molly in her arms.

A look of puzzlement on Tom's face turned into one of recognition. 'Is that little Molly? How she's grown, and how pretty she is with those golden curls and big blue eyes. She is very fair, considering the place of her birth. I mean that the Turks are generally darker complexioned...' He broke off, flushing and looking to Lottie for help.

'I believe that her mother was an Englishwoman who had fallen on hard times,' Lottie said quickly.

Gideon responded with a gentle pressure on her hand. 'No matter what her parentage might be, Molly is everyone's favourite. But if Jem has no objections, I'll leave him to carry on here and I'll take you to see our office, Tom.'

'You go ahead, mate.' Jem stood up, wiping his

hands on his apron. 'It's going to take a few days to get this old wreck into shape anyway. I might even drag Harry away from his desk as there are things he can help with. He's good with his hands.'

'Your father is helping you here?' Aurelia said curiously. 'What can he do?'

Lottie was instantly on the defensive. 'Pa has a good head for figures. He's agreed to take on the clerical side of the business, and it seems to suit him very well.'

'With a Bath chair at his disposal he'll have more freedom of movement,' Gideon said firmly. 'Harry is an amazing fellow. I can quite see where Lottie gets her determined spirit from.'

'I'll second that,' Tom said, grinning. 'You were an example to us all in camp, Lottie. Ruby, too,' he added quickly. 'Two such stalwart ladies put us all to shame.'

Grace moved closer to her son. 'I'm sure that Gideon is well aware of that, sir.'

'I don't think you've met Gideon's mother.' Lottie could see that Grace was offended and that Tom was embarrassed. 'Grace, this is Tom Bonney, an old friend from the Crimea.'

But before she could complete the introduction a shout from Teddy rang around the stable yard followed by the clatter of hobnails as he raced across the cobblestones with Lad at his heels. He skidded to a halt, stood to attention and saluted. 'Lieutenant Bonney, it's me, Teddy Miller of the 97th. Do you remember me, sir?'

'Of course I do, but there's no need to salute now, Teddy. I'm a civilian just like you.'

Gideon ruffled Teddy's curly hair. 'We're going

to see my office in the City. Why don't you come along too?'

'Really? You'd like me to come with you and the lieutenant?'

'Yes, of course,' Gideon said easily. 'I'd like you both to see where Farrell and I are beginning our new venture.'

'I'll come with you too.' Aurelia turned to Lottie with a persuasive smile. 'I'm sure that Lottie is much too busy to accompany us now, but as Tom is only in London for a couple of days I insist that you all come to dinner this evening. It will be good to celebrate our engagement with old friends. Perhaps you would like to join us, Mrs Ellis? I'd ask Mr and Mrs Barker too, but with a newborn baby I'm sure they would rather leave it until another time.'

Lottie stared at her friend in amazement. She hardly recognised this new, gracious and caring person. Aurelia met her gaze with a knowing look. 'Don't look so surprised,' she said in a low voice. 'I've been practising niceness.'

'You're doing extremely well. I hardly recognise you now.'

'Even so, I am the same person and I haven't changed my mind about Molly. I want you to adopt her legally. I gave her to you once, and I truly believe that she needs you far more than me.'

'I'll look after her no matter what. I love her as if she were my own, but you might think differently when you and Farrell are married.'

'No, I won't,' Aurelia said firmly. 'I don't want children and Farrell knows and accepts it as a fact. I intend to settle a sizeable sum on Molly, which she will come into when she reaches her majority. In the meantime I'll honour my promise to pay for her education and upkeep. I will be her caring and affectionate godmother. It's all I can do, Lottie.'

Lottie clasped Aurelia's hand. 'I can't pretend to understand, but if you ever change your mind...'

Aurelia smiled, shaking her head. 'You know me better than that, my dear. Now I really must go, but I'll see you tonight.'

Aurelia's invitation was as good as a royal command, and there was no question of gainsaying her. Lottie put on her best gown, which once again happened to be one of Aurelia's cast-offs and was far too elegant for any but the most formal occasion. Worn over a crinoline cage, the rose-pink gown whittled her waist to a hand-span, and the low décolletage revealed just enough of her firm bosom to tantalise without risking censure. She had intended to wear her hair in a chignon at the nape of her neck, but Ruby insisted that she was well enough to get out of bed and attend to Lottie's coiffure. The result was even better than Lottie could have hoped for, and at her father's request she went to show off her finery.

He gazed at her misty-eyed. 'My beautiful girl, I'm so proud of you, Lottie. I'm so sorry that we were separated for so many years.'

She leaned over to kiss him on the forehead. 'It wasn't your fault, Pa.'

'I missed so much, and you suffered at the hands of my brother. I'll never forgive Sefton for that.' Harold picked up a small velvet pouch from the table by the sofa. 'These were your mother's,

Lottie. They will be the finishing touch.'

Lottie tipped the contents onto the palm of her left hand. 'Oh, Pa. They're lovely. I remember Ma wearing this amethyst pendant and earrings.'

'It was my wedding gift to her, Lottie. She loved amethysts.'

Lottie fastened the clasp of the gold chain. The earrings she was wearing were a pair she had bought cheaply in Poona market and she replaced them with the sparkling amethyst drops. 'How do I look, Pa?'

Harold dashed his hand across his eyes. 'Perfect, my love. Wait until Gideon sees you.' He reached out to clasp her hand. 'He's a good man, Lottie.'

She smiled and raised his hand to her cheek. 'I know it, Pa.'

'I just wanted you to know that if I have to give my daughter away to any man, I'd be content to place your happiness in his hands.'

Gideon was waiting for her in the stable yard. He looked taller and every inch a gentleman in his black tail coat, white shirt and bow tie and black waistcoat worn with tapered trousers and highly polished shoes. Leaning slightly on his cane, he walked towards her and as he came to a halt in a pool of gaslight, the look of admiration in his eyes and the tenderness in his smile made her feel like a queen. The girl who had been a skivvy at the beck and call of the Filbys was gone for ever, and like a butterfly emerging from its chrysalis, Lottie knew that she had come home at last.

She took a step towards him. 'I'm ready.'

'You look wonderful,' Gideon said softly. 'You are truly beautiful, Lottie. I'm very bad at expressing my feelings, but I want you to know that I love you and I can't imagine my life without you.'

'I love you, too.' Lottie met his ardent gaze with a tremulous smile.

'I thought perhaps you had feelings for Tom Bonney. I saw the way he looked at you today, and I know he's a better bet than a semi-crippled ex-sapper...'

Lottie stepped forward, laying her finger on his lips. 'That's nonsense, Gideon. I am fond of Tom, but not in the way you think. He was a good friend to us in the Crimea, but that's all he ever was. There's no need to be jealous of him, or anyone, come to that.'

'I was jealous. I admit it, and the intensity of that feeling shook me to the core. I've been a fool, and I've taken you for granted because I always assumed that we would be married one day.'

'You said as much that time in Kadikoi, but a lot has happened since then. I thought perhaps you'd changed your mind.'

'Never.' He raised her hands to his lips. 'I'm sorry, Lottie. I was stupid but I wanted to prove that I was worthy of you.'

'You don't have to prove anything to me.'

'I know I don't deserve someone like you, although I dared to hope that you still loved me. I was going to do this at a more appropriate time, but Aurelia forced my hand by inviting us to dine with them this evening.'

'I don't understand,' Lottie said, puzzled. 'What difference does that make?'

'She saw through me today. Lady Aurelia is no fool; she could see that I was struggling with the green-eyed monster. The thought of seeing you with a man who clearly has feelings for you was enough to bring me to my senses, and for that I will always be grateful to her.'

He took a small shagreen-covered box from his breast pocket. 'I bought this at the same time that Farrell purchased a ring for Aurelia.' He flicked it open and went down on one knee, despite the dampness of the evening dew on the none-too-clean cobblestones. 'There's only one way I know how to say this, Lottie. I love you with all my heart and I want to spend the rest of my life with you. Will you marry me?'

Torn between tears and laughter, she took the box and the amethyst surrounded by tiny diamond chips glinted in the gaslight. 'How did you know that this was my favourite stone?'

'Your father showed me the necklace you're wearing now. He told me how much you loved it when you were a little girl.'

'I love the ring, and I love you, too. Please get up. You don't have to kneel to me.'

He struggled to his feet, smiling ruefully. 'That wasn't the most elegant proposal, but it was heartfelt. I want the world to know how much I love and adore you. Will you be my wife, Lottie?'

She laid the box in his outstretched palm, and held out her left hand. 'I will.'